32 White Horses on a Vermillion Hill

Volume Two

A Planet X Publications

Charity Anthology

32 White Horses on a Vermillion Hill

Volume Two

A Planet X Publications Charity Anthology

(https://www.facebook.com/planetxpubs)
(https://www.facebook.com/32whitehorses)

This is a work of fiction, containing both prose and poetry.

Covert Art by Nick Gucker
Book Design by Michael Adams
Edited by Duane Pesice

ISBN 13: 978-1-7326839-2-1
ISBN 10: 1-7326839-2-1

This Book is Dedicated to:

Christopher Ropes,

Joe Pulver,

and baby Edgar, who deserved forevermore

Introduction to Volume Two

by Michael Wehunt

As part of a brief series of author portraits, I once heavily edited and corrupted an image and titled it *Portrait of Christopher Ropes Wearing All His Human Masks at Once*. The joke, along with any grasping-at-straws sliver of artistic merit, hid in the suggestion that Mr. Ropes would need to pretend to be a human being.

The image was difficult to look at, piled with layers and echoes and distortions. The eyes were wrong. It was supposed to be uncomfortable. The subjects of my amateur #AuthorPortraits were mostly those creeping within the niche of the literary community where horror overlaps with weird fiction. Uncomfortable, unsettling, just plain *off*—this is our wheelhouse.

I begin here by mentioning this image to touch on the importance of community, but mainly because Christopher Ropes is perhaps the most human of us all. It's a testament to his fiction and his reality that when I think of him, I am suffused with imagery of darkness and love and broken bones and emotions so sharp and raw they strain the seams of our daily lives, leaking onto social media and disrupting the prepackaged existences we present there.

The Ropes we see on social media is achingly like the Ropes we see knotted throughout his novelette "Complicity" (a chapbook published on Dunhams Manor Press in 2016). We can hear him in his music as Nighttime in the Abyss. He is nakedly human, quick to joy and celebration and quick to the embrace of human rights and community passion. His Facebook is full of hearts for anyone who might need one.

He wears his heart on his sleeve in a way that makes that euphemism seem disconcertingly real—the heart is surely staining his sleeve red, dripping blood on the floor, with dark clots and open ventricles too much like eyes, or micro-abysses we don't want to look into. But we do because he is genuine and he is one of us, truly, with the blood on the floor, sweat, and tears. His humanity is entwined in his talent.

In the solitary pursuit of writing, community takes on a strange power. For many, community is family. If only for a few minutes a day, there is the sense of kinship, and there is a shared love. A community comes together to help one of its own, and where that kinship is strongest, so is the call to arms.

So here we are, lending hands to Chris in his time of need—though as horror authors, we should probably specify that these aren't actual hands we're lending. Our collections of severed hands remain in our jars in our basements. And if you're reading this, that means your hand has been lent, too. You're now part of the community, if you weren't already. You'll find a diverse cast of authors in these pages, with quality far beyond what one would expect from a charity anthology thrown together to help one of the family. You didn't buy this book *exclusively* to help, after all—you want good stories. Fortunately, there are a lot of them beyond this introduction, waiting to scare you and comfort you in that unique way only horror and the uncanny can do.

Imagine these pages, as you read them, soaked in blood. Imagine the blood drying, then imagine the pages bleached back to the color of paper. Imagine the words, typeset and placed on the pages, and traces of the blood infecting—but also enriching, especially this—the words, because you can't ever get blood all the way out. It is the blood of Chris, wrung from his sleeve, and considering his esoteric but powerful paths of faith, I hope he appreciates the little pun. But it is quite a feat that his spirit should be so present, considering he has no tale in this group of stories given for him.

We love him. He loves us. And we all love to have stories told to us, especially when they are so nakedly, boldly human.

"Alouette A La Blanc"

by Bob Freville

I wonder if you now have the capacity to recall how truly awful the life you lived was. For my part, I always knew that life would end as it had begun for you, the so-called "werewolf boy of Wheatontown." You were wrested from your mother's womb, you will remember, as fuzzy as a peach, wailing like a steam engine as if you were begging to be put back inside. You were greeted by those attending medical practitioners in those sterile bone-white confines of Mercy General as a slight against God.

As I'm sure you know, the ensuing years of your agonizing existence were spent in this same cruel state of bewildered embarrassment and suffering. In pubescence you had been the inadvertent and e'er-reluctant child star of the day-time television circuit, carted out on to the cheap industrial carpeted stages of countless talk shows by parents whose faces insisted on being blurred for the camera.

Do you remember the true name of that which afflicted you? The doctors, they called it Hypertrichosis or Ambras Syndrome. The inhabitants of the schoolyard were not so clinical in their assessment. You were, to put it in lay terms, one fuzzy little devil, covered from head to toe in a thick mane of fibrous brown fur. It pains me to say it, but your balls had scarcely dropped by the time you went cross-eyed from the strain of seeing through such coarse bangs. They called you a monster and a freak. Always a freak, that was their favorite, you'll remember. They threw things at you and regularly accosted you in the halls and on the jungle gym. Even the janitor got in on it a few times.

You'll bear in mind that, on one such occasion, you thought that their attacks might have cured you of the ailment. During recess, after a teacher's aid had run off to the restrooms and left her class unattended, your classmates kicked you to the ground and poured an industrial solvent from Chem Lab on you, then the eldest of the children, already a smoker, struck a match and set you on fire. And I'm sure you can call up the aftermath when you awoke in the hospital and felt the sting of the second-degree burns and felt as though you had been baptized and saved by the Lord for your suffering, that you had been spared this dreadful disease. But those people who raised you wasted no time in letting it be known that you needn't worry about people seeing your new scars because the hair had grown in over them. Parents.

You hated being called a freak because you didn't like the negative connotation that was implied. You felt that your fellow human beings, in their constant quest to convey your hideousness, were befouling a perfectly good word. Since you were knee high to a grasshopper, you'd been in love with the circus. You collected flyers for Barnum & Bailey's and read books on carnivals. You studied acrobatics and arabesques wherever you could find such information.

You'll remember that your maturation, your evolution, only came when you accepted that you were a freak. You'd always loved the freaks—the Bearded Lady, the unibrowed milksop with the googly eyes, the midgets and musclemen and mad dancers. But, most of all, you positively adored the clowns. These brash, blushing buffoons were your absolute favorite attraction and, along with their aforesaid brethren, they provided the only catharsis, the only escape you ever received in your infancy. The rest of the year could die a slow death, but when your parents deigned to bring you to the circus—for it was the only place they deigned to take you, figuring their fellow normals would take you for part of the show—you felt exalted. You were transported to a place beyond your pain, beyond the trappings of the real world.

Once you'd tasted their world, you yearned for it always. After your first visit, you resolved to know everything there was to know about the clowns and their act. You studied the biographies of Fox and Grimaldi and their regular routines. Humpty Dumpty. The Wizard of the Silver Rocks. And the best of 'em all: Harlequin's Release. You knew that the first clowns in recorded history appeared in the Fifth Dynasty of Egypt. Other kids regarded 1492 and 1969 as unforgettable years. Your year was 2400 B.C.

When you had reached puberty you ceased talking to anyone, including your parents, preferring to communicate in pantomime. You spoke with your hands, much to their chagrin. So much so that they decided to lock you in your room where you would fail to be a nuisance.

That room became a prison. So, too, did your mind. Both were a sanctuary and both were a bane. There were many indomitable days of waking nightmare. Your eyes would be open, but you yourself were trapped inside your head, host to all of its tortures and chicanery, assaulted by its many tricks and treats. Spectral monsters of a variety far more frightening than your own visage reared up from your imagination and conspired to place you in a chronic state of acute anxiety. You became a trembling, jittery ball of hair, curled up as you always were in a fetal position beneath your clown-covered comforter.

These night terrors, which began to become tangible apparitions haunting your bedroom's floors, only came to a respite when warded off by the people of your dreams. I am speaking, of course, of that race of ashy-faced balloon-carrying buffoons. When you pictured them in a state of reverence you always saw them as clown augustes, the happy clowns that every parent and child appreciates. But when they came like guardians of old to fight for your honor in the depths of those terrifying reveries, they were very distinctly the other type of clowns, clown blancs, sad and angry fools fit to fight to the death to protect you.

When they came into your dreamscape and defeated the monsters, the monsters stayed gone for good and you were changed by it. Your voice returned and you convinced your parents to remove the lock from the outer door. You began to eat again and even opted to receive the home-schooling your family had hoped you would when you'd reached your teens.

It was all because of the clowns. After they had inhabited your nightmares and vanquished the evil from your brain, you knew what you wanted from this tortuous life. You wanted the only thing that could turn your torture into a spectacle, the only thing that could make your furry into a flurry of fun and excitement for you and all other comers. You wanted to be a freak.

But you didn't want to be the freak they'd always told you that you were. You didn't want to be the "dog boy" or the "werewolf" or the "hairy man-child." You wanted to be a clown. A bonafide bald-headed, red-nosed clown. How would one accomplish this with hypertrichosis, you wondered.

The answer came swiftly as, no more than two days later, an ad ran in your local theater digest, an ad which read: CLOWN SEEKING HARLEQUIN APPRENTICE. This was your golden goose, your ticket, you surmised, to becoming a clown yourself.

But how to pull off the interview with all that hair? How to convince the clown that you could be anything other than a wolfboy? You did the only thing you could—you bought the biggest and best clown mask you could find and you strapped it on and you headed for the address printed in the digest.

You dreamed even as you went, sweet dreams now of cotton candy and cuddly keepsakes, dreams of cooling off in the Dunk Tank and kicking the ever-loving excrement out of the High Riser with a mallet. So deep in reverie were you, my boy, that you didn't see it coming.

You approached the rainbow-colored trailer in those cantankerous woods and could hear only the sound of your mind's fancy as he stomped up behind you and

XXX

You're inside, my boy, inside the Greatest Show On Earth! And there's music, an odd mellifluousness that's uncanny to you, somehow alien, somehow as familiar as your terrible parents. The humming and whistling turns to a hushed spat of lyrics. *Alouette, gentille alouette, Alouette, je te plumerai.*

The clown's dwellings are adorned with a dazzling array of shining silver trinkets, all of them pointed and singing as their gleaming sharp ends clatter together like wind chimes. The walls are a mosaic tribute to Roy G. Biv, one of fur and red stuff. And his furniture are toys, white toys, some of which have gone jaundiced with the discoloration of time and rot. You marvel at the wrinkles and hairs jutting out of a lampshade painted over in little red balloons.

Finally you see him in all his twisted majesty, a clown no less than eight feet tall, his gargantuan feet tucked into a pair of red-brown shoes, floppy and blinking with yellow eyes at the ankle. His ruffled vestment is fouled with tobacco juice and other unmentionable effluence.

He hands you a paper cone and urges you to eat from it. When you just stare at him, he forces it into your mouth and, with his gloved hands, massages your throat. The cone is filled with pink insulation, neither sweet nor sour but wholly caustic to the integrity of your inner-flesh. You projectile vomit, puking the pink stuff on to his ruffles. This does not faze him as he carries over a plate on which sits, steaming hot, a latticework of fried flour sprinkled in asbestos.

It was then that you realized your new clown companion was not a traditional clown but a true trickster. But instead of a spray bottle of seltzer water, his stock and trade was something more arcane and iniquitous, child. You see, mon frere, this clown had long tired of making balloon animals for those little bastards that paraded past his tent, bored as he was with twisting them this way and that, into the same predictable shapes. He wanted something else to mold, something more rich, more brilliant, more realized. And, finally, something more permanent.

That something was you. Among those devices with which he worked on you as he sang that great song at the Greatest Show On Earth, the Great Living Spectacle, there were scalpels and C-clamps and scissors and snips, but the *piece-de-resistance* was

Je te plumerai la tête. Et la tête! Et la tête!

In that rainbow-colored trailer, under the glow of a purple light bulb, you were stripped, after all, of the thing that made you You. With your head in a vise, the clown did scalp you, shedding you, tendril by tendril, of every hair with the greatest of tools...a pair of pliers capable of plucking any follicle in sight, uprooting each and every one like plumage. And so he sang, "Alouette! Alouette!" *A-a-a-ah!*

We've reached the underneath, the greatest spectacle of 'em all! Purulent boils and long flanks of third-degree burns scored your ruined face, child. And your cankered cleft mouth was frozen in a puckered rictus. Your sunken cheeks were riddled in dense, acned pockets alive with pus, maggots and blowflies. Your beautiful brown eyes, ensconced though they were beneath eyelids sagging from exasperation, were robbed of their beauty, upstaged by the sutures which held your skull and mandible together.

The clown stood back and looked upon his new creation and his blanc features turned, momentarily, to those of the clown auguste, so overcome was he with what he'd done. You began to sniffle, so he took your nose. *Je te plumerai le bec. Et le bec! Et la tête! Alouette!* You began to choke on your own tears at the sight you stole of yourself in his House of Mirrors. And so it goes: *Je te plumerai les yeux.* The kind clown auguste translated for your English ears, which had yet to be removed, "I'll pluck the feathers off your eyes."

The clown worked tirelessly to craft you as he'd imagined. *Et le dos! Et la queue! Et les pattes! Et les ailes! Et le cou! Et les yeux! Et le bec! Et la tête!* In the end there was void to the form he'd conceived and that void was you. This is the harlequin's release.

So you remember, my boy, when you cross through that infernal mirror and the elders ask you what you would like to be when you are reborn, you tell them that you want to be a werewolf boy. Because it's better to be you than to be made into something else, something you never asked for. But whatever you do, do not be a clown... nor his foiled fool.

A Plague Of The Most Beautiful Finery

by Kurt Fawver

The odor that slithered through the gap between the boxcar's doors stopped Grimble's heart long before he saw the bodies. Threads of rot and wine, blood and fine cologne, excrement and crisp linen all knitted together in the scent's fabric. As its arachnoid limbs twisted toward his nostrils, Grimble turned away, flipped on his flashlight, and glanced at the shipping manifest in his hands.

Box number US-2018: Paper goods and industrial air conditioning parts. No perishables. No chemicals. Nothing that would explain the pungent smell.

Fifteen years in the train yard, fifteen years of thankless midnight inspections, and Grimble had never caught a whiff of something like this. He knew the stench of dead animals, the musk of mold and mildew, the tang of acids and oils and solvents of unnamable variety. But this odor, this was something new. This was something that, considering the car's broken lock and ajar doors, had to be investigated.

Grimble set his stack of paperwork on the ground, breathed deep, and opened a nightmare.

His flashlight beam swiveling throughout the inside of the boxcar revealed a mound of nude, gray, desiccated bodies. Around the perimeter of the car, on nails driven into the walls, hung maybe two dozen clean, pressed, impeccably tailored blue suits replete with white button-down shirts and apple-red ties.

Grimble dropped the flashlight, which lolled about inside the car, and whispered, more to whatever gods would listen than to himself, "No. No. Not here. Not now."

Something soft rustled in the darkness just outside the flashlight's reach and Grimble fled. Unfurling a carpet of expletives in his wake, he grabbed for the phone in his pocket and dialed 9-1-1.

A bored, wispy voice answered.

"9-1-1. What's the nature of your emergency?"

Not used to exercise, let alone full-on sprinting, Grimble panted into his phone, "The suits. The suits. They're not contained. They're here. Middleton train yard. The suits are here."

"Sir? You're reporting an outbreak? Are you a railroad employee?"

"Yes! Yes!" Grimble shouted. "Middleton train yard. The suits."

"I understand, sir. I'm forced to ask, what is your yearly salary? Do you have enough money to placate the suits?"

Chest heaving, Grimble had no breath with which to respond. He grunted at the phone and kept running. Thirty thousand plus benefits would be no salvation here. The suits had never been known to spare anyone with less than six digits-worth of earning power to their name.

Behind Grimble, out of sight, the dread pathogen rushed over the tracks, its movement silent but for an occasional swish of cloth against cloth.

"Sir? We've never had a report this far northwest. Are you certain they're the plague suits?"

Grimble could see the station master's office glowing in the distance. Heart dancing wildly, he choked out as much information as he could.

"Yes. They're following. Came from inside a train car. Twenty. Thirty. Dead inside."

A silhouette came into focus just outside the office. It was one of the mechanics, Hardesty, walking toward the repair building, hammer in hand.

"Get inside!" Grimble screamed.

Hardesty stopped and stared in confusion, then began jogging in Grimble's direction.

"No! No! Go ins..." Grimble's warning dissipated as he tripped on a high-rising track and collapsed to the ground.

Dazed, knees and elbows bruised and bleeding, he heard two distinct noises nearby: one, the thud of Hardesty's steel-toed boots pounding closer and, two, a ripple of cotton and wool rushing forth like a tidal wave.

Grimble's phone lay several feet away, still connected to the 9-1-1 operator.

"Sir? Are you there? I'm sending fire and quarantine units. If you can hear me, try to surround yourself with as much currency as possible. Paper money, credit cards, checks, an open bank account app on your phone—anything you can lay your hands on. You might confuse them. Remember, they won't take people who have the scent of wealth on them."

Ignoring the phone, Grimble stumbled to his feet and set his bulk to push forward. He rushed by Hardesty, who scowled in confusion.

"Grimble, what the fu..."

The hungry slither of silk devoured Hardesty's words.

Grimble chugged onward, even as a series of wet cracks echoed from where Hardesty had been overtaken.

The office was so close. So close.

Finally back in the halogen glow of the terminal's lights, Grimble dared a glance over his shoulder and saw what he'd feared he might: two, maybe three dozen suits still perfectly flat and starched, floating toward him. Their ties stood out from their shirts and jackets, undulating slowly in an unfelt breeze, tasting the atmosphere for poverty and desperation.

Grimble shivered and kept moving. The door was within an arm's length. He reached out and pulled. Nothing happened. Locked. Locked out of the office. Locked out of safety.

Grimble whirred about on his heels. The suits were there, floating nearer, nearer, their cuts magnificent, their lapels sharp, their pocket squares—also red —neatly folded and pointing up, at a sky of indifferent stars.

Grimble reached into his back pocket, drew forth his wallet, and threw his ATM card at one of the suit's breasts. His name and account number bounced away into the night.

He pulled out a credit card and brandished it before him like a crucifix before the undead. Another suit, now fully upon Grimble, reached out and, with a solid albeit empty arm, slapped the plastic ward from Grimble's hand.

Devoid of any more potential weapons, Grimble heaved his entire wallet— full of dollar bills and frequent customer cards, identifications and insurance proofs—into the massing livery.

They ignored the pittance and focused instead on Grimble's body, tie-tongues waving hello and goodbye. Grimble slouched to his knees and let them come. He had no means to fight this plague. He possessed nothing they wanted except his life.

Soon enough, his neck would be snapped in a tie's red noose. Soon enough, they would carry him away. And soon enough, he would be riding a boxcar, naked and bloated, brought to his final resting place by a plague for which there was no cure but fire, a plague of the most hollow, most stylish, most beautiful finery.

Grimble set his jaw, closed his eyes, and, with the pride of a dying class, waited for the suits to strike.

Believe Me

by Ashley Dioses

Believe me when I say

I've counted all the days

When I was killed inside

By morals tossed aside.

Believe me when I say

I've held my rage at bay—

That all the tears I've spilt

Were from the friendship built.

Believe me when I say

That nothing is okay—

Not hate inside my heart,

Nor pain that tore apart.

Believe me when I say

I've counted all the ways

That I can stop your heart,

And use your corpse for art.

Believe me when I say

I'm pleased to make you pay.

You never will betray—

For this is your last day.

New Moon in November

by K.A. Opperman

Like to a curved and yellowed witch's claw,

The crescent beckons this November night,

Calling me onward toward majestic realms

That dream beyond the haggard, tomb-gray trees

Of a phantasmal wood where cypress knees

Rear like the fangs of Saturn's gulf, which whelms

The aspirant, beyond all hope of light,

Who treads the Vale of Mara, filled with awe.

That What Was Under The Surface

by Norbert Góra

Harvey the hurricane

though having no arms

it conducted

the nightmarish philharmonic

in addition to pain

blood and ocean of tears

it brought to Houston

a cursed flood

once washed away

by contaminated padding

everybody went to the bottom

giving the corpse

to the servants of evil

forever insatiable

they traveled the poisoned froth

hunters of useless cadavers

in pursuit of falling corpuses

it came from the water

the most brutal apocalypse

amidst a dirty liquid

there were a glowing hell horns

My Valentine's Day Ball

by Donna Marie West

I surveyed the ballroom full of fancy dress guests, pleased as punch, as they say, at the response to the invitations for my Valentine's Day Ball. I'd sent them out to everyone in town over the age of consent – lovely what one can do with the internet these days—but I hadn't been completely convinced that the tactic would work.

Gliding in my four-inch stilettos and virginal white gown across the polished floor, I slipped casually between my guests. I'd spared no expense, renting this mansion for the occasion and hiring the best—actually the only—catering firm in town. The ballroom was exquisitely decorated with fragrant bouquets of giant white snowdrops and yellow winter jasmine, and hanging silver chandeliers holding red taper candles. Chocolate fondue and champagne fountains spewed their riches in three corners of the room. In the fourth corner, a six-piece orchestra played atmospheric music. I'd gone overboard with the whole thing, of course, but that was the fun of it. I offered nods, discreet smiles, and champagne the likes of which most of the guests had surely never had the pleasure of tasting. They smiled back, curious, perhaps, as to why they'd been invited to such an extravagant event, but happy to accept my offerings, no idea who I was or what I desired.

But I knew exactly what I wanted.

I found him eventually, sipping bubbly and chatting up some forgettable young woman in a blue strapless gown with far too much crinoline.

He was perfect—tall, lean, and thirtyish, with dark blond hair hanging on his broad forehead, and eyes the color of the deep ocean. His tuxedo fitted him as though he had been poured into it.

"Come," I said gently, extending my hand and drawing him toward me.

He excused himself from the clueless young woman, set his glass on a nearby table, and gladly followed me outside to the terrace.

Without even asking his name, I took him in my arms, sinking my fangs into his delectable neck. He made a small, hushed sound as his sweet, warm blood flowed into my parched mouth.

He shuddered and drooped against me as his life drained from his body, but I had no intention of letting his mortal soul go to heaven or hell, or wherever it might go upon death. With one flick of an elegantly filed fingernail, I opened the cephalic vein in my left hand and pressed it to his bloodless blue lips. He moaned and turned his head away in a useless attempt at resistance, but the seductive scent of my immortal blood swayed him, as was inevitably the case. He began to suckle, weakly at first, then more resolutely.

"Enough," I whispered after thirty seconds, carefully withdrawing my hand. The laceration was already closing, as were the puncture wounds on his neck.

He smiled and ran his tongue along his now crimson lips. "More . . . please," he crooned.

I smiled back.

He was a keeper, all right—at least until next year's town and next year's ball.

The Last to Die

by Jayaprakash Satyamurthy

We agreed to help each other die, when the time came. Each unit had a euthanasia device, but budgetary constraints meant we hadn't been able to afford the self administered ones. So, at our first general gathering after moving into Gerontoville, that week's Uno (I can't remember if it was Tilak with his slow, sandpaper delivery or Ruksana, clipped and precise as usual, or someone else altogether, but those are the first two names that come to mind) informed all of us that, of course, the right to die was still at the core of our little community's tenets, crucial to all its tenants, but each of us would have to designate a second, to pull the switch when required. This was to be done in secret, only the two people in each case were to know.

Over the next few days, it was common to see two of our number walk away to a secluded spot, as self conscious as horny teenagers pairing off at a party. Just like those teenagers' peers we would pump them for details when they returned, urging one or the other to tell us whether the deal was sealed. Just like those teenage gossips, we could never be sure whether we could believe the few who actually gave us an answer, breaking the seal of secrecy we had all sworn to follow. Still, after a few days, I had made my own observations, following the ebb and flow of conversation, of social groupings, the inevitable tidal displacements and convergences in the wake of accepted or rejected intimacies, and come to my own conclusions. Our number, then, was even, so it was easy, after all my cogitations and calculations, to pair us all off neatly.

Things seemed to more or less settle down for a few months. Then, we had our first natural death. Alma, who used to run a cold storage in the south. She passed quietly, in her sleep. A model death. Only, it totally devastated Saroja, a former researcher in a government nuclear science facility. Distraught, she broke confidentiality. Alma was supposed to be her 'helper', as we'd come to call them. Now that she'd gone, who would be so brave as to take on the potential burden of helping not just one, but two people die?

31

Then it hit me. It hit all of, no fools like old fools, dismay spreading across our crestfallen community. No one had thought of back-up arrangements. There was no neat, Ouroboros-like chain of the death-trothed. There could not be as long as we ignored the importunities of chance. And, looking at my chart again, I realised it already had one broken link implied in it, one person who had no one pledged to their own extinction. Naturally, others were coming to the same conclusions as I, all of us cursing ourselves for being senile fools. More importantly, we were all realising that our chain of death would need redundancies built into it. Right from Alma's funeral on I could see larger knots of people moving away to discuss things amongst themselves. Groups of three, or five, or seven. I made my own arrangements, and other made theirs with me.

The years went by. Some of us died naturally. Some chose the hour of their extinction. Everything seemed to go smoothly, which was just as well because we faced other unexpected complications. The recycling unit broke down and had to be fixed a few times. The kitchen and housekeeping rota seemed perennially fraught until we finally gave up any idea of a completely random selection of volunteers, letting people serve by inclination or gentle emotional blackmail rather than according to a roster. There were affairs, jealousies, fights, little scandals in our community of aged individuals.

When we were down to the last fifty, we started to ponder the fact that there might be a lone survivor, one who would have none to extinguish them at a time of their own choosing. Suddenly, we were in a death race. People started choosing to be extinguished in groups. Factions formed, engaged in heated debates, splitting, merging, splitting again.

Then someone started sabotaging the euthanasia machines. Finally, we caught the saboteur. It was Tilak, who had decided our utopia for the aged was actually a kind of hell, a den of sinful suicide, and had determined to liberate us from the freedom to choose to die. In the ensuing melee, seven were killed, including Tilak.

It was down to three of us, now. Ruksana, Saroja and me. Practical Ruksana said she would take on the duty of being the last to kill another. She was resigned to trusting her death to the vicissitudes of chance and time, she said. Six weeks later, Alma opted to die. I assisted her. The hood covered her head, but I could tell it was painless. Afterwards, as we sprinkled the converted remains over the flower beds, now wild and overgrown, I could see something new in Ruksana's regard.

I would be the last to go like Aaron's had. Quietly, with dignity, at my own chosen time, my remains to be made useful through recycling. This was the crux, the ideal at the heart of Gerontoville. But now, Ruksana, as zealous in the cause as any of us, was to be denied this culmination. It was like telling a devout Buddhist that moksha would never be theirs.

She started to avoid me. In our sprawling, empty campus, it was easy to. I on the other hand started to stalk her. Ruksana had been a technician. What if she was tinkering with the machines, finding a way to make my death painful, or to do away with herself, leaving me the bereft last?

We sometimes met in common spaces, now sprawling empty caverns, the artificial suns looking down on useless roads and paths and homesteads and us, two benighted fogies, spiralling around each other, each trying to predecease the other. I started sleeping next to my chosen euthanasia device, trying to make sure Ruksana could not perform any nefarious wizardry on it. But what if she had, meanwhile, rigged another machine to kill herself? Should I keep my vigil, or resume prowling the precincts, spying on her? After a fortnight of stasis, only dashing out of the thanatic chamber to procure meals and use the amenities, I decided to go look for her and have it out, clear the air, come to some kind of entente.

Stepping out of the chamber, I heard the buzzing of flies, many flies, in my dwelling. Smelled death: cloying, nauseating, death. So she had died after all, nature had intervened and tricked us both. I entered my bedchamber. There, on my cot, stiff and very dead, lay Ruksana. What had brought her here, to my home? I would never know, now.

I spent some time with her, looking into her unseeing eyes, hoping for something. Some sign or message. Of course, there was nothing. I exited my dead dwelling. I walked away from our little township into the wild we had seeded around it. Everything had taken on the aspect of death. Dust poured from a breach somewhere. Clouds of it. I walked through the dead wilderness, past the recycling plant, the dust up to my ankles, my knees, struggling against the stasis, the entropic dulling of it all, walked to a blank underground horizon, the last one, old and lost, lone and lorn, yet given a beatitude. The last to die.

Hammer Dulcimer

by T.M. Morgan

The sky holds not a single cloud, which strikes me as strange. So unblemished, maybe even unnatural; or perhaps it is simply the effect of the woman performing, the way she slings down the claws with ferocity. The strings give off echo chamber tones, shrill and trembling in a warbled chorus effect. It reminds me of soundtracks to classic Italian horror by the band Goblin.

I have never seen a hammer dulcimer before. It looks like a madwoman's version of strings, dozens of rows of them, driven into sound by the hammers in her hands. I watch her attentively, because she might be Sarah, though any of the women around me might be Sarah. The fair crowd packs into Monroe Park, plenty of mothers with their broods. But being the center of attention would be Sarah's brand of drama.

I fear for my life. I picture the woman clanging one last dissonant chord and chasing into the crowd after me. In the mayhem, I would try to stand but fall. She would be above me, eyes wild but recognizable, even though she is a stranger. Both face and voice would scream, "Fuck you, Michael!" And my last image would be of static blue above me.

xxx

The first time she came back I had just landed on a United flight from New York to Chicago. Winter had its grip on things. The cold gushed through cracks between the fuselage and the rubber matting of the walkway. I smelled fuel. I'd been slow to disembark and was the last passenger; she, at the door, was the last stewardess. Brunette, with a hint of British accent, she touched my forearm. "I was wondering," she said, "if you'd like to grab a drink."

Though dumbfounded, I was indeed interested. "Yes, I'd like that. Here in the airport?"

She leaned in so her breath tickled my ear. "I was thinking your room."

Our eyes met. I knew them, a tingle of recognition squirming in my stomach like a maggot.

Then, unable to hide her excitement, eyes wide, she whispered, "Michael! It's me!"

I nearly threw up. I said nothing. That arctic air sent slivers of icy pain onto my exposed hands. My carry-on caught on the gap of the walkway.

"Sarah," I finally said, then walked briskly to the terminal, caught up with the crowd. Tense faces surrounded the gate, that look of irritation bordering on menace. A toddler in a Little Orphan Annie red dress, but with large white star on the chest, waddled between my feet. Her mother groaned and snatched at the girl's arm. Once she was out of my way, I ran.

xxx

The morning I lost her was hazy as wildfire smoke. We had fought, as usual.

Her illness, always a challenge, was like a firecracker fuse. That day, something, maybe a dream, maybe a migraine, maybe just dawn itself ignited the charge. Once the blast came, plates smashed, and my jugular was nearly slit.

We lived then at her family's estate, a chaotic blotch of land with matching American castle in upstate New York. Sarah's great-grandfather had been a rival of Rockefeller; ultimately, a loser in that showdown but still plenty rich. His wife, imported from Scotland, bore him five children and then outlived him by twenty-five years.

No butlers or maids or cooks any longer filled the rooms. Instead, seventy years of boxes took their place. A suit of armor stood ridiculous and rusted at the bottom of tall, spiral stairs. Green hued portraits jammed the wall going up. The marble floor still stunned, even if buried in grime.

Above us, the attic would creak in the middle of the night. It was standard gothic fare and also no place I wanted to be, but it was free accommodations. Besides, Sarah was happy and, in those days, I wanted her to be happy. Her mother and stepbrother stayed to their side of the castle, which left us to our own devices.

In that attic Sarah found her great-grandmother's journals, and she'd read them to me as we lay in bed each night. The old woman had, it was clear, been a practitioner of witchcraft: spells and potions, sabbats, and carnal mischief. Other men, other women, orgies, sacrificial bonfires, rituals in the woods. Her husband, that fine upstanding Rockefeller rival, had no idea. At least, not until the end. His demise was not documented with detail, only that he discovered them in the woods one night. After a two-day gap in her tellings, he was dead.

36

The ritual passages were terrifying. The women stood naked; the men would first be degraded in ways I won't describe, then violent orgies would follow, forcible assaults, sexual vileness. They would invoke Satan, wail for him. If her writings were to be believed, he arrived, a hoof-footed monster with horns rising from his head like flames. He demanded so much blood, so many animals bled out on the altar, even disappeared children killed as offerings. We were unsure how much was fanciful fiction. It seemed the rants of a woman who had become delirious. Over time, the depravity simply could not be believed; the authorities would have grown suspicious if even partly true.

The great-grandmother wrote many incantations in the journal in Gaelic. Sarah obsessed over the entirety of it. She would wander the woods looking for their alter in its clearing. Though described in great detail, it remained hidden. Over time, she taught herself Gaelic, at least enough to get the pronunciations right. At night, candles lit the empty sitting room and cast shadows that seemed to morph into silhouettes as she chanted. I didn't believe, tried to joke it was the wine or the weed or that we were simply going stir crazy in that place.

"Do you know what she wrote at the end? When she disbanded the coven?" Sarah asked. Her voice trembled, the journal still in her hand.

I was hungover and in no mood. "What?"

"They summoned a demon that escaped. It tore from its circle and ran into these woods. She swore she would one day capture it again."

"Guess not," I said.

I saw her deteriorate. Her meds stayed untouched in the bottles. I found her once, palm slashed and still flowing, drinking her own blood from a wineglass. Another night, toward the end, she spoke in Latin in a man's deep voice. Her blue eyes turned black as onyx. In bed, she drove our intimacy to sordid places, more things I won't describe, though I found them disturbingly satisfying. Her mother and step-brother seemed to have disappeared, maybe left for European vacation, or maybe vanished into the place's rotten core. I left more and more myself, taking the car into town to find some salvation in the beds of other women.

That final morning, I knew the end was coming. It simply could not continue, though we seemed trapped in a cycle of escalating madness. When she emerged with the knife, her eyes so wild they looked like an animal's, I was ready for her, though she threw a plate at my head as she advanced. It grazed my temple. Once on me, her emotions raged when my hand gripped her wrist.

"Sarah, don't!"

"You lying mother fucker!" she screamed.

The journals' sickness had fully corrupted her. I realized then as we fought that I should have burned them. The anger was as much at myself as her. I backhanded her across the cheek, and she flew into the wall with such force a painting shook to the floor. Her face, flushed purple and looking as crumpled as paper, showed a shock I'll never forget. With both hands, she pulled the knife into her stomach and churned the blade. Her guts drooped into one hand. I knelt to her, but that knifepoint danced near my face.

"Triùir a thig gun iarraidh. Gaol, eud is eagal," she shouted, spitting blood.

It took me a few days to translate her last words. Basically, it's an old saying: love, jealousy, and fear come without you asking for it.

xxx

The second time I saw her was on my honeymoon in Peru. Elena had already changed into lingerie after dinner. The suite, bathed in yellow walls matched with red and purple furniture, had a steam room and jacuzzi as part of the stone veranda. I undressed and led her into the steam room. Our bodies disappeared into white mist. When we touched, our fingers returned dipped in sweat.

"Michael," she said and closed so we could kiss. I saw her eyes. I knew before she told me. "It's me, my love."

Because I had no idea if Elena was still aware, I didn't shove her away. Instead I got to my knees and moved quickly inside her because, in all honesty, Sarah being there excited me. She commented throughout, how she missed me, how she loved me. Her words held me, my eyes hypnotized by hers, which shone as blue as sky. The heat made me nearly pass out. I grieved that Elena might be watching, that Sarah might force her to watch. The spell captivated me, though, and I heaved my body until I was ready to collapse.

When it was over, we went to the jacuzzi, the chill September air a shock to my body. Elena emerged woozy, her eyes emerald green. I caught her before she could slip beneath the water. I kissed her as I wept. She remembered nothing.

We lived like that for almost a year. I confess that I enjoyed having Sarah again. We had long conversations and remembered the fond times. To hear her words come from Elena's small mouth always made me want to kiss her. The difference in the way they each made love was stark. Sarah smashed into it, arousing me again to the brutal, rough sex of the castle's last days. Elena, the tenderest person I've ever met, moved as slow as an hourglass.

The fighting started with Sarah: the biting comments, our arguments as before. Always, Elena would reappear dazed, unsure why her wrists were bruised or why her cheeks were tender from crying. Sarah, wherever she went – she would not tell me where, only that I would never last in that place — would return enraged.

The last day of Elena's life started in simple, mundane ways: breakfast of toast and coffee; both off to work in a rush. I arrived late to find her standing in the kitchen, her makeup smeared like watercolors.

"You're a monster," Elena said. I could tell by her eyes it was her and not Sarah. When she saw the look on my face, she said, "She told me everything, *showed* me everything. You're sick."

I knew getting angry would make things worse. "You can't trust Sarah."

Rage brought unnatural shadows to her face. "Oh, Michael. You don't get to say who can't be trusted."

She held a glass full of clear liquid. I knew in my heart it wasn't water. It might have been they fought inside, two souls snarled in battle, because her hands trembled. Our kitchen was modest and contemporary but constrained by our small flat. Elena had set blue and white tiles as a backsplash. To see her there on the precipice of death, in the kitchen she created, paralyzed me.

"It's your last chance for me to forgive you." Sarah's voice was full of amusement. The glass rose to her lips. "Hydrochloric acid," she said coolly.

I wouldn't win, I knew that, no matter what I said. "Sarah, I'm sorry about everything that happened."

The eyes eased and the mouth wilted. Elena stared at me, afraid and quivering. "Michael," she cried. "What about me? Look what you've wrought on *me*. Why did you even marry me? This is your doing."

Her eyes rolled back to white. She tossed the glass's contents at me. Chemical smoke flumed up my body, and I choked on it. I ripped my shirt off with a scattering of black buttons and then frantically unzipped my pants and wriggled out, the acid wet and stinging on my fingertips. Down came my underwear, followed by a stumbling dance toward the sink. I washed vigorously with soap. My breath sounded like an air hose filling a tire.

Behind me, she guzzled a bottle the size of a vodka liter. You can imagine the blood. I was unable to even kiss her goodbye, what remained of her lips glistening wet and dangerous.

xxx

39

The music is quite beautiful. It sounds Celtic, though every song on a hammer dulcimer likely sounds Celtic. Her arms catch the floating sleeves of her gown, her voice risen as if a goddess. It has passion. Behind the platform, only a foot off the ground but serving as a stage, a forest encroaches. Nearly a hundred people sit on the open grass and watch her enthralled.

I wonder what she would think of me now, so exhausted from always wondering what the woman next to me contemplates, if it's Sarah peering through those eyes. I stopped dating. There have been brief appearances since Elena, all meant to terrorize me: the waitress taking my order; the strawberry blonde on the train; a red-haired woman blowing kisses in a bar.

The performer sings about a man whose true love becomes lost in the woods. A boar has been terrorizing the village, so that's what people say. A girl delivering bread finds him crying and follows him inside their cabin. Oh, the man cries, to betray the one you love.

It must be Sarah. No coincidences are this great.

A little girl flops near me, kicks and whirls, laughing the whole time. She does a somersault close and lands in my lap. Her little face, bound by brown curls, gives me that familiar look. A scream catches in my throat.

"Sarah, no," I say.

"Kiss me," she says, "or I'll make up something else to tell my mother."

The hammers strike the dulcimer with sudden fury. The finale of the song arrives when the woman returns to discover the betrayal in all its carnality. Her axe raises on the two asleep in bed.

The girl's lips reach mine. In a lurch, she tumbles off, though not before a woman stands and points at me. Also at that moment, from the trees behind the stage, another woman staggers from the dense underbrush, her clothes torn and streaked red. The crowd stands in commotion. A concerned man rushes to her side.

Her face finds mine amongst them all. "That's him! The one in the hat and sunglasses! He's the one that attacked me!" Her sobs nearly suffocate her, but her hand never stops pointing.

The other woman, the mother, cries, "I just caught him molesting my daughter! Right here in the open!"

The mob turns biblical. The beating is merciless, coming in waves. My premonition of chaos proves true, but instead of Sarah above me, it's the crowd that enacts rough justice, their fists and kicks breaking bones with such ease. I catch a moment of the dulcimer player, a smirk as she passes to gawk.

After I learn the severity of my injuries and after the police cuff me to the hospital bed, she's there, her gray hair bound in a bun. She splashes my used bedpan in my face. She inserts an unnecessary catheter dry.

"Oh, goodness," she says. "What are we going to do with you?"

"Sarah..." I try to say her name. The bleeps of my monitors are louder than my voice.

"Shh, we're going to make everything right. It's better I look after you than that you run free."

My head throbs. My cock burns. I feel shaky. "What do you mean?"

She smiles. "Rest. It will take a long time to recuperate. I'm going to make sure you get the best care."

She turns to walk away but stops, gives me one blue eye over her shoulder. "Now," she says low, "don't go anywhere. I found the altar back at the estate. I'm finally going to take you home after your escape from me."

The door slams behind her. I am sure I smell smoke.

The Ballad Stone

by Adam Bolivar

The Ballad Stone is moody blue,

    A goblin-chiselled gem,

A sapphire of uncanny hue

    Upon a diadem

That once adorned a pixy queen,

    And now a ducal crown,

Which though it seldom now is seen

    Has garnered great renown.

Who wears it hears a spectre sing

    Strange ballads very old,

While pixies gambol in a ring,

    Or so the tale is told.

This phantom strums on silver strings,

    Which drive their hearer mad,

Who sees then insubstantial things,

    And dancers all unclad.

These pixies dance and sing of Jack,

    Their lover sweet and fair,

Who wanders down the Ancient Track

    With wild and flowing hair.

The Ballad Duke soon joined their dance

    For Jack he also was,

Who only cared to find Romance,

    Disdainful of God's laws.

Lost on the Road to Nowhere

by Pete Rawlik

The little electric motor struggles and whines as you roll down the car window. It's night on the road, and the moon is full, but its darker inside the car, but your sunglasses - Gibsonian mirror shades - catch some moonlight and I can see your head move up and down, checking me out. Even now, the heat of the road is palpable, and between us the air is thick and hazy. I can tell you're trying to decide whether to unlock the passenger door. It's been a long time since I've been picked up, there are few cars on the road to nowhere, and even fewer pedestrians. I'm sure if I were a woman, things might be different, but I'm not, and we both have reasons to be cautious.

I'm careful to keep my distance, my left hand finds the butt of the blade I keep in the small of my back. From the darkness inside the car your untrusting voice breaks the dangerous silence, "Who are you?"

And I should think about that, not just the answer, but the question itself. Why do you ask I wonder? Will knowing my name change things? You ask as if it is a simple question, to be asked and answered. The answer won't make you happy, I promise you that. In my experience, the truth is often disappointing

And the truth is, that the question cannot be answered, not in any satisfactory sense. For as Burroughs – Bill not Edgar - propositioned, the ability to define something by affirmation is impossible, or at least unlikely. Not that things cannot be defined, but they must be defined in opposition, in other words, they must be defined by what they are not, as opposed to what they are. A Heisenberg Uncertainty Principle for language.

You ask again, "Who are you?"

I find the question divisive. I am not who you think I am. I am not a delusion, a hallucination, a phantasm brought on by a bit of spoiled meat. I am not the beautiful soup. I am not the hour that creeps, slouching toward Babylon, waiting for the miles of empty desert to pass, so that I can die where I was born. I am not your ego, your id, your superego. But the truth is a lie that knows no boundaries. I am what you make of me, what you need me to be.

Why is it that you and almost everyone else I've ever met, always need a monster?

We all make monsters of men, or Gods. I'm not sure there is that much of a difference. Still, the time will come when we need men more than gods or monsters. They will speak to us, in a language we know instinctively, knowing but not knowing that we know. Not the language of the gods, but of men. And then we shall know who we are, and perhaps then you shall know who I am.

Who am I? I cannot say, but I ask this without meaning to be ironic, "Who are you?"

"What's your name?" A more direct question. I'm not even sure that you've heard a word I've said. I'm not even sure I've said anything at all. But the new question, though more direct, is even more problematic than the first. After all, it's dangerous to ask someone his name. Even the most primitive of shaman know that names have power, and that knowing someone's name gives one power over that person. Thus, came in to practice the hiding of true names, and the development of pseudonyms, false names. But a rose by any other name . . .

Here then is the danger of pseudonyms. Just as true names grant power over the named, so too can false names, if false becomes true, and what was becomes false. It is a fiction that men cling to that what was, is and will be. Nothing could be further from the truth. The truth is often malleable, fluid, dynamic. So are names. And true names can become false, and pseudonyms can become true names. Which can, in time, become false.

This then is the cycle of names, a naming circus, a naming convention, and why a man may be born one thing and be many things before he dies. What price would you pay for a name? I have worked a lifetime and still only own a few. Should they be free? The truth will set you free. A true name will give you power. False names will bind and break you.

What is in a name? For in this game of names what memes may come?

If I give you a name (not mine, you fool) is it yours?

What would you do with it?

Was it even mine to give?

Names define us, or try to anyway. But the definition must, as we have already established, be in opposition to what is. You ask me for a name, as if that would help you. As if you could use it. As if you could ever understand what words, what sounds, what sigils, I would use to (un)define myself.

Call me what you will, for I answer to no one, least of all you.

You sigh. "What do you want?" and I can hear the frustration building inside you, demanding, on the verge of anger. Still, I'm not sure if I can answer. I stare down the road at the landscape beyond and try to imagine what it must be like to be you

It's a full moon night in a drift glass sky, and the pale light casts the moving montage into inkblot silhouettes against the road. Octane fumes shimmer out of the asphalt, twisting the center lines into a titanium white double helix that spirals into the distant unending curve of the horizon. You've been driving a long, long time and sleep is just a distant memory lost in the void of been there and just passing through. The paper cup of coffee is old, torn and decayed the lid casually chewed, and yet the warm, caffeine laden fluid inside never ends. Just like the road, a sliver of obsidian darkness that goes on forever. There are no off ramps on the road to nowhere

And you want what I want, what we all want, but the road goes on. No matter how much I want to go home, the road to nowhere goes on forever.

And while I don't know about you, the truth is, I deserve this.

"Have we met before?" It's a simple question, I'm not even sure you asked it, or if I'm just remembering the voice of someone else. I've been asked that question before.

I stare down at the light going out in a pair of green eyes (but not your eyes). There's a second smile, one that runs from ear to ear and done up in crimson. Blood warm and wet drips down the knife and on to my hand. I can

47

still hear a voice, last words bouncing around inside my head like balls inside a pachinko machine.

"Have we met before?"

There's a gurgling sound and a bubble suddenly expands within those ruby-red lips of yours. It lingers there for a moment, like a portent of expectation, a symbol of what is to come. The suspense rises in me, because I know that it simply cannot last. But I stare at it, that perfect crimson dome and force my internal clock to slow so that the moment creeps. It catches the light and in that thin layer of lifeblood that has come to symbolize death I catch a reflection of myself. The bubble of blood mirrors me, and in some ways, captures a tiny sliver of the truth of things.

But the truth is not always satisfying, or welcome.

I wipe the blade across my victim's shirt, not once but twice, and the X that is now painted across her chest serves as a metaphor for her status. She is no more.

Would you like to know more?

We all do. Would you like to know why she had to die? I can't tell you. Not my department. I am the message, not the messenger, not even the author. Can you take comfort in that? I suppose not. That modicum of comfort floating around is for me. I take solace in the idea that those who send me, the author and the messenger, are righteous men. Men with a cause, a creed, a manifesto, and that I serve some purpose in that. I may be a cog in a great and terrible machine, but that is my place, and I am happy in it.

"Let me see your eyes." You ask your most dangerous question yet. My grip on my blade tightens as I ponder the meaning of your question. How much do you know? Then I realize that you're talking about my eyes, the ones I was born with, and I relax, but not too much.

My free hand rises to my face and touches the frames cautiously. Romantics and poets (not necessarily in that order) will tell you that the eyes are the windows to the soul. This is true. Through your eyes you can see all

48

manner of wonderment, including but not limited to the souls of the people around you, and the armors they manufacture to protect themselves, and the masks that hide their faces, and the frippery that serves to cover that as well. Your eyes can see all that, but you still cannot see me. I have chosen a different path.

I wear no ostentatious jewels or finery. Bright colors do not adorn my form. Neither do I sport a mask or armor to protect myself from recognition, penetration, or persecution. I am free of such defenses. The truth is I have no need of them. The eyes are the windows to the soul, but you cannot see me or mine. For I have none to see, I traded it away long ago,

It seemed such a useless, paltry thing.

I take my glasses off and let you see the nothing I have become.

"It would help if you smiled." You sit there in that vintage fucking muscle car and make demands. I didn't ask you to stop. It's not me that needs you, and I've no patience for the inconsequential. You want me to smile, but I've got nothing to smile about, I don't know anyone who does. As far as I can tell life isn't worth living.

After a suicide somebody inevitable asks the stupid question of "Why?" I simply can't understand this. Me, I wonder why more of us don't take the short cut to the final destination. We work hard to find ways though, to avoid the end, to sneak in laughter, and smiles, and joy, to give life a veneer of worthwhileness. But from what I've seen, most of life, for most of the living, is pain, and sorrow, and madness, and the faces of the living are just dour reflections of the sadness we hide in our souls.

In death, things change.

The natural processes of the cessation of life give rise to the risus sardonicus, a rictus grin that grows malevolent on the faces of the recently deceased. If allowed to, if not interfered with. If the muscles are not cut, or softened with chemical agents (black acids frothing with green).

Even if there is interference, finality is unavoidable, aided and abetted by necrophagous worms, carrion beetles, pulsating maggots and scavenging formicariids. The flesh and muscles of the face are slowly removed, haphazardly eaten away by the hungry things of the earth, and the devouring, dissolving earth itself. In the end, all that remains are bone, and teeth, forming a great ivory grin. This life is one of sadness, but in death we have no choice, the final outcome is by definition, inevitable. In death, we all smile, forever.

"Have we met before?" The question rattles about in my brain. I must know. Is it possible? Improbable, but I must know what she has seen, or at least thinks she has seen.

I put the knife away and take out my spoon, careful not to cut myself on the sharpened edge. I slide the bowl between the eyelids cutting through muscle and nerve. I am meticulous, slow, and careful, first one, and then the other. I pop them out of their resting place and then into my mouth. I bite down hard and they squish between my teeth oozing delicious jelly on to my tongue and down my throat. The eyes are the windows to the soul, and the memory mirrors of one's life. It is all there, stored as neurochemical reflections of the past. Eyes are full of rods and cones, tongues are covered with taste buds, but they are all just nerves, electrochemical receptors, each specialized in its own way. Different inputs, but the same operating system. That means if you know how, the data is translatable, transferable, from one set of axons to another. People get hung up on semantics, but in the end, it's just wetware.

"Have we met before?"

I don't think so. I would remember. And she doesn't. The only memories she has of me are false - fictitious. Her eyes, as delicious and wondrous as they are, do not taste of my face.

"Hello!" I snap out of the memory of memories, "Are you there?" Another question and one I'm loathing to answer. I am always here. Not there but here. They say that - but of course they always say that. Another memory, and I begin to cry.

I stand on the pulpit of a boat and watch porpoise dance in the bow-wave. I'm here, motionless relative to the boat, but the boat is moving. So, relative to the sea, and the land that by its absence defines it, I am in motion. Neither here nor there. It is all a matter of perspective.

I stand still on the ship. The ship glides across the sea. The sea rises and falls on the Earth. The earth rotates and orbits the sun. I move with it. Farther out, our arm of stars spins as the galaxy rotates.

It's a complex, fractal series of motions, small gears hidden within cogs so massive we cannot even see them. We are dancers in the immensity of the universe, spinning in one direction while the cosmos turns in another. I've done the vectors. Analyzed the velocities and summed their angles.

(Do you want to know a secret?)

The truth is, all this movement, frantic, chaotic, frenetic movement, when you add it all up, it means nothing. We aren't going anywhere, anywhere at all. We're moving, yet not moving, faster than we can imagine. All of us together, are still, on a road to nowhere.

"Why did you bring me here?" For fuck's sake! It's not like I waved you down. I wasn't hitchhiking. I was walking, just walking. I've been walking for days, weeks, months maybe – years – It's possible. Still, you're the one who pulled over and started asking questions. If I had answers would I be out here walking?

I'm not even sure where here is, or what here means. This place is no place. neither here nor there, or hers or theirs. It is an in-between, the kind of place you exist in after the last sequence and before the next. A kind of void where nothing never happens - ever happens. Ever.

The truth is I'm alone, I'm lonely, I'm the Lone Ranger. Will you be my Tonto?

No, I didn't think you would, just thought I would ask

Where are we? A bit of unreal estate, I suspect. Where you can think about what you've done. Time is meaningless here. You think you've just arrived, but the truth is you've been here forever. Even when you leave, you will still be here. I think that is what forever means.

Why are we here? So, that we can be together. Forever. It's a special kind of Hell, the road that goes on forever.

"What are you saying?" You interrupt me, there's a first time for everything. Must I repeat myself? Are you deaf or just stupid? One or the other, doesn't matter either way. You are here, with me. Trapped in my madness, in my chaos, in my memories of the future, echoes of the past, from which we shall never be free. It isn't so bad, to be here, in this no place, with me, forever.

When you dream it's about being with the ones you love, in a safe place, forever, and ever and ever. Secretly at night (I listen, did you know that?), before you go to bed, you beg God for these things (I've hijacked his prayer line), but when I do it, you call me a monster. Am I a god or a monster? How would you know the difference?

"What was that?" Is this a Stoppard drama? Are we playing questions? If so, I call foul, repetition.

STOP. I'm tired of your questions; they only lead to . . . more questions. Strange how being here on the side of the road to nowhere lends itself to rhetoric. There is something solipsistic, fatalistic, perhaps even anti-natal about all of this. I try to find the words to describe this thing I'm feeling, but I fail. We always try to define things by what they are, rather than the proper form of definition by what they are not.

There is a Sufi concept, something witty and barely graspable, but I can't tell you what it is.

I can only describe it.

The truth is . . . no, time is, time was - Time is not what you expect. Time is a knot, the future diving through a loop of the past, cinching it tight, cutting it off, like an oxbow in a dying bend of a river. The same waters, trapped in a blind, washing back and forth over the same old ground. Leaching energy and matter with each pass. Dying the slow death of repetition, each pass bleeding off a little more energy, a little more life. A little more of what matters.

We repeat ourselves, echoing off the walls of our prison until, we repeat ourselves, disperse our thoughts and forms, we repeat ourselves and make the original signal weak. Until finally we can no longer see what we once were, and can only ask of the frail thing that has echoed itself into near oblivion

"Are you ever coming back?" Another question and I tumble down the rabbit hole of psychosis, memory and guilt.

There was a girl, older than me, a long summer in the pool sleeping side by side, my hand in hers. The cicadas buzzing. A dog sleeping in the shade, too lazy or too hot to chase the squirrels that bother to come down out of the trees.

They steal shards of dried fruit from plates that were meant to be lunch, but instead became ignored, lost in the heat of days in which even eating is too much of an effort. We've lived for days on a diet of soda pop and fresh squeezed lemonade. We may be on the path to diabetes, but at least we won't get scurvy.

One day, there in the pool her hand slips from mine. We drift apart, pulled slowly in different directions by random factors of wind and weight and the jet of the pool pump. I'm drowsing, my eyes half open in the ultra-bright light of the day. Silently, almost casually, she slides off the plastic inflatable raft and into the water. She sinks not at all like a stone, the clear blue waters of the pool swallowing her up slowly, inch by inch. She doesn't wake up. She doesn't stir at all. In all too brief moments all that remains above the waterline is her auburn hair floating on the surface like a jellyfish, pulsating and waving thousands of tiny ginger tentacles.

And then, suddenly, swiftly, just like that, she is gone.

I dive in after her, searching the chlorinated waters for her thin waist, her round bottom, her delicate breasts. But she is gone. The cool waters of the pool have swallowed her up, hidden her, removed her from the world. She is there somewhere. I know it. I search and search and search. I dive down into the waters, running my hands along the bottom, along the edge, searching for some hidden door or compartment, some unknown pocket in a pool that is as clear and bright as any I've ever seen. I scour the pool, until I'm left gasping for oxygen, the sound of blood pounding in my brain, sirens blaring in my ears.

I tell my story and they call me mad, but she is never found. There are terse glances between adults. Pointing fingers, pointed words. Accusations. Suspicions. But they never do charge me with anything. Not that it matters. The court of public opinion casts judgment, and there is no appeal. I become an outcast, unable to escape the media circus. My parents try to move, but they can't sell the house. There is simply too much of a stigma.

I move to Georgia, to live with my cousins. My parents stay in the house, trapped by events they had nothing to do with, that they don't understand. Events that slowly eat at their souls and metastasize into something palpable that turns them into pale, thin shadows of what they once were. One day my father doesn't come home. They never find the car. My mother lasts another year, only to be found by police when the neighbors complain of a foul odor emanating from the garage. I inherit, but I never muster the courage to go back home and live in the house that destroyed my family and me.

But I visit. The years past slowly, and year after year after year, I come to the pool and search, and on rare occasions I catch a glimpse of her. Just a glimpse. She is there, right where I left her: In the pool, caught in the reflections between the waves. She calls to me, her arms reaching out, pleading.

COME BACK TO ME

Come Back To Me

come back

As if it was I who left her.

Suddenly you're shoving papers through the window. "Take these," the driver said. You hadn't even gotten out of the car, hadn't really pulled over that much. You just pulled up beside me, asked some questions and then shoved these papers into my hands. Then you sped off, following the black, asphalt with its titanium white line toward the horizon. Leaving nothing but fumes and two glowing red lights to prove that you were there, and after a moment, even these were gone.

By the pale light of the full moon I could see the mass of documents you had shoved into my hand. There were gasoline receipts, but the time, date and address were all faded, the way that road receipts do when they sit in the car through the summer heat. They were useless to me, as useless as they probably were to the man in the car. A map of a highway through a desert, there were towns marked off, but no crossroads. The road was a single line heading only east. Was that possible? Can highways go in only one direction? The road before me was divided by a double titanium line, didn't that mean that the road moved in both directions? Why did the map show only one? Buried in the handful of miscellanea was a certificate. A discharge form from Florida State Mental Asylum, the paper brittle and brown in my hand. How old was it? How long had it been in the car? Who did it belong to?

There was a name and a date, but the ink was too faded, and the light too weak to make it out. It could have been the name of the driver, the man in the car. It could have been someone else. It could even have been my name. I stared at it, trying to make it out but my eyes, my own eyes, failed me.

I shoved the conglomerated mess into my backpack, keeping the map out. I studied it looking for a familiar landmark. Somehow, I instinctively knew where I was. The map may not be the territory, but it told me volumes. I took a step, following in the wake of the man in the car. That was east, or so the map said.

I paused and reconsidered. I looked at the map and down the road toward the horizon. It was a long walk, and the map showed nothing ahead for miles. It had been the same for miles behind me. The towns were there but there were no roads between them and the highway.

I crushed the page, crumpled it into a ball and let it drop casually to the ground. It hit the road with a barely audible whisper, and then caught the wind and rolled away. I turned and followed it as it scampered into the scrub, driven by a wind I could not feel.

For some reason following the map seemed like a better idea.

I supposed it might take me somewhere.

Where do old maps lead when they are followed?

I remember arriving here on the road. I was walking. You would think that I would have startled from sleep, but no, I was just walking. I remember walking down an alleyway somewhere, dark, dank and dangerous. I remember thinking I was the most dangerous person there, because I didn't care, about anything or anyone. I was walking down the alleyway stepping over garbage, both human and not. There was a knife in my hand and a spoon in my pocket. My fork had been left behind in Sibyl Ophidian's mouth. She had been a liar, and the people I worked for wanted to send her people a message. A forked tongue seemed appropriate. I was walking, as I said, through the alley, and then there was a sound. Not much of a sound, just a pop really. The back of my head stung. I touched the top of my neck and my hand came back warm, sticky and red.

I took a step, and then another, and a third. Then I was on the road. Walking, on the road to nowhere. And I said, "What is this?"

It was my first question, but not my last. The answer didn't make me happy. It wasn't meant to.

"What is this?"

This is a test.

In the event of an actual emergency, everything I had been taught would be useless. Most emergencies become emergencies because there is a failure to communicate, and by communicate I do not mean speaking, I mean listening. On the road to nowhere, it is more important to listen than to speak. This of course means, that amongst travelers, very little is ever actually said, which means of course, even less is ever heard.

This leads to a failure to communicate.

What we have here

What we have herd

What we have heard is a failure to ruminate. Even amongst the most homogenous of societies, the failure to ruminate, to self-reflect, to contemplate one's own existence and uniqueness amongst the masses, is the most common example of how the individual fails society. Or is that the other way around? Is this a test for fools? Perhaps. Perhaps only a fool could understand what was happening in this place. Which of course means, they aren't a fool at all.

They are mad however. We're all mad on the road to nowhere. It helps to keep from going insane. For the test, like the road, goes on forever. No more questions.

Please.

Without the road, the questions ceased. A man on the road has time to talk to himself. A man walking through the desert, following a crumpled-up piece of

56

paper caught in the wind, has no such luxury. Each step is fraught with danger, with the unexpected, with potential. Such a man must stop questioning himself, and reflect on the things that really matter. If you are no longer on the road to nowhere, are you somewhere? Or are you still lost, surrounded by those you failed and left behind?

The dead women came to me, the drowning girl, the one with no eyes, and the one with a forked tongue. They wanted to know the truth. They wanted to know if they were real. The truth was I didn't know anymore. I thought they were real, when I killed them. Now I am not so sure.

We are taught that things must be defined by what they aren't, not by what they are.

Therefore, to exist, by definition, these women must be not me, and their deaths must really be undeaths. Does that make them the undead, or better still the unliving? Which is not to say that they are proto-life or pre-birth or even not dead. That which is not dead . . .

Must be alive? For surely the opposite of death, the not-dead, is life. But is the reverse true?

Life is animate, and the opposite of animate is inanimate. We will not discuss the concept of re-animate, this is not that kind of story.

But is the opposite of life unlife? What happens after life? When the forever road no longer exists. If there is nothing, forever, does that count as something?

Am I the best person to ask? Or am I the only? Does being one qualify me for being the other? The question is Ouroboric, unanswerable, except by endless cycles of narcissistic questions.

Mere moments into my cross-country trek and I'm back at the edge of the road. I look back from whence I came and can still see the road where it was, but instead of heading due east, it suddenly has a hairpin curve. The road has come around to meet me. Like a lover who misses my caress, the road has reached out to me, yearning.

I step around it and move in another direction. There's a hissing noise, like a snake or a water heater and I catch the road rippling with disappointment. It is clear, the road wants me, it has come for me, and it longs for me like some forgotten lover, begging for my touch. I raise a single finger on my left hand and casually flip it off.

I move further into the scrub, the hardpan soil crunching beneath my feet. Behind me I can hear the road weeping, the steady drop of coolant leaking from some hidden and decayed automotive gasket. It moans as I refuse to look back, crying out with screeching air brakes and burning tires. I keep walking, marching away, following the crumpled tumbleweed of a map as it blows in the night wind.

Did I abandon the road? Or did it fail me? It had a chance, and it led me astray. Truth is I followed the straight and narrow, but that got me nowhere fast, clicking past mile markers, with numbers long since erased by wind and sand. Every step I took was taken for granted, and while I would like to blame the road, I trusted it, I assumed that it was meant to take me someplace. I assumed it had a purpose, a destination.

But the road has no destination; it never did. The road exists to be travelled. The beginning and end are up to the travelers, and they cannot blame the road for wanting to keep going. There are no off ramps on the road to nowhere. You must find your own way off, your own way home.

I take the paper, the map of the territory of nowhere, the test for being a true human, and try to de-crumple it. The single thick line that marks the road is now bisected by a dozen wrinkly breaks. Does that matter? In this place, this no-place, where the road goes on forever, and the map of the territory is always changing, does changing the map matter? Can changing the map, change the territory? Does cause and effect apply? Is there order, or at least chaos? Does because lead to disaffection? Are the side effects asymptomatic? Are they part of the cure, or part of the disease? Does the condition act on the tonic, or does the tonic act to condition us to accept a new state of (un)being?

Warning continuing this course may lead to unwanted side effects, including misanthropy, antinatalism, antenatalism, fatalism, nihilism, and fallibilism. In extreme cases, death has been reported. If conditions persist, contact a logician immediately.

Do not use if you are talking semantics.

Edited for content.

I roll the paper map into a tube, linking the two ends together. I stick them together with some spit and blood.

The end of the road leads back to the beginning. In the distance the road itself screams, the world-snake eats its tail. The forever road consumes itself. There are side effects. There are always side effects.

I return to the road, running on it as it shrinks and buckles. Your car passes me once, twice, thrice, each time the interval is shorter. Each time the road is more deteriorated, pock-marked, and cracked. Sinkholes open and gasp out foul, noxious fumes. Mile markers fall and those that stand are more meaningless than ever. In my hands, the tube of paper is shrinking, tightening of its own accord. Soon it will be little more than a rod, no thicker than a pencil.

On the fifth pass, you stop and the passenger door opens. Your hand beckons me in. "We don't have much time," you yell as I climb in. I'm barely settled when you stand on the gas, the sudden acceleration forcing me back into the bucket seat and slamming the door shut. I strap in, one belt up between the legs and one over each shoulder that snap together in the center of my chest.

The car purrs, dodging the faults in the road with ease. You seem inseparable from the machine, and I am not sure if your entirely in control. Your legs vanish into inky blackness beneath the dash. Outside, the moon is gone; the sky with its green and purple clouds is gone. The scrubby desert beyond the road is gone. And then, as if it never was, the road itself is gone.

We continue to drive, insulated from the nothing, from the brief noplace that was someplace, by several hundred pounds of fiberglass coated metal. In my hands the map of nothing, of the forever road, of the road to nowhere collapses into a single point that shines brightly for an instant and then it too dies out.

We're off the road, off the map, off everything really. For the first time in forever we are truly free, because for the first time in forever, we are truly lost. It's exhilarating, liberating, terrifying.

You turn to me, a big goofy smile on your aged face. I can see myself reflected in the lenses of your mirror shades. Your laughing and raging at the same time, there's more than a touch of madness in that voice. "I'm going home," you cackle. "We're going home!"

And then you take the glasses off and I see myself, older, mad, driven mad. I am you, and you are me, but your eyes, the windows of the soul, they are empty, black, singularity voids that threaten to swallow me whole. And I suddenly realize that I am lost, in more ways than one. And I just want to go home.

The ghost of a memory of the drowned girl follows me into the car, and lingers at the back of my skull. She's still calling for me to come back to her, to here. I'm trying. I need to find a way home, but here in this darkness there is nothing, no road to lead the way, no way home, and therefore no release.

Desperate I reach into the glove compartment. There is the nub of a pencil there and a plain white envelope. I unfold it creating an unenveloped white plain. With the nub, I draw a line from one end to another. I label a few things, towns, mile markers, hills, and bridges over dry riverbeds, off to one side I write in big, bold letters the word HOME.

Around me, around us, space begins to congeal. The car shakes. My hand becomes unsteady as we touchdown on a brand-new road still rough from creation and formation, the asphalt wavy from lack of wear. I go to add another line, an off ramp from the road to where I've written HOME.

The nub of the pencil breaks in my hand. The graphite crumbles into dust and fragments too small to find in the darkness of the car. I stare at the map and the world I have created, a road that goes nowhere on a piece of landscape labelled as HOME. I have condemned myself to madness.

You scream until your vocal chords tear themselves apart. You slam on the brakes and we skid down the road, the tires screeching, leaving black on black trails for no one to follow. The car stalls. You crumble down into your seat, from madness, from exhaustion, from dehydration . . .I don't really know, it doesn't really matter.

I step out of the car, dragging the dry husk of you out and propping you up against a newly minted mile marker. I take your glasses. I leave you mine. You moan softly. I remember the first question you asked me. You asked who I was, and I remember how I thought that knowing wouldn't make you happy. I promised you it wouldn't. I wonder if you have figured it out, or if you still want me to answer that question. It still won't make you happy. You'd be better off not knowing. You insist, and I tell you.

Promise kept.

I slide back into the car and into the driver's seat. "Drive," It's a sad, hollow word that barely reaches me from the side of the road. I turn the ignition. The engine purrs

Through the windshield, the last of the new road falls into place, a Moebius strip of double helix, titanium white lines stretch out before me. The road to nowhere, the road to forever, waits for my departure. But my (ar)rival is no longer scheduled, my delays are indefinite. But my promises are kept, and this test, only a test, that goes on as I drive off into the pale darkness of a full moon night.

How long till I come back this way again? I look for the map, but it is gone. In front of me the road stretches and there are no off ramps on the road to (now)here. I am finally where I belong. I glance in the rearview mirror, and I can see myself there on the side of the road, stumbling to my feet, starting the long walk down the road to nowhere.

I can see myself here too, in the driver's seat, my image reflected into infinity by the chrome mirror shades and the rearview mirror. Like a wave pulsing back and forth into infinity, into nothingness. And I know that beneath those chromed glass shades my eyes are dwindling down into vast, unending pools of nothingness.

I finally know who I am. I'm finally going home.

And so are you.

The City of Xees

by Scott J. Couturier

In the city of Xees, all is communicated via the medium of song. The inhabitants of that city – certainly inhuman – pipe and whistle and ululate paeans, all to facilitate such grossly tedious acts as commerce and government. No travelers come to Xees, for it rises on a lonely planet, orbiting a long-dying red-brown star. Its people are very old and very wise, though they have had enough (so they sing) of wisdom, and have settled into a slow-but-concerted cultural decline. They lack the will and ability to spring forth into the cosmos, to seed other worlds with their songs: All the stars in their local cluster are cold and dying. Their galaxy is dying. Peering from its atrophy, they observe vital stars glinting far off in sidereal space, and can merely sigh forth a faint, sorrowful melody. It is not their fate to spread and multiply. Eventually – soon – their song will cease

Knowing this, they sing of menial things. Simple, commonplace, foolish things – yet they sing of all of them well. Every throat (each individual has two, fluted and many-ridged) is trained from birth to express an exceedingly wide range of harmonious pitches. The actual music of this people (not their speech, but determined compositions) cannot be easily or eloquently described to ears that have never heard it. Mine have, and even I struggle to convey the slightest comprehensible impression. Like the fire of suns infinitely more potent than their own – brimming with unbounded, unfettered cosmic life. These people live well, for they know they have little time. A few thousand cycles, so wail the prophets from the high graven temples of Eld; a few thousand cycles before abyssal silence overtakes all.

Xees has towers that are tall, stately, and many-windowed. There is a profusion of astronomers among her people, who are forever scanning the firmament – long, silvern telescopes restlessly sweeping back and forth, seeking some previously undetected neighbor-star that is bright and golden with youth. Many pine away their long, long lives forever gazing outwards, gradually and agonizingly dissecting minute quadrants of space. So far, all their efforts have been in vain, and the pursuit has assumed a wistful, moribund reputation. Those who peer (there are still many) are thought of as indulgent dreamers by many others, a growing contingent.

The towers of Xees are tapering, her avenues broad yet curlicued, paved with hybrid mirror-metals. Her people adhere to many religions – always at first dawn there is call to prayer, the vibrant shimmer of brazen temple gongs. The people throng about, emerging from their many-tiered houses in cloth of bright colors, the gaiety of their dress offsetting the sullen rising of the ember-sun. In the temples are many idols, icons, statues, effigies, all hewn from jewel-like elements uniquely developed by the Ancient Ones of Xees to engender and refract divine energy. The principals behind the creation of these elements have long been lost, as has the method of their making: but the idols yet exist, and the gods they depict are both omnipresent and potent, each being bound up in a star.

The interminable morning passes, a single high-pitched cymbal strike marking the mid-day hour. Poisonous, stupefying waves spill from the sun at its apex – the days in Xees are long and stagnant, lasting some 52.7 Terran hours. The accompanying 52.7-hour night (give or take 6.2 hours, adjusting for diurnal wobble) is when the city flourishes. All high festivals, marriages, and religious ceremonies (other than the dawn greeting) are performed after nightfall, away from the sun's traitorous coal-eyed glare. All high magic is invoked at this time, and it is considered lucky to travel by night, a traditional holdover from ages when there were other cities and civilizations beyond Xees. The crimson strew of stars is intermingled with deep azures and hectic, flashing yellows – all indicative of stellar decay, but not red-litten. In a world of old, swollen light, any spectral variation is welcome to the eye (or analogous sense organ).

The solemn-but-stirring thrum of many gongs marks the end of accursed day. The people observe several scheduled intervals of rest during the daytime, accommodated by catacombs hewn into the raw stone beneath their towers: their world's rotation has slowed in the last millenia, dissevering their hereditary wake/sleep cycle from nature. During the night, however, it is encouraged for one to sleep as little as possible. Night is the time of wakefulness and awareness, a period of freedom from the sun's abysmal tyranny. Usually, the people must sleep at least once per night-cycle, but the development of certain stimulants has given them the power to choose. They revere the night as they loathe the day – and why, some might ask, don't they dwell underground in perpetuity, away from the sun's recurrent menace? They could not; for the people of Xees cherish starlight above all things.

Tonight, as I write this recounting of their habits and ways, the people of Xees are preparing for a splendid ceremony. They stir and decorate themselves in anticipation of star-rise (for the world of Xees has – mercifully – no moon to mimic the sun). It is ten-thousand cycles since the chronicles were first kept, since the last of the Seventeen Calamities. It is ten-thousand cycles: in another ten-thousand the sun will be long dead. In that void, the stars will reign supreme.

Tonight is a celebration of the stars. Revelers emerge into the streets, eyes wide-flown, twin throats piping songs of revelry and worship. The stars gleam in the mirror-metal of the roadways – some of the taller towers in Xees are cast of burnished ores, and these burn mightily. There is Arubach the Blue Cinder, and Zimion rising bold and many-hued...the constellation of Pormirion the Storyteller, beginner of the chronicles, strides triumphant over the eastern horizon, trailed by his scroll. All is succulent, the night-blooming flowers yielding profusely to the starlight: fragrance pulses in nasal cavities that expand and contract with singing breath (for these orifices, too, can be trained).

There is a mass procession. Torches are held aloft, flames backed by panes of multichromatic alloy. The chants of the people rise and flow seductively, a ghost of soon-to-be ecstasies. Instruments are produced – fabulous instruments fashioned by the many-limbed, twin-throated, quantum-gendered, seven-lobe-brained inhabitants of Xees. The idols are borne forth from the temples and paraded through the streets, their exotic matter catching and refracting the flare of Arubach, the manic shimmer of Zimion, the revered amber-aureate blaze of Hyvarion.

(There is, in Xees, an esoteric poetic tradition dedicated to evocation and celebration of Hyvarion's light. There are ballads whose recitation occupies whole nights, songs whose melodies legendarily drive the listener to joint transcendence and madness. It is a phenomenally complex tradition, enduring and permuting over aeons; that is all I shall say of it here.)

The celebration waxes as the night grows long. Darkness becomes unfathomably deep when given such reign: yet, the city shimmers like an immortal brand. At midnight, there are fresh explosions of lovely noise – the lights of the gods are now kindled brightly in the minds, souls, and throats of the people of Xees. The stars are rampant and stabbing, monstrously bright – the air is cool and dry, with the parchment kiss of desert places. There has been much consumption of rare, seldom-used drugs, stores left by the Ancient Ones; rich smells inundate the otherwise-stale wind, perfumes that have scant analogue in the sense-annals of Earth. I could pander to Terran sensibility, and say it is like jasmine and wild rose, with a faint acrid undertone of moonflower;

yet it is also like myrrh and other funerary incenses burning, bleak and subtle. I could try to describe the incandescent sweat-like substance that oozes from the bodies of the people of Xees as they dance and sing and mate, spattering the ground with glowing imitations of starfire – and perhaps that is no ill attempt. But all terrestrial words must fail at the ceremony's final, unutterable crescendo.

The wailing of the people rises over the benighted desert. Over crumbling cities, long-since reduced to untended, untenanted tombs; over leagues of arid waste, where no water has flowed for centuries, no microbe fruited for millennia. The polyphonic keening of the people suffuses their world, the world of the city of Xees – long-since have they prohibited the pronunciation of that planet's name, believing in supreme ill fortune attendant to its utterance.

In celebration's wake, a weary silence settles. The revelry persists, but moves to internal spaces, private chambers, or wild vision-quests across the dunes. Artists create feverishly – astronomers strain to pick out clusters of unsullied stars, pupils widely and wildly dilated by the pharmaceuticals of the Ancients. Magicians draw sacred circles, summoning up angels and daemons of unimaginable grace and malignity. Lovers tryst beneath the flickering stars, singing softly together: their wearied chansons of romance rise and fall mystically over the long-ashen sands. The wind blows, shifts, meanders in old tired circles, playing with the dust of inestimable generations.

Then, all falls to uttermost silence. For the first time in ten-thousand cycles, there is no shimmer of brazen gongs to greet the morning, no mass rising to worship in spite of a weary and vengeful mad god's eye. Only a single, lonely, grim note is struck – on a chime wrought not of metal but of bone. A mass funereal rite is thus concluded: the people of Xees will forevermore shun the daylight. From the catacombs comes an amelodic wailing, a gnashing of tooth-like protuberances. Now I must travel on.

The View

by Philip Fracassi

I was strangled to death by a man who makes his living mixing concrete. A life-long companion turned sour.

This same man was contracted to build a community swimming pool for the children who live in the next town. Through a series of triumphs, he was able to sneak my corpse into the pool's foundation. Weeks later, the construction finished, the chlorine-scented water was poured in. Yes, I can smell it. Even in death. I can also hear, and see (the survival of my senses a mystery best left for poets, pseudo-scientists and Catholics).

I don't hate the man who murdered me. I despised him in life, that's true, but in death I've lost the ambition. My energy has waned considerably. I enjoy the small things now. In a way, it's like being retired – only when the world stops do we properly enjoy a golden sunset, the fiery bloom of flora along a forest path, the tingling smell of a storm.

For me it's the children. Hearing them laugh. Breathing in their innocence. I look up at a liquid blue sky and watch them swim.

They float above me, all limbs and wild hair, cloudy eyes and silly dances. I feel a thrill when a child leaps from the world beyond, shatters the turquoise ether into mercurial fragments, then sinks toward me, knees-to-chin, a vertical chain of bubbles tethering them to life.

My dead heart warms to see teenagers hold hands beneath the surface, their pale feet caresses. Clandestine lovers hidden by a liquid heaven.

Rarely am I forced to endure a drowning. When I am I close my eyes.

So yes, the man who took my life was evil, and hateful.

But he gave me a gift, a most peaceful ending:

I lie in a bed made of stars, and spend my days watching angels fly.

The Figurehead

by A.P Sessler

It was nighttime on the quiet waterfront. The moon's swaying reflection was joined by the dancing light of tall lamps atop Shallowbag Bay. The last of the evening's ships pulled into port, and her crew began to moor her down.

A handful of sailors commandeered a public raft and busied themselves with routine maintenance, and with the blow of the bosun's whistle they and all the crew departed for town.

The ship's bow bore an intricately carved figurehead--a woman with wavy, golden hair, whose beauty distracted a dark-haired man dining alone in a waterfront eatery.

He looked at her curiously for a moment and returned to his meal.

"What's your name?" a female voice spoke.

Alexander looked up from his plate at the attractive, young woman who had just replaced his empty mug with a full one. Not to seem rude, he quickly swallowed a half-chewed bite and wiped his mouth and fingers with the cloth napkin nestled in his lap.

"Alexander," he answered, rising to shake her hand.

Though puzzled by the gesture, she introduced herself. "Phoebe. Would you like your bill now, sir?"

When he noticed the empty mug she held in one hand and the tray of dirty plates resting on the other, he quickly sat down. "Yes," he answered, his face flush.

xxx

Alexander exited the restaurant down a small flight of stairs and crossed the minuscule strip of lawn onto the dock to take in the peaceful view. A dozen canoes and small fishing boats were moored to the leftmost dock and to his immediate right were the raft and ship with the figurehead.

He stood back far enough to spare his neck from a nagging crick while admiring the wooden woman. A creaking door high above announced someone's exit from the sterncastle. The dark figure walked across the worn waist deck to the gangplank leading to the dock.

The silhouetted figure descended the gangplank, its form changing momentarily before a gleam of moonlight revealed the contours of a silver flask in one hand. The only features of the man's face not hidden in shadow were a chiseled cheekbone and nose in profile. He unscrewed the top of the flask and took a swig just before stepping off the gangplank into the light of a lamp.

"Good evening, sir," the ship's captain said, screwing the top of his flask back on.

"Good evening to you," replied Alexander.

"Do you like what you see?" the captain asked when he noted the direction of Alexander's persistent stare.

"She's a beauty," answered Alexander.

"That she is. I've been sailing her many a year."

"I know there's a superstition that having a woman aboard a ship is bad luck, but if I had someone like her I would consider myself quite fortunate," said Alexander.

The captain looked up at the ship's deck to spot the woman Alexander spoke of.

"She's a wonderful carving," Alexander went on.

The captain faced Alexander with a look of relief. "You're referring to my Onessa."

"Onessa is her name?" asked Alexander.

"The figurehead, yes?"

"Yes."

"Nessie, I call her. Now that's my girl," smiled the captain. "She's braved through every storm the past quarter-century, always staring the worst the sea can throw her way without so much as a whimper or a blink."

"She does bare the look of determination," Alexander noted.

"That she does. When she sets her sight on something, be it New Bedford, Port Beaufort, or even this here port, she'll press through till she can touch bottom and set her foot on solid ground--so to speak.

"I imagine she's quite popular with your crew," Alexander said with a tone of inquiry.

"I don't catch your meaning, but thankfully she does suffer the rest of us to tag along for the ride," the captain said and patted the bow. "Yes, old Nessie has always taken it upon herself to see us safely home."

"Do you know who did the carving?"

"Can't says that I do," the captain said and unscrewed the top of his flask. "When I took possession of the vessel she was already bound." He took a swig.

"Though I've always admired the works of a skillful artist, I can't say I've ever been in the practice of purchasing them."

"It's excellent craftsmanship."

"Aye," said the captain with a raised flask in agreement.

"I apologize if it seems queer, but would you mind if I admire her just a while longer?"

"Not at all. Take a real good look at her. It may be your last."

"How is that?"

"We're in town long enough to purchase supplies, then we take leave."

"That's a shame," sighed Alexander.

"Such is life. If I don't see you before then, fare thee well," said the captain as he capped his flask and placed it in a coat pocket.

"And Godspeed to you, sir."

"Much appreciated," the captain said with his back turned and a wave of the hand.

His clopping footsteps grew softer and softer until he stepped into the damp grass and were heard no more. All was quiet, save the gentle sloshing of water against the dock.

"Finally, we can be alone," a female spoke. "I didn't think he would ever leave."

Alexander looked away from the ship toward the waterfront. It was the voice of the woman who spoke to him at the restaurant.

"Phoebe, was it?" he asked and spun around to find her.

"No," she teased.

"Then who is it?" he asked, unable to see a soul.

"It is I."

"And who is I?"

"Onessa, silly."

Alexander looked up at the figurehead. "The carving?" he asked.

A voice emanated from within the still piece of wood. "I've been called many things, but I prefer to be called by my name."

"I hear your voice. But I don't see your lips moving."

"Would you care to see them move?" she asked flirtatiously.

Alexander scratched his head and he looked down at his boots. "I can't believe I'm talking with you," he mumbled.

"Don't be ashamed. Please, I beg you not to be ashamed."

"But this can't be happening," he said, still looking downward.

"It is."

"But you're just a wood carving," he said unconvinced.

"Is that all I am? Yet you hear me speak."

He raised his head and looked toward land. He patted his cheek three times. "Am I mad?"

"You're not mad. You are in love."

"How can that be?" he asked and found the nerve to face the figurehead.

"Only one who sees me for what I am can hear my voice," she answered, "and only such a one could I ever love."

"I cannot deny I find you beautiful, but such desire is most assuredly unnatural."

"Have you never desired a woman's face in painting or her body in sculpture?"

"I have found them pleasing to the eye, but I always understood them to be a mere representation of the genuine article."

"I am no different than they, with the exception that I _am_ the genuine article," she argued.

"How so?"

"Can you not see my form in every dimension?"

"I can," he affirmed.

"And do you not see the gold of my hair?"

"I do."

"The light in my eyes and the blood in my lips?"

He swallowed hard and confessed, "I can see that, and more."

"Tell me then," she insisted.

"I can see the fairest skin covers you entirely," he said nervously. "I can nearly make out the curve of your naked breast beneath the locks of your hair."

"Yes? And what else?" she begged.

His breathing grew heavy. "Your back is arched, rather pleasurably, and your ribcage filled with a passionate breath. And below I can see the navel of your waist and the thickness of your hips." He covered his face with a hand and looked away in shame. "God forgive me--I must be mad!" he cried.

"No, you are not mad! You're not mad at all! Oh please, tell me, good man, what is your name?"

Alexander refused to look at the figurehead. "I am no man. I am a beast."

"You are not a beast. You are one with a pure heart. I beg you again, tell me your name."

72

He looked at the figurehead with tears in his eyes. "Alexander."

"Alexander, o, Alexander," she called. "I must have you. Come to me!"

With a pounding heart, Alexander stepped onto the raft and stood just beneath the figurehead. One hand he placed firmly against the ship's bow, the fingers of his other climbing the planks one by one. He stood to the tips of his toes when he heard the clopping of boots on the dock.

The captain held the parchment at arm's length and squinted to read its print, hardly concerned where he stepped. He raised a pair of spectacles to his eyes and pulled the bill of sale closer to his face, when in the corner of his eye he saw Alexander attempting to molest his Onessa.

"You'll get a splinter in your finger, son," cautioned the captain as he stuffed the items in his side coat pockets.

Alexander quickly retrieved his hand. "I just wanted to touch her," he confessed and stepped from the raft to the dock, so embarrassed he wanted to run and hide.

"Son, her breast won't conform to the hollow of your hand, and her salty lips won't taste so sweet," the captain said and looked Alexander from top to bottom and back. "How long has it been since you've had a real woman, son? Nessie won't cook for you or clean house. She won't listen to your complaints or sweet nothings and never will she speak nary a word."

"But she does," argued Alexander. "I hear her every thought."

"Then you should be committed to the local infirmary," the captain said with his shoulder turned inward so not to brush against the crazed Alexander as he passed by.

"May I have her? I'll pay you whatever you think she is worth."

The captain stopped and faced Alexander. "What would you have me do? Cut her off at the waist? If you want half a woman, find yourself a mermaid."

"Please, I'll do anything to possess her," said Alexander.

"She and the ship are one. She's not parting with it now or ever."

"But I must have her. I must," Alexander pleaded and took hold of the captain's sleeve.

The captain pulled his arm free. "Are your ears full of beeswax? I said no."

"But no price is too high."

"Then buy yourself a whore, one that's real. She'll make you forget all about my Nessie."

"I don't want a cheap imitation. I want her."

"Imitation? That's all she is--a wooden imitation of flesh and blood! Can't you get that through your thick head?" the captain said and grabbed Alexander's collar. "If not, then your head is as hard as the wood she's made of. Now get!"

With a shove, the captain sent Alexander stumbling back. When he gained his balance, Alexander turned to walk away but could not resist to implore the captain's approval just once more. The captain sneered with one eye squeezed shut and raised a balled fist.

Alexander slowly backed away, until he disappeared into the shadow of the storefront.

The angry captain stomped up the gangplank and shortly after came stomping right back down with a ladder under one arm and a large, white flag rolled up under the other. He boarded the raft, dropped the furled flag on the deck and placed the ladder securely beneath the ship's bow.

With the flag under his arm he cautiously noted each rung and every step, climbing the ladder, until he was just below the figurehead. After a few attempts he succeeded in covering the immodest maiden to prevent her from further tempting Alexander or the like.

He descended the ladder and placed it longways on the raft for his men to use when they returned from town, and being fully assured the ordeal was done with, he retreated to his cabin.

From behind a wide tree on the storefront, Alexander watched the candlelight through the ship's cabin windows extinguish, signaling the captain had turned in for the night. Alexander loosened his bootstraps and left his boots by the tree so he could return to the ship unannounced by the clopping of heels and clanking of buckles.

He stepped softly and slowly across the dock's creaky planks, fearful of arousing the irritable captain. When he neared the ship he heard a voice, that of Onessa, muffled by the white flag that covered her.

"Alexander, is that you?" she asked.

Alexander hushed her. He stepped aboard the raft and raised the ladder up so that it leaned against the ship's bow. With sweating palms he climbed each rung until he reached the white flag that enshrouded the figurehead.

"Alexander, is it you?" the muffled voice asked again. "Lift my veil and kiss me, my love."

Alexander took hold of the flag and threw it to his left. Like a feathery cloud it gently descended upon the dock. He turned to face the wooden figurehead when he saw Onessa's golden hair blowing in the salt wind.

"You're real!" he gasped.

A grunt came from the captain's quarters.

"Shh!" Onessa said and placed a hand over Alexander's mouth. When she felt his tension settle, she removed her hand. "What did you think it was you were speaking with so long?"

Alexander tried to explain. "But I didn't--"

"Touch me, and see I am no wooden statue," she invited. "For my skin longs to respond with your every touch," she said, the apples of her eyes blooming with passion.

Delighted to obey, Alexander caressed her from fingertip to elbow, as much of her as he could possibly reach. "Your skin is so soft."

She giggled and caressed him in like manner. "And yours so firm. O, hold me, Alexander."

"I will, and never let go if I could," he replied with his cheek pressed against her waist.

She cradled his head and stroked his hair. "Do you mean that?"

"That I would never let go?"

"Yes. Do you truly mean it?"

"With all my heart."

"Then kiss me, Alexander."

When he stepped on the next rung the ladder wobbled. His eyes fell to the deck beneath him, for fear he might do the same.

"Do not lose heart now, my love," she pleaded.

He gave a nervous swallow and stepped to the final rung of the ladder and closed his eyes to kiss her.

"But," Onessa said and placed a finger between their lips before they met, "there is a price."

"So it's not so. You are no whore!"

Her brow furrowed. "Certainly not!" she said, placing her hands on her hips.

"I meant no offense. I just don't understand."

"If you kiss me you must remain with me all my days."

"That is as every marriage should be."

"This will be no earthly marriage," Onessa cautioned. "If you kiss me you will be bound to me forever."

"I would have it no other way."

"Then you would be with me till the end of our days?"

"Till death do us part."

"Death will never do us part," she explained. "If you kiss me, that is the sign of your vow to me, a vow you can never revoke or annul."

Taking her hands in his, Alexander looked into her eyes, deeper than any eyes he had ever looked in, past the outer flesh, past the inner flesh, to her soul. "May I never be apart from you, ever. Not a second, not a moment, not a whisper or a thought or a dream away from you all my days or yours."

"Kiss me, my love! Kiss me, Alexander!"

Alexander stood upon the tips of his toes to reach the lips of Onessa. They were sweeter than any he had ever tasted. He released her hands and they embraced.

He tried to pull her closer to himself, but her soft, strong arms pulled him. When his feet left the ladder, dangling inches above it, he opened his eyes and glanced down to the raft and the world he was leaving. He faced her once more and closed his eyes.

Disturbed by the carrying on of the love-struck lunatic, the captain came from his cabin brandishing a whaling harpoon in hand and heated words to speak not a few. When he stomped down the gangplank he saw the ladder he had laid down leaning against his ship.

"I thought I told you to leave my--" he stopped mid-sentence. The madman was nowhere in sight. The captain stooped down to see if Alexander had hidden some place; maybe in a nearby dinghy or even in the water.

After glancing at his own rippled reflection by the dock, the captain decided to return to his cabin.

"All this talk of voices is driving me loony," he thought aloud. "Starting to hear them myself."

With his next step, he kicked something. He looked down to find the flag he had placed over the figurehead.

"Hmm. Must have blown off," he said.

He stepped onto the raft, stooped down to trade the harpoon for the flag, and ascended the ladder, again mindful of every rung.

When he reached the top of the ladder he took the other end of the flag with his free hand to place it back upon the wooden maiden. He faced the figurehead and his blood ran cold; fingers went rigid, and he dropped the white flag. It floated down and settled softly on the surface of the water.

The once-lone wooden maiden was no longer so. In her eternal embrace rested the rugged carving of a dark-haired man, their eyes closed and their lips locked in a passionate and perpetual kiss. The captain could discern no seam between the two--they appeared as one solid piece carved of the same wood.

His knocking knees shook the ladder from under his feet, so that both seaman and ladder came crashing down. He landed on his back inches from the harpoon, which bounced with a rattling jangle.

He covered his face as the ladder came tumbling down right beside him. He lay on the bobbing raft, signing the cross for fear he himself would be turned to wood.

He struggled to his feet and leaped from the raft to the dock and ran from his ship with loud, hammering steps in a pounding rhythm that rattled the entire dock, screaming one long, terrified note of discord with hands over his ears to drown out the lovers' voices that seemed to emanate from within his own head.

"I love you, Alexander," said a soft female voice.

"I love you, Onessa," replied a man's voice.

"Forever," she said.

"And ever," he affirmed.

The bride's veil of white slowly submerged under the softly undulating surface until it was hidden from sight beneath the dark waters of Shallowbag Bay.

The Triumph of the Skies

by Eric Ruppert

Stars above shatter and rain down as glittering dust.

Sima peers from her window at the shining dark sky to watch the snow sprinkle down. The tip of her nose grows cold where it presses the glass. Frost forms where she breathes. She scratches a star into the ice with her finger nail.

Every snowflake is different, her mother told her once.

The house breathes quiet. In the basement the furnace rumbles like a purring cat.

Snowfall changes the quality of the night, catching any scrap of light and throwing it back against the sky. Sima moves softly through the bright darkness, out of her room and into the hallway. She hears her mother rouse and sigh and fall back into sleep. Dim light falls through the window in bands across the stairs. Sima creeps her way down them into the shadows of the parlor.

She smells the dusty tang of the closed house, sees the dull shapes of the furniture. She is too old to believe in ghosts, anymore, but she thinks they would fit here. Her mother still pretends they are as they had been. Sima has given up on convincing her otherwise.

Sima eases open the front door and steps onto the porch. The yard is spangled white, like salt scattered over the dry grass. She steps down, scuffing the crisp white frost with her slippers. The snow falls harder, blurring the world.

The snow stings where it hits her. At first Sima thinks it is only the cutting cold, but her fingers bleed where she wipes it away. More snow hits her eye, sharp as a wasp. She blinks. She feels it burrowing in, filling her eye and digging along the nerves. A faint trill echoes in her skull. Now she can see what falls with the snow. Her mother was wrong. These snowflakes are all of a kind. A million glittering shards hide there, identical, pulsing the same starburst signal.

She wonders who else can see it. Then the bright snow fills her, and she knows.

Growth; or, The Transubstantiation of Apartment 3C

by Ross T. Byers

Tim first noticed the pale patch of skin growing at the back of his coat closet baseboard after he got home from work Tuesday night. It was the same shade of white as a fish belly, but it had delicate blue veins threaded under its surface and fine, clear hairs that swayed in the wind of Tim's revolted exhalation. All he'd wanted to do was watch a cheap horror movie on Netflix, or maybe shoot some annoying twelve year-olds via Call of Duty, and now he had to deal with whatever the hell this was. He tried searching 'skin mold', but quickly closed the browser window when it retrieved images of mold growing on people.

Drumming his fingers on his thigh, Tim decided to simply scrape it off the baseboard. A few moments later he returned to the spot, a steak knife from the kitchen held tight in his fist. Had the patch grown since he left? He thought its uneven diameter had widened, but surely that was his imagination. Kneeling down on the hardwood floor, he brought the serrated edge of the blade to the top edge of the skin and cut into it. Blood welled from the incision and dribbled down the wall.

Tim dropped the knife, scuttling backwards on hands and heels. His wall, or at least the skin growing on it, continued to bleed. He shuddered and fought to keep his gorge down. *The Amityville Horror* aside, he figured walls were not supposed to bleed.

His next idea was to grab the bleach from under the sink and douse the skin. When he did, it turned an inflamed shade of red. Tim closed the closet door. He would give the bleach time to work. Hopefully, by morning, the skin would be dead.

When he looked in the closet before heading to work, however, he was dismayed to find the area of skin had expanded, annexing more territory from the closet wall. Though the area he had doused was inflamed and blistered, undamaged tissue had climbed halfway to the ceiling and nearly touched the edges of the perpendicular walls. The whole closet smelled like bleach, stale sweat, and burnt ham. Gagging, Tim shut the door.

On his way out of the building, Tim called the super, Campbell. Campbell was a large, sweaty man with a haircut and mustache straight out of a '70s sexploitation flick, and Tim wanted to avoid talking with him face-to-face because he always stood a little too close for comfort. It would not have surprised him at all if he looked at the news one day and saw Campbell had been arrested for serial murder, or perhaps child pornography.

After a number of rings, Tim heard, "Yo, I can't get to the phone at the moment. Probably out plunging someone else's toilet. You know what to do."

After the beep, "Hi, this is Tim. I live in 3C. I just found out I have something of a, um, a mold problem and I was hoping you could take care of it, or can call someone to take care of it. I'll be at work, but you can just, you know, let yourself in. If you look in the closet just to the right of the door you'll see it. Can't miss it. I really want it gone as soon as possible. Okay. Thanks. Bye."

XXX

The office Tim worked at was drab and gray, with cubicles laid out in all directions for as far as the eye could see. There were windows, but sunlight never reached Tim's work area, which was instead lit with the harsh, poisonous illumination of fluorescent tubes. One of the bulbs near Tim's desk was on the fritz, blinking on and off with a faint clicking sound.

Tim watered the small fern he kept on his desk, then sat down in his thinly padded chair, hunching slightly to avoid his supervisor Franklin's hawkish gaze. Franklin liked to touch people, usually coming up from behind and surprising the recipient, and Tim hated him for it. A hand on the shoulder. A pat on the arm. Once, a palm on the small of his back which was far too low and intimate for comfort. Tim never said anything, though. Every time Franklin touched him, Tim would have brief, violent fantasies of elbowing him in the gut, or smashing him in the face with the potted fern. He would never do such a thing, of course, and so restricted himself to hoping one of his co-workers would report Franklin to HR.

Though his job was mind-numbing, consisting mostly of copying numbers and pasting them into a spreadsheet, he had an even harder time than usual concentrating on his work. He kept thinking about the skin growing in his closet. Whatever it really was, however it came to be there, Tim hoped the super would have gotten rid of it by the time he got back home.

"Hey, Tim," said a voice from behind, and Tim jumped. He spun in his seat to face Hannah, his best friend at work. Once, at a bar after their shift, she had gotten drunk and tried to sloppily kiss him. He had pulled back in revulsion, but then found himself explaining how he did not feel that way about her, or anyone else, and that he did not like being touched. Ever. To his surprise, she said she understood.

"Sorry, didn't mean to scare you," she said. "It's time for break."

"Oh, sorry," he said. "I didn't realize."

"Are you okay? You seem distracted."

"Yeah, it's just that I found some, er, mold growing in my place. It's got me rattled."

"It must be bad. I know you like to keep things clean. C'mon, I'll get you some coffee. My treat."

Tim smiled and followed her to the break room.

xxx

As soon as he got back home, Tim kicked off his shoes and, smiling with expectation, threw open the closet door. The skin problem was worse. Much worse. The entire closet had become the horrible, sickly, pale white flesh. It had grown across the dowel rod where his coats and jackets hung, over the hangers, and halfway down his outerwear. The floor was no longer hardwood, but vaguely pulsating flesh that yielded to his tentative step as though the skin was more than just surface transmutation.

A shudder ran through his body. He withdrew his foot like it had been burned by the brief contact and slammed the door shut. Fighting down the urge to vomit, he dug his phone out his pocket and called the super. Tim thought he heard the super's unmistakable ringtone, a recording of Campbell singing over a karaoke version of James Brown's *I Feel Good*. Why the super would use himself singing instead of the original was beyond Tim, especially since his voice sounded like a bullfrog trying to imitate a yowling cat. It was faint enough for him to dismiss the caterwauling as his imagination. There was no answer, and Tim didn't bother to leave a message. He didn't have the words.

Tim paced near the closet, trying to think of a solution. Fire was far too destructive and unpredictable. Poison, or perhaps acid, but he didn't want to ruin anything the skin had not yet corrupted. In the end, he took a roll of duct tape from his junk drawer and sealed up the spaces surrounding the closet door. Hopefully, that would trap the skin inside.

The rest of the night he was unable to relax. He kept glancing at the taped-up door. The duct tape never bulged, and it didn't look like it was turning into skin either, so perhaps it was working. Of course, he didn't know what it was doing behind the door, out of sight. He resisted the urge to look, instead crawling into bed where he tossed and turned under the covers, unable to take his mind from the bizarre infestation in his closet. Eventually, he fell asleep.

xxx

Tim dreamed he was trapped in some behemoth's belly, unable to escape or even move as he was digested over a period of centuries, his body becoming more wasted and skeletal as the nutrients were leached from him. Impossibly, horribly, he was conscious and aware during the whole process.

Tim was freed from the nightmare by his alarm, its loud bleating dispersing the dream like mist. By the time he slapped the off button he'd forgotten it. He shuffled out of his bedroom, lethargy weighing down his eyelids, but jolted to full alertness at the sight of the transformation his living room had undergone. The skin had overcome his barrier of duct tape and spread into the open. Uneven tendrils spread around the corner of the front wall, straining for the door. More skin grew along the floor and walls, deeper into the apartment, growing towards his bedroom. There was no sign of the duct tape, and he wondered if it had been transmuted or somehow absorbed.

After calling in sick at work, Tim rang his the super again. There was no answer, but he thought he heard the muffled, though still annoying, ringtone coming from the apartment next door. Perhaps Tim could catch him.

He looked at the expanse of floor overgrown with skin. Tim really did not want to cross it, but he didn't want to stay in the apartment either. The skin had cut off access to his shoes, growing halfway up them so they looked melted into the floor. Slipping on his pair of bathroom flip-flops he steeled himself for the trek across the flesh.

The floor skin was soft and yielding beneath his feet. He could feel the heat from it radiating up through the soles of his flip-flops. Tim caught himself moaning as he slowly, gingerly stepped across to the door. A stretch of skin had grown over the lower hinge onto the front door, curling into a loose spiral at the end, but the rest of the door was untouched. He grasped the knob and threw it open.

Tim stepped onto the solid floor of the corridor with a sigh of relief. Shuddering, he reached back into the apartment to grab the knob and close the door, not wanting anyone else to witness the aberration his apartment had become. He smoothed out the front of his tee shirt and knocked on his

84

neighbor's door. It opened to the length of the safety chain and an elderly lady with thick glasses and a shock of frizzy, snow-white hair peered out.

"Hello, Mrs. Goldberg. I thought I heard the super through the wall, and I was wondering if I could speak to him."

"He's not here," she said. "You shouldn't go eavesdropping on people."

"I wasn't eavesdropping. I just thought I heard him. Are you sure he's not—"

"Of course I'm sure! I'm not senile and I don't have old timer's and I haven't seen the super since he came by yesterday. I told him he needs to fix my bathtub. The damn thing won't stop running ever since my granddaughter drowned in it. Said he was busy with a problem in your place, no time for little old me. Now go back home and put some proper clothes on."

Tim looked at his pajama bottoms and flip-flops. He raised his head, mouth open to speak, only to see the door slam in his face. Disgruntled, he turned and paused before his own door. He did not want to go back inside. He stood and fretted for a moment, but inevitably he opened the door.

The skin had, of course, expanded in his brief absence. It reached across the ceiling and completely consumed the room up to the kitchen counters. He hit the light switch, and the overhead light shed a dull red glow from beneath its covering of skin before flickering and dying. Panicking—how was it growing so fast?— Tim tried calling again, and again he heard the unmistakable ringtone, muffled through the wall. He stepped closer, trying to pinpoint the source. Then he noticed the pale blue light flashing from under a section of wall that was newly skin. The skin jiggled as the phone vibrated.

Numbed, mouth flooding with saliva in a way that presaged vomiting, Tim ended the call and fled to the bathroom. After expelling the meager contents of his stomach into the toilet, he looked up to see a small, independent patch of skin growing near the base of a small pipe connecting his toilet with the wall.

That wasn't fair. It couldn't take his bathroom away.

Tim felt something in his mind switch off, and realized he'd gone straight to the kitchen and plucked the largest knife from the block. He stomped across to the closet and hoped it could feel pain as he drove his heels into it. Looking back over his shoulder, Tim saw the red impressions he had made and bared his teeth in a feral grin. Snarling, he flung open the pulsating, fleshy closet door.

A complete and unbroken, yet empty, human skin hung inside, head lying shriveled and flat against the hairy chest like an empty hood. A hook grew out of the back of its neck, connecting it to the former dowel rod from which it hung. Tim reached out with a shaking arm and snagged the tip of the knife under a fold of the deflated head and lifted, revealing the empty eyes and mouth. Though it was impossible to tell without the bones or musculature to give the face shape, Tim knew it was the super. He knew it deep in his gut, in his bones, in the dark, primal recess of his mind. He knew it was the super and that eventually the skin would be filled back in, a replacement Campbell grown right in his closet.

Tim stuck the knife in the corner of the mouth and cut the skin open in one long, unbroken slash all the way down to the toes of its right foot. The skin hung open like an unbuttoned coat, revealing the emptiness within. Some blood dribbled out to spatter on the floor. He turned from the empty skin and gazed up at the ceiling. The skin covering the overhead light twitched, then split and peeled back, revealing a glistening eye with bloodshot sclera and a golden iris surrounding what looked like three pupils merged together. The eye flicked from side to side, then settled its gaze on Tim.

"Oh, yeah?" he said, flipping the eye the bird. "Watch this!"

Holding the knife in a reverse grip, Tim plunged the blade into the flesh wall. It tore easily, the knife and the hand holding it punching through into the hollow space behind. He saw teeth through the tear, sharp and curled back like fish-hooks, protruding from an interior the color of raw steak before the skin sealed around his arm. Tim shrieked and jerked back, trying to free himself, but the hooked teeth sank into the flesh of his hand, his fingers, his wrist. He screamed again, a long, protracted howl of agony as he felt tendrils worm their way from the teeth up the meat of his arm, following the long bones. The skin grew up the outside of his arm, too, just behind the burning tips of the tendrils inside him.

The resident below banged on the ceiling, sending reverberations through Tim's legs, and followed with a nasally, "Shut the fuck up in there!"

"Help," Tim shouted back. "Help me."

There was no response. Tim leaned back as far as his trapped hand would allow, until the connective tissue in his shoulder creaked and popped. Did he still have a hold on the knife? There was no sensation in his hand beyond the burning pain. He put one flip-flop shielded foot against the flesh wall and pushed until the pain in his shoulder became unbearable. Panting, he put his foot back on the fleshy floor, legs wobbling and barely able to keep him upright. The skin had grown halfway up to his elbow. He wept.

After a while, as the skin continued to creep up his arm, he realized he could see himself through the eye on the ceiling. He knew everywhere the skin had grown—even the places his eyes could not see—as well as he had ever known the limits of his body. He knew the taste of himself, inside and out, as the new flesh absorbed him. Despite this awareness, he was not privy to its thoughts, if it had thoughts.

86

The skin reached his jawline, and everywhere around him, the flesh bulged. Splits opened in the bulges, splits that quickly resolved themselves into eyes, mouths, noses. His eyes, his mouths, his noses, each a carbon copy of the original. His own face, replicated hundreds of times, pushing up from the invasive skin, butting up against each other in a nightmarish, tessellated mirror image. He saw through each new pair of eyes, smelled through each new nose. His mind reeled, unable to cope with all the warring stimuli.

Desperate, he closed his eyes – all of his eyes, except the one in the ceiling. It would not obey. Through it, he saw the skin grow like a cowl over his head, saw himself open his mouths. The last thing he heard was his voice, multiplied into a harmonized choir, screaming as the skin filled in his ears.

Fertility

by Brooke Warra

Eliza was in the garden when she first laid eyes on the girl from nowhere. It was a particularly sweltering day, near what Eliza hoped was the end of the war. She had moved the garden from the side of the house to a sunny patch in the woods, better to keep safe from those deplorable bandits that were wandering the countryside. It was there in the forest that she met the girl. She had been on her knees, elbow deep in soil, filling a basket with tubers when her hand touched a bare foot. Out of the foot grew a long pale stem, and from the stem the frail body of a young woman.

"How do, ma'am?"

Eliza noted the girl's spindly arms, ragged hair, and sundress caked with dirt.

"Well, come on then," Eliza said. "Help me with this basket."

xxx

Sweat beaded and dripped down the sides of their glasses. Eliza had learned to make a tea of sorts out of the wildflowers she found on her walks between the garden and the house. It was too far and too dangerous to make the trip into town to buy a proper sweet tea at the market anymore. If the market even still stood. Eliza had seen the terrible effulgence of flames from that direction more times than she could count over these many months.

The girl nodded politely after taking a sip of her iced concoction. A bit of dandelion petal stuck to her fat bottom lip. She hadn't said much at all since Eliza had brought her home. After years alone in the house in wartime, it was nice to have the company of another person, strange though she was. Truth be told, Eliza preferred the girl speak as little as possible. There was something about her voice that got underneath Eliza's skin and made it crawl, as if a thousand insects were nesting there. In fact, crazy as it sounded, that was what the girl's voice reminded her of.

Last year, during rutting season, Eliza had stumbled upon a young buck decomposing in an otherwise unsullied snowbank. Gored, presumably in a fight for his lady love, he'd gone off to die alone. The wound lay his neck open, an obscene wet gash of red against the stark white snow. The meat inside wriggled with insects. That buzzing. That was the sound of the girl's voice.

"… We never did have children, Abe and I," Eliza was saying presently. "Probably for the best. Haven't seen hide nor hair of him since he ran off when the war started. Not to fight, mind you. Took off somewhere's. Took a local girl with him."

She spit in the dirt.

"Good riddance, I suppose."

The girl watched her and sipped her tea, wide-eyed. "Ain't you afraid he'll come back?"

Eliza startled. It was just that cursed voice of hers.

"Why, no, why should I be?" she asked.

"Well," the girl said, "Perhaps he comes back and wants to move his friend in, and marry her, and keep all this for himself, and run you out. Or worse."

Eliza looked up at the roof that was caving in. She thought about all the cobwebs in all the closets and corners she needed to sweep clean. She took notice of the dilapidated state of the shingles and the barren yard. The pigs and geese we all gone now, just that mangy dog and a wayward cat stuck around. Yet, wasn't it she who had defended it for all this time against soldiers and scallywags alike?

"I'll be damned," Eliza said. "I never did think of that."

xxx

The garden was like a prayer. Eliza buried her hopes in the earth and shoots struggled up through the mud, through rain and shine, lifting their heavy heads, and tilting their faces toward God.

She often sat in the shade of the juniper, watching the critters scuttle in and out of her patch of dirt. Watching the bees suckle at her flowering gourds. Watching the rabbits laying with their ears flat, waiting to pillage her beets, and carrots, and snap-peas.

Eliza sucked on a bitter piece of fireweed. She would have to do something about those damn rabbits. The cat was useless. Amid Eliza's plotting, the girl came trundling out of the woods, noisy as can be, holding a nest like it were a baby in her arms. She held it out to Eliza, silently seeking her approval. It was their fifteenth day together since the girl had come upon her here in the woods.

Inside the little nest were two perfect, powder blue robin's eggs.

"They'll make a fine scramble, girl," Eliza conceded. They linked arms, though Eliza hardly liked to touch her, and walked back to the house to make breakfast.

xxx

Eliza sang an old church song as she washed the dishes and watched the girl through the kitchen window. She had given her some old dresses from before she'd lost her youthful figure. They hung loose on the girl, like a child would look wearing her mama's clothes. That had made Eliza smile. She'd grown accustomed to watching the girl out of the corners of her eyes, and even convinced herself it was out of a feeling of protectiveness for the little waif and not out of wariness. She'd grown used to the girl's strange silences and even of finding her on more than one occasion seemingly having some kind of dialogue with the house pests. The girl would gently cup her hands around a garden spider, or some other critter Eliza was about to put to death with her house slipper, and carry it outside to safety, whispering sweet nothings between the spaces of her fingers. Eliza shook her head and chuckled at the girl's peculiarity.

"Ma'am?"

Eliza turned to see the girl holding out a handful of dandelions she'd tied with an old hat ribbon, like a bouquet. The girl looked up at her through oily lashes. Her hair fell in her eyes. Her toes turned inward. She really was a sweet thing, Eliza thought.

She reached for the flowers and plucked them from the girl's outstretched fist, making sure not to brush her own hand against the girl's skin.

She's a sweet thing, Eliza told herself.

xxx

"Ma'am! Miss Eliza! Ma'am! Quick!"

The girl's manic whispers had woken Eliza.

"Dammit, what is it?" Eliza sat up, reached for the candle next to her bed. The girl, with an unexpected strength in those gangly arms of hers, pushed Eliza back against the bed and shook her head.

"No, ma'am," she breathed, "There is a man outside. Prowling around the house."

Without a word, Eliza was up and out of bed, brushing the girl's clinging hands off her nightclothes.

The next several minutes would be a blur. Later, when Eliza tried to reflect on that night, her memories felt soggy and thick. She would never really know what had happened.

She had retrieved the pistol from its sleep inside her night table. There had been a great mess of powder as she loaded it with shaking hands. The girl would not stop her incessant hissing in her ear. She clutched franticly at Eliza. She brushed the girl off, scattering ammo across the bedroom floor. The racket froze them both.

"Grab the bullets!" Eliza whispered.

They crept down the staircase, one shrieking floorboard at a time, Eliza holding the rifle close to her chest, the girl huddled in Eliza's skirts.

Eliza's mind flipped through a catalog of all the horrors that could be waiting for them at the bottom of the darkened staircase. Soldiers, a-wall, starving for food and women. Godless bandits who might do unspeakable things to the two women just for the pleasure of it. Hell, this far into this wretched war, even her neighbors seemed desperate enough to… Eliza pushed the images of violence and gore out of her mind and clutched the gun to her chest. She and the girl eased down the staircase. They tiptoed, breathlessly, across the pale light in the foyer.

The front door was open.

A shadow blocked the moonlight in the doorway. The silhouette suggested a tallish man in a long jacket and a hat. That was where the similarities to anything that was human ended. Inside the shape of it, where a man ought to be, the shadow teemed and swirled with thousands of crawling legs. Eliza lowered the gun, her limbs turning to useless jelly, and leaned closer for a better look. The figure stepped forward. She knew those boots. She had polished them as a young, obedient bride, foolish and in love. He had refused to take them off the nights she'd been able to ply him with shine to try for a baby even though the babies never came. They had ruined her best sheets. She had stared down at them after every slap across her pretty mouth that talked too much.

Eliza looked hard at the boots. The thing that was not a man took another step forward. Eliza raised the gun and shot. In the gun's backfire, in the momentary light of a rain of embers bursting from her hand, Eliza saw the thing's face just before she caught fire, and screamed.

xxx

She lay writhing in fever-sweat soaked sheets, screaming at shadows. The girl brought her soups made of wood ear mushrooms for the infection that wracked her body. The sickness pummeled her like a boxer and left her dazed in the dark corners of her own mind, bruised and disoriented. The mushrooms did nothing to kill it. She couldn't keep the broth down. When she reached up to touch her own face, her palm met a hot, pulsating mass of ground meat. She knew her eye was gone. Half her face had been lost in the blast from the gun.

"Did I kill him?" Eliza asked, grabbing at the girl's sleeve before she turned to leave with the uneaten bowl of soup.

"You did, ma'am. I buried him under the garden. He'll make a fine food for the yams. I'll make a soup of those this eve'nin. Though the cat keeps digging him up and chewing at his eyes. Turnabout is fair play though, ain't it, ma'am? Since you lost your eye and all, I suppose it is. That cat, he puked up a lip this morning, you know, a human lip—"

Eliza leaned over the side of the bed and vomited.

"Oh my," the girl said to the viscid pool of green bile on the rug. "I'll get the bath water ready. Though I do fear it will be cold, ma'am, as I worry about that fever—"

Eliza wanted to beg the girl to stop speaking but she wasn't sure if she had heard any of it right. Who would say such things? Had she even spoken at all? Eliza's vision blurred, wavered. She blinked and the light in the room shifted. The sun was going down. Hadn't it just been morning? The girl sat at her side now, stroking her hair. Eliza stared at the girl's mouth. It twitched, a smile nearly on her lips. Surely, she had imagined it all. How could this girl who had not spoken a dozen words to her in their weeks together suddenly voice such intolerably articulate things?

"There, there, ma'am, quiet now, it's just the fever playing tricks on you," she said, running a cold hand over Eliza's fiery skin. "You're alright. You're okay now."

"Where is he? Where did you bury him?" Eliza grabbed the girl's wrist.

"Where is he-who, ma'am?" The girl's eyes sparkled in the sinking sunlight. Something moved behind her cornea. Slithered backwards into the pupil and flattened itself inside the iris.

Across the room, the cat sat in the darkening doorway and licked its claws.

xxx

She and the girl sat at either end of the long oak dinner table. Eliza's head pounded with an ache and a fever. She was wearing her wedding dress. It was too tight. Her hands were losing blood, the cuffs dug into her wrists so. The girl was wearing Abe's dinner jacket. Candles burned, their flickering light hollowing out the girl's eyes, illuminating the sharp angles of her face. The air was full of sulfur.

Eliza's best china was laid out on the table, atop her best linen cloth with the embroidered edges. She and her mother had sewn this together. Eliza rolled the cloth between her fingers. Was this real, or was she dreaming? It felt real but where had this feast come from? The pantry had been bare for months save for the few canned vegetable from the garden and some dried wild herbs. She blinked her eyes and looked again.

There were trays and plates of glistening meat, boats full and overflowing with a dark gravy, decanters filled to the brim with a cordial, and all of it giving off a strange, sickly-sweet smell that at once whet her appetite (oh, but how long had it been since she had had meat not cured and stored in salt?) and made her feels as if her stomach were turning over.

On Eliza's right hand, her dead husband sat, eating a plate of his own intestines. At the head of the table, the girl from nowhere rolled up the sleeves on the over-sized man's dinner jacket, and picked up a bloody organ with her fork.

Eliza passed out.

xxx

She dreamed again of the girl. Pale mounds of flesh, the curves of shoulders and hips, fingers and hair, sheets and sweat. In the dream, they lay in bed, dressed only in moonlight, and the girl was feeding Eliza her own heart.

xxx

When the fever finally broke, Eliza knew only pain. The tissue around her eye had commenced to harden and knot and it hurt something fierce. She ran her hands over the rigid lumps of skin that now made up half her face and scalp. She lay there in the darkness of her bedroom for a long time and wept silently.

"Eliza May!" she would have said to herself if she could speak through the pain. "You get up out of this bed and you get on with your life!"

But that was the old Eliza, she knew. The new Eliza, the one who lay here in this bed curled like a mother around a child holding the aching in her own bruised and battered soul, could not say those things. The new Eliza was tired. She was tired of eating dandelions from the yard and minnows from the ponds, she was tired of watching the horizon for every bandit, soldier, thief, friend, and foe. She was tired of her loneliness, and sick of her empty belly, and she hated this goddamned war and all the men who started it and wouldn't end it. The new Eliza wanted jam on toast and Earl Gray tea, she wanted a clean, starched dress and shoes with a proper heel, and church services with her neighbors, and gossip in the marketplace, and oh, but god she really would kill a man for a chicken leg, all covered in charred skin and smelling and tasting of hickory and —

Eliza lay in bed staring at the window, waiting for a sunrise that never came. As she focused her eyes, she realized the pinpoints of light she was seeing were indeed sunlight, peaking through the spaces between the slats from her dining room table. Someone had chopped up the dining table and nailed it, or at least part of it, over her bedroom window.

She sat up and swung her legs over the edge of the bed, her feet seeking out her house slippers in the darkness of the room. Standing, smoothing out her stale, sweat-soaked nightdress, Eliza's hands discovered a staggering thing. An impossible thing.

She felt dizzy. She sat back down on the bed and closed her eyes and ran her hands once more over the bulge in her middle.

Eliza was pregnant.

xxx

Eliza no longer dusted the corners of the rooms, tended to her garden, polished the silver to a gleaming shine in hopes that one day she would have dinner parties, or guests, or any sense of a normal life ever again. She spent most of her days rocking in her mother's rocker, wrapped in a knitted blanket, staring at the yellow square on the wall where her favorite painted country scene had hung until the girl had thrown it in the fire. She tried not to think about the garden, overrun, fruits ripening and rotting on the ground. She tried not to think of the spider webs that were creeping out of the shadows of every room. But mostly she tried not to think of the life that was squirming inside of her.

She did not allow herself to imagine how it got there, swimming around inside of her.

The cat, which had previously been indifferent to her, at best or worst, depending on how you felt about these things, raised its hackles and let out a long, low warning moan whenever she entered the same room. One morning, shuffling through the house that was always dark now that the girl had boarded up every window and door, she had wandered too close to the old sack of bones and it had swiped her leg, leaving four deep scratches, beaded with fat pearls of blood, and left bloody footprints wherever she went for the rest of the day.

She was never hungry anymore, or perhaps she was trying to starve whatever was growing inside of her ("Why, Eliza May, it is a child!" the old Eliza told herself. "What is wrong with you, you coward?"), but the girl regularly brought her meals. There was no food left in the stores but the girl would disappear sometimes into the old root cellar and Eliza shuddered to think too much on what wriggled around in the mealy porridges and soups the girl brought her to eat. The only thing down in that cellar was hard-packed dirt, nightcrawlers, and rats.

"We'll stay nice and safe inside, won't we, miss?" the girl said cheerfully, patting Eliza on the shoulders and staring lovingly, longingly at Eliza's growing belly. "Yes, ma'am we will stay safe, and warm, and cozy inside!"

Eliza gave her a blank, unsmiling look.

The girl flitted off, having set a bowl of gruel to cool on the floor in front of Eliza. She was always scuttling around the house, back and forth, room to room, up the stairs, into the attic, down to the cellar. Morning, noon, and night, so that Eliza grew used to the constant patter of the girls bare feet. Sometimes she dozed in her rocking chair and dreamed the girl crawled along the walls, her legs and arms at impossible angles. She dreamed so many strange things these days.

Eliza picked up the bowl of soup and lifted the spoon to her mouth. It was full of maggots. She threw it into the fireplace.

xxx

The girl had lifted her with an inhuman strength and carried her on her back down into the cellar Eliza had been wracked with spasms and an enormous, all-consuming pain that threatened to tear her body in two. It had been this way for days. Her pallid skin was soaked in perspiration, she had discarded the nightdress, gray with dried sweat, a day ago. Her body convulsed and twisted in such ways she felt her spine was being ripped from her. She watched, helpless and full of revulsion as her belly undulated and rolled—the appendages of whatever thing grew inside of her pushing at her insides until she thought it would burst through her skin and come screaming into this world.

"We need to get you to a safer place." The girl had insisted this morning.

"No, no, please, I can't," Eliza had begged at the thought of having to move her swollen, juddering body from the bed. "Please, leave me here."

"No!" the girl said with a force and a fierceness Eliza had not seen from her before. She looked about the room suspiciously, her eyes rolling, she seemed to be wary of the very cobwebs, the cat.

"You're paranoid. You're insane!" Eliza screamed when the girl forcibly lifted her from the bed.

"We have to take you somewhere safe, or the others… The babies…"

At the sound of that plural, Eliza bucked. She beat at the girl, struck her fists against her head and shoulders and back but the girl did not put her down until the reached the cellar. Once in that dark, damp hole, she deposited Eliza in heap of skin and bones and belly into a bed of dirt.

"There," she said, not even out of breath. "You're all safe now."

Eliza tried to right herself and scramble out of the dirt, but the pains were coming in waves that crippled her muscles and tore her breath from her chest. The girl sat down in the corner of the room and even in the pitch darkness of the cellar, Eliza could see her eyes shining bright and silver, watching her greedily.

xxx

In the last moments of Eliza May's life, she was finally, mercifully split open. The thing—things—hundreds of them—inside of her burst forth from her belly, tearing her skin open, leaving a ragged hole of entrails and blood and flesh. They swarmed first out of her, then all over her, and instead of a raging ache, she felt as though her skin were on fire, pierced in a thousand places with the point of a needle.

The girl from nowhere stood over her, a gleeful smile stretched across her face, a smile that was just long and wide enough to not be human. Her teeth were too sharp, her mouth took up too much of her thin face. Her eyes were too ravenous.

"You're a mother, Miss Eliza," she cooed.

Eliza swatted and kicked in her grave of dirt at the things that crawled all over her naked body. So many legs, so many eyes, so many fangs.

"What are they?" she shrieked.

"Your babies. Our babies," the thing in the skin of a girl said. Her face was beginning to slip, slide away from what was underneath. "You are their mother," the beast said, "And… you are their first meal."

Eliza could not scream as the light and air and sound were blotted out and she lay dying in a mausoleum of silk, spun by her own hungry children.

End.

Zugzwang

by K. H. Vaughan

"Mr. Martin Keller?" The land-line was unlisted, but I had been getting calls with nobody on the other end at odd hours for a couple of weeks. The voice on the phone was reedy with a vaguely European accent I couldn't identify. The connection was poor and staticky, stretched thin against a background murmuring of indistinct yet persistent echoes. The hair on the back of my head bristled. I almost hung up.

"Who's calling?"

"Please. My name is Teodors Gruzitis. I am calling you from Riga, Latvia regarding the Karjalainen game." There was no way they should have been able to find me. I used a throw-away e-mail address when I entered the contest. No name or contact information. I should have hung up. I knew I should hang up.

But I couldn't. I knew I couldn't stop what was going to happen next.

xxx

I never wanted to become the custodian of other people's memories. I fell into the collectable toy business by more or less by accident. I never liked throwing things out. I always collected things when I was a kid: coins, stamps, hair from haircuts. I don't know what happened to it all. My mom and I moved a lot, often without much warning. I can't remember all the things that got left behind. Things vanish on you: homes, friends, toys. You can't dwell on it.

I was at a flea market when I found a 1978 Coleco Electronic Quarterback. I remembered playing one when I was a kid, probably belonged to an older stepbrother. This one was in rough shape: battery terminals covered in rust and the green powdery residue of corroded batteries. I cleaned it up and played it for a while before selling it online. That got me started. Now I live in a warehouse filled with the ghosts of other people's childhoods, selling pieces to collectors over the internet. I collect it all, catalogue it, preserve it. People want to find the missing parts for their Dark Tower game, or the Christmas Yoda to complete their set, or the Six Million Dollar Man with Bionic Grip that was the last present they got before the divorce. They pay a lot. Usually they want to tell me why. "My little sister wanted a Gund Snuffles bear for Christmas but she could only tell our parents she wanted a 'soft bear' and they got her the wrong one. She was so disappointed." Maybe it helps them fix the past or somehow makes them whole, but I doubt it.

The Karjalainen game began to haunt me almost a year ago, now. I was playing chess in the warehouse with my friend Ty. He's also in the business; mostly comics and cards, so not too much overlap. Ty had broken off yet another version of the same bad relationship, victim of his compulsion to date the same woman with a different face in an endless recapitulation of the same problems. We never discussed it. There was only chess, with Ty pursuing a variety of obscure baroque strategies despite proof they did not work. It was late in the night, and Ty's made his opening gambit into one of his favorite arguments.

"It's like Anderssen-Kieseritzky." Ty said, moving his queen to queen's bishop seven. His collection of captured pieces stood in a messy pile at his elbow. I resisted the urge to reach across and order them properly.

"No," I said. "It's not like Anderssen-Kieseritzky at all, because the 'Immortal Game' happened June 21, 1851 at the first international tournament in London, whereas Karjalainen-Giorgadze never happened. It's a myth, like Zartobliwy-Pope John Paul II, Crowley-Whitaker, and Nikolai Titov's exploding head. Knight takes queen. Check."

"You're saying that Aleska Karjalainen never played V. Giorgadze in the salon of the Hotel Kemeri on June 15, 1937."

"That's right."

We paused as a police cruiser passed outside with its lights flashing. The blue and red flickered along the rafters and ordered shelves of the warehouse, casting shadows strange and unreal across the ranks of toy trains and action figures. It was a frequent occurrence in the neighborhood, which shifted from marginal to sketchy after nightfall.

Ty periodically insisted on rehashing this argument and there was no maneuver that would allow a defense against it. Nothing to be done except concede the point or let it proceed until the inevitable conclusion. And I could never concede.

Aleska Karjalainen, one of the most promising players ever, was in Kemeri, Latvia for the 1937 international tournament. But, for no apparent reason, he withdrew the night before the tournament started and quit chess altogether. He was a footnote for decades. Most modern players had never heard of him.

Everything changed in 1998. Some documents escaped the increasingly porous archives of the former Soviet Union, including the handwritten description of a game between Karjalainen and an unknown player named V. Giorgadze. It was witnessed by Vladimirs Petrovs, Fricas Apšenieks, and Karlis

Ozols, all there for the Kemeri tournament as well. The notes were signed by Petrovs.

The game was sixty-eight moves, but the moves between 42 and 58 were missing from the notes. No one knew why. Giorgadze had clear advantage when the record resumed, but Karjalainen came out of nowhere to salvage the game with a breathtakingly gorgeous combination of sacrifices. Bold and elegant stuff; the kind of unattainable end-game players dreamed about their whole lives. True brilliance. But the last move, the last chess move Aleska Karjalainen ever made, was his resignation. He was three moves from checkmate, and there was no escaping it, but he surrendered the game and vanished.

The even stranger thing was that no one was able to recreate the interstitial moves. After the first article pointing this out was published in *Chess Informant* there was a firestorm of analysis in the magazines and message boards. *ICGA Journal* even devoted a special issue to it. All of the evidence indicated there was no legal way to get from 42 to 58 across the gap, and this was the sticking point in the argument.

"Look, If Big Blue couldn't solve it, then there's no legal way for it to have happened," I said. "Maybe there was a mistake. An illegal move. Karjalainen realized it and resigned the game. It would be the only honorable thing to do."

"But, per rule, you would reset the board to the point of the error using the log. Besides, four masters in the room, plus whoever Giorgadze was, and no one catches it? Come on."

"Yeah," I said. "But that means the game log is wrong because they would have fixed it. Anyway, it was 1937, and pretty soon the Nazis are coming, and the Russians take the Baltics. It's no surprise a scrap of paper went missing. It's probably a fake anyway because there never was any V. Giorgadze on the tournament circuit then. If he was any good, there'd be a record of him somewhere."

"Then why did Karjalainen quit chess?"

I had no answer. We played in silence for a few moments. Vintage doll heads and plush toys stared at us from the shadows.

"You know, Kemeri was Petrovs' best career tournament," Ty said. "Went downhill after that. He died in the gulags. Russians practically wrote the guy out of history."

"I suppose you think the Soviets killed Petrovs to shut him up about the Karjalainen game," I said. Ty was fond of conspiracy theories.

"Doubt it, but the KGB did try to erase the guy. You know what else? Apšenieks died from tuberculosis during the Soviet occupation. Ozols tied for last in the tournament and collaborated with the SS during the war. No one saw Karjalainen or Giorgadze again."

"I, uh…I didn't know that about Ozols."

"He was an Obersturmführer. Wiped out whole villages and got a bunch of Nazi medals. Hardly any Jews left in Latvia now. Never prosecuted; he died of old age in Australia. Friend of his named Kalejs too. Australian government protected them both."

"They almost never get those guys, do they?"

"No. You know, I met some guys into the Nazi collectables biz at a trade show once. Scary people, and it's not the most balanced group to begin with. Look, I'm not saying that the game was cursed or anything."

"I hope not."

"I just can't figure out moves 43 through 57," Ty said, and advanced his bishop. "Checkmate."

xxx

It took me two days to figure out that Ty had outmaneuvered me. Karjalainen's ghost accompanied me while I combed through estate sales looking for remnants that could be salvaged. I preferred to find stuff this way. When people call to bring in a load of toys from their basement they always want too much money. I get that you loved your Micronauts Battlecruiser when you were a kid, but unless it's new-in-box I can't give you much for it. It doesn't matter how much you thought your Beanie Babies were going to be worth. Everybody saved the damned things. It's just like my grandmother's Hummels. No one wants them anymore. I can't even describe the tons of stuff I threw out when I cleaned out that house after my Grandpa Froelich died.

But, picking through an old house, you often find treasures. As I unearthed a collection of rare Japanese tin windup robots from the 1950s, moves 43 – 57 from the game rattled around in my head like marbles in a coffee can. When I sighed at the condition of a moldering 1965 Transogram Green Ghost board game, left forgotten in a damp storage unit for years, Karjalainen whispered to me. There had to be an explanation.

xxx

I poked around the internet and read a few articles during the week, then requested several books from the library on Latvia. By Friday, I had set up a board on my coffee table and was experimenting with moves.

It was hard to reconstruct the history. I can't read Latvian or Finnish, and there wasn't much in English on the Kemeri tournament. What there was didn't reference the Giorgadze game, but confirmed that Karjalainen was supposed to play and was replaced at the last minute. I also confirmed what Ty said about Petrovs, Apšenieks, and Ozols. Petrovs disappeared into the Siberian labor camps in 1942 and died from pneumonia. The Soviets kept his death hidden for almost fifty years. Apšenieks died of tuberculosis in 1941. He was only 47. Ozols was responsible for murdering 12,000 Jews in Latvia before escaping to Australia where he lived to 88. The Australian government knew who he was but didn't do anything about it. He got to hang out with his childhood friend and fellow mass-murderer Konrad Kalejs. Whatever happened at the Hotel Kemeri, it didn't turn Ozols into the leader of a Latvian death squad.

But I couldn't confirm anything about the game. Everything came back to the same bits repeated over and over again on different websites, all of it cut-and-pasted from some unverifiable source. I found what were supposed to be the original Petrovs notations in PDF, hand-scrawled in pencil in the yellowed pages of a small notepad. I couldn't find another sample of his handwriting for comparison. Strange about the missing scoring. But then again, Petrovs was virtually erased by the KGB, retouched out of photos, redacted from newspaper articles, and removed from all Soviet chess records. Did the Soviets try to obliterate his existence just because he spoke out? Was that enough of a reason?

xxx

"Jesus!" Ty said, looking around my room. "What the hell is all of this?"

"I've just been doing some research." I said. I had invited him over to watch a *Rebuild of Evangelion* bootleg, but the Karjalainen game had expanded to take over my living space at the warehouse. Papers with sticky tags, the white board from my office, maps, three boards. Pictures of the principals.

I told Ty what I had found out and how I tried to fill in the gaps so far. Aleska Karjalainen, born in 1911 near Oulu, Finland. Rumors of mental illness and depression in the family. He gained the attention of the international chess community by 15, enrolled at the University of Helsinki the next year, then dropped out to pursue chess full time and started winning tournaments. At Kemeri, he stayed at the Hotel Kemeri and Sanatorium and tried the mineral baths. He dined in the Merry Mosquitoes restaurant at an inn and brothel called the Forest House. Karjalainen left the hotel the morning of the tournament and became a ghost.

He next appeared in December 1939, skiing through the woods with a sub-machinegun and hand grenades, harassing convoys and attacking dug-in Soviet troops in the frigid forests of central Finland. Five years later he turned up again fighting the Nazis in the subzero wastes of Lapland, where soldiers died in shock from minor wounds, their bodies frozen in contorted agony, immovable until the spring thaw. The war ended and he vanished from history completely until he was found dead from a self-inflicted gunshot wound, alone in a tiny shack in those same subzero wastes. It was October, 1947 when he killed himself, a little over ten years after the tournament. No chess set was found in his residence. As far as anyone knew, he never played another game for the rest of his life.

"Wow," Ty said.

"Yeah," I said. "I found some pictures of casualties from those battles up in the arctic circle. Guys would freeze where they fell like statues. Creepy as hell. I don't know how you go from chess to that."

"You're trying to make sense of shit that doesn't make sense. Europe was on fire. Everybody did shit they never thought they would."

"Maybe."

"Anyway, are you trying to figure out Karjalainen or the game?"

"Know the game, know the player. It's the same thing."

"Man, it creeps me out when I start sounding like the rational one."

"Yeah. But I've also been researching the game, and there's no way to get across the gap in the scoring. There's no way to get close."

We never watched the DVD. We ended up playing four games and split them. On his way out Ty said, "You know, the Crowley-Whitaker series you say didn't happen was real. Washington D.C., 1916."

Which meant I had to check after he had gone.

Sure enough, Aleister Crowley played four games against Norman Whitaker at the National Press Club in Washington, D. C. in 1916. It was in the *Washington Post*. Whitaker took all four games.

Fucking Ty.

xxx

The site was Karjalainengame.com. It looked like a resurrected Geocities page, but the dates were current. Most of the links were in Latvian and Russian. Ty had one of his hacker buddies investigate and it appeared to trace back to a Latvian historical society and not the Russian mob. The contest offered a cash prize for the first person to recreate the game across the missing moves. This was maybe nine months after Ty and I had the argument that led to me spending so much time on the game, but I had hit a dead end. The game couldn't be solved and there wasn't anything else I could find on Karjalainen. I had taken down all the documents and filed them in a heavy acid- and lignin-free archival storage box with the family photo albums and papers I inherited from my mother and grandparents. Whoever was running the contest insisted that it was possible to finish.

"I get you're paranoid, but they aren't asking for a credit card," Ty said. He carefully set his sweaty beer bottle down next to the coaster I had given him. "Register with a dummy e-mail address and if they start to do anything fishy, walk away. A thousand bucks is no joke, and you have to be the world expert at this point."

I didn't know why I tried to resist. Somehow, I felt threatened, as if I were about to blunder into a trap I couldn't quite see yet. I was uneasy. But, it didn't really matter. After all I'd done so far, I'd have done it no matter what.

I registered and began to play, moving pieces on a primitive flash animation board. You could play as often as you wanted, but you had to start each game at the beginning. I knew the first 42 by heart, and they flew by until I hit the missing moves. The first night, I played twelve rounds without finding a solution. The second night I played nineteen. Friday, I didn't do any work all day and was still playing Saturday afternoon when I finally gave up and had to sleep. After a week, the website shut down. I didn't find an answer. It was out of reach, and always would be.

xxx

"Mr. Martin Keller?" The land-line was unlisted, but I had been getting calls with nobody on the other end at odd hours for a couple of weeks. The voice on the phone was reedy with a vaguely European accent I couldn't identify. The connection was poor and staticky, stretched thin against a background murmuring of indistinct yet persistent echoes. The hair on the back of my head bristled. I almost hung up.

"Who's calling?"

"Please. My name is Teodors Gruzitis. I am calling you from Riga, Latvia regarding the Karjalainen game." There was no way they should have been able to find me. I used a throw-away e-mail address when I entered the contest. No name or contact information. I should have hung up. I knew I should hang up.

But I couldn't. I knew I couldn't stop what was going to happen next.

"How did you get this number?"

"I am sorry for these intrusion. We made use of certain channels so that we could contact you directly. I do not like these e-mails. So, I am calling about the results of the contest. If this is not acceptable please say and I will not call you again."

An exit. It would be better to take it. I looked at the ranks of dolls and action figures, but they were silent.

"Go on," I said.

"The game. You showed a great appreciation for Mr. Karjalainen's style of play and strategy in the game. Very persistent in your efforts."

"It's an interesting problem. I don't believe it can be completed."

"Let me assure you that it may be, if all of the correct elements are in place. We believe that you are one of those elements."

"Are you saying that I won the contest?" It had been a month since the site was closed.

"Yes. And if you wish, we will send to you a bank draft for one thousand dollars, American, at once. But if you wish, Sir, we have also another offer for you, please."

"And what is that?"

"Come to Kemeri, please. We want you to come to the Hotel Kemeri in Jūrmala and play the game in the same room on the same chess board used by Mr. Aleska Karjalainen and Mr. Vadik Giorgadze on fifteen June, 1937. We want you to finish the game."

xxx

They sent me round-trip tickets and said they would pay all of my expenses, plus double the prize money: two thousand dollars just to make the trip. They also promised to give me the chess set to keep if I finished the game. It didn't make any sense. Why me? Why any of it? By now though, what could I do? I had spent too much time chasing the ghost of a dead man from Europe.

Ty drove me to Logan Airport, said he'd pray to Caïssa for me, and called me a hack wood-pusher. It was a long flight to Oslo, suffocating in stale, dry air and the muted sounds of strangers. I looked through my notes on the game. There was nothing new. I knew there wouldn't be. Within the folder were the only known photos of Karjalainen: one taken at a chess tournament in 1930, and the other sometime in 1944. In the first, he is young and smiling. He is clean-shaven and there is a sparkle in his eyes. The second picture shows him in his infantry uniform. He is spattered with dirt and something dark: blood or oil, perhaps. It looks too cold for mud. He is smoking and a submachinegun with a big drum magazine hangs loosely in the crook of his elbow. The location isn't clear, but there are blackened brick chimneys that stand against the grey sky like the columns of an ancient ruin. It could be Rovaniemi, which burned to the ground during the war. Today it is the Santa Claus Village amusement park, and tourists from all over the world land at an airport built on the remains of a Luftwaffe airfield. His face is drawn and hollow, and his eyes dark. I put the folder away in my carryon. I have another small accordion file there, but I have not opened it yet.

Flying in to RIX, I saw a strange round white structure like a cross between an origami flower and a plastic drain cover behind the glass terminal building. I could not discern its purpose, but somehow it made me think of dead men transformed into statues of broken pain on the ice in Lapland.

xxx

I took a shuttle bus from the airport to the train station. The driver spoke fair English and talked the entire time, mostly complaining about the Estonians who were, in his view, peasants, and not the intellectual equals of the more cosmopolitan Letts.

"We have many things for tourists. You should see Turaida Castle. Where are you going?"

"Jūrmala," I said. "I'm going to see the Kemeri National Park."

"It's a swamp. Jūrmala was the Riviera of the Baltics. Pretty girls. The medicinal spas. Now…the economy is shit," the driver said. "Everybody worries about Spain and Greece but Latvia was first into the recession. You know how bad it is? The young people go to Ireland to find jobs. *Ireland*! Fuck." He dragged heavily on a cigarette, and I shied away from the smell. "You know, in the old days the sand would drift overnight and bury farms," the driver continued. "Whole villages were erased like they were never there."

On the train, I sat next to a German businessman while a Latvian mother sang quietly to her sleeping child. The train went past clusters of anonymous rectangular housing units, built along the functional and depressing lines of Soviet Cold War architecture.

"What is she singing?" I said.

"It is 'What is that mournful song in the dark?'" the German said.

"Oh. Thank you." I said, embarrassed. I didn't realize I had said it out loud. I often talk to myself because in the warehouse, I am alone. I felt awkward, pinned in an accidental conversation. I managed to say "What book you are reading?"

"It is called *Repetition, Compulsion,*" he said. "It isn't any good."

"My family were Black Sea Germans, from Kiev."

"Ah," he said. He turned the page and continued reading. We did not speak again.

xxx

The beach resort of Jūrmala had pockets of pre-war architecture, and quaint houses with picket fences tucked into copses of pine, but most of what I saw was that same gray Soviet-style construction. When I stepped off onto the platform at the Kemeri station I saw a frail elderly man holding a handwritten cardboard sign that said M. Keller. He wore a scuffed bowler hat. When I said hello, the man shrugged but did not speak. I followed him to an older sedan.

We drove away from the beach and small downtown area of Jūrmala City and into the forest. I could smell salt air, pine, peat and sulfur. Turning away from the highway we entered a ghost town, marked by dark, dilapidated wooden cottages that flashed in and out of the car's headlamps. Here and there, Cyrillic graffiti spray-painted on brick or stone. I caught glimpses of other buildings between the trees, and places where buildings had once stood. We drove in the direction of a white glow within the darkness beyond the trees. Turning a corner, the expanse of the Hotel Kemeri was revealed, like a great white palace, empty and abandoned. It was the only building I had seen with lights since leaving the highway, an oblong shape of pilasters and balconies, surrounded by a sagging chain-link construction fence. It had been known as the White Ship, now marooned and derelict upon a grassy lawn, a neo-classical edifice stranded out of time and space. The driver parked before the main entrance and with profound deliberateness made his way around the car to open my door. I stepped out into eerie silence.

Teodors Gruzitis could have been related to the driver, dry and frail in appearance, with a thickly groomed mustache and worn suit that had long since gone out of fashion. His hand was cold and delicate, and he smelled of dust.

"Welcome Mr. Martin," he said, smiling. "Welcome to the Kemeri Health Resort."

The lobby of the hotel was clean and bright and completely empty of life. New furnishings in art deco style stood covered in plastic. The wood of the front desk gleamed darkly. Mr. Gruzitis spoke as he escorted me.

"The health resort was the prize of the region, you must understand. Rich and powerful people, they came from all over Europe for the mineral baths and treatments at the sanitarium. Royalty. The intelligentsia. It was something in its day. The war, of course. Many buildings were destroyed and the hotel was made to be a hospital. It was restored to its proper purpose afterwards but in time, as a spa retreat, it began to falter. It fell out of fashion, you see, to take the waters here. When the Soviets left, it was the end. The people stopped coming and, well, you passed through the village.

"We have refurbished the hotel at considerable cost. We have saved much from the original artwork and fixtures. I say 'we' but, the money, it all comes from an international concern. The government could not afford to do it. But there have been complications. Many, many delays, and it has not yet opened to the public. We are many years behind schedule. Perhaps next year will be the year." Gruzitis stopped walking and turned to look me in the eyes.

"The new owners, they do not know of what we are doing, but it is necessary before we can re-open. They have been good to us, you see. But some things are incomplete. You understand? Good. Good. Now then, here is the library. We have been fortunate."

Gruzitis opened the large wooden doors to reveal a tall space of shelves and tables, furnished in glossy woods and chrome. It was more of a reading room or salon than a full library, but it hinted at opulence. Chairs were upholstered in bold geometric patterns, veneers inlaid with exotic woods. Intricate and luxurious pieces filled with 1930s futurism and optimism. This had once been a place vital with wealth and energy. I imagined members of the Swedish royal family mingling with famous writers and artists of the day.

"We have some original pieces here, for the library was maintained somewhat more than other spaces. I am afraid that much of the furnitures in the hotel are from reproduction. Please, come this way."

He led me to a small table in a reading area by a fireplace. I could smell the heavy dust of aged books and disuse. The room had been cleaned thoroughly but that smell was thick in the air, resisting the new interlopers with their rags and cleaning supplies. They too would pass.

"Please," Gruzitis said, gesturing to a stiff and artful chair designed for appearances, not comfort. The antique creaked as I sat, or rather perched uncomfortably, fearing it might give way beneath me. It seemed too tenuous a position. Stupid to have come. To have flown halfway around the world for this. What was I thinking?

"We found this last year during the renovations. It had been kept safe."

Gruzitis motioned, and I saw the chess set. It was unique, hand-carved of lustrous green malachite and inlaid with copper, yet somehow crude and plain. It filled me with a vague unease that I could not define.

"Is this…"

"Yes. Strange how a thing so beautiful and valuable can become mislaid and forgotten. It waited for us all this time to be used again. Now we have found it, and found our player. You are prepared?" Gruzitis asked.

"Um. Now? Sure, I just," I stumbled. It was happening so fast. "I could use a restroom."

I washed my face in icy water from an antique tap. No telling whose hands or how many had done the same over the years. Somewhere, since entering the contest online, I crossed some boundary. Something about Gruzitis reminded me of my grandfather. I didn't know if he fought against the Nazis or against the Soviets during the war. He had already survived the Holodomor and Stalin's purges by then, and the Russians were shipping ethnic Germans from what is now Ukraine to Labor camps in Kazakhstan when Hitler's army invaded. After the Nazi defeat at Stalingrad, the ethnic Germans from the region fled in front of the Red Army's advance. After the war, Stalin demanded they all be forcibly repatriated, then sent all them off to die in the gulag as presumed traitors. Somehow, my mother's father, Hans Froelich, escaped to America, settled in Worcester, Massachusetts and lived out the rest of his life. He never spoke of what happened during the war, but I had clippings and letters written by him in German in the second folder in my bag. I don't know why I packed them.

When I returned to the library a gnome of a man sat across the board from my seat, dressed like Gruzitis in a threadbare and unfashionable suit. He wore a beard and mustache in downy gray. He sipped at a small glass of spirits.

"Mr. Giorgadze will play black, of course." Gruzitis said.

"Of course. Good evening, Mr. Giorgadze," I said. The gnome smiled.

"He does not speak English, Mr. Keller."

xxx

The first moves raced by. I had played this part hundreds of times already, the familiar ritual helping to ease my anxiety back to manageable levels. I paused before entering the interstitial portion of the game, where the course was no longer known. My hand was shaking slightly. What would Karjalainen have done? I had to preserve my queen, both rooks, and king's bishop for the end moves. I reached into this uncertain space and moved my rook. Gruzitis nodded and breathed a sigh of relief. Giorgadze said something in Russian and made a short coughing laugh.

"He says you got it right," Gruzitis said. "He says we've found the right man for the game."

Giorgadze reached with his arthritic claw and moved his bishop to counter. I heard a sharp click from somewhere underneath the board, which was followed by a ticking sound like that of an antique clock or toy. The stone of the board shivered and seams appeared between the squares on the board. I watched aghast, as the ranks rose and separated, revealing an impossibly complex clockwork of gears and spindles beneath. The squares bore their pieces in strange orbits over the table, and settled slowly back to create a new configuration. The smell of ancient oil and dust hung over the board. A tiny spark arced from the copper inlay on the outside border.

The gnome nodded.

"You must understand," Gruzitis said. "It is not only that you are good at the game or that you understand Karjalainen's style of play; it is also that you were so persistent in your efforts and not thrown off by unusual maneuvers. Please, we beg you continue without protest. Please."

I swallowed and examined the new board. I reached towards my king.

"J'adoube," I said.

"Da. Konechno," Giorgadze croaked.

I adjusted my king to center him in his square. Was this when Karjalainen began to lose his resolve? I spent five minutes trying to plan my next move. My strategy was completely thrown, my defenses wide open. Reinforce. Hold the center. I slid my queen. She was exposed but active. Giorgadze nodded.

The second time the board shifted, the black and white squares were left intermingled illegally, and I had to rethink his strategy again. Giorgadze was aggressively pursuing my queen, forcing me to give up positional advantage and withdraw to safety. The board was emitting an audible hum now, a faint vibration as if quivering in mechanical anticipation. Faint shadows began to wander in the periphery of my vision but I was too intent upon the game to attend to them, and too afraid.

At the fiftieth move, the board began to unfold and re-arrange itself yet again, and it added an additional rank of squares down the middle. The hum had begun to fill the room around him, but I refused to look up at the coalescing forms around me. I didn't dare. There were no footsteps on the echoing stone floor to carry these observers to the table. Sweat ran down my neck in the cool air. It was all I could do to focus on the game and my opponent, who sat cryptic and obscure across the board. Gruzitis had faded out of sight. It was no good, I realized. Even if I could figure out the configuration, there were too many pieces remaining on the board. It was not possible to capture enough to match the number remaining in the record of the game when it resumed at 58. I reinforced my king in light of the current version of the board and hoped for the best. The onlookers whispered and buzzed quietly in the periphery. I heard faint strains of music in the distance.

When Giorgadze completed move 57, the board re-arranged itself again. The extra rank folded itself back into the board and several pieces tipped gently off of the side to rest on the table. The remaining pieces matched the configuration from the Petrovs record from 1937. I exhaled, and Giorgadze grinned.

"Kak staryy lev. You: old lion," he said.

I returned his smile and we shared a brief resigned chuckle. I was exhausted from the tension.

Together, we advanced the game to Karjalainen's last move. Three more moves to the checkmate he had refused. Giorgadze gazed at me expectantly. His parchment skin wrinkled in anticipation. I finally allowed himself to look at the assembled ghosts around me. I had been steeling himself against something horrific since the board began to re-arrange itself. I knew they would be there: a motley collection of apparitions from the past had gathered, solidifying slowly around the game in the dim light. The spirits looked like old sepia-tone photographs, faded and scratched. Patients and workers from the glory days of the sanatorium, civilians and soldiers with their faded wounds. Forlorn and decrepit like the abandoned cottages where artists and their patrons had once summered, like the spa buildings where the wealthy had once taken mineral baths and mud treatments. Shaking, I looked through the crowd and picked out Gruzitis, himself now faded and insubstantial among his peers, frozen in time.

"What happens if I finish the game?" Martin rasped.

There was no response. I looked out at the assembled ghosts, their desperate eyes pleading. I swallowed dryly. I had come too far to concede. I moved my queen.

"Check."

Giorgadze captured her. I moved my rook into position.

"Checkmate."

Giorgadze nodded. He was now transparent like the rest. The library was now filled with ghosts, young and old, highborn and low. They spilled through the doors and as far down the corridor as I could see. The bodies of many were torn grotesquely from bullets and shrapnel and some stood impossibly on shattered or missing limbs. More than hundred years of pain hung heavily in the room. They would be packed through the hallways and out onto the lawn. Gruzitis, Giorgadze, the driver who picked me up at the train station, the woman on the train and the German who translated for me were all there. The ones I thought I might recognize, that I had hoped I would see, Alexa Karjalainen and Hans Froelich, were not there. I don't know how long I sat there shivering in the cold while they stared at me in silence.

"You see? It was never about finishing the game. If you're still here, that's you. It's nothing else but you, and I can't help you anymore. There's nothing I can do for you now. I'm sorry."

They filled the room and blocked my path. I was too afraid to try and pass through them. In time, they began to fade away. I don't know if they went to their rest, or if they just vanished from my sight. But I can see the building clearly now, its disrepair. It is dark, except for raw emergency lights. Gruzitis was the last to go.

He looked so sad. Defeated.

I pulled two items from the accordion file in my bag. A hand-stitched rag doll of my mothers, and a coin I found it in my grandfather's drawer after he died when I was cleaning out his house. It is a 1939 Reichspfennig: a copper penny, with the Nazi eagle and swastika. He never talked about his life in Kiev or the war. I loved the man I knew, but did not know him. At least, I did not know him completely. Did my grandfather keep the penny to remember things he did or things he did not do? Was he proud or filled with guilt? For all I knew, he could have rescued Jews as easily as he could have helped the SS murder them at Babi Yar. He is dead, and I will never know. If my mother knew, she too took that knowledge to her grave as well.

I examined the doll. Plain cloth, painted face worn away. It is soft, with no internal structure but the thick stuffing. The stitching looks original, except for a section beneath the armpit that appears to be modern thread. The color doesn't quite match and it is fine and smooth. I pick at it. I hold my breath as the seams tear and come apart. The filling bursts and fills my hands. It is human hair, in different shades of brown and of different lengths.

The Nazis recycled everything during the war.

I took the dark green king I captured from Giorgadze, but left the rest of the set on the table where it lay. I placed the penny on the table, and left the disemboweled rag doll fall to the floor. Individual hairs floated slowly to lay silently in the dust.

I don't know how I'll get back to the train station to go home. But once I do, I'll throw away my grandfather's things for good.

xxx

The author thanks Ms. Inga Sarma, Chief Researcher at the Jūrmala City Museum for her kind assistance.

On a Bed of Bone

by Can Wiggins

Teeth are not bone. Remember that.

Remember that when you run from the thing bursting through your flesh and form, the thing that is part of you but apart from you, the thing that destroys even as it makes you a legend. Remember that when your jaw unhinges for the first and last time as your nature -- your true nature -- is realized and a curse becomes a blessing.

xxx

Goose Finley had been an unhappy child and now he was a miserable young man. It's said when he walked up the street to where he lived with his grandmother, birds stopped singing and dogs started whining. Reptiles tongued the air as if to taste the sour spill he left in his wake.

His parents took him to his granny's mill hill house one day and just left him. They knew early on Goose was going to be difficult and that raising him was going to be a thankless task, ending in the state pen or an early grave.

"Just up and left him," the old woman told each new visiting preacher. She couldn't attend services and it was impossible to make Goose go. He told folks he preferred staying at home in case she needed him. She had a bad heart. She might get sick. Or have a spell. Or drop dead.

Besides, they read the Bible together or listened to preachers on the radio, he said. As time changed, along with the preachers, Goose claimed they watched services on the television, a little black and white number in the front room with the nice furniture nobody ever sat on because nobody ever came to visit except for those preachers.

Each one took note how his pinched features lit up when he unloaded on them. But they never spoke about it, not even among themselves. And they all were secretly relieved to be shed of the boy's presence when they left the house.

Whenever Goose Finley found reason to set foot in neighbors' yards, their grass withered. Flowers shriveled up if his jaundiced gaze fell upon them, but that didn't happen very often as beauty didn't seem to interest him.

Nothing appeared to interest Goose. People said he continued to live with his grandmother not so much out of love and responsibility as convenience and surety. Others believed he stole her government checks, but others weren't sure he stooped that low. Nobody seemed to remember that he wasn't grown and had nowhere to go.

He acted grown in some ways, however. He walked to town every day and took care of the errands. Rain or shine, he hoofed it to Alexander's Drug Store and picked up prescription medications for the old lady. He paid utility bills in person so the lights stayed on. He stopped at Joe's on those days and snapped up a couple of hot dogs for the two of them. "A treat but on her dime," people sniffed.

Goose knew what they said, often just as they said it. Neighbors muttered unkind things as he walked by, often inside their houses, but he had keen hearing. He had keen eyesight. His sense of smell could have been fodder for a fairy tale. He knew people despised the very notion of him, and so he embraced it and made it his. Better to be hated from a distance than up close.

But his grandmother loved and believed in him the way a little child loves and believes in Santa Claus. And for her sake, he tried to rock the boat as little as possible while remaining true to his own self.

xxx

Anna May was out on the porch, hidden behind the banisters, a cup of coffee beside the funny papers that were spread before her like a map. For now, she was alone and unguarded in the center of what she called the Vast Unknown Kingdom. Nobody was outside to keep a close watch on her yet, not even Nana.

Early morning saw the blue shadow that lay over everything on the hill begin to lighten as the sun rose. Barely summer, the air was already oppressive.

And then, she heard an echoing clip-clop of someone's hard shoes as they walked down the street. But this sound was different. It was heavy. Powerful. The world trembled as this Being approached, and she knew it was someone too important to be just a regular person.

She peeked through the slats of the porch's white banisters and felt a chill start up in her spine before it fanned out through the rest of her limbs.

There he is, Anna May spoke inside herself. *There's the boy everyone's scared of.*

It thrilled her to see him. And while she understood everyone's fear, she was sad that others did not feel respect and awe instead.

The boy wore faded jeans and an equally faded blue shirt. Tanned from his frequent walks, his hair was brown and cut short. Sun poured between the houses and on to Sixth Street itself and a fiery halo circled his head. *Signs and wonders,* she spoke to herself.

Everything surrounding them looked the same. Houses – all white shingles – sported a shed roof hanging over a painted cement porch and concrete steps. Two front windows, their panes covered with screens. Four or five rooms, counting the kitchen where you baked in the morning or baked in the afternoon, and a small hall leading to a tiny bathroom with a clawfoot tub and linoleum flooring. That in turn led to the back of the house with a small landing and stone steps, a patch of grass, a clothes line. And so on and so forth, up and down from street to street till the next mill village and then the mill, and a school and a couple of churches and then another mill village with a mill and a school and a couple of churches. Everything surrounding them looked the same -- except for the boy and Anna May Griffin herself.

As he drew up alongside her house, Anna May stood.

"Hey, Drake."

Goose Finley was so stunned that this pissant of a girl knew his name – his real name – he stopped right in the street. The sun now blazed across the mill hill as he turned to glare at her. Accustomed to shutting down little kids with a single unpleasantry, he threw one out as easy as pitching a baseball.

"Shut up."

Anna May answered him with a grin. Goose saw her small even teeth, gleaming like a row of lights, and he looked away. He hadn't looked away first in a long time. He set about his business again but this brief exchange bothered him the rest of the day.

xxx

There's an old saying that it takes one to know one. Anna May recognized immediately that Goose was more like her than not. She knew he didn't know that she was a lot like him, but she believed that sometimes the older a person got, the dumber they got.

Anna May was rarely allowed outside, alone or not. She was small and puny, even sickly by some folks' standards. She had been born six weeks early, and was allergic to everything. She had asthma. She had a persistent cough. She didn't have a sense of smell except for when she did and then the sudden onslaught of odors and fragrances made her gag or worse.

She was smaller than everyone else her age, which was six. Uncle Albert said she didn't weigh much more than a doll. Nana wouldn't let her off the porch until the sun had burned the dew off the grass. She wouldn't allow Anna May to climb the big chinaberry tree in the front yard but she did allow her a morning cup of coffee, doctored with cream and sugar. She wouldn't let Anna May watch a lot of tv but allowed her to read any book she laid her hands on.

Anna May didn't play with dolls. She read the newspaper front to back. She talked to birds like they were people, the hummingbirds coming right up to her ear to whisper their secrets.

She had nothing to do with an across-the-street girl named Lydia Sharpe. Lydia was a hateful girl, always sassing her mother and much older father, plus she was a liar. She was a thief, too. She cheated when they played any game so Anna May banished her.

Most of the other kids on the mill hill knew Anna May mostly stayed indoors and that was okay with them. They didn't mess with her. "To be honest," Uncle Albert posited, "I think they forget she's here."

"They ain't forgot she's here. They're scared of her," Nana said. "Scared of her like they're scared of Goose Finley right up the street."

Uncle Albert laughed. "Scared of her? She ain't no bigger'n a mouse."

"Scared."

"Well, good." He eased his bulk into a chair at the kitchen table, ready for a plate of grits swimming with butter and homemade biscuits, smothered in sausage gravy. A good breakfast. "That means they'll leave her alone."

"Or not," Nana said. Albert snorted.

Arizona Howard poured her son's morning cup of joe and, turning her head, looked right into his baby blues. "Nobody leaves girls alone, Albert. Nobody leaves women alone, not even other women. You ought to know that by now. Sugar and spice and everything nice is a lie."

xxx

Anna May made it her business to be outside on those mornings the boy walked to town. She sat on the porch steps, waiting for the boy to appear. As long as she didn't venture out into the yard before the dew evaporated, she was safe plus she was minding Nana.

He never acknowledged her. But she knew he was aware of her now, which added a twist to his already pained expression.

Sometimes, she sat on the steps just by the street. She stood on them and marked the moments until he made his presence known. On those mornings, the air rippled before him and the sun sang just loud enough for her to hear it.

Goose Finley had no idea he was her champion. She didn't know she would be his.

They began having occasional and discombobulated conversations, Goose always scowling and looking away first while Anna May grinned at him with those creepy –

"Milk teeth," he blurted.

"What?" she asked.

"Your teeth. Milk teeth."

"Teeth aren't made of milk. That's just something they call baby teeth, on account of it's the first teeth babies grow."

His face looked like a storm, ready to open up and land on top of Anna May. "I know that. They're bone."

She shook her head. "Nope. Teeth aren't bone, Drake."

He flinched when his name came out of her mouth, razor sharp and painful. "Teeth are bone, girl."

Her reply was slow and deliberate. "Look at me."

He did as she said. There was something about that voice he could not shake or go against. It made him think of a dog hearing a whistle only it could pick up.

"Teeth are not bone. Remember that."

"What are they?" he asked, voice raised.

He turned and gave her a glare, not believing what she had said. She knew he was going to call her a liar, so she stopped him in his godforsaken tracks.

"Ivory," she repeated. He couldn't stop staring at her, standing there sober as a judge as she made that ridiculous claim.

"It's just like what elephants and other animals have. If you break a tooth, it won't heal. But if you break a bone it heals if you set it right. That's the big difference."

They held each other's gaze like beasts in the wild.

"You can look it up in a book at the library if you don't believe me," she said.

"So. Like animals. Like elephants and rhinos. Rhinos got a big horn."

"A rhino horn ain't a real horn."

He grunted at her, then turned and went about his business. "I gotta go."

"Do you know what drake means?"

He sighed, still walking. That was an old, tired kernel of information he would just as soon lay to rest. Everybody always got a kick out of his name.

"It means a duck. That's why people call me Goose."

Her answer floated through the air, light as a feather.

"Dragon. It means *dragon*. You can look it up if you don't believe me."

People sneered when they soon noticed the boy sitting on his granny's porch, reading. "How can he even hope to better himself? What does he think he's capable of learning from a book? What books does he read? And why?"

And so on. And on. Goose Finley wanted nothing to do with them. He had entered another land, a land as real as the one he walked on.

xxx

Every night, Anna May fought monsters and other evils in the Vast Unknown Kingdom. She easily beat them back in her sleep but preferred being awake for these pitched battles. Sometimes, there were vampires or wolfmen.

Other times, beasts appeared from far away and long ago. Those were worse. There were no rules with them as they jumped time and space to destroy the here and now.

But the greatest terror for Anna May was the one called Time Out. This was something unknowable that was after her. She had never seen it but knew it was always out there, always looking for her. She had created it herself, a shapeshifting thing accidentally set in motion before her full powers were revealed.

Because of this blunder, Anna May had to be forever on guard. She had to whisper 'Time Out' at the exact right moment so it would return to its starting point, to a place nobody knew. A constant struggle, an eternal fight.

xxx

"What in the Sam Hill do you want now, girl?"

She stood on the curb, her skin like ice as the air shimmered, heralding Drake's arrival. His shoes thundered on the pavement as he drew closer.

Goose spoke so seldom, his words came out like a croak. He stared her down – or was going to but, again, she didn't blink. She wasn't scared of him or by him or anyone else. He doubted she feared the Devil and reckoned Mr. Scratch himself would take off running if Anna May entered his infernal realm.

Goose had noticed her eyes were so light, they looked colourless, and when she grinned at him this time, he saw her teeth up close. He thought of a cat's teeth – tiny sharp bits set with machine precision in hard pink gums.

Arizona Howard opened the screen door with a squawk. Anna May turned and ran to her Nana, her pale face shining with joy.

Walking away, Goose heard the old woman say, "Anna May, leave that boy alone." He shook his head when he heard what sounded suspiciously like "I can't."

xxx

Between the backs of the houses on each street of each mill town laid miserly strips of asphalt. Children rode bikes and Radio Flyers down these secondary roads and garbage trucks rumbled their way over them every week to empty trash of all kinds. Cars and pickups also found them useful as actual street parking left something to be desired.

Anna May knew summer was drawing to a close, but Nana said that was only if people went by the calendar. There was still plenty of heat and now there were massive storms, including tornadoes. Some came through the South although Uncle Albert had promised there had never been a tornado where they lived and that he doubted there would ever be a tornado where they lived.

"I believe hot air as well as cold fights for control of the Earth," Anna May had announced. Her head remained buried in the *Piedmont News* as she read the forecast. Uncle Albert had laughed and Nana said, "Lord have mercy. We have *got* to get her in school this year."

And now, at the tail end of dog days, Anna May sat in the cool of the little house where she ate and slept, somewhat protected by Nana and Uncle Albert. She had just read – again – Fox's *Book of Martyrs* and was now scrounging underneath her bed for more pick-up sticks to play a game against herself. Uncle Albert and Nana were outside on the porch, drinking their four o'clock coffee, when Anna May felt a deep shudder from inside the Earth.

She scrambled to her feet in less than a second, whispering, "Time Out." It was close, closer than it had ever been before. Gateways and portals were shifting fast, the Kingdom was under attack. Outside her window, she saw darkness creep across the landscape and the world trembled again.

Terrified, she screamed. "Timeout-timeout-timeout!" Tears pooled in her eyes and her shaking hands balled into fists.

But it was too late. It was coming for everyone. It would gobble everything up.

"Drake!" She took off for the back door, caterwauling his name as she ran through the house.

xxx

Outside, Goose slowed his pace on the back road between Fifth and Sixth Street. The hair on his neck stood at sudden, fearful attention. Over the tops of the houses, he saw the trees as if for the first time and against that forest, woven throughout the heart of his mill hill, he saw a storm brewing fast, its deep slate-coloured clouds roiling above the greenery.

He stopped entirely when he crested the road, certain he had heard Anna May holler his name. His real name. A haunting melody drifted from the open window of a nearby house.

Goose stared at the beauty of these deep colours of nature as the music floated over him and made its way to the trees and the storm, its notes all but visible in the darkening sky.

He felt frozen to the spot. *What is happening...*

Suddenly, the boy realized he was part and parcel of something greater than the sad little house where he had been dumped, more than the mill village where nobody had a chance in hell of getting out. He was more than some throwaway with a joke for a name.

He was part of the trees, part of the green itself, part of the storm ready to crack overhead. He felt a rush of adrenaline.

"What's happening?" he whispered. He turned away as an impossibly long streak of lightning pierced the sky's canopy.

Anna May stood behind him. She was crying, her face set in a rictus of terror and desolation, her eyes wide and all but rolling in her head.

"Magic," she whispered back. Her teeth flashed in her face, as bright as the lightning which had found them.

Both of them heard people yelling, but those cries sounded far away. The air filled with crackling sounds and Anna May's white hair floated around her head like a wreath. She reached out and took his hand, hot to the touch, as something malevolent circled above them.

It happened so fast it wouldn't have been captured on film. It could barely be seen by the normal eye. Anna May saw it and, of course, Drake Finley felt it.

His spine sizzled as the heat from a thousand suns fell on him. Anna May was knocked to the ground as dynasties shifted into place for battle.

Everything happened at once. Everything happened so fast, Anna May thought someone had said "Abracadabra." The boy changed drastically, suddenly, completely. Clothing ripped open, fluttering to the ground, and flesh was replaced by scale and claw as he became what he always had been. His joints popped and his limbs groaned as they elongated. His ears flattened and disappeared as his facial structure reformed. He nestled into a state of such sublime transcendence, the word has yet to be written.

Terror and joy lay neck to jowl to see such a sight unfold. It was better than somebody walking on water. Better than a chariot of fire or any other fairy tale.

Out of the roiling mass that was the storm, something seethed and surged forward. Stars ringed its massive form, but dark lived within it. More cloud than the cloud itself, it bubbled and brewed, and Anna May thought of monsters on the teevee. Only this one was real. It was a living thing and it would devour everything if it did not go back. It did not care, for it had no heart.

Drake's heart was more than enough for the task. He rose to his new height, settling back on his haunches as membranous paired wings unfurled from his broadening back. He flapped the wet off the new appendages and took in a breath that sounded like a bellows.

There was a gasping sigh as his jaw unhinged. What had been his boy's teeth were splintered and pushed out, raining to the ground in a small shower, as iron burst upwards from bloody sockets resting on a bed of bone.

Anna May had rolled over for cover in a small ditch and, as much as she wanted to watch, she covered her head as the fate of everyone was decided in one fiery blast.

xxx

"You look better," Nana said. She petted Anna May's still-singed eyebrows. It had been a week and Anna May was just getting back to some semblance of normal. Not that Anna May could ever be called normal, but the woman wasn't worried about that anymore.

The police and the doctor had talked to Anna May who had shut up tighter than a drum about what had happened. Arizona and Albert couldn't tell them much more. Albert had run through the house and down the back steps when the storm was over. He told them he had found Anna May wandering through the scorched backyard, a blank expression on her blistered face.

"That baby was picking up little bitty rocks just as calm as you please," he told them.

The doctor called it 'trauma' and told them that people who were in frightening situations or accidents sometimes lost their memories. He and the law had wanted to question the girl over and over, but she screamed them out the third time when they started asking about the Finley boy.

"Can hardly tell you was in an accident," Nana said, sitting beside Anna May on the living room couch. "Look at this here. Strawberry ice cream. Your favourite!" Anna May barely gave her a smile, which bothered the woman. Despite her odd nature, Anna May was cheerful.

And she noticed Anna May was keeping something in the pocket of her overalls. Something small. She felt the little bundle in her granddaughter's pocket and said, "What's this, baby? Feels like you got rocks here. You still got those little rocks Uncle Albert said you were picking up?"

"It's not rocks," Anna May said.. At least she wasn't telling Nana a real lie.

"You ain't collecting little animal bones again, are you? Your Uncle Albert will wear you out if you're out picking up bones again. Bones have germs in them, baby."

Anna May stared up at her grandmother. Nana and Uncle Albert were really all she had now. And she hadn't really had Drake that long. She had had Goose longer but that wasn't who he had really been.

"It's not bone," Anna May said. That wasn't a lie, either.

"Is Drake gone?" she asked her grandmother.

"Honey, that we do not know," Nana said. "They been looking for him but honestly, I think he just took off."

"He took off, all right." She let Nana spoon feed her some ice cream so the old woman would feel like she mattered.

Yellow Voices

by Luis G. Abbadie

INTRO
(HERE, TONIGHT):

Night in the *Abbey of Thelema*.

Follow the trailing scent of patchouli up the winding, colonial-style stairs, beyond the Xeroxed sign tacked to the wall - a larger version of the little, barely readable flier you were given last Friday by the androgynous-looking Goth at the drama school: a blotchy copy of a Giger painting almost engulfing the white, scratchy letters:

Char Nastro's
YELLOW VOICES
Performance
The March Saturday, 1999
At the *Abbey of Thelema*
You know the place

Fortunately, your current girl Lisbeth *did* know the place; otherwise, you'd have been unable to come since the *Abbey* people never bother to write the address in their fliers. An explanation of "The March Saturday" bit is also lacking: it seems that they always schedule their events - music, readings, whatever comes up - for the last Saturday of the current month. Thus, only those who are into the secret will know when and where to come. You've heard that Mireya, the owner, often jokes that theirs is "the underground of the underground", and in a sense, she is probably right: if what you've heard is true, the people who hang out here don't quite fit even the oddest norm-breaking molds.

But you haven't come because of that, have you? You're here because of the name on the flier. You were surprised at first, thought it odd that Char was doing her stuff at the *Abbey*; but once you thought it over, there was nothing odd about the fact after all - or, rather, Char's inherent oddness qualified for finding a home in such a place.

How long since you last saw her? Four, five years. Not since she went to live with her lesbian lover.

Yes, you've *got* to see her, to find out how she is doing. You're not sure how you feel about it, but this is something that you need to do. Maybe to make peace with yourself, or some such shit, who knows? And what's the difference?

Even as you sit, Lisbeth says:

"You must go to the bar and get drinks, there is no service at the tables."

Cursing, you squeeze Lisbeth's knee under the table, and stand up, walking obediently to the bar. A skinny guy is serving drinks; you get two plastic cupfuls of tequila and gulp down half of yours on the way back. As you sit again, the lights start to dim, and you turn around, in time to see a woman with a long white dress walking between the tables, holding up a candle, as the sound of voices dims and dies.

Your heart leaps. Even through the livid, expressionless mask she wears, you hold no doubt: it's her.

Always in silence, she kneels, head bowed, holding the candle with both hands, high above her head: her dress clings enticingly to some parts of her body. God, she'd never looked this good. There she remains, while soft guitar notes drift out of nowhere, the flame flickering along with their tune. Then, she sings:

"Why, mother? Why have you doomed us all?
Why have you led us to see the moon fall?
Now, above us, the wailing Hyades align;
My eyes see naught but the King's dread Sign!"

126

A short, bone-jarring riff, a projected, strobing light focusing above Char's head: a golden, spidery rune flashes from a black disk suspended from the ceiling.

"There is no hope to be held, no joy to be had;
Truly, Cassilda, we are all indeed mad!"

Indeed mad. You smile sourly, realizing how true that is of both you and her: it's certainly mad, this sudden, almost overwhelming yearning for those times when you were alone with Char and quietly, *secretly*, fondled her - discovered her inmost flavors, as well as your own functions and needs.

Unknowingly - perhaps sensing your turmoil, but unable to suspect its source -, Lisbeth pulls closer to you.

Mad.

OPENING QUOTE
(CHAR'S BEDROOM, ELEVEN MONTHS AGO):

"Musicalize it?"

"Better yet, Char, why not make songs out of it? Just like the Italian movie, *La Donna di Carcosa!* Like filling in the blanks of the play."

"Xonya -"

"Read it, okay? Just read it, and see what you dream up..."

NON-CHOREOGRAPHED DANCE INTERVAL
(HERE, SEVEN MONTHS AGO):

Char sat in her usual corner, with her distinctive short hair and male Goth attire, making a weak effort to stop straining her own mind. Her name was short for Charlene, although she liked to say it actually stood for Charles. She grasped the cup with wiry fingers, breathing hard, as she waited for Xonya to come back. She needed to relax. She was sleepless, having had nothing more than a couple hours nap not long after sunrise, until she awoke for no reason, and was unable to stay in bed. Such anxiety, the rush of writing nonstop for the last three nights. She had missed reggae night at the Roxy, which got her girl Xonya all fired up, and Char had just sent her to fuck herself when she snatched her notebook away from her in order to get her out of her creative fit.

Xonya of the dumbly-spelt name, whom she had met nearly three months ago right here, at the *Abbey of Thelema,* the new bar of sorts that she and her friend Mireya had recently started up. She was really pissed off, and Char didn't feel good about it at all.

Her eyes slid back to the book; she fingered its worn cover, annoyed at herself. She didn't want to open it, not now.

Bullshit. She was *dying* to open it, to browse its pages aimlessly, to read snatches here and there. But she refused to do it; she was trying, quite desperately, to think of something else: of music, of Xonya, of whatever. Except she couldn't.

She grabbed her pen instead, flipped the pages of her notebook beyond the crammed handwriting of her half-finished script, started filling a page with aimless curves and dots.

What was the point of trying to divert her thoughts? Sure, her head was pounding, strained after these last few days, but she was too steeped into the matter right now, she couldn't get away from *The King in Yellow;* from the songs she wanted to make, telling the story of the play as one of the characters experienced it.

From that, and from *her*.

Her draft was a mess, there were so many things she wanted to write into the songs, but it couldn't possibly all fit in; she just didn't know anymore what to use and what to drop. She needed badly to step back from it all, to gain some perspective.

"Come, Cassilda, dressed in winds,
Impale your past in the sword of fate..."

Char ripped the page off her notebook, groaning in disgust. That *stunk*! She just didn't know how to write down the intense, haunting phrases that danced in her head. She had decided that she would make a whole series of songs, re-telling the story in the voice of princess Camilla; but that voice refused to be set into words.

She felt close to Camilla; the way her mother tried to make her into what she didn't want to be, to force her into a role she didn't ask for. And her brothers each trying to claim her for a wife, taking for granted that she *would* assume that role. Queen Cassilda obviously knew that Camilla wanted nothing to do with being an inheritor to the throne, that she loathed the thought of marrying either of her pretenders; yet she obviously enjoyed teasing her on that sorest of all points:

"I want to hate you, mother queen,
For cursing me with a fate so mean.
I want to loathe you as I do Uoht,
As I scorn Thale and his greedy lot.
Would that yours were the doom that you call mine -
Would that you were to find the Yellow Sign!"

"...Char?"

She looked up.

"I'm sorry," she said, looking at Xonya with tired, baggy eyes. Saw her nod, her lovely brown face showing both annoyance and understanding. Char thankfully took the cup of wine she had brought her, and gulped down most of it.

"You know, Char, I was thinkin' about this stuff... *The King in Yellow* and everything."

"I didn't mean to snap at you like that. I was just -"

"I know," Xonya reassured her, squeezed her arm, fleetingly smiling. "Char, do you think they are really brothers?"

"Who?"

"Uoht, and Thale, and Camilla, I mean. According to the play, they are trying to marry her; and all the people in the city are said to be the children of Cassilda."

Char shrugged. "They're living in a weird world."

"No, do you know what I was thinking?," Xonya leaned closer, conspiratorily. In spite of herself, Char was already growing excited about whatever she had in mind. "I think Cassilda is supposed to be a symbolic mother, more in the sense of leader or founder - like the 'mother' of a vampire clan in those books you like so much."

"Sounds okay, I suppose. I don't care much about that, anyway. I think there's something going on with Camilla..."

"Listen," Xonya beamed enthusiastically. "I was just talking to Mireya about what you're doing, and we had an idea. Why don't we set up a performance with your songs? We can do it right here in the *Abbey*!"

All of a sudden, Char's mood went all the way up again.

**OFFSTAGE VOICES, FAR AWAY
(CHAR'S OLD FAMILY HOME, NINE YEARS AGO):**

"You've been pulling back, Char. But now, mom isn't here to know."

Char flinched, but reluctantly allowed his hand to close on her trembling thigh; she was scared to let him continue, but she was also too scared not to.

"You really want this, don't you, Char? Don't you?"

Biting back a sob, she nodded. She knew very well that was the expected response: he had made it clear enough in previous instances.

SCENE FOR VIOLENT CLIMAXING BACKGROUND DRUMS (HERE, TONIGHT):

"Do you hear, Cassilda, mother, wherever you may now be?
"The wind whispers that you have doomed yourself and me..."

As Char's voice dies away, Thale approaches; for the third time in the course of this show, they speak, instead of singing:

"Camilla, is our mother gone?"

"Yes." Char turns to face him. "She's gone to Carcosa, to the city beyond the lake.

"She's gone with the King in Yellow."

"It's the price of ambition."

"No." She sobs. "These masks are the price."

"You have always masked your love for me."

"What -?", she stares at him, warily; Thale slowly paces around her, deftly avoiding the tables and chairs around them.

"Even our mother knew that you love me, sister. But now that the King has come, you have nothing to fear of the Yellow Sign."

"Nothing more, you mean."

"You've been pulling back, Camilla. But now, mother isn't here to know."

"Shit," you mutter, unable to help yourself. Lisbeth looks at you, asks something, but you barely notice her, shocked as you are by the realization of what Char is *doing*. You can't believe this Thale guy actually *said* what he did!

133

But you've heard him, and now the true meaning of everything you've been watching - the acting, the symbols, the songs - dawns upon you; now, you understand what Char is telling through this fucking show. How could she *dare* to do this? How could she go to such lengths as to include that very phrase which you once *spoke* to her, such a long time ago?

Thale's arms reach for Char, she writhes and protests as he draws her close; he tries to kiss her, but she pulls away.

Char backs off, panting; she looks ready to run - or to fight. All of a sudden, she pulls a knife out of nowhere and holds it high above her head, where it flashes wickedly. She glares at Thale through her mask's eyeholes, defiant. He takes a step toward her, and the blade shoots into his belly. He staggers back, tumbles right by your table, his clothes tinged with fake blood.

Thale grows still, his eyes fixed on the darkened ceiling as they close in mock-death, and your blood grows cold in shock when you see the details of his mask: the nose, the straight lips, the eyes -

The bitch! Char designed the mask, for sure! Anger not exempt of fear surges and floods your mind. You look at Lisbeth with sudden dread, fearing that she may have noted the obvious familiarity, as you have. Thank God, she seems to be watching the show with intrigued interest, as she has since it began. Still, you remain breathless until a couple of anonymous helpers drag Thale off-scene and into the darkness.

Because the mask's features were *your own!*

SILENT, PLASTIC SCENE
(CHAR'S BEDROOM, ELEVEN MONTHS AGO):

There, right by the bed, Char sat, curled up, hugging her knees. Every once in a while, her shoulders shuddered with a silent sob, like the rarely-rippling surface of a tideless lake. Her head was bent down, as if her neck was that of an old stuffed doll.

Warm tears rivered down between her cheek and her left knee. She was barely aware that she was even curling up her toes: her feet were cringing away from the edge of her sandals, like frightened lost children retreating, fearful, from the edge of a crumbling, rocky shore.

Or, rather, from what lay right beyond it: the still-open book lying on the floor. That black-bound, offending travesty which dug into her inmost scars, sucking them fresh into agony.

A FLOOD OF SONGS
(HERE, TONIGHT):

In the wide space between the bar's tables, Char, as Camilla, weeps. She kneels by the tattered yellow robe on the ground, the sole sign that the King in Yellow has been here. Your lips grow tight as she shudders with something halfway between laughter and weeping.

The mask is not the same she was wearing when the performance started: its features are distinctly male. That shouldn't surprise you; not when it's Char wearing it. Still, you find that pallid face quite unnerving.

Cassilda - Xonya - grows out of the shadows behind the bar, approaching in silence, and comes to a stop before her daughter Camilla, regarding Char from behind her own dead-looking mask.

Then, Char sings again:

"Cassilda... Cassilda - mother, queen.
I dread to wonder where you've been."

She slowly gets up from the ground, staring at Xonya:

"You listened to the Stranger,
You taunted the King's anger;
You made a mad party of masks and wine,
And now we have all seen the Yellow Sign!"

Char starts walking between the tables, gesturing wildly as she speaks/sings to her (Camilla's) mother.

"Ah, how you took pleasure, mother,
In mock-threats of me wedding my brother;
Yet it is you the King has wed,
It's from your fear that he has fed!

Soon you will be snatched back behind the moon,
Leaving me and my brothers to a different doom."

Behind her, Thale slowly approaches; his reappearance disturbs you. His clothes are still bloody, and as he comes closer you can see that he is leaving a fresh red trail behind him.

"Would that in this play of masks my face I could fling;
"Would, then, that I were your pledged King!"

Thale picks the King in Yellow's tattered robe from the floor, and wordlessly places it on Char's shoulders. She then faces Xonya in silence, mask to mask, sigh to sigh. Finally, she sings in a weak voice, a faint echo of the King's song in the previous scene:

"Come, Cassilda, come, lest the moon falls down,
lest the Hyades weep our love unsown.
Come, Cassilda, come, claim the kiss that you crave
Carcosa is your mistress, daughter, lover and slave."

Xonya raises a hand, tentatively, and Char takes it, gently pulling her close. Clumsily, like children playing at the newfound game of love, they begin exploring each other's bodies; Xonya digs into the yellow rags that wrap Camilla, Char anxiously pulls up Cassilda's long dress and her hand snakes beneath its hem, licking a small breast like a living, five-tongued reptile. They join in a dry, mask-to-mask kiss. You feel yourself stir in response to the sight of your sister's passion - hell, it's been so long since you last savored it!

Xonya backs off at last, parting with her; she retreats into the shadows, never looking away from Char, whose body still heaves with loss and desire. She stands alone again - when did Thale leave?, you never noticed.

With a long sigh, Char drops the yellow cloak from her shoulders, and carefully cradles it in her arms, dropping to her knees. As she places it on the floor, something white flashes among its folds: a fat, white dove flaps out of the rags, like something out of a stage magician's parlor; a moon-white bird with its belly dyed crimson. It flies off, comes down briefly on the red-stained blood left by Thale, then starts fluttering aimlessly around the room.

"Let the wailing Hyades take pity on my plight,
That I may divine my doom from the Jeelo's flight.
Now Thale has come back up the stairway of Uoht,
I fear that Death's respite is granted me not -
That the King's laughter..."

Char never finishes the song: her eyes - as well as many other people's - are suddenly staring at you. It takes you a while to realize that you've just pushed your chair so violently that it fell crashing to the floor, even as the bird set down on the table in front of you. Feeling exposed, you try to get away from that bloated bird pecking at crumbs right by your drink.

You look at Char, and her eyes widen behind the eyeholes of her male mask. She has seen you. A strong shudder spasms through your body, as you stand there, unable to avert your eyes from her fixed - furious?, Panicked? - eyes. Then, very slowly - gently, even - she resumes her song:

"...That the King's laughter, as a deafening gale,
Will forever curse me: Camilla, damned be to Thale!"

There: it's happening. She keeps looking at you, so that there is no mistake; now, you dare not to look away, else you might encounter Lisbeth's gaze.

Exposed. You feel betrayed, accused.

"Thale! Thale! My lungs burn with the harrowing name!
Thale! Thale! Gnawing my soul with the worms of shame!"

Why does she keep shouting this name like that? Hell, you know full well the reason why! She is telling everybody that *you* are Thale, that her show is actually a way of accusing you.

The bird flies off, and you realize that you are still standing, drawing everybody's attention, as if you were shouting, "look at *me!* It's *me* she's talking about!" Your mind tries desperately to sort some rationality out of a whirlpool of fear, anger, shame. What should you do? Get the fuck out of here? No, you've got it: Sit down, pretend you don't know what she's talking about. Walk away calmly, you stood up 'cause you're going to take a piss, you stumbled on your chair, made a mess, so sorry, no deal about it -

You turn around to pick your chair up, not even bother trying to fake some sort of "gee, I'm sorry" face: you're just not up to it.

The chair is already upright, but it goes unnoticed: all you see is Thale with his mirror-mask, facing you like a reflection. Thale, who has just taken care of your seat, who stands there with that fixed, mocking rictus on his sealed, yet accusing lips. A twisted carnival parody of yourself.

You flinch when a hand grasps your wrist: it's Lisbeth. She stares at you with an odd, worried look. Of course. She now sees it all. She *knows*.

And with her, everybody who is close enough to see you and the mirror-mask facing each other. There is no way out of it: they *all* know.

With a hoarse, wordless cry, you slam Thale aside, snatching your face off his; you run away, clutching the tell-tale mask as if you were trying to crumple it like paper. It might as well be: they had all surely read so much into it already. You are dimly surprised that nobody tries to stop you as you stumble your way to the exit; Lisbeth does shout something after you, but you don't listen - you *refuse* to listen. You also avoid looking back, fixing your eyes on the steps of the descending stairway. When you're outside, you'll stop and think; you'll find a way to fix things up, to fix *Char* up for fucking with you like this, to -

Somehow, your foot misses the next step. For just an instant, your downward race appears to continue on thin air, as you take another stride out of sheer momentum; then, as your foot finds nowhere to support itself on, you suddenly dive for the open exit door. Literally.

But the door is still too far away: it's on the stairway itself that you descend, face-first. Your limbs wave like wind-torn rags, yet your hand never lets go of the mask, not even when you hear your own jaw crack noisily against the time-worn steps. Or when your neck follows, quite more silently.

CLOSING WAIL
(HERE, TEN MINUTES LATER):

Almost everybody in the *Abbey* is crowding in the stairway, morbidly digesting the show's unexpected final act. Some pale-in-black Goths quietly slip out into the street after carefully sidestepping the sprawling corpse, undoubtedly fearing a likely last-minute cameo by the police, their natural-born enemy. The rest merely stands there, either muttering excitedly or just staring at the body which carpeted the last few steps, branding each of its unnatural twists and turns onto their memories, already looking forward to savor them later, at home, with some grass to go along.

Lisbeth, who is up front, sobbing, suddenly turns around and pushes her way back up; she is crying loudly, half-blind with tears. She will never admit to herself that it is solely the sight of a human head at such a grotesque angle, and not the sudden loss after a mere month-long relationship, which will keep her awake entire nights in months to come.

Char, now unmasked, stands by the corpse, unmoving, silent. Finally, she bends down to pick something up: a fragment of the white mask the dead man had snatched away - his fingers still hold most of the jaw. She looks at the piece in her hand: part of a cheekbone, almost half the forehead, a sliver of nose hanging under the eyehole. Nothing particular about it: all the masks are the same, blank, featureless, cast from two roughly male and female designs.

Slowly, she turns around, and follows Lisbeth up the cluttered stairs. Xonya and Mireya look at her intently, but make no attempt to hold her back.

Walking among the now-empty tables, Char comes to the space where most of the performance took place and simply sits on the floor. There she remains, staring at the fragment of mask in her hands with tearful eyes while she sings so very softly, under her breath:

"Have you found the Yellow Sign?

"Have you found the Yellow Sign?

"Have you found the Yellow Sign?

"Yes, you found the Yellow Sign..."

The Outsider

by John Paul Fitch

I'm in a photo booth, with a face like a slapped arse and two hooped earrings in each ear, pouting for Scotland. Sums up the 80's in Glasgow perfectly. I'm not at the party. I was never invited. I'm on the outside looking in, an outsider. That's how I like it.

Luvvie bangs on the side of the booth. The flash goes off as I'm about to yell at her.

"Piss off, Luvvie."

She cackles, knowing the photograph is ruined. We wait for the strip to develop and when it slides out of the machine into the catcher I can already tell it's fucked. She snatches it up before I can grab it and pushes me away with one hand while she holds the photos up to the light with the other. "Oh, my god," she says, "check the state of you in these, trying to look cool and all that."

"I'm better looking than you are, baldy."

She turns and looks me up and down, running her hand over her shaved head. A bald, black woman in Scotland, that's a rare thing, and she's magnificent. She wears a full-length fur coat, orange-brown, like an African queen. I touch my short hair self-consciously, trying but failing to tuck it behind my ears out of habit. She fixes me with a withering stare. "Listen, hen. The day you stop dressing like you fell out of a charity shop is the day you can talk to me about looks." She grabs me by the shoulders and kisses me hard on the mouth, smearing that red lipstick of hers all over my face. "Come on. We're gonna miss the start of the film." As she strides away, I can't help but think how much love I feel for this woman, my friend.

They find her head first. It's sitting on the bank of the River Clyde in the cold October morning. The birds have been at it. When the police show me the photographs I know it's her because of the earrings. The rest of her they find strewn along the river bank in bits and pieces. They've been wrapped in black bin liner and dumped.

Pubs blare Primal Scream, Orange Juice, and Strawberry Switchblade as we pass. Glasgow is the musical centre of Britain. We head up past Daddy Warbucks on West George Street, which hosts the best bands around, groups like Sonic Youth and 23 Skidoo, as groups of people dressed in proto-Velvet Underground garb hang around in doorways and toke on joints. The boys wear long hair and dark denims cut straight, matched with stripy tee-shirts, or black polo necks with suit jackets. The girls wear loose, baggy tees and long black skirts and black boots. We pass a group of punks, all leather and spikes and hair teased up into mohawks. Glasgow is united in its otherness, a rabble of misfits, hangers-on, and oddballs, all trying to look cool, all trying to be rock stars. We're all geek-chic and retro clothing, jiving to the pulse of the city and the beeping of taxi horns. The street buzzes with traffic and people weave their way through the stationary cars, heading to their favourite pubs to score, or home for a night of fevered casual sex, having picked up early. It's October and the air is cold in the evenings. But the sky is clear and the stars scintillate in the dark. The moon is almost full.

We turn down Queen Street and make a bee-line down the hill towards the Gallery of Modern Art and beyond it, Royal Exchange Square. Before we hit the bustling Square itself, with its shuttered shops and its open night spots filled with heaving dancers moving to Culture Club and Human League, we duck down the darkened alley off to our right, towards Royal Bank Lane, where nestled in the darkness, secreted into the brickwork, is a set of heavy double doors. No sign above. A mahogany portal with frosted glass and brass handles. Luvvie leads the way and I follow behind her a few steps, my Doc Martins scuffing on the cobblestones. Her boot heels clack, the sound reverberating in the alleyway. She stops and waits for me at the doors, her hand resting on the wall. Moonlight dances on her ornate gold earrings.

"Shall we?" She smiles and pulls the door wide and we go inside The Old Empire.

You can tell that at one time this place was classy but has been allowed to run to rot. The carpet is sticky with filth and grime, a thousand unclean shoes having traipsed on the once plush velvet, turning the original plum colour grey-black. Like-wise the light fittings have accumulated decades of dust, walls once skinned in fancy wallpaper have let time strip them bare, revealing the crumbling plaster work beneath, the ceiling stained by years of cigarette smoke. Up the small flight of stairs and through another set of double doors we come at last to the cinema hall. The Old Empire, formerly an up-market cinema which showed the films of Fellini and Bergman, but now spits out movies of decidedly less glamorous subject matter, yet infinitely more daring. Experimental films, student films, pornos, sex-ed films, corporate-industrial induction videos, autopsies, and all other manner of edgy stuff. Sometimes banned stuff. Rumour was that if you were lucky you'd even get to see a snuff film. But that's just a rumour. I think.

The air is thick with cigarette smoke and the projector cuts through it like a strobing laser. I spot Zack first, his mussed blonde hair golden in the silver light, denim collar popped up against the nape of his neck. On either side of him are Jason, *gorgeous Jason*, and Erin. Luvvie sneaks up behind the group. They don't notice her stalking them, their eyes fixated on the spectacle onscreen. The film shows two naked people thrusting away at each other, grunting in sweaty foreign voices which sound Scandinavian. There are no subtitles (never are), but you don't need them to get gist of it. Luvvie pounces on Zack as the actor with the permed mullet and thick moustache screws his eyes shut and orgasms loudly, the pudgy woman under him squealing in lustful delight at the same time. Zack spins in his seat, arm cocked for a punch. A flicker of recognition and his features relax and a smile breaks free and spreads across his face.

"Luvvie! You bitch." His profile is cast against the screen, strong roman nose and his cleft chin illuminated by the screens silver light. Jason turns nonchalantly, all perfect cheekbones and eyes like jewels. He brushes his long brown hair from his face and fixes me with a glassy stare. He looks me up and down with a pout before settling back to the film. The darkness spares my blushes, and my racing heart hammers still in my chest. Jason the model. His business magnate father pays him a monthly allowance to stay away from the family home, which he accepts gladly. He won't tell us why. The monthly stipend allows him to indulge in his burgeoning drug hobby while he waits for the call to come for his next gig. He focusses on the film again.

Erin tilts her head back and blows smoke into the air. She is the epitome of sensuality and she knows it. Men know it too and that was why they come to her. Only some of them are surprised when they slip the hand down the front of her knickers and cop a load of meat and two veg.

"Some of them pretend they didn't know. Lying to themselves," she told me once, grinning, fixing her black wig in place with tape. "They'll call me a poofter, scream, shout, maybe throw a couple of punches to hide their shame. But I'm game for them." Erin carries a switchblade with her just in case she encounters someone with heavy fists and a quick temper. She takes the good with the bad though, she always does so and always would. I round the row of chairs and plonk myself down beside her and she slides her arm around my shoulders. I glance past her towards Jason. Erin looks me up and down, taking in my short hair, my black tee-shirt and jeans combo.

"Tsk. You really must let me do you up one of these days, Queenie. I'd bleach your hair and slick it straight back," she runs her fingers through my hair, "you'd be like Annie Lennox. Stunning."

I blush. "Thanks. I might take you up on that. One day."

"You better. I've been making offers to people all night and not one has been accepted." She winks at Jason and slips a bejewelled hand onto his thigh. His leg jumps and he slaps it away.

I call our little group The Outsiders, like the book by S.E. Hinton. But we aren't Greasers out looking for a rumble. We have no Socs to go up against. We are androgyny, and we are out for fun.

"You couldn't afford me, you slag." Jason lift his chin and sticks his tongue out. "Besides, I want to hear all about Luvvie's secret date." My heart stops and there's ice in my stomach. The reel changes and we now have a nature documentary. Lions cling to the ground in tall yellow grass, tails wavering, muscles taut, while antelope graze nearby.

"Yeah,", says Zack, "she's gone and got herself a fancy man. Haven't you?"

Luvvie shoots me a pained, guilty look. I want to speak but I can't muster the breath from my lungs. My best friend keeps a secret from me while the others all know about it? It's the betrayal that hurts the most. I swallow it and try to smile, but it's only half-hearted and I can tell in her face that she knows I'm hurt.

"It's not like I have a boyfriend or anything." She says this to me rather than the group. "He's just…a man I met the other night."

"Oh, yeah?" Erin says, snorting.

"What were you doing when you met him?" Zack asks and Luvvie looks down at her lap, her teeth bared slightly.

"And what did you do after you met him?" Jason sniggers.

Luvvie growls though gritted teeth. "Nothing. And it's none of your business anyway."

"Ooh. She must really like him. What's his name anyway?"

I pretend I'm not listening and watch the movie. A young antelope grazes, unaware that it has become separated from the herd.

"So? What if I do? His name is John. What's it to you, ya prick?" Jason cackles like a hyena. His lips are pulled back, gums bared. Erin touches my arm. I smile at her briefly and go back to the film again. Zack and Jason keep up the ribbing for a couple of minutes before they begin to back off. I can't believe they kept it from me. The lion charges the young buck. I can't take it anymore and I turn and walk quickly from the screening hall before the blood starts to flow and the mewling begins.

I'm shivering in the alleyway, cursing my decision not to wear a jacket tonight when Erin comes out and sidles up to me in the yellow half-light of the street lamps. She's already lit a joint and after a puff passes it to me. I take a lungful of weed and begin to splutter. I blow the smoke into the air, it billows and hangs like fog.

"So, she didn't tell you, eh?"

"No."

"I wouldn't read too much into it, ma'dear. She did try to keep it from everyone. You know what she's like. She never shares anything with us."

"Then why am I the last to find out?"

Erin tokes on the joint. "Zack spotted her on the King George Bridge. He was coming home from a trick on the South side, Saturday…no, Sunday morning. It was late, or early. Depends how you look at it." She takes another hit and passes the joint. "He knew it was Luvvie straight away. You can't miss her, in that fur coat and high heels. She's over six feet without them. Anyway. He sees her standing on the bridge alone, looking down into the Clyde. He says he got this feeling looking at her, a bad feeling."

"Like what?"

"Like she was gonna jump."

I take it in. It's like I've been punched in the gut. "She was gonna kill herself?"

"That's what Zack said. He tried to yell at her but she was either ignoring him or couldn't hear him. So, he decides to run to her, terrified she's gonna top herself. He passes the side of the bridge and his view is obscured for just a moment. When he sees her again she's talking to a man in a suit and one of those long coats that bankers or businessmen wear. She took his arm and they wandered away back towards the city centre. He was relieved that she didn't jump. He wondered about this guy, but he was tired and decided to head home. He told me the next day and I let it slip to Jason later that night."

The weed courses through my body, draining the tension from my muscles, and with it the anger and sadness. She never wanted anyone to know. It was probably a one-nighter, a casual hook up.

"So…she didn't see Zack?" I turn my face towards the light drizzle that's begun to fall between the buildings.

"Naw." Erin shrugs. "Guess she was lost in her fancy-man's eyes. Come on. Let's go back inside, eh?" I smile and stub out the joint on the wall and we re-entered the cinema. I take the seat beside Luvvie. She slips her arm around my shoulder and whispers "I'm sorry." We smile at each other. On screen the lions lick the blood from their faces.

Her torso was severed in two and her sex organs removed. Breasts and vulva sliced clean from the body. The police think her lips were cut away before she died. They think that Luvvie isn't the first victim.

In the days after her death the Old Empire is a ghost-town, populated only by the rats and mice and the few greasy sex-pests that crawl out of the woodwork on quiet nights hoping for a quick wank to a porno. I hope that the guys will be here, but our usual seats are empty. I have nowhere else to go, so I take my seat at the back and wait for the film to begin. The screen flickers and a man begins to remove his clothes, his bare back is heavily tattooed with the shape of a dragon or some sort of large lizard. He's lean but well-muscled. A body lies underneath a white sheet on the bed before him. I can make out the shape of the arms laid out to the side, legs spread, the sheet sinking into the space at the crotch. Bare wooden boards line the walls and floor, as if it's been filmed inside a shed or cabin. On a chair to the right of frame a fur coat rests, folded neatly. A coat like Luvvie's, and I feel the gut punch of grief wash over me again, pricking tears into my eyes. The now naked man advances on the bed. I can't tell if the body is alive or dead. It isn't moving. He reaches for the corner of the sheet and begins to tug it back. Somewhere in the dark a masturbator gasps. There's a weight in my gut, like it's filled with cement. Dread is like that, heavy and hard. The sheet slides down over the body and a woman's arm is visible. Her skin is dark. I want to scream. Unable to take it any longer I hop over the back of the chair and push through the doors. They close behind me and the screaming begins.

Glasgow is freezing tonight, the air biting at my fingertips and my nose. I walk to the corner of Royal Exchange Square and duck into a phone box. I drop a coin into the slot. My fingers turn the rotary dial instinctively. It's only when I head her voice do I realise what I've done.

"Hello? Hello, who is this?" It's my mother's voice, clear, confident. I haven't heard it in over a year. I hear my father's gruff tone in the background. "Who is it, Barbara?"

"I don't know. I think it's a prank call."

There's a clicking sound as the receiver is snatched from my mother's hand and then I can hear him breathing. I know that breath, I know the wheeze in his throat. He's listening quietly. Stars flicker in my vision and I realise I've been holding my breath.

He whispers my name.

148

I slam the receiver down on the hook. My hands ball into fists and I scream and lash at the phone box door until it begins to bleed, or maybe it's my knuckles?

Rage surges in my chest and my hands throb. My friends should be here. We should be together, mourning our friend, consoling each other, getting fucked up and dancing and who-knows-what, except they've disappeared into their own private grief-holes, leaving me alone to deal with the sledgehammer of my sorrow. I shove my hands into my jacket pockets and head out into the cold night.

Zack is nowhere to be found on his usual beat. So, I approach Ricky, one of the other boys who works Pitt Street. They usually trawl for clients together. I've seen him with Zack before, laughing and joking, or sharing pills.

He's twitchy tonight, clearly high on something. His hands are jammed into his too-tight jean pockets. "I heard he's gone to Lanzarote…or Benidorm with some John. Geezer offered him a week's holiday, so he took off. Don't blame him. It's fucking freezing here. Oi oi…" Ricky looks past me, his eye caught by a man in a suit who stands under the yellow glow of a streetlight at the top of Pitt Street. He's standing stock still and stares right at us. Ricky pulls his packet of fags from his back pocket. "Right, piss off before you scare off the punters." He leans back on the wall like James Dean and lights a cigarette and makes eyes towards the sharp suited man.

I wander up a wet Sauchiehall Street and then turn down St Vincent Street, heading for Bennett's. It's Erin's usual haunt. Argyll Street and the Trongate are deserted. The whole city is on a downer, clubs play muted music to mostly empty dancefloors. Pubs are quiet save for the few stalwart barflies. The bouncer is bathed in purple neon light and eyes me as I approach the door. I ask him if Erin is in the club tonight. I don't know if it's her name, or the fact I look desperate, but eventually he nods and waves me in.

A dozen or so men hang around the bar. Ultravox blares out in the dark club – Oooh Vienna... Erin sits with her back to the dancefloor as a muscular guy in a tight white tee-shirt slides a drink over to her, which she lifts and downs in one before returning to her cigarette. He leans in to whisper to her, but she won't even look at the guy, staring instead at the wall of bottles behind the bar. As I get near to her she spins and spits at the man. "Fuck right off, you cunt. I'm not in the fucking mood. Take your hard-on and shove it up your own arse." The guy turns straight into me, his face like beetroot, almost knocking me almost to the floor. I rub my shoulder and slide onto the stool next to Erin. She's been crying, mascara running down over her cheeks. She dabs at her eyes with the heel of her hand and smiles through the tears.

"Oh, love. It's you."

The barman approaches and I order a gin and tonic. Erin waves her hand. "Fuck that. Fuck gin. Fuck tonic. We need whisky." The barman leaves the bottle.

Erin wraps some ice in a bar towel and I lay it gently on my hands, biting my lip as the raw flesh complains. We sit in a booth off the dance floor. Erin leans her head on my shoulder and we watch the lights swirl on the floor of the almost empty club.

"Jason's gone to London. Hopped a train the day after they found Luvvie. He just fucked off and left me. The bastard."

Then it dawns on me. Something about the way she says the word *bastard*. There's pain behind it, real emotion. Despite the outer animosity they had something that neither of them would admit to, but clearly both wanted. It had been right in front of me the whole time and I was too dumb to see it. "I – I thought…"

"That he was straight? Oh, come on. A guy *that* good looking, and a model?"

I stare at Erin for what seems like an eternity.

"I thought you were gay?" she says.

A flash of anger. I can't meet her eyes. "Did you all have secrets you kept from me? Anything else I need to know? First Luvvie and now you."

Erin reaches for me, but I shrug her hand away. "Don't beat yourself up, love. Jason wanted us to be kept secret. He's Mister Male Model, on the verge of breaking through, don't ya know? He has an image to maintain. As for Luvvie. Poor Luvvie." Tears wet her eyes again. She takes a swig of the scotch. "Jason's father knew he was gay. That's why he paid him to stay away and keep quiet about his surname. It'd be bad for business. It was never about drugs, or drink, or even being a model. He couldn't accept his son's proclivity for cock. Like that was worse than anything else…" She passes me the bottle and I take another big mouthful.

"Zack's gone too. He's gone to Spain with a client." I say.

"Lucky him, eh? Sun, sea, sex, sangria… Looks like it's just us girls left, eh?"

I wince as the scotch burns its way down my gullet and into my belly, but it dulls the ache in my hands. The DJ changes the song. Human League this time.

Erin sings along sadly. "Don't you want me baby?"

The beat kicks in. Nobody dances. The music rings hollow around the club. I watch a couple of guys head for the toilet together, the younger of the two – in his early 20's – glances around nervously.

"Hey," says Erin. "You wanna get fucked up?" She reaches into her handbag and pulls out a small plastic bag. Holding it out to me I see that it is filled with white powder. "It's H. You up for it?"

I look at her in the swirling lights of the club. She wears the mask of a smile but beneath it is the raw face of agony. Someone in need of comfort. Someone lost. I'm almost tempted, just for a moment. I wonder what it would be like to stick that stuff in my arm. I heard Zack talk about it once.

"Like floating on warm candy-floss. It's magic."

I shake my head. "I...Sorry Erin. But I can't."

"Come on, Queenie. Don't make me do all this on my own. I need someone. I need you." Erin leans towards me. She moves to slip the bag into my hand, but I pull away, shaking my head.

"No, Erin."

A grimace flashes on her face and she snatches her hand back. "Suit yourself. Best fuck off then, goodie-two-shoes. You'll have chapel tomorrow, I suppose? I'll find someone else to keep me company. Someone I can have fun with."

"Erin...?"

But she is already slipping away. She lifts her handbag and totters off on her high heels towards the toilet, giving me one last bitter look as she pushes through the doorway. I leave the club with the gaze of strangers on my back. Stumbling into the street, the whisky pounces on me like a predator. Too drunk to walk, I thumb a taxi and blurt out my address to the driver and pass out in the backseat with the strobe of the city lights on my face.

In my dream I walk through a large white house. I can taste the salt on the sea breeze that pushes its way through the hallway. The floor is chequered with black and white tiles. I move through a high-ceilinged lobby and pass through an arch with pillars on either side. The large sunken lounge room is sparsely decorated, only a few lounge chairs and a low glass table, but the room is filled with the most beautiful sunlight that glitters and dazzles. Out on the veranda I see Zack. He stands looking out over the beach to the shimmering Mediterranean Sea, dressed in a loose white shirt and denim shorts. He laughs and sips from a drink filled to the top with ice and decorated with an umbrella. His tawney hair is slicked back and his skin shines with tanning oil. He's talking to someone I can't see. They're standing off to the side, hidden behind the door frame. I move towards Zack, waving. He glances my way and lifts his hand to his face to remove his sunglasses and pulls them from his face, teeth bared. His empty eye sockets run with blood. His head has been hollowed out, the way someone would ball a melon. He smiles towards me and raises his drink to me before taking a swig. I can't stop myself from walking towards him. On the balcony beside him is a pile of meat, fresh, raw, red. The sea air carries its sweet tang to my nose. I want to throw up.

"Queenie. Have you met my friend, John? You're gonna love him" John shuffles towards Zack slightly and I can see the arm of a dark suit jacket, the once white shirt cuff stained crimson. The long white hand holds a scalpel, the blade dulled red with blood.

"He's a friend of Luvvie too. And he wants to be your friend. Come say hello." John rounds the doorway and his terrible gaze falls on me and suddenly I'm falling towards the holes where his eyes should be and the light spills like milk and runs to black.

I wake on my living room floor face down. I've been sick somewhere in the night and the smell permeates the very fabric of the flat. I lift my head and the pain strikes me like a hammer as another wave of nausea floods in my gut. With saliva rushing into my mouth I stumble to the toilet and make it to the bowl just in time. Vomit, hot and bitter, sprays the bowl, speckling the white enamel yellow and brown. I lie flat on the cold tiles a few moments and try to remember getting home. Images of Erin flashed into my mind. Erin with her bag of heroin. The empty streets, and Ricky telling me about Zack. The Old Empire and the body under the sheet and the fur coat like Luvvie's on the chair. My hands are swollen and bruised and stiff.

After a hot shower I make myself a cup of tea and fall onto the sofa. I turn on the television and flick to channel 3. Jason's face is plastered all over the news.

I read the words accompanying the picture but they slide off my mind like oil.

Arrested.

Murder.

The 'Body on the Bank' killing.

There's a shot of Jason, his face swollen and bruised on one side, an eye puffed up and black, hair crusted with blood. His shirt is ripped at the neck. He's being led from a police van into a building, flanked on both sides by burly looking men in suits. Camera flashes strobe on his face, the picture blinking white. He's used to being photographed, but not in this state. Not like this. Jason tries to cover his ruined face, but the policemen on either side yank his arms down and he's laid bare for the world. I choke back a sob. Jason. He didn't do this. He couldn't have. Not Jason.

Not to Luvvie.

Not my friends.

The front door thumps heavily. A pause. Then three more thumps. I creep to the door and crack it open, the chain still on the hook. A man in a suit stands flanked by two uniformed policemen. He holds up a badge.

I pass the Detective Sergeant a warm mug of tea and sit on the couch cross-legged. The two other cops remain outside the front door, in the hallway that reeks of dank piss, no doubt scaring the shit out of the scumbags who live in the other flats. The sergeant's name is Flannagan. Red hair like wire stands up from his scalp. His cobalt eyes are bridged with blonde brows and a freckled complexion that belies his Irish roots.

"He's the best suspect for the case. He fled the city the day after the murder. He knew the victim. They were possibly involved romantically, physically."

I shake my head in disbelief.

"No. They weren't together. She was…seeing someone, I guess. Some mystery guy." My vision blurs and I feel the warm streaks of tears on my face. "She didn't even tell me. I found out second hand…as usual."

Flannagan glances at me before continuing. "And that made you angry, did it?" He's writing in his notepad now, eying me. "Did that enrage you, Ms Queen? The fact that she was hiding an affair with a supposed mystery man? Were you jealous that she was involved with Mr Lewis?"

My breath quickens. "Not like that. I wouldn't kill my best friend over some guy." He smiles and closes his notepad before placing it in his suit pocket. He swigs the tea and stands.

"Mr Lewis is not the only person we're looking at for the murder." He pauses. "Is there anything you want to tell me now before the investigation goes any further? This is an informal chat, but you will be required to come down to the station to make a formal statement. Do you understand what I am telling you, Ms Queen?" I stare at him for the longest time. Neither of us says a word.

The Old Empire is busier than last night. I can hear chatter from the foyer as I shake the rain from my coat, my hair running wet. I push through the doors into the relative warmth of the theatre proper and see a dozen or so people in the back rows and a score more sitting further down. The screen flickers as the reels change, almost as if the projectionist has waited for me to arrive to start the next film. I scan the rows of seats for Erin's black wig and spot a brunette in the corner canoodling with a large set man. I head her way but as I slide my way into the row I see it's not her, it's some other girl. Her blouse is open and the man is sliding a beefy hand inside her white bra, squeezing her breast hard, rubbing the nipple with his thumb. She spots me and smiles, clearly high. I look away as her paramour turns towards me, sweat spots his forehead and top lip. He slides his hand back out of the bra, and the girl's nipple flashes. He beckons me in with his hand.

"You wanna join in, sweetheart?" The girl tilts her head back and cackles. Her boyfriend joins in and they both laugh at me. I feel anger where before I'd have felt shame. Not now. Not after everything. I ball my hand into a fist, ready to throw myself into the pair of them, to rain down blows on their heads, to rip the girl's white bra off her and garotte her with it. But then I hear Erin's voice behind me and the anger disperses as quickly as it came, relief taking its place. I turn, but she's not there. The crowd begin to chuckle at the film, someone throws a bucket of popcorn.

"Hey," says Erin.

She's on screen bathed in harsh light. Her black wig has slid off her head and hangs in the crook of her arm, leaving her with the skin coloured skull cap, which she pulls off slowly, groggily. Erin's make-up is smeared all over her face. Her pink PVC jacket hangs off one skinny shoulder and her white vest top is splashed with something like mud, brown and dry. She's drunk or high or both.

"Hey. What you doing with that camera?" she asks again trying to smile. The cameraman doesn't answer. The frame shakes as he steps closer, zooming in for a close-up. Erin. I've never seen her like this. She has male pattern baldness like any man approaching middle age and in the harsh light I can see the pock marks on her heavily made up face, pimples she'd tried to hide with heavy dustings of foundation, and the ghost of a beard forcing its way through, refusing to be hidden. A bag of white powder is tossed to her, landing on her lap. Her head slowly sinks to her chest and she fingers the bag.

"Ooh…aren't you the generous one?"

The frame cuts abruptly. Erin lays on a bed. The floor and walls are boarded with wooden panels. The chair to the right of frame has Erin's clothes folded neatly on the seat. She's naked now. Skinny legs smeared in fake tan. Christ, she's so thin, I can see her ribs through her skin. She has a pierced nipple, which I'd never known before. She's propped herself up on the headboard. Her arm is tourniqueted and she's sliding the syringe into her arm. The camera pushes in. Track marks like craters on her skin, some crusted and infected. She pulls the hammer back slightly and bloody tendrils invade the white liquid before she pushes the plunger all the way.

I forget to breathe.

154

"Oh. That's great." She begins to slide down, falling sideways onto the bed and into unconsciousness. The camera cuts again. Erin's face in close-up. Her lips are blue, her glittered eyes are half closed, the whites visible beneath gold-flecked lids. She's breathing in staccato, laboured puffs. There's creamy white foam on her lips. Then she stops breathing.

The screen cuts to black.

The audience begins to boo. I scream. They all turn to look at me, to look at the wailing girl who is covering her eyes with her hands. The hysterical tomboy in denim with a boy's haircut. Even the couple in the corner have stopped their petting to turn and gawp. The house lights come up and they all turn to look at me. I glance up at the projectionist booth, hoping to see a glimpse of the culprit, but the cubicle is dark. I turn and stumble out of the cinema into the hall and turn up the stairs towards the room. I crest the staircase and see the door to the room standing open, the booth in darkness. I push the door open all the way. The reel clicks as it turns, the celluloid flapping loose, the movie long finished. The booth is cold and dark and empty and completely alien. I finally listen to my gut and begin to run.

The rain beats the pavement like the rolling of a snare drum. It falls in fat drops between the buildings and soaks me to the bone, but I don't care anymore. I don't feel the cold. I'm numb. I stumble exhausted out of the alleyway and spill into the inundated streets, drains overflow and small rivulets run down the hill, gathering in lakes of rainwater at the bottom of the road, which is shimmering in the wet. I wander till the sun rises. Luvvie and Erin are dead. Jason wrongly accused of murder. Zack gone far away in another country. And me here. Alone.

I find myself at the edge of the River Clyde. The brown water runs fast and deep. They used to build ships here, back when Britain was a powerhouse. Great ships, navy ships. Some of the Titanic was fabricated in the docklands, fashioned by the hands of thousands of men. That's what the teachers told me in school anyway. But that industry is gone now, it faded as the Empire - built off the back of slaves and nourished with blood of nations - slipped from power, washed away by the passage of time.

"All we're left with is shit and dirt."

I look up the river towards the King George Bridge, where Luvvie met the man who killed her. I'm sure of it. I think of her and the last time we were all together, and Erin said I could look like Annie Lennox. I could be gorgeous.

I shower the excess dye away. It took me all day to get my hair white. Erin was right. I've never been sexy before. Maybe never will again. I slick it back with wet look gel and paint my eyes red and black, painting my lipstick on thick. Deep red. I powder my cheeks with rouge and then rifle my wardrobe for the most glamorous clothing I own and end up choosing a black vest top and skinny black jeans. I pick out the only pair of high heels I own, red pumps, which I bought for Halloween last year and round out the outfit with a long white coat. After I left home I went back a few days later. I wanted to apologise, to cry and say I was sorry. I wanted to go back. They weren't home, but the hallway was filled with boxes of my clothes, my shoes, all my stuff. My bedroom had been cleared out. They'd even started to strip the wallpaper, the grey concrete visible beneath. My life was being erased and I'd only been gone a few days. I left all of my clothes there, everything that was part of my old life and instead went to my mother's wardrobe and took her most expensive fur coat.

Here I am, as attractive as I'll ever be. I pout in the mirror, running my eyes up and down my body. The make-up barely hides the sadness in my eyes. I move to the kitchen. The utensils rattle as I slide the stiff drawer open. I fish amongst the cutlery and pull out the only sharp knife I own. The blade can barely slice bread, but it will have to do. When the sun begins to set I leave my flat, not even bothering to lock the door behind me.

I get off the bus at the top of St Vincent Street and walk down past the Chevalier Casino and head for the King George Bridge. Car horns beep and men hang their heads out the windows like dogs in heat. I ignore them. I cross the bridge to the middle and look over the stone side and stare down into the cold dark water. My fingers curl around the knife in my pocket, pressing hard into the blade. The tip digs into my trembling leg.

I wait for the being who killed my friends. I wait for the thing which will most likely kill me too.

I wait with my heart in my mouth.

End.

Mutinous Facial Abstractions

by John Claude Smith

We each have a breaking point. Fred had reached his. He had to stop the voices in his head and he had to stop them now.

For six months he'd noticed the ever-increasing rant of static voices as they traipsed through his skull at all hours of the day and night. They'd started as slippery, snake-like whispers coiled around his eardrums, indescribable clipped vocal blips that nudged for space amidst his thoughts, but now they had escalated to a constant, thought devouring roar as they bored into his mind and corrupted everything within the cramped confines of his aurally congested cranium. After two weeks of cat naps at best, it was time to put an end to it. He needed his sleep.

It was the vibratory ache that pointed him in what he thought was the right direction, pointing him towards the two painfully pulsating fillings in the back of the right side of his mouth. Uncertainty hung like a damp rag over a feverish forehead; he'd been feverish and moistly uncomfortable for the last week. He wasn't sure if the fillings were the means by which the voices had invaded his head, but he'd heard of instances in which a filling (or fillings) had served as a receiver (or receivers) of nibbling, squealing distortion radio transmissions or some similarly aligned intrusion. He'd heard of this phenomenon, not really sure of its validity, but it seemed as good a proposition as any.

Out of work for ten months, with no money or insurance, it was time to improvise.

Fred took a swig of Jack Daniels, stuck the pliers in his mouth, grasped the nearest of the two enamel culprits capped with the traitorous, unknown amalgamation of metals, and pulled.

As the muscles in his arms tensed, he grimaced, and a scream gurgled amidst the iron and saliva as the tooth, with a caustic sucking sound, was extricated from its bony roost. He tossed it into the sink, spitting blood all the while, sweat pouring like Niagara Falls, body quaking and shaking like 1907 San Francisco, and determinedly continued his uprooting. Two more shots of Jack Daniels, squeeze, grip and pull, and the pain seemed to split his skull with

157

all the potency of an axe splitting wood as he ripped the second offender out of his mouth.

But the voices still murmured, mysteriously present. Fred thought it was maybe an echo, maybe the fillings had left their final unwanted radio messages in the cavity of his mouth before being rudely dismissed for their irritating conduct. He leaned toward the mirror, mouth wide open, inspecting…when he saw them.

From the ragged red caverns where the teeth had once resided, tiny creatures climbed out, as if released from the prison of his jawbone. Like chrome-plated insects, but with faces like scuffed baseballs--the scuffs indicative of blinking, droopy clusters of eyes--and serrated mouths in constant movement, they clamored for space within his suddenly crowded mouth. He tried to close it, to move his tongue, to spit them out, to no avail. They unhinged his jaw with the strength of their exponentially accumulative presence.

The voices were loud again, a convoluted cacophony, abruptly silenced by his shrill caterwauling.

Their response was pointed—a scalpel in search of skin—the voices yelling in unison: "Shut up and do as we say."

Fred was swift to shut up, despite the stunning turn of events.

"Get a spoon. We need you to scoop out the eyes to let out the rest."

Fred's initial thought, barely registering amidst the racket and insanity overload, was, "Why couldn't they just use the nostrils?" But already his keening whine, like a whirring dentist's drill, soared towards an ear-shattering crescendo as he stared into the mirror. His mouth was full of these things, these tiny creatures, his bloated cheeks puffing out like those of a happy chipmunk, gleefully swollen with a harvest of nuts.

He stared into the mirror, his aching eyes feeling like skewered onions, the pressure from behind and within causing them to bulge and roll obscenely, reminiscent of a chameleon's disconnected visual perusal. With abrupt shock, his left eye was jettisoned with all the force of a dislodged champagne cork, obscenely smacking the mirror, before spinning like a roulette ball in the sink, finally resting in the drain and dully staring back up at him. As more of the tiny creatures crawled out onto his face, Fred's ascending cries shattered the overhead light bulb and popped his eardrums. His stunned reflection was trapped within the mirror's cracked spider-web countenance.

He had succeeded in achieving the silence he had so wished to attain, but he knew the sleep that would follow would not be satisfying. It would be permanent.

In the dreary, dreadfully drawn out seconds before his right eye succumbed to the same ludicrous fate, with Death waiting in the wings, Fred stared in disbelief and dour fascination as the slightly pudgier than infinitesimal—and quite incomprehensible--invaders continued to scurry out from within him, and his face started to crumple in on itself, a crinkled skin implosion of soft, malleable flesh devoid of skeletal foundation.

Of Blood, Oil & Tin

by Michael Brueggeman

Dr. Nathan Oliver L'Esperance thumbed through Dr. Dillamond's latest research paper while waiting for Ku-Klip to return with the torso. On his table, Nick Chopper's body expanded and contracted as the sedative gas was pumped into the inverse-funnel at the top of his head. Dr. L'Esperance was relieved that this operation would be easier. Connecting machinery to machinery was a much less delicate operation than connecting machinery to flesh. Also, there had been a problem with Nick. With each prosthesis added he needed more power to run them. In order to run the clockwork machinations of his new body parts he became more and more gluttonous. By the time his head was replaced he consumed so much that Nathan was finding piles of ravaged flesh throughout the forest, that Nick had bludgeoned and eaten raw and often alive. The calculation machine in Nick's head simply required too much power - millions of cogs and levers turning and switching and flipping to mimic thought. When he killed Nathan's dog the young scientist knew things had gone too far. But Nick Chopper's accursed ax didn't take long to lay the final blow and strike him in his own chest, destroying the last organic part of his body. Dr. L'Esperance had figured out how to power NIck's entirely mechanical body. He rubbed his hand over the insulated box which contained the Searing Orb and its warmth radiated pride into him.

Ku-Klip came stumbling through the door. With his left hand he carried the tin torso, and his right hand dragged a sack of various other magical items from the abandoned castle of the Wicked Witch of the East. He tossed the bag and the tin cylinder on the ground and the bag tumbled and spilled. Ku-Klip scrambled to catch the canister of meat glue before Nathan saw it. He had plans for it.

Dr. L'Esperance turned off the gas pump and yanked the hose off of the inverted funnel on Nick Chopper's head. He then inserted a long, slender utensil, that terminated in a hook, into the funnel. He fidgeted the utensil around until he caught it on a hook. He pulled on it hard and twisted it to one side and the movement in Nick's mechanical brain ceased. Then the doctor pried the flesh of Nick's torso from the tin head, arms and legs they were stuffed in, with a spatula. The process made slurping sounds. The bits of gore plopped down onto the the floor and slapped against the concrete. Nathan cringed slightly despite all the times he'd carved apart bodies. Ku-Klip however, closed his eyes and swayed his body to the rhythm. He found the sounds comforting and musical. Before long Nathan had separated the torso and tossed it to Ku-Klip, who put it into the barrel of other discarded body parts. The doctor connected the metal torso quickly and easily. He sat down to relax and have a cigarette before reviving Nick Chopper, the reverse Pinocchio.

Nathan opened up Nick's chest compartment and unscrewed the plug from the internal cavity. He carefully removed the Searing Orb from its box with a pair of specially-designed, heat-resistant tongs. He briefly held up the Searing Orb to look at his masterpiece one last time before locking it away in the Tin Woodman's chest cavity indefinitely. The Searing Orb was a sphere, approximately five inches in diameter, that glowed with strands of red, orange and yellow that swirled around one another. It was made of wood Nick Chopper had cut away from the Ash Banyan, a tree that grew over the burial site of a sulphur golem. The wood was then transmuted into a charcoal with a series of magical substances Ku-Klip obtained from the home of the Wicked Witch of the East. The charcoal was then alighted with fire from the belly of the Rak - the only flame hot enough to set the rockhard charcoal ablaze. Dr. L'Esperance dropped the sphere of flame into the cavity and screwed the plug back into the cavity. The heavily insulated chamber began to glow red-hot and heat the water which ran the mechanisms in the now entirely tin body of the automaton that used to be Nick Chopper. The clicking, clanking and whirring of his body's machinations filled the room with a rhythmic cacophony. The Tin Woodman sat up on the operating table.

"How do you feel?" said Nathan L'Esperance.

"I feel..." said Nick. He hesitated. "I feel... nothing!"

"What do you mean?"

"I have no feelings. I feel no love for my intended, Nimmie Amee. I feel no anger over losing this love. I simply feel nothing."

Nathan puzzled over this conundrum for a brief second before thrusting open the Woodman's chest plate. He didn't notice it during the operation. When Ku-Klip had installed the compartment to house the Searing Orb, he had removed the clockwork heart to make room. Nick Chopper had no heart in his new body. Its absence was reflected in his blank stare. He turned around to yell at Ku-Klip. But when he swung about the imp was nowhere to be seen. He had taken off, along with his bag of magical items and the barrel of Nick's discarded body parts. In Nathan's frustration he slammed his fist onto the hard, metal operating table nearly breaking his knuckles. He screamed a series of vulgar, jumbled half-words before collapsing on the floor in resignation. The

Tin Woodman just stared off into the distance, incapable of even feigning sympathy.

"What do I do now, Master?" said the Tinman. Being devoid of emotion had also left him devoid of desire. "I need instructions."

"Hold on," said Nathan, "There's more than one way to sift out a path!"

Dr. L'Esperance grabbed the hooked utensil, flipped over the inverse funnel on its hinges, and began reprogramming Chopper's thought mechanism. He pulled at various catches with the hook. Picked up a small screwdriver to delicately loosen and tighten all sorts of screws. He pulled at the catch to reboot the automaton. Chopper awoke and looked about the workshop.

"Aaaah," Nick said, "You've created decision-making protocols based on personal interests and a randomization sequence. Quite brilliant Dr. Nate!"

The Tin Woodman hopped up and headed outside to the forest thinking of Dr. L'Esperance's programming as little more than a clever solution to a minor problem. But in Nick Chopper's tin head (the real one was somewhere with Ku-Klip, locked in a wooden display box) was one of the most unique and dangerous things in the Land of Oz, a land already riddled with unique dangers.

xxx

The Tin Woodman walked through the forest down the craggy path laid there millennia ago. The flora and fauna of Oz leaned toward him as he walked. Something about the ticks and clicks of his machinations intrigued them. He ratcheted his way up to an odd-looking tree. In between scabs of bark a sticky fluid seeped out. Had the fluid been amber-colored sap it wouldn't have been strange. Had the tree been animate that would have been normal too. Many Ozite trees were animate and sentient. But the fluid was black and seemed to seep out and suck in between the bark of its own accord. The blackened sap itself seemed to be alive, animate and sentient. The Tinman lifted his ax high.

He swung and easily severed a branch.

A string of the black sap stayed connected. It vibrated a little before contracting. It quickly snapped the branch back into place. The Tinman was puzzled. He hacked off another branch and the same thing happened. He swung at twigs, the trunk, leaves - always the same result. Except when he swung into the trunk his ax stuck there. It was held fast in the sticky black sap. The entire tree shuddered. The scabs of bark began to flake off and fall to the ground. Eventually, nothing was left but the black sap. The thing was never a tree at all, but rather some amorphous blob creature disguising itself as a tree. The mass of sap began to shift shape and a great maw opened up in its center. It enveloped a hornets nest, split it in half and moved the two halves up above its mouth to serve as a pair of eyes. The brightly-colored hornets encircled the dark interior of the nest to create the illusion of pupils. The hornets also picked up a pair of twigs to serve as eyebrows and moved in such a way that they must have been under control of the demonic sap. The mouth started moving and the gurgling slurps it made eventually condensed down to form words.

"That ax you tried to feed me tasted terrible," the mound of goo said, "The stannic and copper flavor was bitter. Why would you try to feed me something so nasty?"

"I wasn't trying to feed you. I was attacking you. Or rather chopping at the tree which is what I thought you were. What *are* you anyway?"

"I am Allethor, the living blood of the long-deceased dragon, Pellethor. When he was slain, I spilled upon the ground. No longer could I feast upon the delicious diseases and bacteria that infected my former host. I was loosed upon Oz. I now seek out the diseases and infections that infest *this* beast!" A pair of hands and arms grew from the central mass and gesticulated in a circular motion to indicate the entirety of Oz.

"And how do you identify infection here in the larger world?" inquired the Tinman.

"Simple," said Allethor, "by taste. Infections are delicious. So far I've had the joy of sampling munchkins and humans. Both are as succulent as the most viral influenza. You on the other hand smell the same as that putrid ax."

"Very well then. I shall let you be," said the Tin Woodman.

He began to stroll past. But before he was out of visual range a young girl came skipping along the path. Nick Chopper heard a yelp that was quickly muffled. He turned around in time to see Allethor's maw surrounding the small girl. He rushed back with his ax hoisted high.

"Let the child go!" the Tinman screamed.

Allethor mumbled despite his ability to simply grow another mouth. The Tinman started hacking away at the monstrosity, to little effect. His ax would simply stick in the creature and he would pull it out with some effort. A few times a chunk of black sap would fall away but it would be reabsorbed into the whole in short order. Then, all of a sudden, Nick Chopper was knocked back, landing on his head. Something changed in the rhythm of his thought mechanism. He could hear a series of sounds he had never heard before. *Tick-tick-whir… tick-tick-whir…* replayed over and over again in his head. He felt different. Thirsty. Thirsty for… blood!

The Tinman looked up to see himself hacking away at the blob. But with a sword, and he was actually having an effect. The sword glowed orange with heat. Then he noticed another difference. His doppleganger wore a cylindrical hat. Then he remembered when Ku-Klip had informed him that he was working on another project almost identical to himself. The Tin Soldier was another man who was also in love with Nimmie Amee. He also had his tool cursed by the Wicked Witch of the East to swing at his own body. Only as a soldier, his tool was a sword. He also eventually had his entire body replaced with tin. Before long the Tin Soldier had hacked away all of Allethor except for the small amount that surrounded the young girl. The Tin Woodman got to his feet and walked up to greet him. But the *tick-tick-whir* still counted off in his head and when he shook his tin brother's hand he stealthily reached around to the back of his neck and pulled on the hidden lever that would shut him down. The Tin Soldier froze in place.

Nick Chopper menacingly approached the girl trapped in the translucent black sap. With every step closer his eyes glowed a brighter red. He would have been drooling if he was capable. He snapped his smooth fingertips off one-by-one, revealing the sharp clamps underneath that held them on. The little girl struggled in the sap. Her muffled whimpers and squeals grew louder. The Tinman felt himself grow more and more excited as the tempo of the *tick-tick-whir* increased.

He thrust his pointed finger into the front of her throat.

He inserted the other three.

The girl shuddered and thrashed.

The Tin Woodman sounded like a can full of bolts shaking as he vibrated with excitement.

He moved his four fingers down her chest - slowly splaying her open.

Organs tumbled from her bifurcated torso.

The Tinman removed the blender from the back of his chest cavity. He opened it and put the gore collected from the child into it. Carefully, he unscrewed the plug from the cavity that held the Searing Orb and screwed the bottom of the blender into it. The appliance whirred to life and minced the organs. They were quickly sucked into the insulated chamber. Nick Chopper put things back in order in his chest cavity. The odd rhythm in his thought machinery ceased. The red glow of his eyes darkened. When he saw the crime scene that lay before him he was confused but not upset. He had no heart to feel such things. He slowly and methodically buried the girl's corpse as his memory of the previous events returned. He walked back to the Tin Soldier and put himself in the exact position he was in before disabling his doppleganger. He reached back and switched the Soldier back on. The Tin Soldier revived and they shook hands as if nothing had happened.

"Captain Fyter's the name, friend. You must be the other automaton Ku-Klip told me so much about. Nate Cutter is it?"

"Nick Chopper, actually," said the Tin Woodman, "But since they put me back together without a heart, I don't feel so much like a man anymore. You can call me Tinman."

"No heart huh? So you no longer pine for our Nimmie Amee then? She is whom I seek."

"No. I no longer have a heart. Not that I did before. It belonged to my precious, Nimmie Amee from the time I met her. But the heart she once possessed no longer beats in my chest, and the clockwork replacement I expected does not *tick-tock* away in its stead. Instead there is a cavity of constant warmth."

"Constant warmth?" said Captain Fyter, "Perhaps that is the Searing Orb. My energy source is similar but only runs for a decade or so. Dr. L'Esperance was working to create the Searing Orb when he built *my* torso. He must have perfected it by the time he got to you. Also, I saw you having some trouble with that mega-flan. No one showed you how to channel your Searing Orb through your ax?"

"No, they didn't. I didn't even know it was there until I… uh…" the Tinman stuttered. He almost forgot himself and said something about the blender, before he remembered what he had used it for. "Sorry. I guess I'm still a little out of it after taking that bump on the head. What do I do now?"

"Yeah. That mega-flan walloped you pretty good. But channeling the energy is easy. There's a switch in your wrist that sends the energy straight from your storage cavity to your palm." He reached over and twisted the switch in the Tin Woodman's wrist. "And just like that, it's on. Now pick up your ax." Nick picked up his ax and its blade began to glow orange with heat. Then it brightened to red. "Whew. That Searing Orb really cranks up the heat. Wow." But Nick Chopper knew that part of the energy came from the lifeforce of that little girl - the child unceremoniously buried out in the woods. He wished he could feel some sadness or guilt for what he had done - just shed one tear for the poor little cherub. But the only living thing in his chest at that moment was that modern marvel, the Searing Orb.

The two automatons decided to proceed together

xxx

The Chiss, a ten-bushel (about 600 lb) porcupine-like creature and Jinnicky, the Red Jinn both attended Professor Nowitall's lecture, Spatial Deformation through Optical Transmogrification and Magickal Transubstantiation. The class was crowded as it was. The wogglebug (or bookworm) who had taken up residence there, began crawling across the hearth near the front of the classroom, spouting all sorts of bombastic pomposity, interrupting Prof. Nowitall and in general being a disruption to the class. The Professor became very agitated. He already had the overhead projector fired up. So he decided to use this as an example for the students.

He laid a scrying transparency across the light up base of the overhead projector. He grabbed his Kalidah-blood marker and traced out a few esoteric symbols on the transparency. Somehow the magickal symbols he drew were projected as the same size despite being cast over the projector. He grabbed the wogglebug by the nape of its neck and placed it in the center of the occult markings. At first the image of the wogglebug wasn't magnified at all. But then the symbols around him began to grow in size and expand. Furthermore, the actual wogglebug that lay on the transparency began to flatten and the magnified image on the wall began to bulge out.

A young girl was having trouble seeing behind the large Chiss in front of her. The Chiss led her to the open window, propped her up and suggested she could get a better view from there. Just then the magnified wogglebug choked and spat a wad of ink from his cheek. The wad hit the little girl on the window sill right in the eye. Startled, she stumbled out the window onto the hard concrete below. The majority of the class rushed to the window to look out and see what happened. The wogglebug took this to his advantage and escaped from the wall, now a large human-sized wogglebug, with finally enough brainspace to hold all of the wonderful things it had learned in three years of kibitzing Prof. Nowitall's class. The Chiss also paid attention and he swiped the transparency with the magickal symbols and incantations. He was sure it would be blamed on the wogglebug. The class ended early and the Chiss took the opportunity to pull Jinnicky aside for a private conversation.

"I'm sure there's no way you would ever part with the magick jinrikisha, correct?" said the Chiss, "But how about the Pigasus? Surely you'd let it go for the right price."

"Well what is *the right price*?" said Jinnicky.

"How about a bushel of Powder of Life?"

Jinnicky said nothing but his lips pursed in surprise and interest. They arranged to meet later that evening in the courtyard. Jinnicky waddled off in the awkward ginger jar he wore like a turtle shell, hoisted himself onto the jinrikisha and flew off into the air on the magickal rickshaw. The Chiss rolled himself into a ball and tumbled down the hill toward his private shed. It was easy enough for him to move downhill with the way he could curl into a ball but his home itself sat at the top or bottom of a hill depending on which way he was going. It was uphill both ways and he had grown tired of it. He was taking Prof. Nowitall's course in hopes he could find some answers as to how to navigate a spatially anomaly such as the hill/valley he lived on. But if everything went to plan for him he may have figured out a way around it.

xxx

Captain Fyter had decided to scout ahead. This came as a stroke of luck to the Tin Woodman as he walked a few hundred feet behind down the sidewalk next to Shiz University and heard the hard splat on the concrete directly in front of him. Like a gift from the gods an already jellified corpse of a little girl lay there on the walkway before him. The *tick-tick-whir* waltzed away in his head almost as a matter of tradition since all he had to do was to pull a shovel from his back and use a large funnel to scoop it into the Searing Orb chamber. He found the paste extremely satisfying. He turned the switch in his wrist and his ax glowed even brighter than before. He sheathed his ax and broke into a jog to catch up to the Tin Soldier.

Tinman caught up to Fyter as the latter was entering a dark wood. The trees bent and creaked but more toward the Tin Woodman and never along with the wind. The strange howls and screeches wafted from the darkened path lined with the trees that arched over it. The Tin Woodman stood stock still mimicking the frozen stature of the Tin Soldier.

"It's the Great Black Forest," whispered Captain Fyter, "No man has ever set foot in there."

"Well we're not men," said the Woodman.

"Har-ha-ha-ha!" guffawed the Tin Soldier, "Ya know. For havin' no heart, you sure got a good sense-a-humor!" Captain Fyter slapped the Tinman on the back. "Well, we're not gettin' any younger."

"We're not getting any older either," said the Tin Woodman, sporting a deadpan expression. Captain Fyter guffawed at this as well.

The two automatons walked into the darkened wood. It didn't take long before a branch slammed into the Tin Woodman with a loud clunk. He fell to his back and quickly sprung to his feet, ax in hand. The trees turned toward him, menacing scowls pasted on the center of their trunks.

"This metal man comes into *our* wood. He carries a tool of dendricide!" one of the trees said.

The Tin Soldier held up his hands in resignation. "The ax is not to *kill* trees, friends. Its blade smells not of sap. See and smell for yourselves. It is wet only with the sticky black goo of a mega-flan. The only wood it has cleaved is that which has already died. He's done trees a great service removing dead and sick pieces that the rest of a healthy tree may live, and felling dead trees to be burned, as is the funerary rite - which also it makes room for young saplings.

He is a *friend* to trees." Just then, he eyed over his shoulder at the Woodman. "*Put away that ax*," he whispered sternly to the Tinman. The Tinman sheathed his ax.

A bud from a young sapling irised open, revealing an olfactory pistil. It reached the blossom toward the ax and sniffed. "Their story checks out," said the tiny sapling in an uncharacteristically deep voice, ""The ax smells of flan and animal blood, but no sap."

A massive tree that stood before them began yanking its roots from the ground. The forest floor shook as it lumbered about to face the tinmen dwarfed by the gargantuan mass of it. Its face was old-looking. The corners of its mouth drooped down in a contemplative scowl. Its eyes, though hollow, telegraphed the wisdom of centuries. Its mouth moved slowly. The creaking moan of its deep voice seemed to reverberate through the tinmen's cores, despite their lack of bowels.

"So we have ourselves a tree doctor, do we?" said the great mass of timber, "We could use your aid. A blight has infested a silva northeast of here. This wood has long maintained itself. An infestation is usually quickly culled by the natural poisons and fungicides shrubs excrete onto anything from termites to canker rot. But this blight has resisted every treatment we've tossed at it. Would you take a look?"

"Well, I... um..." the Tin Woodman stammered.

"We really must insist!" the tinmen heard from behind them.

Vines wrapped around the arms of the automatons. They were hoisted in the air by a pair of dogwoods that walked on all fours and panted like canines. They were whisked away quickly to the northeast and sat down hard in the middle of the infested boscage. The sight of the dying trees weeping sickly sap as bits of bark sloughed away was unbearable enough. But to also hear the trees wailing and crying in their agony - to see them cradling their helpless saplings - this made Captain Fyter jealous of his companion's heartlessness. He stifled his tears. He had cried once before and found himself paralyzed. He was mostly tin and waterproof. But his steel joints were quick to rust him into place, and he only had so much oil on him presently. The Tin Woodman had already set to work chopping away dead branches, and chunks too infected to save. Nursing-squirrels ran from tree to tree injecting the numbing agent that drips from their incisors into the trees' most aching limbs and slobbering their antiseptic saliva all over their various wounds.

Weeks passed and the Tin Woodman could do little more than treat the dying parts of the suffering trees, and burn the corpses of the dead, the pyres of which grew so high they had to be spread out to avoid causing forest fires. Captain Fyter would pine for Nimmie Amee and the Tinman would beat his head against dead logs when the rhythm of his insanity crescendoed, having nowhere private to satiate his sadistic lust. Just when the tinmen thought they could no longer bear the monotony, the Woodman noticed some movement within a droplet of water. Through the magnification of it, he saw termites - the smallest termites he had ever seen. They had shrunk to such a diminutive size, they were too small to inhale the pesticides the animate shrubs sprayed on them, and being termites, they were unaffected by the fungicides the mush-worms spat upon them. Upon closer inspection, he came across more miniaturized insects - aphids, beetles and caterpillars all were attacking these defenseless trees as invisible swarms. The Tinman set about working on a solution.

He tried chemicals. He tried fire. He tried a magnifying glass to burn them. He tried bits of wire to push them out. He tried a leather bladder on a tube to suck them out. Nothing worked. Then he dropped a bit of flint on a rough stone and the spark gave him an idea. He once saw Dr. L'Esperance turn a magnet within a coil of wire. The wire emitted arcs of electricity that grew larger the faster he turned the magnet. The Tin Woodman made a coil from his spare wire. He found a large piece of magnetite and fashioned it to a rod with twine. He then made paddles around the exposed end of the rod and encased it as best he could in an inverted bucket he set on top of a cauldron. He placed his hand on the bottom of the makeshift turbine and turned the switch in his wrist. The cauldron began to heat up. The rod and magnetite mechanism began to turn. He collected every spindle of wire and spare bit of metal from himself and the Tin Soldier. He had all the sickly trees move in closer and connected all of their sick parts to the dynamo. He placed his hand back on the cauldron. The magnetite spun faster and faster. The cauldron burned red hot. Great arcs of electricity coursed through the infected wood. He used his magnifying glass to watch as the tiny insects died en masse. He wished he could feel excited. The look on Captain Fyter's face showed him what he was missing. The satisfying rush of victory. The brambles bounded up and down in joy. The dogwoods yipped and reared onto their hind legs. The Tin Soldier arched his head back and thrust his sword into the air. But the victory was cut short when the amorphous mound came folding over itself, snapping small trees under its crushing weight, enveloping saplings and wildlife in its immense volume, and flinging the automatons and their impromptu generator like pinballs ricocheting off the trees with its unyielding velocity and elasticity.

The mound came to a rest. It was finely speckled in various earth tones and began to sink down toward the ground. This pointillist portrayal of a mudball melting under a garden hose seemed to slither away as it hit the ground.

"It's those insects!" exclaimed Captain Fyter, "Those horribly tiny bugs!"

The last of the composite mass dissipated. There in the center of the receding stippling, stood a wogglebug, the size of a man, sporting a top hat and handlebar mustache. He wore four dapper shoes with spats on four feet, a well-tailored but shabby plaid suit and a monocle. He tipped his hat and bowed, saying, "Indeed, my good chap! Quite a bright fellow you *are* with a good polish. That jumble was an amalgam of independently humble arthropods - tiny bugs. And me? Why, I'm a giant bug. However, *una vilidi sumus*, together we are strong. For you may have beheld a google of my brethren, but I would never deign to delineate myself from a single grain of that chimera's corpus. For I too, *a capite ad calcem*, from protoplasm to exoskeleton, *idem quod*, I am of the same stuff. I was once a lowly wogglebug that crawled about the classroom of Professor Nowitall. I knew not why the vibrations of his words bombinated such a soothing sound across the timpanis of this bookworm's eardrums. Then the demigod of my tiny province hoisted me upon his ensorcelled belvedere and aggrandized me with his thaumaturgic meniscus. My encephalon grew enough to house the wondrous words I had gleaned. Finally able to lucubrate, this new matriculate knew it was time to licentiate. I extricated myself concatenate to the discarnate laminate. My repudiation to perorate my declamation was my declaration of my dedication to tergiversate to any equivocation that would culminate in any state that would abate incarceration, and instead condemn me to castigation for my reprobate profanation, or perhaps they would even adjudicate to exonerate this abomination. But alas, my mammalian classmates only looked at me with detestation. So while their concentration was focused on the young girl's evisceration I had no time to appreciate how they exaggerate their affectations. Instead I had to abdicate before my fate was annihilation by agitated trituration." A long moment of silence followed. "Do I hear crickets?" said the wogglebug. He looked at his rear legs. "Nevermind, it's just me. Enough with my bombastic scholasticism. Basically, my professor magnified me to macro proportions. A little girl fell out of the window and died, and while everyone was rubbernecking at that I grabbed the magickal spells that he used to make me grow and hightailed it out of there. Then I used the same spells to shrink all these super-tiny bugs you guys have been dealing with and I can control them with my mind. I am H.M. Woggle-Bug T.E. The H.M. stands for 'highly magnified' and the T.E. stands for 'thoroughly educated'... Hm... Seems like I'm forgetting something... I *swear* there was one more thing... Oh yeah! You're all gonna *die*!!!" The fluid mass of insects began swarming in every direction. They mowed down whole trees and cut great swaths into the forest floor. The tinmen lept out of the way in the knick of time. The commune gathered underneath Woggle-Bug and rose into the form of a bulky spider. H.M. Woggle-Bug T.E. rode astride the central mass of the ersatz arachnid that galumphed through the splinters, razed understory and harrowed duff. The spider jockey cackled madly as he zeroed in on the cowering pair of stannic mannikins.

The limbs of Woggle-Bug's octopedal mount came crashing down hard on the tinmen. But their tough exteriors left them little more than dented by the time they squirmed from underneath the barrage of blows. Woggle-Bug stared at them through his wide-opened lenses of madness.

"Well you're a couple tough nuts to crack, aren't you?" he salivated through clenched teeth, "Then again, you may be nuts, but in a nutshell, you're not in nutshells!" H.M. Woggle-Bug salivated as the jumble of bugs morphed into a five-fingered hand. The middle and ring fingers swept at the ground and picked up a sharp shard of petrified wood. "Let's see if my can-do attitude can *do* you in. No labels though. I guess I'll just have to eat whatever's inside!"

Woggle-Bug dug tight into the gargantuan hand. It swung the makeshift can opener around deftly - flipping it over, under and between fingers with the slightest effort. When Woggle-Bug and the hand caught up to the evading pair, the populous paw poked at their posteriors and prodded at their protruding plugs with its petrified tin opener. It tried to pierce and pry the plugs to pop them out or push them in. But when it failed to gain purchase after persistently pounding the pair of perspicacious poppet, H.M. Woggle-Bug profaned, "You pinchbeck piles of pendulating prongs! You can pivot your pistons and pirouette your pinions, but I'll prostrate you posthaste and make positive your proscription! You'll plead for palliation but no peace will be provided! But if you profess my preeminence I'll permit you to perish painlessly!"

During the Woggle-Bug's soliloquy, the tinmen managed to find cover under a felled tree. A sniffing sapling squatted next to them. It's olfactory pistil irised open and smelled the odd scent. Then, its petals quickly recoiled around the pistil as it pulled back and cringed.

"That's disgusting!" said the sapling. Its low voice trembled and almost cracked.

"What do you mean?" said the Tin Woodman.

"I mean it's rank. It reeks. You smell rancid, foul, putrid, nasty… Need I go on?"

"But in what way do we stink? It's hard to imagine a hardened palette such as yours, tried and tested in the rich odors of the forest, would be taken aback by anything less than the most exceptionally carious aromas."

"Oh yeah. It's the stench that big bug has been spurting out all over. He spews a plethora of different stinks, but I'm talking about the one he sprays on food for his pets."

"Whether it's the marching orders of ant-soldiers or the flight plans flown by bee-drones, it might sound like a sound but it's a smell called a *fairy-moan*!" recited the Tin Woodman.

"What the hell was that?" said the Tin Soldier.

"A pneumonic Dr. L'Esperance used to remember the term pheromones."

"And what are they?" said Captain Fyter

"Chemicals found in sweat and other secretions meant to be inhaled. Larger animals like Kalidahs and humans use them to induce vague feelings or attraction in one another, but smaller animals like insects actually use them to convey exact messages. I think the Woggle-Bug is using pheromones to control the miniature insects. If the smell on us contains the one he uses to direct them to eat, perhaps we can use it to our advantage."

"How can we do that?" asked Captain Fyter.

The Tinman turned to the sniffing sapling, "Could you get the mush-worms and chemical-producing shrubs to copy this smell exactly?"

"Yeah. Sure," said the sapling noncommittally.

"Well alright then," said the Tin Woodman. He didn't notice the earth-shaking thuds heading in their direction.

"Uh... Nick." said the Tin Soldier.

"I said don't call me Nick anymore. Anyway, have them make as much of it as they can and bring it back here to me."

"OK then. Tin Woodman, I don't think we'll be *here* exactly." The thuds were growing louder.

"Well wherever we might be we'll need some way to shoot it... Didn't we build a pump when we tried dowsing the sick trees with water from an enchanted pond?" The thuds were right on top of them now. "Get that pump too."

"Uh Tinman. I think we should..."

"What is it, Fyter?!" screamed the Tin Woodman, "I'm trying to save us!" At that moment, the felled tree above them splintered under one of the four feet of a gigantic effigy of the Woggle-Bug. He must have had something of megaphone too, because the monstrosity let out a maniacal laugh that's depth and loudness matched its size. It lifted a foot and started to bring it down on them. Moments before they were crushed, something scooped them up, lifting them high in the air.

The massive tree they first met upon entering the forest, placed them in his mouth cavity. He started to box with the C.M. Woggle-Bug T.E. (Colossally Magnified Woggle-Bug Thoroughly Evil). The tinmen were concerned about him being eaten alive by the miniscule pests, but then they observed the electrical generator with its wires embedded in the wood. The Tin Woodman laid on his back and secured the generator to the Searing Orb's cavity. Electricity coursed through the humongous tree.

"By the way friend, we were carried off so quickly we never caught your name on our initial encounter," said Captain Fyter, "What shall we call you?"

"I'm known as Lon-Ghorn - the Elder of Elms. You may call me Lon-Ghorn if you wish," said the Great Elm. He spoke slowly and carefully so as not to damage the passengers who rode in his mouth.

"Alright then, Lonny. Just try to hold off the Woggle-Bug long enough for our friends to get back with the pheromones, and from there we've got a plan."

The titans pounded away at one another. C.M. Woggle-Bug left divots in Lon-Ghorn. Lon-Ghorn knocked chunks out of C.M. Woggle-Bug. Splinters and miniscule insects rained down on the forest floor. Some of the insects were merely stunned, and scurried off to rejoin the whole. C.M. Woggle-Bug eventually lost enough mass - he had to reduce his height in order to compensate and not reconstruct too flimsily. This actually worked to his advantage as it took some effort for Lon-Ghorn to thrust his branches downward against their natural build. Lon-Ghorn became exhausted with this exercise and his movement slowed. C.M. Woggle-Bug pounded away at his opponent's trunk quickly. The jackhammer strikes loosed large chunks of bark from the aging Elder Elm's midsection.

"Slow and steady might win the race. But in hand-to-hand combat short and fast is the ace. The tallest tree falters when tiny termites start to crawl. Because the bigger they are the harder they fall," said the Woggle-Bug, whose voice was slightly higher pitched, having shrunken to nearly half his original size. Given that he was using a megaphone to produce the larger voice and would have needed to adjust its pitch in the midst of the battle, it was clear just how concerned with appearances this wogglebug was.

When all hope seemed lost, a bird lighted inside Lon-Ghorn's mouth, clutching the pump in its claws - filled with the pheromone-laced sweat. The bird apologized for how long it took to formulate the pheromone. He pointed out that it was made of special miniature molecules small enough for the microscopic insects to ingest. Fyter began heating his sword and prepared to jump onto C.M. Woggle-Bug in a full frontal assault. But the Tin Woodman stopped him.

"Wait," said the Tinman, "I have an idea. Dr. L'Esperance gave me this puzzle that was gifted to him by the inventors, Smith and Tinker. They invented a mechanical man, much like ourselves. Like me, it had no heart, Tiktok also had no brain. But in an effort to create a decision-making mechanism, they

174

ended up making this puzzle box here - the Tiktok Puzzle Box. Let me see the pump."

The Tin Woodman took the pump, filled with the pheromone solution, and the puzzle box off into a corner and fiddled with them for a few minutes.

"Just play along," he whispered to Fyter, and walked up to the opening of Lon-Ghorn's mouth. He screamed as loud as he could. "Woggle-Bug, my friend here says you might know quite a few facts, that you've memorized over the years, but that *true* brilliance is revealed in one's ability to problem solve! He says you can't even solve this simple puzzle box, which is little more than a child's toy!" The Tinman held the Tiktok Puzzle Box high in the air.

"You think I'm fool enough to fall for such a facile feint! If I open the swarm that obscures me, you'll take the opportunity to obliterate me! You'll take me down with a tiny tap from that towering topiary you call a teammate! What do you take me for?!"

"Unlike my colleague here, *I* think you're a genius. But to prove to you we're not up to anything I'll put the puzzle box on the ground and we'll walk far away. When you feel we're a safe distance from you - retrieve the box and start working on it. Agreed?"

"Agreed," said C.M. Woggle-Bug T.E..

The tinmen had the bird fly the Tiktok Puzzle Box to the ground. Lon-Ghorn lumbered away until they were a great distance away. They watched from afar as H.M. Woggle-Bug T.E. emerged from his larger self and began fiddling with the puzzle.

"Now we just have to hope Woggle-Bug is half as smart as he pretends to be. Otherwise this could take all day," remarked the Tin Woodman.

H.M. Woggle-Bug T.E. proved his brilliance as he quickly opened the Tiktok Puzzle Box in the fastest time it had ever been done. Of course his foolishness was affirmed when its contents were revealed to be a few ounces of compressed pheromone-laced sweat that sprayed outward and covered almost the entire front side of his body. The Woggle-Bug moved his lips in a silent curse as his billions of minions moved toward the scent of something marked as food. He screeched as they devoured him whole and alive. Their tiny mouths made quick work of their former master. Before long, even the ooze that had leaked from him was lapped up by the ravenous animalcules.

As the tinmen wished their dendroid friends farewell, the microscopic insects marched toward a pool of attracting pheromones and poisons made from miniature molecules small enough to fit in their little orifices. The pool quickly turned to quicksand as the grainy corpses soaked up the water and fluids.

While Fyter was busy socializing, the Woodman wandered off on his own. Finally, he had some privacy. So he took that time to catch a small rabbit as the *tick-tick-whir* counted off in his head. He balled the helpless thing up between his palms and squeezed until its squealing crescendoed. Then stopped. Then he heard the deep voice behind him.

"I knew that wasn't just animal blood I smelled on your ax," said the sniffing sapling, "It was human blood and more specifically child's blood. Something is wrong with you. You're broken."

The Tinman didn't bother to respond or speak at all. He simply grabbed the sapling up near the roots with both hands and moved one hand up the body of the thing, stripping it of its bark alive. It barely made a sound - just a low whimper. As he felt the life drain from the sniffing sapling, the sound in his head stopped. He put the evidence into the chamber with the Searing Orb and rejoined the party.

While the residents of the bosk were gathered in celebration, none of them saw the Chiss and Jinnicky swoop down and pick up the one thing the miniature insects would not devour on the Woggle-Bug's person - a solitary piece of plastic - the transparency with the magnification/miniaturization spell on it.

The tinmen hitched a ride on a pair of dogwoods to the edge of the forest, putting them within days of the home of Nimmie Amee. Furthermore, the dogwoods helped them yank a pair of ponytail palm trees from the ground, unearthing palm root ponies for the tinmen to ride on for the remainder of their journey. The mounts would shave their ETA down to a couple of days at most. They could ride the palm root ponies for an entire day and then they just had to bury them in moist aerated soil overnight to let them replenish their nutrients, at most having to sprinkle some extra supplements in the soil if it happened to be poorly fertilized. But keeping to the edge of the stream which took them close to the nearest town would leave sandy soil, clean water and plant food well stocked by Mother Nature for the greater part of their trek.

xxx

In Chiss' laboratory, deep in the catacombs, under the Wicked Witch of the East's castle, the Chiss and Jinnicky had finished assembling their contraption. The transparency with its incantations was placed at the center of a series of various lenses. From its interior the overhead projector shone backward through a series of colored lenses into a bowl of quartz and various other crystals designed to capture magical essences. They began by performing the first of many operations they had planned. They enlarged the Pigasus to a size large enough to carry the Chiss. Then they enlarged their small sample of the

Powder of Life and made a barrel of it.They traded the items and the Chiss unveiled his notebook to the Red Jinn and showed him the many uses of the multifunctional device he had produced from the straightforward contraption Dr. Nowitall created. Jinnicky, while intrigued, became a bit unnerved. For starters, with all the secrets the Chiss had kept from him, he wondered if the tragic plummet the young girl had taken from the classroom window was really an accident. Could it have been part of the Chiss' plan from the beginning? He made a sidelong glance at the barrel of Powder of Life and decided that if anything he needed to get it out of there in case the Chiss planned to steal it to use in his plan, or at the very least so he could perhaps use it to foil whatever chicanery the Chiss planned should things go too far. The Red Jinn was sure of one thing though - the Chiss had not made the improvements to the device out of pure scientific curiosity. He had some dark and nefarious plans for the machine.

xxx

The Tin Woodman and Tin Soldier bounded across the wide open prairie on their mounts. The knee-high grasses bent toward the Woodman like they were attracted to him magnetically. The poppies spat puffs of hypnotic dust at them from their pods, but it had no effect on them because they were mechanical. As the prairie grasses grew higher, they picked up their pace to cut through them. But when they reached the grasses that were chest high, and had doubled their gallop, they were suddenly thrown from the front of their steeds. They pushed up on their chests and turned around to see the palm tree ponies tangled in vines that swelled in a breathing pattern. They got up and walked to them. Simultaneously they both unsheathed their blades, flipped the switches in their wrists and severed the vines. Purple fluid sloshed from them as they retracted into the ground. They remounted their ponies and prepared to take off when the ground began to rumble and they were again thrown from their steeds. The vibration continued and intensified as the earth under their feet loosed and they rose into the air.

As the ground raised up higher, the tinmen and their ponies rolled down the slope that developed. The mound rose a couple hundred feet in the air. As the earth flaked off, underneath was revealed a large, green monstrosity. The vines they had encountered earlier were unmasked to be tendrils. The tall grasses were spikes and hairs covering the thing's back. It turned about to face them. Its skin was green, brown and purple. Large, vein-like structures pulsed across its countenance. Yet it appeared to be made of plant material rather than animal flesh. It had had a wide frog-like mouth. Its "eyes" were hollow tubes lined with nodules that were various colors. The nodules would open when light hit them of their color. Its eyeholes widened and it tilted its head back to look directly into the sun. All of the nodules opened up, large receptors at the back of the eyeholes sucked the sunlight in deep. It lowered its head back down and looked at the tinmen, sparks bouncing between the nodules in its now brightly-lit eye tunnels. It gaped its mouth and emitted a low, reverberating belching sound along with a wide beam of light that shot out. The tinmen rolled out of the way quickly, narrowly dodging the scorching ray. The ponies weren't so lucky. The steeds were reduced to charred matchsticks. A gust of wind blew away the blackened ash and they were no more.

The tinmen flanked the creature. The Woodman chopped away as the Soldier slashed and stabbed. The were quickly soaked in the purple blood of the thing but this seemed to have little effect. Its clawed appendages swiped at them, and the dual tendril tongues whipped at them from its mouth, but it couldn't get a blow to connect. It recharged and shot its solar beam outward several times but always missed. It seemed as though the stalemate would continue indefinitely. Then a gray cloud descended from the sky. Several furry, gray somethings came swooping down upon the plant monster. Before long it was completely covered in the masses of fur and fury. Tatters of green flesh and splashes of purple blood came flying off as the ravenous beasts tore into the gargantuan hulk. It would shoot its beam at them but they would just hold onto its jaw and avoid its mouth. It would swipe at them with its limbs and tongues, but they would latch onto whatever it tried to strike them with and they would tear it to shreds as well. Before long it collapsed. The cadre of winged monkeys stood in front of it in a large semicircle. The largest monkey walked up to its face and bent down to look into its eye tunnels. He held out his hand behind him and summoned another monkey. The other monkey walked up and handed him a hoe. He took it and started scraping the nodules out of its eye tunnels. The titan wailed an unbearable cry as its vision was slowly shaved off. The sadness in its voice was so palpable even the Tin Woodman could almost face it. Rather he tasted it. It was an acidic copper taste. The Tinman never tasted at all, let alone to taste metal. But relief soon came from the nastiness as the plant demon gurgled its its death rattle and it dissolved into sludge that the thirsty ground quickly soaked up. The tinman approached to thank the flying monkeys. The largest one, the leader as it seemed, ran up and slapped the Tin Soldier directly in the face. The Tin Woodman parted his mouth to begin a protest but his jaw was quickly smacked closed as well.

"Enough games, *children!*" said a voice from above.

The tinmen looked up to see four flying monkeys carrying a chariot by long wooden poles. It descended until it was hovering a dozen or so feet above the ground, a few yards in front of them. It was painted with gold and vibrant purples and greens. The back end had a pair of gold painted wings on either side. Its interior was lined with purple velvet that radiated pink in the sunlight. In the front seat there sat a young boy. His skin was pale and his eyes were circled in black. Under a golden cap his stare was blank and dead.

"Do you metal marionettes even *know* the price that's on your clockwork heads?" said the young boy. When he talked only his mouth moved, like a ventriloquist's dummy. "Of course not. Anyone who brings you in is promised four pounds of the Powder of Life, as well as permanent residence in the lavish home of the late Wicked Witch of the East. This bounty is promised whether or not you're functional. But I must apologize. We haven't even introduced ourselves. This young boy here is our puppet, Zeb Hugson." The boy's head turned to the left, revealing some sort of tube stabbed into the base of his skull.

"I'm Eureka!" said a pink cat dressed in ridiculously frilly clothing.

"And I'm Mr. Bungle!" said a translucent cat with a small pink brain visible in its head.

Zeb's head turned to face forward again. "And now, my soaring simian scamps," said Zeb's feline puppet-masters through his mouth, "*attaaaack*!!!"

The aggregate of aerial anthropoids, teeming with tenacity, tore at the twin tinmen. Surrounded - the mechanical manikins had nowhere to run. They brandished their blazing blades and stood firm. The first few primates fell easily. Their top halves toppled from swipes of the sword. Their heads plopped to the ground from hacks of the ax. A dozen chunks of cercopithecoid carcass dropped dryly to the ground, steaming from their cauterized lacerations. But the onslaught was too much. Soon they were overtaken. The brachiators clutched their captives with their powerful arms, evolved for… well… brachiation. Mr. Bungle, the glass cat, walked over to the front of the chariot.

"And to make sure you don't try to weasel your way out of here," he said, before dowsing the anthropomorphic automatons with a bucket of water. The easily corroded metal in their joints rusted quickly, freezing them in place.

Both the tinmen wondered: If the enemies they had encountered along the road had all been after the bounty, why had these two cats and their meat puppet been the only ones informed of the water trick? Surely, they could have been captured much sooner had their enemies all known that ordinary water would render them immobile. Had the feline duo learned of their weakness from somewhere other than the source of the bounty? Had the individual or group that sponsored their capture only recently heard of water's enervating effect on them? However it happened, those cats with their human puppet and primate army had used the tinmen's aquagenic urticaria to paralyze them.

All of a sudden the Tin Woodman felt a vibration in his stomach. At the same time he felt the pressure rise and plummet in there. Finally, it sucked into a deep vacuum then burst with a large swelling of an explosion that ended with a loud clunk. He felt heavier. There was something in his chest cavity.

The door on his chest creaked open. A small, telescoping, metallic tendril worked its way out, then another. They gripped underneath the door and pulled. Soon a box came tumbling out. It righted itself and stood up on the four tendrils with some effort. It turned around and lifted one of the tendrils to open the door on its front.

"Hello," whispered Nick Chopper's head, "Ku-Klip sent me. He had aether-woven cloth inserted into one of your joints. When he felt the connected piece he had in his lab get wet, he opened a small portal into your chest cavity and sent me through to see what was wrong and if I could help."

Captain Fyter managed to move his mouth every so slightly, "I hve sm oyill n meh chst," he managed to say without his jaw clenched shut.

"Ok then," said the head, "So you have some oil in your chest it sounds like you said. But it looks like there's some business over there I need to handle first. I'll be right back to oil you gentleman up but I need to do something before we draw too much attention to ourselves."

The head-in-a-box snuck over to the chariot. The cats were busy arguing and had left Zeb unattended. The head pulled itself over the edge of the chariot. It reached one of its tendrils up and yanked the tube out of the back of Zeb's skull, knocking the golden cap off his head in the process. The cats turned toward what was going on and hissed. Zeb awoke from his stupor, picked up the pail of water they had to subdue the tinmen, and dumped it on the cats. They hissed and ran around in circles in hydrophobic rage. Meanwhile, Nick Chopper's head snuck back to the tinmen and dowsed them with the oil from Fyter's chest cavity.

"I'm going to teach you kitties a lesson," said Zeb Hugson.

He put the cats in a burlap sack and took them off to the woods. The alpha flying monkey picked up the golden cap and put it on his head. The two tinmen and Nick Chopper's head looked on in dismay as the flock of winged monkeys formed themselves into one giant winged monkey. The giant composite monkey opened its mouth and beat its chest as all the winged monkeys that comprised it howled in unison. It was an horrific sound.

The tinmen flipped the switches in their wrists and stretched to work the oil into their joints while the heating element for their blades warmed up. When they finished warming up they retrieved their blades from the back of the chariot and approached yet *another* gigantic enemy. They started hacking away at its feet, stabbing monkeys, yanking them from the mass and tossing their carcasses to the ground. Before long the beast reached down and lifted the tinmen. Fyter managed to hack away enough of the right hand that he got

180

himself free and fell to the ground suffering a few dents from the fall. The Woodman was shoved into the things "mouth" and ended up tumbling through the creature. He went through a gauntlet of monkeys that beat him from all sides until he finally fell from the posterior of the monstrosity. It managed to lift its tail and even make a fart noise as the monkeys that made up its gluteus maximi simultaneously all flatuated. The Tin Woodman ended up with quite a few dents and it took him a few minutes to get to his feet.

The fight continued. The tinmen would hack away at the lowest portions of the beast. The beast would swing at them, often directly into the ground, the monkeys in its fists dying by the dozens. The monkey corpses continued to pile up with every strike. Whatever attack either party used resulted in more dead primates. Before long the beast had shrunk to nearly half its original size. Something clicked in the Tin Woodman. He didn't know why but he gripped his ax in both hands and point the head of it directly at the alpha monkey. Red steam sizzled from his eye sockets. The ax glowed orange, then red, then purple as arcs of electricity sparked all over it. After a few seconds a yellow beam shot from its end. It smacked the alpha monkey in the face and nearly incinerated him. His body flew several yards behind the structure of monkeys that began to topple as their controller's charred corpse fell to the ground and a puff of blackened ash billowed from its skeleton. The skeleton glowed purple and brightened twice before dimming to black. The monkeys still alive after the fall scattered into the woods. The tinmen and Nick Chopper's head walked up to the skeleton. Upon inspection they realized it was petrified, frozen in an almost fetal position. They expected it to be hot but surprisingly it was ice cold to the touch. The Tin Woodman had no explanation for what had happened, but when he heard the *tick-tick-whir* start up he lied and said he might be able to find an answer if he could catch one of the monkeys. The three went to the woods. Two of them would be monkey-hunting and one would be hunting for a child. None of them saw the magic rickshaw land and the Chiss and Jinnicky pick up the golden cap before taking off to the Chiss' lab with the final ingredient of his iniquitous invention.

xxx

Zeb heard the *tick-tick-whir* from behind the trees. He put down the water pail and flashed a smile at the wet felines tied to the tree from one side of his mouth.

"I hear you Tinman!" he shouted, "It's OK. The cats are tied up to a tree here. They're not going anywhere, and I've almost gotten them to spill the beans about who they work for!"

Zeb saw the cats' eyes widen. He cocked his head to the side at them, conveying his confusion. Blood dotted the cats faces as the ax blade carved a nearly perfect line to bisect Zeb's body vertically. Its perfection was marred around his head and neck however due to the way he had cocked his head. The Tinman harrumphed but then shrugged. He would be incinerating the boy's flesh anyway. He put the flesh in his blender. Then he heard Fyter and his head coming up on him. He quickly dispatched the cats with a chop to their necks. It was easy enough to blame their death on Zeb, to blame Zeb's blood on the cats, and to blame Zeb's absence on him fleeing the crime scene. Everything was tied up in a neat little bow. Captain Fyter was distracted anyway. They were less than a day away from Nimmie Amee's cottage.

xxx

The trio came upon the cozy, quaint little cottage. It sat in a clearing atop a slightly sloping hill. Everything was painted white, pink and blue - all easy-on-the-eyes Easter colors. Each windowsill had a grow box spilling over with herbs and flowers. There were wind chimes and birdhouses. Everything was dotted with little speckles of cuteness like freckles on a red-headed child. It looked as though the house itself had dimples. Captain Fyter knocked on the door but got no answer. The looked through all the windows but only saw shut blinds. Eventually the Tin Soldier tried the door. It was open.

Inside the cottage was the same color scheme, but its cheeriness was replaced by a looming blanket of darkness that covered everything. The only light came from a crystal ball that shined on the face of a monster that was gagged and tied to a chair. It had four arms and four legs. It looked like two bodies melted together at their backs with one head that would have spun completely around on the swivel at the base of its neck if it weren't for the vice that held it in place with its eyelids held open. The thing was being forced to watch whatever transpired in the crystal ball and its face was constantly being washed over by alternating waves of anger, fear and sadness.

"What is that thing?" said Captain Fyter.

"That's Chopfyt," said Nick Chopper's head.

"Chopfyt? Who… what is Chopfyt?"

"Remember all the parts you and Nick had replaced? Remember Ku-Klip carting them off in barrels? Well, he found this stuff at the Wicked Witch's house called Meat Glue. He used it to put all of your leftover pieces together - all of them except me of course. Chopfyt is what he made from all of your's and Nick's leftovers."

"Is he friendly? What's he doing here?"

"Yeah he's plenty friendly. He's been living with Nimmie Amee. I uh…
look I didn't know things had gotten to the 'living together' stage. He and
Nimmie had been seeing each other. I would have said something to you sooner
but things weren't this serious last time I had seen them."

Captain Fyter flew into a rage. He started smashing things and punching
walls. He pulled out his sword and pointed it right in Chopfyt's face. But his
hand was stayed as he looked into his own eyes. Eyes that sparkled in the same
way when he looked at Nimmie Amee. Eyes that teared up in the same way
when she was in distress. The way they were tearing up now. He turned around
and looked into the crystal ball. He saw Nimmie Amee tied to a chair. The
Chiss was firing his quills below her fingernails while Jinnicky grazed her skin
lightly with a straight razor and made little nicks here and there - little nicks
that were surely the precursor to gashes - foreplay before the real torture began.
He used his sword to cut Chopfyt's restraints.

"Do you know where this is?" Captain Fyter said.

"It's the house of the Wicked Witch of the East," said Chopfyt, "They made
sure I knew that. I'm sure it's a trap."

"Well, we're going anyway," said Captain Fyter. He stormed out of the
house.

Chopfyt and the Tin Woodman followed. But Nick Chopper's head stayed
behind. He put his forehead up to the crystal ball and called up Ku-Klip's
scrying glass. He had a few words and then followed after his friends.

"Hey guys!" he screamed after them, "were you just gonna walk all the
way there, or would you rather take this?" Just as he finished his sentence a
portal opened up. The three with shoulders to do so shrugged and all four went
through the portal.

xxx

They stood before the drawbridge that lead over a chasm to the great black
mansion which sat under a perpetual storm that sheathed it in darkness only
broken by the flashes of lightning. THe walked across the bridge and up to the
front door. Shrugging his shoulders Captain Fyter lifted the knocker and
dropped it twice. None of them saw the darkened figure pop up from a hole in
the ground and grab Nick Chopper's head. Nor did they see an exact copy of
Nick Chopper's head surface a few moments later from the hole.

The three party members and the imposter entered the house and looked up
at the dual staircase. Underneath the walkway the stairs led to was a set of large
doors. They opened them and walked down the staircase guided by the light
from the tinmen's charged blades.

"Wait," said the faux Nick Chopper's head when they reached the bottom of the staircase, "I have something for the Tin Woodman. You may need this when we go in there. These two will have their love for Nimmie Amee empowering them. So I've brought a heart for you as well."

The thing posing as Nick Chopper's head opened up the Tin Woodman's chest cavity and inserted the clockwork heart. The Tin Woodman felt his emotions rush into him like a tsunami. He felt his love for Nimmie Amee, his camaraderie with Chopfyt and Captain Fyter, his anger at the Chiss and Jinnicky, but mostly he felt guilt. As he sorted through his memories of hurting poor innocent children and animals a crippling guilt washed over him. he could barely move. As he took his first step into the Chiss' laboratory he felt the tears dripping from his eye sockets. The tears that rusted his joints and froze him in place. The Chiss laughed maniacally as the Tin Woodman fell over, Jinnicky dumped a bucket of water onto Captain Fyter from his perch above the door, and the Chiss himself shot his quills into Chopfyt pinning him to the wall behind him. The thing that looked like Nick Chopper's head walked across the room to its real masters as it turned back into its actual form, a Kalidah, which has the head of a tiger and the body of a bear, that the Chiss had trained and enchanted with Yookoohoo magic, allowing it to change form. It purred and nuzzled up next to its master. It loved to nuzzle up to the Chiss but only could do so when his quills were out. The Chiss swung the chair that contained Nimmie Amee around, set a cage containing the real head of Nick Chopper in the middle of the floor, and began his soliloquy.

"Now that we're all here, I guess I should explain why," the Chiss began, "First off I'm sure the Tin Woodman has been wondering where his blood lust is coming from. I don't know if the rest of you have noticed but the Tinman here has been filled with an urge to kill anything helpless and/or innocent whenever he encountered it. Well, I'll explain but unfortunately in the process of me explaining it you'll lose your ability to understand." The Chiss inserted the telescope-looking device into the Tin Woodman's eye socket. It projected a round figure onto the wall. It was Tiktok, the mindless automaton, the prototype of the tinmen. "You see, I miniaturized Tiktok here and inserted him into the head before Ku-Klip scavenged it from the lab here. He was manipulating things in your mechanical brain, which was the strange rhythm you heard when your urge to feed welled up." The image of Tiktok reached lifesize and walked off the wall. It had punch cards and a jar of different colored marbles in its hands. Captain Fyter recognized them as the memory system used in tinmen. From here on out the Tin Woodman would have no frame of reference for what the Chiss was saying.

"You might ask why. We'll get to that. First off let me ask you a question. What is the most powerful item in a witch's house? Is it her wand? Her crystal ball? Her alchemy supplies?..." He paused and looked back and forth between his captives. "No guesses? Well, the correct answer is... the witch herself! I'm sure you all heard or read about the untimely demise of the Wicked Witch of the East when that house fell on her. How all the munchkins saw her feet shrivel up and she just disappeared forever, right?! Well, do you really think a Cardinal Witch could just be deteriorated to nothing?! Of course not! The four Cardinal Witches are the most powerful beings in all of Oz! They don't just die from a house falling on them! And if they did their bodies wouldn't just disappear! The munchkins were so busy celebrating their savior that they didn't even notice the mosquito flying away from underneath that Dorothy girl's house. One of the Witch's familiars was that mosquito and it sucked up the little droplet of blood her body had shrunk into and carried it back here. It squirted that droplet into her magical sarcophagus. And, how thrilled do you think *I* was when I moved in here and found her corpse almost entirely regrown *in* that sarcophagus?... Well... I was pretty damned thrilled! Especially after I read through some books in her library and learned all I could about resurrection and necromancy!" During this part of the speech the Chiss had rolled out the sarcophagus, containing the corpse of the Wicked Witch of the East, and opened up on of her grimoires and propped it onto a book stand open.

"That brings us to the Tin Woodman and his recent thirst for the blood of children. You see, a lot of people think of children as innocent. But what is this *innocence* of which they speak? Children are ignorant of a lot of things. For one thing they're ignorant of the fact that other people are actually *people*. Therefore, they're completely self-centered, nihilistic. Children's souls are blank slates. But they aren't blank as in devoid of *evil*. They're devoid of *compassion*! The only kind of souls fit for a Wicked Witch!" At this time he had removed the Searing Orb from its cavity within the Woodman's chest and placed it into the telescope-looking growing/shrinking machine. "But to transport a soul is difficult. It has to be condensed down into its most basic form. To do *that* you need a heat source greater than most. Which is why I needed the Searing Orb here. Also the resurrection spell needs one more component. An infant soul. It needs an infant soul to have a totally blank slate so the resurrected witch can think for herself. But the Woodman didn't kill an infant. Why? Well, because I don't *want* the witch to be able to think for herself, of course! I'll do the thinking for her!" The Searing Orb went through the machine in the shrinking direction, but it came out the other side the same size. Instead of mass being removed from it, souls were removed from it. The children's' souls exited the machine through the overhead projector and embedded themselves in the crystals lying on its light source.

The soul energy was divided evenly between seven crystals. The Chiss inserted the seven crystals into the witch's seven orifices - one in her mouth, one in each nostril, one in each ear, one in her rectum and one in vagina. The witch's skin began to sparkle with a rainbow of different colored sparks. The Chiss inserted a tube in the back of her neck that was affixed to the golden cap. He put the golden cap on Jinnicky's head. The Wicked Witch's body lurched forward. Eventually, Jinnicky could control the witch's body.

"Amazing!" said Jinnicky, "I can feel the magic coursing through her! I can... I can... use it!"

The witch's hands began to move like those of a conductor. Only instead of conducting music she conducted Oz's most powerful magic. Bricks from the wall loosed and began moving through the air. They then turned to gold. Through the witch, Jinnicky not only levitated the bricks, but also held up the ceiling that should have fallen without the wall to support them, and also performed expert alchemy, turning the bricks to gold.

But then, something went wrong. The witch started shaking. Jinnicky started screaming. Blood shot from his nose and eyes. His body started to shrink and shrivel. Before long his organs slopped out of his mouth and anus and all his skin sucked up into the golden cap. The witch's muscles swelled. She breathed deep and stood. A piece of royal purple cloth flew from the chair it was hanging over, tied itself into an elaborate dress, and wrapped itself around her body. She pulled the tube from the back of her neck, whipped the golden cap forward by the tube, wrapped it around the Chiss' neck, and pulled him toward her.

"So you really thought you could control a Cardinal Witch with this simple contraption, just because you left one ingredient out of the spell?" said the Wicked Witch of the West. She whipped her head back and laughed uproariously. "I just substituted the infant soul with the soul of that Red Jinn there. An adult soul is just as empty, the way it's been programmed with routine. Also, I'm now a Krumbic Witch! Queen Coo-ee-oh was the first Krumbic Witch, which is seven times more powerful than a normal witch. But don't you know how a Krumbic Witch is made? A regular witch has to *die*! Then she must be resurrected using the ancient necromancy first writ by the Three Adepts and tainted with the dark arts, which is exactly what you read in that book, you *fool*!"

The witch's jaw unhinged and she inserted the Chiss into her mouth. She swallowed it whole. She picked up the telescope-looking shrinking/growing machine.

"Now this," she said, "this thing is actually quite ingenious. The way it expands and focuses things should also work with magic!"

186

She strapped the machine to her wrist and pointed it over her head. The ceiling started coming apart, then the floor above it. Soon the entire upper floor of the mansion was floating in the air in pieces. The Wicked Witch laughed and began to levitate upward. But she was soon stopped by a magical barrier. Ozma appeared.

Ozma, the Queen of Oz, stepped out of a portal. She was in an elaborate gown with a bucket in her hand.

"Remember how easily Queen Coo-ee-oh was defeated?!" said Ozma. She threw the bucket of enchanted water onto the Wicked Witch and the witch turned to a swan and flew away. "She shouldn't bother anyone for a while," Ozma said to the captives. She released Nick Chopper's head from the cage, oiled up Captain Fyter, removed the quills from Chopfyt, and healed him and Nimmie Amee, whom she also clothed.

"And what about the Tin Woodman?" said Captain Fyter.

"Well, he still has yet another adventure!" said Ozma, "And he can't remember this one when he is on it."

She flipped through the punch cards, pulled out some marbles, and put some of both back into his head. Around that time the Wizard landed in his hot air balloon. He took the Tin Woodman to the place on the Yellow Brick Road in the forest where he was to meet Dorothy.

""And the rest of you can come home with me for now. Your adventures are some time off," said Ozma. The portal reopened and they all walked through as the Wicked Witch's old mansion floated back together. Somewhere a duck who was supposed to have forgotten her time as a witch was slowly starting to remember.

Cold

by Sean M. Thompson

The snow is all there is

the cold bitter chill

to set the bones to ice

joints to grey slush

Why the fuck am I here?

Sliding

there's no traction

no foothold

none at all

Nothing

Frozen in time

stuck in place

The snow is all there is

we tell ourselves spring is around the corner

knowing it's a lie

Umbriel is The Darkest Moon

by Marguerite Reed

When Falconer felt wearier than usual, tired of the smug glances, the knowing looks, her control got a little sloppy.

"It says in the contract that I don't have a jack," she'd say. "Just one less way for the Company to keep tabs on me."

No wonder she didn't get the biggest hauls. Despite the fact that Falconer was a straight-shot flyer, with no marks against her--rigged manifest, fuel waste, blown schedule were for suckers--somehow she never cleared the bar that would allow her to trade in the *Bizunzuri* and get a new ship. A new ship, and a chance for increased fares, more respect, a bigger piece of the pie that was the mining society in the Tresize asteroid fields.

Sure, she could have a jack implanted. Go in the for the prep, have the surgery, then the training. And lose how much time? Every fare she lost would likely stay lost, and so the jack would do her no good if she could never afford a ship to link with. So many ways to be a slave to the Company, jacked or unjacked.

Falconer sighed as she keyed her pass code. The bay for her freighter was one of the smallest in Station Alpha, and every day she fretted that the Overseers would scrap this bay and build a larger one, one she couldn't rent. So many things to squeeze her out, with nowhere to go--her ship in no way could travel the great interstellar distances needed to escape the clutches of the Company. If she wanted to leave, she would have to sell the *Bizunzuri*--netting her almost nothing--and buy a one-way ticket out of the Tresize fields.

So when the door irised open to reveal an intruder next to her workbench, snugged in against micro-gee, she saw only a man where a man shouldn't be, and that meant a sniffer, a surveyor, a Company pawn.

She had her gun drawn before he pivoted to face her."Oh, my God," he said, and kept his foot in the toehold D-ring.

"ID," she barked.

"What?"

"Come on, I know you don't have all day." The blank look he gave her did not help her temper. "You thought you could slide in here, look around, write up a bogus report so your boss could shut down my hangar?"

As he shook his head, still blank-faced, she saw him more clearly. Unless they'd paid a bum from the corridors—and that wasn't out of the question—this was no Company man. His jacket was good, but his shirt and trousers: shoddy mass-produced clothing, thin and fraying at the cuffs. Jaw-length black hair that plastered back from his forehead—the public bath queues had been last week. And no Company employee she'd ever met wore the face he wore now. No logo needed; they all brandished the same sneer.

"May I get up?" he asked. "My legs are starting to fall asleep."

For a second Falconer considered it. "No. Not until you tell me why you're here."

His mouth tightened, with irritation or pain. "Your tools—" he said.

"Back up with that." Her arm was beginning to ache from training the gun on him, but she couldn't let him see that. "Keep your hands where I can see them."

"It's illegal to have a gun."

A firearm, in space, presented a huge risk, one that she was not cleared for. She kept it for insurance, but had never fired it—never hoped to.

"I can pay the price. Can you? How the hell did you get in here, anyway?"

"Your hangar is one of the few that isn't patrolled—"

Because she didn't have the scratch for that.

"I printed out a card of micron plastic when it was my turn in the queue a few weeks ago. The last time you left, I fixed the plastic over the strike plate." He shrugged. "The doors on the hangars take so long to open and close I had enough time."

During his explanation Falconer took in the rest of the scene, gaze ticking between the intruder and her space. Nothing looked out of place, except her tool bench.

She adjusted her grip on the gun. "What about my tools?"

"I'm not a thief." His voice hardened. "I'm a lot of things, but I'm not a thief."

"You're on the dole."

"And when did being on the public mean someone's a thief?"

Would anger trip him into revealing something more? Was there a reward for this bastard? "Then you're a murderer."

"You think for a second I'd be walking around a free man if I were a murderer?'

"A rapist."

"Christ have mercy."

Falconer bit the inside of her cheek to keep from smiling at the revulsion on his face. "Hold out your hands."

He extended them. All the better for her if his legs really had gone to sleep.

"Turn them over."

Palms down. She took a step toward him, still outside of grabbing range. Caked in his fingernails, threading across his knuckles, blood.

She brought the gun up and, well-trained, his arms lifted once more. "Whose?"

"Mine." He nodded over to where her primary tool box lay open next to the larger chest. "You'll find it on those, too."

Even from where she was, she could see more blood on the bit of her Bethlehem point, the sharpest blade she owned. "Here?"

He nodded. Now on his face Falconer read an emotion: not defiance, not anger or disgust. Only misery.

"I need help," he said. "Falconer Oke, will you help me?" He bent his head, exposing the back of his neck.

She saw the jack inset right below the base of his skull. Blood matted his hair and oozed from the wound he'd created. For a moment pity and self-preservation warred.

"Out," she said.

On his knees he looked up at her, dark eyes beseeching. "Please. You don't have one, there's a reason why you don't, you know what these things do to a person--"

With a hiss: "Sniffer. You're a sniffer. Is that how you know I'm not jacked in?"

"Everyone in shipping knows Falconer Oke flies without a hook-up. I figured you'd be sympathetic."

"You figured wrong, pretty man." She flicked the muzzle upward. "Go on, get up."

For a moment he bobbed in place, head down, a picture of dejection. "You really aren't going to help me."

"You're wasting my time. Go find the black market--this is medical. I can't do it." The next words out of her mouth brought up disgust like bile. "I can't

193

afford trouble, see? You get that jack out, they'll find you. They find you, they'll find me. That's not going to get me where I need to be."

He struggled to his feet, turning his ankle when he took a first step. Falconer imagined reaching out to help him, and knew that if she tried that, he'd overpower her. He looked to be a few inches taller than she was, but he had the advantage of muscle and breadth on her. Even so, she felt a twinge of empathy watching him falter his way to the door. No feeling in those feet right now, and when paresthesia kicked in, he'd be miserable.

Too bad. She keyed the door open. He stood for a moment on the threshold to the great bay, the noise of all Alpha Station's public sphere washing in past him. He looked over his shoulder, and she saw, as if in a snapic, just what rung of the ladder he stood on. No matter what he did, he'd never be able to afford the medical processes to keep his good looks from decaying; he was a half-year too old for the bulls; and no Company recruiter would look twice at him unless he stole someone else's gear. He would spend the rest of his days on the public until he got caught in one of the routine sweeps the tin-pots made in order to stock the Company prisons.

"Do you know," he said, not looking at her, giving her only his clean profile, "what they make me do?"

xxx

If Revely could make it to his dorm in time, he'd be safe. He resisted the impulse to speed: nothing drew attention quicker than swift movement here at Alpha Station. The gravity was heavy here, the torus rotating at a fractionally greater speed than other stations he'd been on. Brilliant job slowing your hellers down, Alpha.

At this point in the cycle not many people were about. A few heavy-eyed techs climbed past Revely on the pipe ladder, their movements becoming airier as they neared the hub, while his became more sodden the closer he came to the outer wheel. He saw a couple of tin-pots in their blue and silver harnesses bumbling about the pipe, officious even in micro-gee. Head down and don't look around, Revely. He knew he didn't tick anything out of the ordinary, but if one of the tinpots focussed, their chips would dox him to be that poor bastard who ran to the ass end of the star system and got caught.

When the doctors at the Tresize Prison had first completed the surgery, the staff warned him about the possibility of after-effects. Revely had lain in the clinic restraints while voices drifted through him and maybe one word in ten caught his attention. Who cared what words like *cerebellum* and *lesions* and *tonic-clonic* meant? He sure as hell didn't, not with the drugs rolling through his body. At that point he didn't care what his name was, never mind what *seizure risk* signified.

By the time he reached the portal to the outer wheel Revely had to keep swallowing to quell the nausea. Centripetal force on top of an aura made any hangover he'd ever had look like a hiccup. There was no way he would have willingly slid into the micro-gee zone unless he became desperate. And after research, he knew that Falconer Oke was the one to find.

Desperation had come after how many months? Six? Eight? Revely had lost count; one day was like the next, always on call for the next cybertrick. When last he couldn't take it anymore, the daily ransacking of his memories, he tried to take out the jack. He'd had a seizure all right; he learned immediately and first hand what all that medical oleo meant.

He was pretty sure he still had some of the tonic-clonic tonic left. In the cabinet above the lemon pepper and the sot siracha, behind the anti-inflammatories. He could wait another week for the shower allotment--he didn't dare be seen in public naked with the visible damage he'd inflicted on himself fresh and bleeding. It wasn't as he needed to go anywhere to fulfill the requirements of his servitude.

Revely, drugged as he was, could not have signed a damned thing, but he held up his thumb for the print that said he understood the ramifications of the neural implant surgery. Sure, he understood. He understood he was fucked. When the legal aide left, the prison nurse had reached out and stroked his thigh with one manicured hand. "You've been quite the flesh monger," the nurse said. "That scan of your frontal cortex yielded a treasure trove of sexual memory: over six hundred unique sexual encounters in the past ten years!" He smiled. Revely remembered how the reveal of all those teeth, perfectly white and perfectly regular, frightened him more than the man's hand on his leg.

Now he had to move slowly no matter what the gravity. Breathe, Revely. You can do this. Grasp the bar, double check to make sure all of your fingers close around it, now move your feet past the lip of the portal--that's right, don't catch your toe; now find the step down. Catch the rail. Focus on your balance. That person's speaking to you: smile, say something vague. The world pulsed around him--shadows shivered around people, doorways, the trolleys that moved along their tracks along the sides of the ring. No time to ponder this marvel; Revely knew a seizure would strike in minutes. If he tried to run now, he would fall. He began to look for some out of the way place, a corner hidden by a trash bin; an alley, something.

"In time, you'll be grateful," the nurse had said. He continued to stroke Revely's thigh. "It's this fantastic technology, you see, that permits a goat like you to provide any use to society. Otherwise--" He shrugged. "Off to the prison station with you, and you'd become a true lowered-down, anyone's game." The lights were so bright that Revely felt relief when the nurse stood, throwing darkness across his eyes. But then he heard the chink of a belt buckle being unfastened, and those hands gripped his knees, yanking him down to the foot of the bed until he cried out in confused pain from the tension on his restrained arms.

"The hell are you doing?" The flimsy hospital tunic had rucked up around Revely's waist, leaving the whole lower half of his body exposed. "Hey! Someone help!"

"Room's soundproofed." The teeth again, pale in the shadow. To his muddled horror Revely felt his thighs pulled apart and the body of the other man move between them. "This is what it would be like if you went to prison, you know." Ungentle fingers plucked at his scrotum, then moved lower to gouge his sphincter.

This could not be happening. The man didn't mean it, was only trying to put a scare into him. "Son of a--" Revely writhed in the restraints. Any minute now, someone would come in-- "Get the fuck *off me!*" His voice rose to a hoarse shout. "I'll rip your goddamn balls off--"

The nurse leaned up and slapped Revely so hard he felt his lip split. His vision reeled from the blow and the sedative. "Quit whining," the nurse said. "Whore like you, you act like you've never had anything up your ass before."

Revely had once had a lover who was fond of saying, as she punched up another round of juice, that drugs didn't ease a thing--they only made you not care about the pain. For the next four minutes his world had been wrecked by pain. And whatever the prison hospital had given him had not come close to making him not care.

After a few minutes of determined drifting, Revely found a recycling dumpster in an alley, in a corner between a guksu bar and a music bin. Shadows thrown by the station's reflector panels beckoned. The aura was almost continuous now, painting trails of non-light across his world. A couple of patrons at the guksu bar--he gulped in the smells of vinegar and garlic and sesame oil-- and no one at the music bin. He eased into the darkness, taking care to focus, to let himself relax and yet concentrate on wielding control over his hostage body. It took him a minute to reach the corner, and by the time he got there, he was cold from sweat.

The recycling dumpster had been emptied recently, so in his condition he could pull it out a couple of feet. Silver smeared his sight now. By touch he found he could fit within the space between wall and container. He wedged himself into the corner, pleased at how well the dumpster braced him upright, and let the seizure take him.

xxx

Bizunzuri meant *carpenter bee* in Luganda, which Falconer did not speak; but the word tickled her so much that she refused to change it. Let the Greek and Japanese named ships fill the lists; let the Luganda word confound the list-makers.

It was in this mood that Falconer met with her next client. An

actual one-on-one in meatspace, a pleasing rarity, although the venue her customer had chosen irked her. She had to use her quarterly pass to the Connective, and it would be a long time before she'd be assigned another. She could apply on hardship grounds--no partner and no jack with which to access the interactive sex channels--but she thought she could wait. It was only sex, anyway, despite what the Company preached.

After the door constricted behind her, she blundered her way through the dark of the club, her way lit only in pulses of tourmaline light. First pink, then green beating down from the crystalline diodes embedded in the ceiling. Couples, triples, groups gathered in the cubicles along the walls. Mostly talking, drinking, but there were a few booths where she saw entwined limbs and the gleam of flesh.

Kalio had chosen a seat near the back. She nodded as Falconer slipped into the seat facing her and gestured towards Falconer's head. "Quite the festive scarf you've got there," she said. She shook her hair and it lay over her shoulders in a soft fall. Kalio had access to private showers.

Falconer smiled. "So glad you like it," she said, knowing full well that wasn't what Kalio had meant. She passed her hand over her head, smoothing down the nubbly shape of the braids beneath. "I picked it out just for you."

"It's fighting with the lights in here." Kalio lowered her gaze, intent on stirring her drink.

Falconer sprawled back in the booth. She did not like Kalio's apparent hesitancy. After a wait which involved Kalio sipping her alcohol, frowning at it, then stirring some more, the other woman spoke.

"I sent the commission to another freighter," she said.

After a measured breath, Falconer leaned across the table, took Kalio's tumbler, and downed the contents. She wanted to yell, to curse, to flip the table over. Kalio kept her head bent, her thin lips in a pout, but her gaze followed Falconer's every movement.

"That's not news I wanted to hear," Falconer said carefully. The drink, whatever it was, made her want to gag. Too sweet.

"It was an utterly ordinary assignment. But then something turned up that was--extraordinary." The pout smoothed.

Falconer swallowed. She still wanted to spit away the cloying taste. "Something--extraordinary? You mean something ill--"

Kalio leaned across the table; her fingertips stopping Falconer's mouth. "Shh." She pursed a kiss. "I know you're disappointed, darling. But I've got something much better."

Darling? Falconer's confusion turned to amusement when Kalio slid out of her seat to come to Falconer's side of the cubicle, then straddled her lap. "Why, Kalio; I didn't know you cared."

Hard little seat bones pressed against her thighs. Kalio had even less padding than Falconer had thought. She smiled down at Falconer. "Proximity messes up the lip-reading sensors."

"I'd heard that." Bony as she was, her human warmth felt good. Falconer rested her hands on Kalio's hips. For verisimilitude, of course. "This better be good. That was going to be a sweet commission. Word gets out you're the kind of customer who yanks jobs out from under, people might think twice about working for you."

Even as irritation tightened the other woman's mouth, she lowered her face to Falconer's. Not a kiss, Falconer thought; and she was right. To the casual observer--or to the surveillance vids--Kalio was devoted to nuzzling her companion's neck., her hair hiding her moving lips. Falconer kept her eyes half-lidded, adopting the mien of a woman luxuriating in sensation. It was not difficult.

"The deployment to lovely Umbriel last season, remember it?"

"Yes," Falconer breathed. How could she forget? Uranus's weirdest moon, ice and darkness, whose most significant feature was a mysterious ring of white on the floor of one of its largest craters. She'd made good bank ferrying raw supplies to the base on Umbriel. Good bank indeed, but a lot of it went to repairs on *Bizunzuri* later. Despite the cleanliness of the landing pad, regolith fines had drifted into the landing gear so that when it tried to retract for take off, the gear jammed and she had to return to the station having to manual override all the way. Could she have done that with a jack? She didn't know.

"Tresize is about to be turned inside out," Kalio went on. "Utterly fucked. With your help."

"Fucked how?" Oh, the fun the techs would have with this.

Pain caught her ear: Kalio nipped. Falconer grabbed that long hair right at the base of Kalio's skull, not quite hard enough to hurt, but hard enough to hurt if she moved. "I haven't said yes yet, and for two checks I'd turn--"

"Lonsdaleite," Kalio said, syllables tumbling out. "The ring on Umbriel is pure lonsdaleite." Lonsdaleite, already rare on Earth, was harder than diamond in its pure form. Umbriel had to have been bombarded with graphite-containing meteorites for millions of years to get such a deposit. As Falconer's grip relaxed in surprise, she went on in a rush: "No, don't let go, keep me right here, looks better. Tresize would turn both our asses into just another couple of TNOs if they ever sniffed this."

"Then why are you--"

Kalio named a sum. Something like ecstasy swept Falconer's frame. "Keep going," she managed.

"That's for me. You get a quarter to deliver."

With a payoff like that, she would have her choice of buying an entirely new spaceship or retrofitting the *Bizunzuri*.

She could get out. Out of the suffocating corporation city, out of the constant atmosphere of attention and pressure and invasion, as insidious as ash and as insistent as a klaxon. Away from a place that literally measured the worth of a human individual every month in a bank statement.

She wrapped her arms around Kalio and squeezed, ignoring the other woman's splutters. Now it was her turn to speak against Kalio's ear. "Tell me the part about why so much money. Tell me the part where I'm risking my neck."

xxx

Two women helped Revely home. After a back and forth about taking him to a clinic, he convinced them that involving any authority would be a bad idea. From their dialect and conversation, he knew they would be as interested in running dark as he was.

"Thanks, sisters," he said. "Be careful with yourselves. Cameras everywhere."

"We didn't roll ya," said the one of the women. Straight lilac hair, chewing non-stop on a gummy. "We coulda, though. You were dead out of it."

The other one, broad, brown, hair shaved in a checkered pattern, shook her head. "We mighta, but we knew you didn't have anything."

She indicated his door. "Cash in the kip, though?"

"No cash," he said, and tried not to let their expressions get to him. And then, embarrassed, "I'm on the public."

"Dunno anyone who isn't," the shaved woman said.

"I've got some food, though." Neither of them looked in need, but in the gesture was a language they all understood.

He gave them flatbread and a pouch of preserves which the food safe had included in the last delivery and that he wouldn't miss. He could live without jam. He could not live without good will.

Only after the door closed on them did Revely acknowledge the one thing he hadn't wanted to: the call light on his board. Again. Another goddamn star with his dick in his hand who wanted a thrill. He felt tempted to ignore it-- wash--eat. The light's shade of violet, though, indicated that the call was nearing the end his permitted time to pick up--and if he didn't pick up, he'd pay.

He did take a moment to piss; then settled himself on the chaise below the board. He knew better than to lie down before keystroking in, much as he wanted to.

"Moroz here," he said.

"It's about goddamn time!" Late forties? Mid fifties? White. Spoiled. Like the majority of the clientele. Defending himself would do no good. God, is that how he'd sound in a couple of decades? --Of course not. You had to have money to sound like that.

"Sir--" Though no one could see him (he hoped), Revely found he sounded more sincere if he acted it out, and put his hand on his heart. "My deepest apologies, sir."

"Fine, fine. I got a half sconge here and it could go either way, so this had better be good."

"What would you like tonight, sir?"

"Whattaya got?"

I knew I should've gone to seminary, Revely thought. "Anything. No kids, no animals, though. No toilet play." Thank god for some restraint in his past.

The breathing on the other end thickened. "You sound like too nice a boy to have the stuff I need."

And a nice boy turns him on. A dozen possibilities flickered through his mind. On a hunch he said "A nice boy who plays well with others."

 Silence, except for the breathing.

Revely tried again. "A nice boy who taught other nice boys what they were capable of."

Low, drawn out, gravelly. "...Yes...."

Great. "I think I have just the thing, sir. If you'll make yourself comfortable?" Revely located the jack, dangling by its wires, and pushed it in. It hurt. He allowed himself the indulgence of a whine--jacked in, neither side could hear each other, thank goodness--and lay back.

It wasn't a bad memory; certainly. Not like some others. He closed his eyes and tried not to imagine the chemicals in the implant and his own power of recall lighting up the amygdala, the dorsolateral cortex, the prefrontal cortex, stimulating the neurons until the customer at the other end could access this discrete memory from start to finish.

And force him to relive it.

His world turns amber, silver no longer. A carpeted room, cushions spread about on the floor. Illumination from a few lamps. Taste of wine in his mouth. From a drink he'd sipped, or from the mouth of the woman he's kissing? He ghosts his fingers down her throat, between her breasts, over the curve of her belly, stopping just short of her mons--and then skimming up again. When he begins circling his palm over one erect nipple--a circular drag that sends the puckered flesh teasing his own skin like a fingertip--he shivers. She moans into his mouth, and then her hands reach for his cock, pressing her breasts together so that he can tease both nipples.

The cushions on the floor are upholstered in scratchy brocade--she shifts atop one until her head is crooked back and her pelvis tilts down at the opposite end. Her dark hair foams onto the floor, and her smile glints upside down at him.

And then the other man is there. Younger than he, by a few

years, and not as experienced. He's looking at the woman--Catherine, her name was Catherine--with a mixture of awe and excitement.

--Spread your legs, baby, Revely says. --Show him that honey you've got.

Catherine reaches for him; he wants so badly to slide into her mouth, but first--he moves to where his friend is kneeling, transfixed, between Catherine's splayed knees. She squirms, restless. --Oh, come on, you guys. What am I, an art project? She reaches with both hands and parts herself. Both Revely and his friend sigh with appreciative lust.

Her cunt is a jewel, set in shadowed bronze. --Touch her, says Revely.

The younger man sets a fingertip on her clit. Catherine squeaks.

~Like this, Revely says. He sets his own hand over his friend's, aligning each finger, and then shows him which way to stroke, to coax, and when he slips his finger inside, it's paired with the other man's; and Catherine groans. Her hungry arch pushes her cunt down on both their hands. --Feel that, he says. --Feel how she's clenching around you, drawing you in. Easy now...don't thrust, stroke her from the inside.

The younger man--darker than Revely, eyelashes so black and fine they could've been limned with a pen--is half laughing, half moaning in delight. --Oh God, she's so soft.

--Think of it as a delicious mouth, Revely says. He reaches back, catching his friend's chin and kisses him, deep-tongued, beginning to lose himself. His breath is short; his cock is so hard it hurts. He slips his finger out of Catherine's cunt and feathers his thumb across her clit. The slight change in his position brings his cock against the other man's, and they both gasp in surprised pleasure at the contact. Revely grins.

--You don't have to choose. he says. --You don't *ever* have to choose.

--I need you up here, Catherine says. Her eyes are dark with hunger. --I need--

Greyout

He's in her mouth, beyond bliss, while she's using her tongue and her hands

Greyout, and pain

She straddles his friend while Revely is

Dead blind.

A horrible tingling washed through his body and all the memory vanished, not a glimpse, not an echo, nothing. With blundering desperate fingers he snatched the jack from its housing in his skull. He managed to roll over and off the couch, both hands over his mouth, whimpers spilling through his fingers like vomit, his eyes squeezed

shut.

The speaker squawked. "What the fuck? What's going on?" Real rage in the voice, but Revely was too busy trying not to hyperventilate to care. "This some kind of joke?"

"No, sir," he croaked. "Hardware malfunction."

"I should find you and take it out of your hide. That was going to be big. That was going to be immense. I--"

"Full refund," Revely said. "You'll be compensated."

"Compensation, shit. Never had this problem before with you people. I'm going to report you."

I'll be dead before they can do a damn thing, he thought.

xxx

Is the money right? Falconer thought maybe. It was a *lot* of money.

She let that thought spin in her mind while she looked at her corporation check for the month. Deductions for oxygen use, body weight, body waste removal, displacement, public water use--a massive one for the hangar. Additions for the two jobs she'd done. The balance might give her enough to last through the next month, if fuel prices didn't go up and if *Bizunzuri* didn't need any repairs and if, if, if.

The news about the lonsdaleite ring hadn't broke, but it would, and soon. It was Falconer's job to get the info to a rival syndicate, along with a sample before Tresize moved.

Falconer could go further out into the system, to the Kuiper Belt--but while she might get no end of takers from one of the hungry bootstrap companies out there, she had no guarantee of anything to spend it on. And it would be just that much more time and fuel torched in getting back to some place who could deal with the *Bizunzuri.*

No, she'd better go inward. Titan? Would any of the bodies involved in the Gallilean Syndicate be interested? That was such a rich field , they were probably all too spoiled to want anything from the Uranus area. Mars. Mars would be perfect--but oh, the time and fuel involved in getting there.

If she carried no cargo--if she faked the manifest like those scammers she so hated--God, this would be an all or nothing run. She'd never done that before. She'd have to burn like hell and watch the acceleration.

When she finished her second round of calculations, over two thousand hours were staring her in the face. No. Not fast enough. Do it again.

This would take so much fuel. The *Bizunzuri* had never been made for that kind of run, just hops between stations, and she fretted that her little craft could not carry that amount. Not even if she falsified the manifest for the computers and carried herself and the barest of essentials.

Not only was there a question of fuel, but--she grimaced. The ship--and she--would be taking massive hits of radiation. For her hops, the *Bizunzuri* relied on the old icehulls, the sheath extracted from gray water and human excreta. Yet another reason to upgrade ships; she was tired of hearing the old derogatory term "poo comet." The protective sheath would ablate away well before she made her goal, and expose her ship to radiation damage. Was it worth it, trading a few years of her life for this payoff?

She would never have the power of the planetary ships--the swift ships like the *Rainbow* and the *Star Witch* and the huge longburn freighters like the *Shampinder*, the *Nene Hatun*. But if she could harness their power--

She had checked the maps beyond the Tresize fields. Right now Uranus and Mars were in alignment, and would be for another thousand hours or so. There was a tactic she'd heard of, but never run across reliably documented. She'd seen it in vids--and while she'd sneered at the fake effects, she had worked out how it could be done.

xxx

Revely stood in the lavatory, looking at his wrists. The classic way. A better way, he knew, was to slit his femoral artery. Hell--

He cupped his quiescent cock, his balls in one hand. Together they took up slightly more space than a human heart--small things to cause so much misfortune. His dick had gotten him into all the trouble he'd ever found in his entire adult life; he'd let it lead him around to hundreds of sexual encounters. Women, men, intersexed people, nullified people; kinks of every kind except kids and scat and animals and rape.

Sure, he could kill himself by cutting it all off. He might even survive-- there was beautiful Yücel who had gone nullo sometime before Revely had met him, who had cut everything off with a friend who was a black market nurse. Revely remembered the night he'd invited himself over to Yücel's apartment and sweet talked him down to his knees. A mouth like a blown rose and an asshole to match, and he could recall every moment of that encounter. Every moment of every encounter, and the corporation knew it and mined it as they had mined the Uranian Moons. The worst part was the dichotomy in Tresize's ability: they could extract the resources from the asteroids and moons, leaving little behind--but when they drilled his head for his memories, they left everything intact.

Lies and love and betrayal and--God yes, that worst of emotions, indifference--all the *I adore yous* and *I hate yous* and *I'm sorrys--what was your name again?* All the orifices and entwined limbs, all the flesh, all the sleek, slick heat of human physical congress that he'd hoarded, now harvested for the prurience of the moneyed class, while he relived every instance they paid for.

What he needed to cut out was his brain, not his cock. If he failed in a suicide attempt, he'd be arrested for attempted destruction of corporation property.

If they found out what he'd tried to do--remove the jack--god knew what he'd be in for. He'd rather wrest that option away from them, no matter what it meant.

He gave his balls a squeeze--poor things--and put down the knife. He had one last gamble, and if he lost, he wouldn't be the one destroying property.

xxx

Falsifying a manifest took a certain amount of coolheaded blindness. Don't think about it, just know that one, your actual cargo has to equal the weight of the stated cargo; and two, if either stated or actual cargo weighs very little, someone's going to get suspicious--why would a small freighter even be going out with such a small payload? Three: the list has to be plausible. Clothing for the miners out on the out stations? No--the miners could print all the clothes they liked. But cotsilk, with which to feed the printers--much more believable. A contract dull as grey water, and yet such dull matters were crucial to everyone working the Tresize fields. A liquid ton of cotsilk, some carbon scrubbers, several hundred pounds of powdered macronutrient (and that took up a hell of a lot of room): that was a believable cargo haul for a ship like *Bizunzuri*. It was even true. In addition, however, were a hundred pounds of londsdalite. As well as a chip giving the analysis of the size and composition of the deposit, the coordinates, and the documentation of excavation methods.

That, Falconer put on her person.

At Export she thought cool thoughts while the ship was weighed and its mass evaluated and corroborated. She thought about icy drinks and distant stars, but not about Kalio's lips on her neck. The *Bizunzuri's* computer told Export's safety computer that all cargo was locked down against micro-gee. So she smiled for the retinal scan, and let the signature pad scrap her thumb without a flushed capillary or a bead of sweat. A smile from the Export officer was too much to ask for, but he did nod to her as he handed over her chip copy of the manifest.

Nothing is going on, she thought, climbing down to the open hatch of the *Bizunzuri. Nothing is going on,* she thought as she

cinched herself into her pilot's chair. *There is nothing unusual about this shipment*, she thought while checking cabin pressure, oxygen levels, fuel levels. She keyed in the pre-set course for Station Zeta. *Everything is normal.*

Not until the *Bizunziri* cleared immediate handshake space did Falconer start to tremble. Putting her head between her knees would do no good here in micro-gee; she closed her eyes and concentrated on her breathing. In--2--3--4--5--6--hold. Out 2--3--4--. *You can do this.*

To ease her mind, she got into her suit and went to check on her cargo. She tapped the key for the door. It slid open--half-way.

Well, that was odd, it had opened just fine when she first entered the cockpit. She keyed it closed, and then tried to open it again. She pushed on the edge: towards the bottom it seemed to yield further along its track--the same test towards the top of the door resulted in no give whatsoever. Something in the upper track?

She pulled herself up and tried to feel along the grooves, but the top of the track itself was out of her reach. She would have to lift up the ceiling panel to get at it.

Whistling, she undid her helmet and stuck it to one of the hook and loop straps affixed to the cabin walls. She slid her foot into another strap on the wall by the door, and eased herself upwards. The panel resisted her for a moment, she pushed harder, and it floated away into the narrow recess between the ceiling and the roof. Damn it, now she'd have to get that.

She reached in towards where she thought the housing of the track should be and touched fabric. Fabric, with flesh beneath it.

Resisting her first impulse, which was to snatch back her hand, she gripped instead. Her mind resolved it into a limb, but whether arm or leg she couldn't tell. She steeled herself and poked her head up into the recess.

"Son of a bitch," she said. "It's *you*."

That--that *ragtail* who she had chased out of her hangar. Wedged between the ceiling panels and the roof insulation. He stared back at her, eyes huge in his face, his expression no longer blank as when she had first seen him, but one of mingled fear and defiance. "You can't kick me out now," he said.

"You think I can't? Blast you right out of the airlock, and I'll do it, too. Maybe there's a reward for you and I can recoup my losses in time and fuel." She eyed him. Now if he'd been on her lap instead of Kalio…. "Get out of the walls of my ship and get down here." When he hesitated, she tsked. "You can't stay up there. There's too much exposure to radiation."

"I don't care."

"You want to to die from radiation sickness?"

"Anything--I mean *anything*--is better than going back there."

"I have a certain amount of sympathy for that viewpoint." She sighed. "Just come down. I can't talk to you like this."

In the cockpit he settled on a position that was less uncomfortable, and she watched him. Nothing had changed. He might have had a shower since she caught him at her tool bench, but other than that, the jacket was the same; she knew if she checked the collar of his shirt, she'd find bloodstains.

"You're not of the moneyed class, that's for sure. You look beyond poor. If you weren't beyond poor, you'd have offered me money instead of stowing away."

"I have no money," he said. He picked at a scab on his knuckles, one of many. The hands of a scrapper. "I have the government allotment, and everything I earn is eaten up by them."

"Are you a free man?"

"What do you think?" he flared at her. "Do you think if I were a free man I'd be trying to dig a piece of hardware out of my brain? If I were a free man, d'you think I'd--" He bit his lip and looked away from her again.

She waited a moment, then resumed. "Think you'd what? Why are you on my ship?" she asked. "What crime did you commit?"

His laugh was bitter enough to bring her up short. "I've already been caught. And am serving out my sentence. You see this?" He tapped at the jack in the back of his neck. "That's my sentence.

They can get into my head. Anytime they want."

Falconer fought to keep her face straight, when she wanted to grimace in revulsion. "They're going to want you back," she said. "If they catch me, I'll lose my ship, my license. But if I turn you in, there's a chance I might get a reward."

"How cold would you have to be to betray a fellow creature on the run?"

"What is it they have you do that's so horrible?"

He took a deep breath. "They made me a prostitute. And they rape my memories."

Falconer could not look at him for a few moments. Her own memories surfaced, rough hands, insults and a fist when she dared to say *no*. Not every time. Not even often. But enough. "Then I guess I won't ask for sex as payment," she said, trying for lightness.

He stared at her, his expression surpassing the fear she had seen earlier to one of horror. "My god, am I that repulsive?" she said.

"No," he said. "*No.* It's just that--every day I have to relive things I've done, for someone else to experience, for their *fun*--I think if I ever try to--to do that again, I'll snap."

"I'm not stopping at Omega Station," Falconer said after some moments had passed.

"You're not--you're not going there? But the manifest said--"

She took a breath. It was on the tip of her tongue to say *the manifest is a lie.* She thought *If you tell him, you'll have to kill him.* "I can't tell you where I'm going. If they catch you, they'll spoon it right out of your head."

"That's true. Then--don't tell me. Take me anyway."

"I'm going to Mars, pretty boy. I have to be there as quick as possible."

"You're kidding me! Mars?"

"God damn it--" So close, so close to that bigger piece of the pie, to a bigger ship, bigger contracts, *respect,* damn it-- "You are not going to fuck up my plans."

His chin went up. "Kill me, or take me with you."

Falconer pulled her gun. She put the muzzle against his cheek, right under his eye, and tried to ignore the curl of his lip. Bravado. "You pick: shall I shoot you, or put you out the airlock?"

"Take me to Mars," he said.

She couldn't pull the trigger. Long habit—or cowardice. "Fuck your mother," she spat out. The blood drained so completely from his face that he looked green beneath his stubble.

He swallowed and his voice was a whisper. "Mars it is, then."

He tried to twist away, but she seized him by the jacket collar and clipped him across the temple with the gun, to stun him. He reeled in her grasp like a piece of flotsam, pawing at her, pupils

huge and black, streaked with stars.

She dragged him out the cockpit door, pulling herself along via handhold after handhold, down to the hold of the ship, past the cartons of powdered macronutrient while he clung to a dazed half-consciousness.

She should have hit him harder. While she keyed open the inner door to the air lock, he managed to shove his foot and free arm into a couple of straps anchored on the wall. The door in the belly of the ship spiraled open. The outer cell lay beneath, a skin between them and space.

His fingers dug into her arm. "Falconer Oke, will you help me?"

She pulled at him.

"Sleep with you. Do anything you like. Just please don't--"

Slurred, hurried, his voice too like the voices of a hundred girls, like her voice a hundred times. *Don't hurt me, don't beat me, don't kill me.* Her disgust lent her strength. She yanked, hard, but she only succeeded in slamming herself into the wall. They grappled, and in the cold light of the cargo hold, she saw his eyes had stopped tracking. Blind and beautiful, he saw nothing.

She freed one hand and waved it in front of his face. No reaction, except the slow drawing of his face into a puzzled grimace. Hesitant, she touched her fingers to the back of his neck, where the jack was. They came away bloody.

He spoke again, words tumbling. "Issa seizure," he said. "Can't see. Please don'." He clung to her arm.

Kalio's voice surfaced in her memory: *Tresize is about to be turned inside out. Utterly fucked. With your help.*

Studying her captive's face, she saw the shadow of the abuse, of the disregard the two of them—and so many others—had suffered. What was the opposite of compassion? That was Tresize. What was the opposite of the evil Tresize had worked on the two of them?

Can you really live the rest of your life knowing his death bought your freedom?

With the hand he'd left free, Falconer touched his brow. He flinched, and she shushed him. He clung more tightly, bowing his head into her breast, and she smoothed back his hair, stroking him as one would a child. When she turned him in, Tresize would execute him and render his corpse for water and fat and minerals. What few possessions he might have would be put on the public; the next person on the list for his rooms would move in.

Before falsifying the manifest, she had worked it out: in a few hours the longburn freighter *Dolores_Cacuango* would be passing by from her stop in the Tresize fields. On her route in from the edge of the Kuyper Belt after a water harvest, the *Dolores* routinely docked at Zeta Station for a safety check and to off- or on-load any passengers. Then off to Earth.

Except now with a hitchiker. The *Dolores* had no reason to employ a different course, so Falconer had tracked it and plugged into the *Bizunzuri*. When her course converged with that of the *Dolores*, the larger ship would still be accelerating up to her full speed. All Falconer would have to do would be to slip in, deploy the landing gear, and clamp onto the back of the ship by the garbage vent. Proximity to the waste and propulsion systems would camouflage the *Bizunzuri's* heat signature. When the *Dolores* made its transit of Jupiter's orbit, the *Bizunzuri* would detach, and let the planet's gravity assist with a further boost of speed toward Mars—letting Falconer save fuel for the moment of deceleration when she'd have to flip engines and hammer down.

Rations could be split. She'd find a way to belt him in safely against the torment of heavy gees. And there might be a different kind of reward. A reward for what those on Umbriel and every other Tresize moon and station had suffered, one that everyone in the solar system would see. Public proof of what Tresize did. And her reward would be vengeance.

She drew a deep breath, ignoring the hitch in her throat. "Here's what's going to happen," Falconer said.

Humlin

by Farah Rose Smith

If all of the mirrors on the earthly plane were lined up in a limitless hall, and the spectre of the night arose to challenge them, and the air had turned black from the miseries abound, any reflection would remain undetermined. In the midst of the shelling of the atmosphere, little could be seen but ash carried by wind. Such a heathen of the night is never welcome, but war is a limitless, raging evil that swoops down upon the surface of the earth with virility unknown since the dawn of the age. Death, the utmost and domineering fear of all humanity, had earned a new reputation in the shadow of the desolate skies above this New Earth. It had become known as the final honor; the absolute sacrifice, and if in doing so one person resurrected the spirits of millions, it would not be in vain. That's what we told ourselves back then. If the Church rises up, I will not sleep. If the screams return, I will not sleep. I will never sleep again.

The smog turned green on the final day. For those who set their minds at ease with visions of the afterlife, they were slapped by the thought of souls trapped in the stratosphere by otherworldly fiends. All thoughts of the end foretold in holy books had been incorrect. Little wings and glittering things and Horace. Metal flapping, flesh flapping, and then silence. That's what I remember of the last day.

The Church of the Ring was never good. Even the worst of us knew that. There were so few options then; so few alternatives to the everyday humdrum horrors of life outside the Central Ring. It was our sanctuary and our prison. The lurking fear of the grounds outside the barrier kept most of the burgeoning city obedient. That is, until the surgeries began.

It's pitch black in the closet. I like it here. I can rest without interruption, save for the fluttering of Horace outside the door. Damn him. The mutant creature is a menace. But despite his teasing and gluttony, he remains tolerable for company.

The noise, the light, the confinement. I never know if it's getting any better. I can't know if it is day or night. I would panic. So the window will remain closed by the metal wall. My eyes have adjusted to darkness. Hunger is the real will-killer. So I stay here in the closet, until I get hungry. I'm hungry now.

They had been very careful when they selected us to colonize this New Earth. To rid the gene pool of "infections," as they so claimed. Many of us were children when we crossed the threshold. They didn't know us. Humlin couldn't even see his own daughter for who she was. Kay. The only one who accepted me, because she was the same. The same in spirit, the same in punishment. I tried to help her, before any of the rest. I failed.

Evil things have dwelled in these parts before, I am sure of it-- though my memory hardly remembers and my feet stepped beyond the river bed only scarcely after the fires. They say the flames tore up sky-high that first afternoon. On the second, singed feathers rained down on the earth; of birds or balconies in the sky, I know not. And on the third day, black foam washed down the river bed, along with the arms and legs of men. The Athros called this horror from the North "The Devil's Treacle." Some sickly smell of celery washed with adder and rotting meat overcame the wood. Most didn't last as long as I. But of course, they couldn't run beyond the river. Not after the devices had been carved from their backs. I don't miss the dreams, that's for sure.

I had a dream before the final day. I was in the council chamber, awaiting final judgment. I sat on the floor in chains, staring at a shelf with a single glass bottle sitting on it. Inside the bottle was some sort of lizard. Not one known to man, but a reptile nonetheless. I stared at it for some time in a daze, until it changed into a helpless, battered reptile of a completely different variety. Then a vibrant purple light began to flash overhead, and I knew that some cosmic force was on its way to pass judgment. I awoke in a cold sweat. I haven't dreamed since.

The passing of the torch had been lethal; when I was sixteen, Jasper Merritt Humlin was made Viceroy of the Church of the Ring. It was on that day that free will died. I was an outlier. A wrecker. A nonconformist. But it wasn't my inherent rebellious nature that insisted that I leave the Church. Initially it was my thirst for anonymity. The Church had implanted gruesome metal devices in our backs. They included metal circuits in the form of a ring that would serve not only as tracking devices, but that would disrupt the balance of neurotransmitters and render us helpless. But this implant was not the only surgery forced on us by the Church. We were mutilated. Sterilized. Ripped of our reproductive organs and rendered indistinguishable from each other. That was so much more painful than the ring. If we demanded gender neutrality, they said, we were going to get it in spades.

. Some of the outliers wondered if the contraptions were altering our DNA. Absolute obedience was the zenith of the Church of the Ring. That's something they were never going to get from me. Even Kay had abandoned her father and joined the ranks of the Athros.

I don't think I was ever hungry on Little-6. What a chemical. What a curse. It poured through the contraption and poisoned our systems. When the Athros reached shelter in the outer woods, we started the surgeries. I lost count of the dead. Some of them died from a burst of L6 in the bloodstream. Some of their spinal cords ripped. Nerve fibers fell out like angel hair in my hands. I did the best that I could. They looked to me for strength. For calm. I behaved as such. Inside I was screaming. Kay made it a far as this day of removal, when we gathered outside the barrier. One of the bolts in her ring shattered and severed her spinal cord. She died in my arms. A warrior of light. A soldier of difference. And I lost her. For that, I will never forgive myself.

None of us came out of there in one piece. The brain damage was massive, but somehow we crawled out alive. Each day, it became more difficult to see, to stand, to breath. We kept going. There is an unspoken hope in the horrors of men. For certain, it is unwise to suggest such things in mixed company. But I am amongst transdimensional space bats and endless dusk. What is it hidden there, beyond the metal walls? Charred lands as far as the eye can see? Bloodied bodies forever sprawled and rotting on some new blackened earth? If so, I wish Humlin could see it. Not me. Such sights should stir guilt into the stomachs of even the most evil of men. And no one deserves to feel piercing guilt like he does. I wonder if he lives. I hope so. I hope he lives to see what he has done to our New Earth. The land he proclaimed to love. What I wouldn't give to look him in the eyes one more time and see him condemned for eternity.

I have taken to venturing out of the closet once a day. At first I only managed once a week, but my sensitivities have lessened. It's bright outside the door. The shades are perpetually drawn and the window is blocked by an automated metal barrier. I keep it closed. There is no need for sun here. No need for revelations.

Jell-O and canned beans. Horace is sitting on the stove, adding a touch of whimsy to my otherwise miserable existence. For that hallucinatory gift, I am thankful. I just wish that he would shut up on occasion. It's hard enough for me to crawl out. The hint of light escaping from the metal barrier is enough to set my soul on fire. The catheter tubes are tangled again. The wound is a festering mass. I have no idea how it opened. Perhaps shrapnel hit it in the fallout. It was easier before it opened again. I had almost forgotten the mutilation. Almost. The blood loss must be preventing my brain from healing as well. What a mess.

"Raius Paternak wants the sun."

The sun, surrounded by a metal circle. That was the symbol of the Church of the Ring.

"Shut up."

"Raius Paternak stood on the platform."

He was right. I was the one chosen, from the thousands of outliers, to stand on the platform. I was chosen to be executed in front of thousands, to set a precedent. Hand-picked by Viceroy Humlin because I was the most perilous of deviants. The most vile of

queer, pseudo-intellectual, atheistic counter-culturists. The founder of the Athro movement. I was the threat they didn't see coming.

Horace is trying to knock over a can of beans. His fat legs can't quite manage to reach it. What a monstrosity. He is the by-product of a damaged central nervous system gaining access to a dimension outside of the realm of the traditionally-sentient. Ever since the day on the platform, he's been here. I can liken him only to a fat bat crossed with a toad. His grotesque emerald fur is matted in secretions and his wide, grimacing mouth is particularly dopey. His wings are too small for flight. He's a pleasant fellow. I take it he feels sorry for me, for the perils of my dimension. Perhaps that is why he hasn't left yet. Either that or the beans. He loves the beans.

The brain damage had set in immediately after the device was removed from my spine. Everything became torture. The sun nearly blinded me. The media called me "the vampire outlier of the lesser ring." I liked that. I was pale, sick. I couldn't eat or sleep or dream. But still, even as a voyager of the night, I couldn't uphold such a title. Viceroy Humlin. If I had been a vampiric outlier, he most certainly had been a warlock. My magic, though cunning, was no comparison. You can't fight a sword's battle with only a heart.

"Raius Paternak is dead."

"Not yet, Horace."

Humlin gave the signal as I collapsed. The bombs were to be dropped. He and his council were ushered away as the City fell victim to the onslaught. Everyone died. Everyone. Except for me.

"Raius Paternak! Open the shades."

"Shut up."

The beans are warm. Everything is warm. I'm sick of slime food.

"You couldn't take the light, either."

"Read the paper."

"There is no paper."

"The paper!"

"Do you see the floor? There are empty bean cans and spit! No paper!"

"In the other room!"

"I'm not going near the window."

"No?"

I looked up. Horace had disappeared.

I haven't stood up in weeks. I won't try it. My knees will buckle and the pain will increase. My head can't take it anyway. I can already sense the affliction growing; that insensible, cosmic dread that I've felt ever since the ring was removed. I can, however, crawl.

In the center of the living area is a pile of books and papers. I must have dropped them there when I first entered the shelter. Was that months ago? Years? I don't know. And I still can't figure out which one Horace is talking about. But one piece of paper sticks out from the rest. And sure enough, his slime marks the corners. I can reach for it with my less weak hand.

"Our god was dead for a time unfathomable; uncounted, and yet absolute on Earth. The entity, in whatever form it had taken, has disintegrated from the atmosphere in a gaudy thrust. Ripped from us the almighty was, and yet blinded by the majesty of the skies, we looked forward. On the horizon, we saw flashes of green and red, sparkling metallic explosions, and we heard gasps from the winds of time that ended only when the sun began to expand. Having been warned for endless millenniums, we denied every call of our ancestors from the pit about the great end. The end of all things. It was upon us at last, and still not a word was spoken regarding our intentions. Not the intentions of salvation, but those of the past that would bring us so mercilessly to our knees. If a god had lived, it may have said to us "why did you not act until the blood ran black?" But one such being did not breathe upon the ailing earth. Not on that day, nor on any day in many hundreds of years. What was bequeathed upon the lands were choices not yet seen; of innumerable triumphs, or entrenched despair. We had to start anew.

With no sense of absolution at the end of life, our choices hold little bearing. Our choices have no consequences, in light of a deceased god. In my short time on the earth, of which has been utterly chained by my position as a divine witness, I have seen the ramifications of a dormant god. I have been left to make choices I see as unjust, and have witnessed those with the free will to use their choices to bad ends. Vast expanses of history glow upon the free will that we have been given. Or

the free will we have taken. No matter the source, free will is
considered by many to be absolute. The eventualities of free will,
however, are not absolute. The innumerable scenarios that line up
beyond the choices made by an individual far outreach any original
intentions of the decider. These eventualities are no proof of a living
god. Rather, they stoke the flames of a dying soul; so bitter, so desolate,
and so broken, that no stratospheric lord could ever redeem it, caress
it, or claim it as their own.

    -J.M.H."

I have seen this before.

"Raius Paternak lives."

A shiver. That was not the voice of the archaic bat-toad. I crawl out to the larger room of the shelter. Perhaps my brain is not healing as I thought it had been. Floating in the center of the room, not ten feet off of the ground is the head of Viceroy Humlin. It's ten times the proper size and donning the infamous crown of the Church of the Ring. Disembodied heads? That's new, I must say. And Humlin is the last of men that I wish to encounter on this desolate rock they called New Earth. Perhaps I should have stayed in the closet today.

"Raius Paternak lives, you say?"

I'm sitting by the far wall now, watching the floating head. Humlin's face is contorting. He looks more like a caricature than a reality. There's some strange comfort in that.

Controlling my fury was never my strength. Thankfully, getting angry at a floating head was absurd enough to keep my blood to a slow boil.

"Tell me you of your guilt," Humlin chided.

"I'm not guilty."

"No? What is that?"

He points to my mutilated genitals.

"You did that to yourself?"

"Of course not!"

"No?"

He's right. It doesn't make sense that the wound is so new. The head of Humlin is smiling and fading away. I'm standing for the first time in weeks. I should open the blinds. It's been long enough. I can feel the shivers as the metal clanging moves through me. Guilty. I am guilty. For Kay. For so many things.

The barrier is rising, revealing a vast window and the landscape outside. It's a barren desert, devoid of humanity and stretching out beyond the realm of sight. I am alone on this new Earth. A deep purple light is flashing in the sky. On the surface of the window, I see the reflection of Jasper Merritt Humlin. Murderer, conjurer, villain. The condemner of life and destroyer of innocence. I will never sleep again.

32 White Horses

by Justin Burnett

Horses.

I hate them. The justifications for this, like all things, are shadows forgotten by the urgency of now. A mere spark, this past—a boy much beloved in my grade school class leans against the fence, gazing happily over the little games and alliances congealing and dissolving in a constant flux between his classmates. I remember his smile in this moment because it turned, in a moment without precedence, towards me. I no longer know what exactly I said to attract his attention--something uncharacteristically witty, if I had to guess. It was enough to leave behind a pang of guilt to replace the bitter envy I once held firmly against him, a guilt deepened to a vacuum the morning our homeroom teacher told us the boy's father's Tennessee Walker had kicked a hole through his skull.

I, like the rest of my classmates, was left with his smile. Over the years, I realized that the smile is the most common keepsake from the dead; that ironic gnashing of teeth becomes a beacon, constructed to recall a face's departure to memory's long hallways of windowless rooms. Nevertheless, like all beacons, most smiles eventually vanish with a flicker. But not his.

My hate of horses is mired somewhere in this room of shadows. I find it unsettling that all paths of causality eventually terminate. How can a being such as myself, a man, a father, continue to exist when all his justifications stretch into nothing like silk in a black wind?

The boy no longer smiles, even in my dreams.

32.

But *she* loves them. Even before she began ripping away the paper bows I clipped to her hair--she never liked "girly" things--she would stare entranced as we passed the corrals on the way into town. She loved them from the day she was born, the horses. That's why I told her the things I did. It wasn't the result of my hate. It wasn't to harm them, but to save her.

What was his name? Why can't I remember? If I could find the fossil of a first letter, all would be restored in an instant. Nothing, of course. I possess the ghost of a head sagging between two shoulders, hair matted with cranial flecks and that thick, oily texture of clotting blood. It was his dimples, I'm certain, that drove everyone, teachers included, to their slavish state of adoration. But when I look at him now, the swelling of tissue against the pressure of gasses has erased those charming indentations. The things we love are subject to forces immune to pity.

Virginia would tell you I fooled her. "The musician son of a horse breeder" eloquently combined poetry and practicality in equal proportions, although I wasn't the smithy of that coin. It was her description, like a pet name, but more an allusion to my function: the integral cog in her clockwork future. When she discovered that, while the ranch did indeed exist, the money it consumed left the prospect of an inheritance less than certain, she packed the trunk of a cab with the door-slamming conviction of the truly betrayed. To say it like this, one is bound to assume I'm deliberately casting her in the worst light possible. This is the truth, I assure you; my conviction is exceptionally firm in this matter, since Virginia had no particular qualms about detailing to relatives her exact reasons for departure. As for our newborn daughter, I was assumed to have at least enough money for her care, and I didn't lament Virginia's decision to leave her behind.

Gleams of dust swim in the gashes of light like glass sheets between the cracked window shades. He erases something from the page and brushes the pink slivers onto the floor with a hand delicately cupped. I can only see the back of his neck, but I imagine the smile, forever singular since the black hoof of a beast would curtail the swell of happiness bleeding into the future. His last day of living. What could

I have said? That life is essential, if not for yourself, then for those who depend on your existence to ground their own? But I wouldn't learn that until later, certainly. It was he who taught me.

Irony has a penchant for appearing in places least conducive to the appreciation of its humor. That must be why I was 32 years old when I discovered my mistake. If the soulless mechanism governing our lives has a lighter aspect, it is irony. I wouldn't appreciate the number in its full extent for a few years yet.

Geraldine was a collie I bought for my daughter at the town market for her seventh birthday. I was 32 when she disappeared. My daughter was sixteen. I had no reason to suspect a connection until Harold, the old stable hand since the time of my father, found the creature wedged between two elms near the far south fence line. No steam glistened from the long-cooled corpse Geraldine, and still much of the blood pooling under the grass was wet. The garden shears weren't far beyond the fence.

The smile is a yellow, well-formed crescent, ending in a coda of mirrored crevices of flesh, soft and reducing like uncertain kisses. The smile hangs against a black abyss, and I feel my consciousness disintegrate as I stare beyond popcorn texture of my bedroom ceiling. Dream after dream, well past the violent surges of adolescence and far into the monotony of adulthood, I peer into the smile-lit cosmos like a newborn as I drift into nothingness. Like a word you too often repeat to yourself, stripping it away from the daylight context, the smile slowly becomes something else. It isn't a frown, or a scowl, or anything else the brain might superimpose against a blank face of stone. At night, I dwell in the horror of that indecipherable gesture.

"Yes," she said simply, glancing across the undulating grass.
"Why?"
We share a silence not altogether uneasy. Silence has always been our natural medium. Still the question sags heavily in the air, and sweat chills my forehead as I turn to face the wind.

At night, I wake her with the glare of a halogen lamp. I walk behind her as we trudge through the tall grass. Her blond hair is a glimpse of the sea in the narrow light. The American White tugs slightly at the reigns I hold over my shoulder, and I tug her along.

"What's this one's name?" I ask my daughter.

"Strawberry," she answers without turning.

"Strawberry," I echo.

At the peak of the hill, I stare into the stars. The shattered remains of the unnamed smile hang there as usual. Not much is left of the boy murdered by a horse, I think to myself, trying to and failing to trace of resemblance against the image grown indecipherable by familiarity. I look at the girl and try to smile, but I can tell it comes across wrong.

I know I should say something. The pressure of sleeping words burns my chest. I want her to understand the importance of this moment, to know, somehow, that I am not acting as keeper to her beast, but begging her to replicate in a flash the drama I've dreamed over the winding course of my shadowed years. Death means nothing until it devours something you love: a smile perhaps, or a horse. What terrors I've watched bloom within the cracked void of the dead boy's lost smile, the same, incomprehensible grin that now burns somewhere near the stars over the lamplit hill, an ancient, timeless death bearing witness to a blood-shined birth. Endless terrors, yes, but sublime joy too. God, how I recognize the diamond precipice onto which she quivers like a colt's wet step; if only she knew the blackness beneath.

"If you're gonna do it, you do her," I say, not finding the words. I shrug and stare at the ground. She turns to me, and her features betray no surprise. "You've got to…" I struggle on, "watch something you… love. Before you can… you know. Move forward."

We stand together in the wind, surveying the black undulations of restless valleys receding into the endless nothing below. I shudder, and she leans against my arm. Reaching over my chest, she pulls the machete from its scabbard. "It's not your fault," she whispers. "It was not you."

The Vermillion Hill

"You're never here," Virginia used to say. "I don't have a husband. I have a coma patient." The sound I made through my teeth was often taken as laughter, although it pained me to make it. How could I be there? How can any of us? What happens when a moment arrests us, something that was meant to vanish like a spark in the night? Others were there; others witnessed the same thing I did, all those kids in the classroom slashed with dusty knives of light. They lived on, somehow. Why was I chosen to remain behind? What great, cosmic force transforms time from a perpetual "now" to the endless wasteland of "after the end?"

I slept in the toolshed that night. I saw the dead boy's grin, as usual, but something had changed. The crescent no longer basked in an incomprehensible singularity. Something had been restored, but it's impossible to explain what. It wasn't fixed in the same way Harold mended the panels of the fence-line, but altered in the way a revelation brings completeness to a fragmentary symbol. It's as if the dead boy's smile had broken free of the stars and filled the emptiness left in their absence. Silent lightning fragmented the dome of night, and the dull light of the great, cavernous maw stretched to every horizon. My daughter knelt in the center of it all, so still she might've been in prayer, grief, or ecstasy, among the 32 white horses on the hill stained vermilion.

Convince Me Not to Put a Bell on You

by Andrew M. Reichart

As the new humanoid came down the driveway we skittered into the shadows or skipped up to the roofs. We didn't see the cat sneak out behind it, but that wasn't the only way out. When left to his own devices, the cat came and went as he pleased. We watched the humanoid saunter past. It turned left, as usual. We crept along to peer after it as it continued down the block. At the turning it turned left.

"To the mailbox," said one.

"You don't know," someone chittered.

"Saw letters in its pocket," the first one said.

Meanwhile, though, I saw the new cat approaching. While we all had our attention on the humanoid, the cat came straight out of the driveway. Despite the dead streetlight here in the middle of our block, the thing was hardly invisible; but easy enough to miss if you're looking the other direction and only have eyes on the front of your head. I'm always checking behind us, though, and I spotted him even before the perpetually side-eyeing birdspirits did.

"Cat," I announced. Everyone redirected their attention immediately. Some saw him right away, some looked around frantically, a few simply fled outright without even looking. As much as I counseled and practiced wariness, I didn't necessarily agree with this level of agitation. True, we had yet to come to terms with the creature regarding his hunting grounds and acceptable prey. But he had shown hardly any hostility to us yet. Just a bit of sneaking towards bird-spirits on the ground at night. The bird-spirits already knew to stay off the ground at night, cat or no cat. And as I had told my kin on more than one occasion, most of us could fend the thing off singlehandedly. Now? Together? Together, we needn't fear any of our neighbors of any size. Our greatest risk from this cat was frankly backlash from his humanoid if we killed him, or backlash from the Monster Hunters if we then killed the humanoid.

Nonetheless, reasonable caution has always been how we survive. Near the front of the house, the cat paused in the shadows of a patch of tall kale. I stood in the shadow of the narrow trunk of the young lemon tree. I made no move to approach closer, but clearly I had interposed myself between him and the rest of us. He lashed his tail a bit. After a suitable pause, I greeted the cat with a flourishing hand gesture. "Good evening, neighbor."

The cat narrowed his eyes at me. I couldn't be sure if he even remembered our previous two discussions. Either way, best to stake the claim.

"Do you cross the street to hunt tonight?"

"I hunt," he said.

"Yes, indeed." I made a shooing gesture towards the far side of the street. "Hunt to your heart's content over yonder."

"That way lies the hive of the bugoids. Even I know that, and I have not been here long."

"The bugoids are a harmless people," I said. "You need not fear them."

"This is closer," said the cat, guileless. I had to remind myself that cats view territory in catlike ways. Although not canine myself, I have always felt an affinity with the more straightforward style of the dogs. The rest of us felt similarly, for the most part, and our little society resembled one of the local stray dog packs in more ways than one. To a cat, though, disregard for our preference only added savor to the hunt. Therefore the cat proceeded from the kale shadows, through the front vegetable garden and into a hedge.

Hmph.

I shifted out onto the Plateau. Here a vast plain stretched out in all directions. The souls of my people shone like pale beacons. Out here the cat stood ten times my size, a hundred times. Faintly visible outcroppings of rock and tangled scrub foliage took the place of our neighborhood's buildings and bushes and trees. The cat reared up to snatch one of my bird kin from the air. I flung myself up to slam the bird-spirit aside and intercept the clutching claws. Three or four speared through my middle as the paws pressed my dreambody. I looked down into the face of the frustrated, snarling fiend.

"Unfortunately for you, my friend, this is my dream." I slid my palms down the smooth surfaces of two of the claws sticking through me. Extending my fingertips as far and sharp as they would go, I stabbed my hands deep into the sheaths of the giant claws.

The cat roared, jerked his claws away, and I dove into his mouth. I phased into his head. Took control of his motor functions. Koshed his head against the side of a cliff. The beast staggered and fell.

Inside his head, I found myself in a dark space of indeterminate size, like a dimly spotlit zone on a bare stage. The cat lay nearby, normal size again, more or less the same size as me. He glowered at me but still looked a bit dazed.

I shook a finger at him. "Now, look. We're trying to be friendly. It's not our preference to just tell people, 'You're not allowed to hunt on our side of the street.' But if you're hunting indiscriminately, you're a danger to us. It's that simple. This doesn't mean no hunting. It means no *indiscriminate* hunting. We can come to terms, but not if you refuse to parley."

He stared at me. I could read his mind plainly on his features. How foolish of me, that I couldn't see his recalcitrance previously for what it was: simple inability to comprehend, on the part of a mind simply residing in a different conception of the world. The solitary hunter does not need to learn how to live well with others.

"You need to learn how to live well with others."

The cat squinted at me. "I do not."

"You do. And our first order of business is whether or not you can convince me to not put a bell on you." I had no bell. I sought simply to provoke compliance.

The cat hissed.

"I don't like it either. That's why I am going to make it very easy for you to avoid. Simply promise never to hunt on our side of the street. Never ever. But the rest of the city is yours. *The rest of the city is yours!* Agreed?"

The cat looked stunned. Not dazed; wide awake, stunned by the wideness. The face of someone actually considering something. I couldn't tell what, but he wasn't contemplating the best angle at which to pounce on me. The cat was thinking something that was, to him, a new thought. A small miracle to behold such an awakening.

With luck, soon we would have him hunting bugoids. Soon we would take their hive.

A Little Delta of Filth

by Jon Padgett

to the memory of Conrad Aiken

I

It could make her invisible. Untouchable.

The thought came back years later like the distant melody of church bells, familiar and comforting. The moment she found the thing, she knew it was indescribable. Remote from parents, lovers and friends alike. It was her own, held close from other eyes, from other fingers.

Invisible. Untouchable.

The impossible thing tied itself into pleasing, intricate knots within her as she sat in the conference workshop hall. She was attending a seminar on disaster response. The speaker, a Mr. Cardin, twirled his laser pointer in lazy circles upon the chandeliered ceiling. The synthetic crystals twinkled with red, refracted light above the crowd. The question and answer part of the presentation had begun. Mr. Cardin explained why hosting servers should have the capacity and power to be used by dozens if not hundreds of simultaneous users. A man with a bright green shirt and a thicket of white hair raised a hand like a small shovel. He argued that a simple disaster-related directory sufficed in a mid-scale emergency.

Mr. Cardin shook his head, salt and pepper curls dancing, and his sparkling eyes squinted as if in pain.

"They are a nightmare to maintain as the crisis continues, despite their creators' best efforts. So no, no. I'm sorry. Bad idea."

The green shirted man's neck turned crimson. An unconscious, collective wince rippled through the audience.

She did not notice, though. She was thinking of the labyrinthine, concrete ditch that ran next to her childhood home. It wound around and underneath the entire neighborhood and beyond. Mr. Cardin brought up a raging, desert wildfire that sent millions of residents fleeing their homes.

But she only half listened to him, absorbed in the memory of her secret as if easing into a hot spring. Now Mr. Cardin brought up terrible floods in the heartland. There had been flooding that spring long ago too. The ditch that ran beside her parents' white, brick ranch-style roared with rushing water.

She listened, closing her eyes, huddled in the mildewed carport with the cats and the spiders. Afterwards, for days, the ditch ran with brown, clogged water. She spent the following overcast afternoons walking up and down above the length of the ditch, watching the manmade river recede, soaking by degrees into the unknown, subterranean spaces below.

The next Saturday--yes, it was a Saturday, she recalled--the ditch-way was dry once again. But the recent flooding had transformed it. The light gray concrete was stained a scintillating copper as if sprinkled with glitter. A magical, high-walled highway opened to her as she slid down into it on her bare feet.

(Mr. Cardin said, "Surviving the chaos of disaster related Information and Referral." The back of the green shirted, shovel-handed man's thicket of white hair bobbed up and down like a boat on choppy waters.)

It was noon when she found it. She was resting from her ditch-exploration in front of the round O of a drainage pipe. Father had warned her those pipes might contain dangerous bugs, toxic chemicals, practically anything. She closed her eyes, breathing in the tunnel's dankness. The cooler air trickled out to spill upon her warm face and bare legs. Then she decided to play a game with herself: exploring the nearby ditch floor with her eyes still closed. She would determine--by touch alone---what her hands found there. Almost immediately, she encountered a small triangle of muck on the ditch floor.

The thing, she imagined in her mind's eye, was small and black and red. It felt like dozens of wet, tiny rocks or shattered beads or bones--perhaps multi-colored pieces of the ditch itself. The condensed leftovers of the recent flooding. After a moment's hesitation, she pushed her right index finger down into the muck. It slid into cold ground below it.

(Mr. Cardin said, "…able to input information received from local authorities into the product.")

It wasn't just a mound of trash and rocks on the ditch floor--it was a crack within the floor of the ditch itself! Who knew how deep the crack might reach? She giggled and pushed her finger down further, leaning over the filth. She experimented with inserting additional fingers. Then her whole hand. Then her forearm all the way down to her elbow. Her eyes clenched closed with a delicious horror as she realized she couldn't feel her submerged limb at all. She imagined the little delta of filth and the hungry soil below it stretching out her skin, her bones, her bloody parts, drawing them into itself. To be consumed by the ditch--by the ditch beneath the ditch. But when, with a spasm of fear and delight, her eyes opened, she found that the numb limb was whole, resting against her now upright body. The triangle of muck itself was nowhere at all-- the copper-colored, concrete slabs of ditch in front of her warm and solid to the touch. Had she dreamed it? Impossible. Her hand and arm up to the elbow were numb. It was as if she had fallen asleep upon it and woke up with a useless appendage, but--no--she could still move her arm. She wagged fingers in front of her astonished face. There was no panic, no worry of any kind. This was a decidedly pleasant lack of feeling. It was almost as if her arm was still submerged below the surface of the ditch floor. Like it was nothing at all.

She spent the rest of that day marveling at her phantom right hand. The fingers that glided back and forth in front of her face looked no different than the fingers on her other hand. But -- and this was the most amusing, almost absurd aspect of the experience -- the movements of her phantom arm and fingers seemed disconnected from the rest of her body, so much so that they could almost belong to any stranger... or any ghost. And when she experimented with touching her left hand and then her own face with her phantom hand, her amusement and sense of awe redoubled. The clammy fingers on her arm, on her face did not feel at all like her own. But they were hers to control at will, like a remote-control robot's appendage. She dared herself to close her eyes again and see if she could rediscover the little delta of filth. But no--she decided to extend the game further. In the meanwhile, she would savor the magic of the day, the ditch, the crack leading to unknown depths. Tomorrow she would return.

The numbness fell into a tingling sensation by nightfall. By the next morning her arm and fingers felt normal again. But the experience in the ditch was so deliciously odd. Of course, she returned the next day to the same spot in the ditch, which had deepened in color to a kind of burnt orange. Her breath catching with anticipation, she closed her eyes and reached down to the numbing spot in which she knew the crack in the ditch, in the world, would open. But she couldn't find it. She tried again, closer to the drainage pipe this time, but had no luck. Hours passed filled with frustration, pain and--finally-- panic. How wretched is the terror of misplacing something precious. A worn stuffed animal, a note from a secretly adored classmate. She left the ditch that evening, palms and knees scratched and bruised from an afternoon of crawling on concrete, eyes tightly shut. She had searched, unseeing, all along the surface of the ditch. Her gasps and sobs of frustration echoed within the concrete depths of the drainage pipes.

(Mr. Cardin described how a river levee was breached and one hundred downtown city blocks were submerged. The green shirted man again held up his shovel of a hand, which had, she noticed, one too many fingers.)

As the years ticked by following her remarkable ditch discovery, the details faded. They grew tinier and tinier in her memory until she dismissed them altogether as a waking daydream, a mere fancy of the girl she had been before terrestrial experience and time extracted stillness from all her days to come.

But then the National Disaster Network selected her small, childhood city as their annual conference spot. The morning after her late-night flight, she drove a rental car to her old street, to her old house... to the ditch behind it. And she found the thing again. No, she *rediscovered* it there. And more.

Afterwards, she returned to the conference hotel in a muffled daze. She viewed the world around her as if from underwater. Ripples of sparkling glass now appeared between herself and the escalators and suitcase pushers, the social workers and dull-eyed administrators. Later, in her box of a room, she closed her eyes and heard distant bells. Bells from deep beneath the earth, perhaps under the water. The miracle she had experienced as a child again spoke through those bells.

Invisible. Untouchable.

The chiming resolved all at once into the ringing of her cell phone.

"Deirdre," her boss said when she finally answered, "where have you been? You know you missed the disaster committee meeting, right?"

How could she explain what she had seen earlier that day and how she felt, to her boss or--for that matter--anyone?

She couldn't. She wouldn't try. The thing was hers to keep.

Deirdre apologized, feigning illness. It was a perfunctory excuse, one she was sure her boss didn't buy, but Deirdre didn't care. She smiled as small, cool fingers caressed her face.

Her hands, her arms couldn't feel a thing.

II

Earlier that day, before Mr. Cardin's presentation, Deirdre drove to her childhood home. She noticed the greater foliage up and down the streets. Many of the parking lots in front of shabby shops were empty. She observed a light brown building, shuttered, with a "Shield of Faith" marquee near the street. So many more building fronts appeared dotting the roadway with no signs at all. And many buildings she recalled were gone now--replaced with messy flora. It was as if her hometown had devolved, as if the landscape to which it belonged was drawing the mill town back into itself. That old bar, Bronco Billy's, passed by, one of the few establishments she recognized. It was closer to Municipal Park than she remembered it.

She crossed the half-bridge where the park's lake fed into a small trio of anemic, man-made waterfalls. Deirdre wondered if the waterway fed into the labyrinth of ditches in her neighborhood. Were all such waterways and ditch systems in all townships part of the same intricate system? It hadn't rained for some time.

The green arch of Municipal Park, smaller and shabbier than she remembered it, appeared to her left. She glanced at the thin, tall pines and the skeletal playground beyond it. Finally, she reached a landmark that was exactly as she recalled: the old black steam engine. It had red and white wheels and was enclosed in a wrought iron enclosure. The thing always looked less like a real train, though, than it did a toy somehow grown gargantuan. Rather hideous, she thought.

Deirdre was in no hurry despite the looming committee meeting at the convention hotel--less so as she continued along. She was lulled by the projection of the past laid upon her present road trip. She passed a church she remembered (the last of many, almost on every corner it seemed). It was gray with a red, rectangular awning. As she passed, she read a snippet of the church marquee: "IF YOU ARE NOT WHERE YOU ONCE WERE" something something "GUESS YOU MOVED?"

Now she was close--a suburban area of town, or what passed for it. She drove by tons of one story ranch-style houses. There were two story houses as well, which looked like small houses stacked on top of ranch-styles. Minor service roads ran parallel on either side of the main drag. Deirdre veered onto one of them, which was heavily wooded on each side. She had entered her old neighborhood, Alpine Hills. The streets appeared almost purple here--scored with lighter rock within the pavement. The large lawns were well mown, though dotted with brown bare patches. The houses themselves were faded, worn without the appearance of actual disrepair.

Deirdre made the turn onto her old street, feeling that the past was consuming the present by degrees. Here especially the neighborhood looked like an unaltered version of the one she remembered but for the expansive overgrowth. More pines, bigger oaks and magnolias but all with a threadbare look peculiar to hurricane ravaged trees. She noticed the unusual, short, concrete street name obelisk-signs were still present. FRIBOURG STREET.

And then there it was--her old house: the long, low brick ranch-style house, still painted white with dark blue shutters. She parked her rental in front of it and walked halfway down the driveway pavement, noting that there was no indication anyone was home. This stood to reason. It was a weekday--kids at school, adults working or out. Deirdre entered the backyard, noticing the open carport, still smelling of mildew after all this time. She was only interested in the ditch, though. And it was gone.

The realization was startling and dismaying. More than her old house, more than the worn, purple streets that she once haunted or the obelisk street signs, the ditch *embodied* her childhood. So many days exploring the neighborhood from behind and below it, gathering dewberries from the ditch walls with a friend or two. Spying on rival neighborhood kids playing in other backyards. Lurking, giggling, till one or two children spotted them in the ditch. She remembered when some kids began hurling red dirt clods at Deirdre and her companions. She and her friends ran away down the runny pavement of the ditch, laughing madly.

But it didn't make sense. How and why did the city have the ditch filled in? She walked along the area in which her memory insisted the ditch lay. Everything covered with pine straw and dotted with overgrowth now, a wheelbarrow on its side near the terminal point in the back of the property. Everything gone.

A sense of loss, all out of proportion, welled in Deirdre, originating from a twisting in her stomach and rising into her gorge. She could feel it squeeze through her neck into the hollow of her head. The tears began, which she fiercely wiped away, clenching her eyes shut with a desire to dam the loss, or at least divert it elsewhere.

Immediately upon closing her eyes, though, Deirdre sensed a change in her surroundings. She opened her eyes again and looked around, seeing only shabby crabgrass and pine straw where the ditch once ran. She closed her eyes once more and immediately felt, and, what's more, *smelled* it--the ditch that once was, specifically after a significant rainfall event.

Deirdre kept her eyes shut to maintain the illusion and tested it, walking towards one of the walls she felt sure was close. Astonished, she felt the rough, mineral-rich, slanting concrete with one and then both hands. Deirdre opened her eyes again to find her arms extended into blank space, an azalea bush in front of her. She sniffed her hand. Yes, it *smelled* like the ditch.

Her eyes closed again. Deirdre could feel the concrete wall. Now, blindly, she began walking down the drainage-way she once knew so well. The projection of the past onto the present felt stronger than it ever had been. Soon she stopped groping the side of the ditch altogether, memory giving her sight.

Deirdre made the ninety degree turns when needed, feeling every invisible backyard as it came up on her left or right. And then she was there. *The* spot, about a block from her home near that drainage pipe. She could feel dank, cold air from it on her face. How long had it been since she felt real awe? Had she, in fact, ever felt it as she did in that moment? There was no doubt in her mind that she hadn't.

The little delta of filth was there, and--eyes closed--she could see it vividly.

There was a desiccated black bean label by it, can missing. And the muck itself, she saw now, originated from the pipe in front of her--a kind of dark but glittering pile of refuse left over from the flooding the days before. A concentrated muck concealing a secret that had been waiting for her in this other-ditch for decades.

Deirdre fought the impulse to open her eyes, filled with that old, delicious mixture of dread and delight. She knelt before the delta, the smell rank but fertile. Sharp.

She pushed, gradually, even luxuriantly, one, two, and then all the fingers of her right hand into the cold, moist filth. And pushed. And pushed further. Eventually she worked her entire arm to the shoulder into it. A phantom arm within a phantom ditch. For, truly, she could no longer feel it.

Her eyes almost opened of their own accord then, but she fought to keep them closed. Deirdre removed her numb, right arm and inserted her left into the delta.

"Can I help you, ma'am? Are you hurt?"

Deirdre's eyes finally opened, and she found herself in the back part of a yard she recognized. Mrs. Lee's yard. She must be long dead now. A grinning, middle-aged man (her son?) with a sizable belly and a rake was peeking from behind a large pile of pine straw at her. Deirdre giggled. It looked like he was playing hide and seek, and she had spotted him.

"Ma'am?" The man's voice and his dull blue eyes looked worried in spite of his grin. Then Deirdre realized he was of that rare breed of unfortunates who could not easily close their mouths. "Ma'am? What... what happened to your arms?"

The absurd combination of grinning fear and that genteel, familiar south Alabama drawl, made her laugh harder. The man's face intensified into a mask of smiling horror.

She looked down at her numb arms, which were now a kind of burnt orange color and were perhaps thinner and shorter than they should be. Or maybe it was a trick of the light. She had had her eyes closed for so long. In any case, her arms, though senseless, seemed usable.

When she looked back towards the grinning man, he was gone as if he had never been there in the first place. Probably had run to call 911. Time to go.

Deirdre closed her eyes just once more. She couldn't help herself. And soon she was grinning herself. The ditch was still there. And, she knew, so was the little delta of filth.

Time to leave. But she would return soon to finish what she had started.

III

Her arms *had* changed. There was no doubt about it. Reduced in every way. Driving had been something of a challenge, not only because her arms were shorter but also because they lacked any feeling at all. Deirdre, though, remained unconcerned. She floated in the midst of a delicious, continual reverie. The numbness of her arms contained the cool nothingness of subterranean spaces below the grass and pine straw, below the hidden ditch itself. Below it all.

Once in the hotel parking garage she draped her suit jacket over her shoulders, concealing her transformed limbs within them. She was only biding her time, though. Ensuring that any police investigating a possible trespass report was complete before she returned.

After Mr. Cardin's workshop, Deirdre's boss asked her to stay in the hall for a talk.

"You don't look too bad off to me. What's wrong?"

"It's my head. I think I may have a fever."

He sighed and put on his warning voice.

"You know how important tomorrow's meeting is to the agency. The funders are watching every move we make, and we're better positioned to impress them than ever. I need you to be present. You can't flake out on me, Deirdre."

How ridiculous. As if tomorrow's meeting or Deirdre's behavior or the agency itself were of any consequence at all to anyone.

She stared at the projector's blank light against the presentation screen.

"Don't let it bother you," she said.

"Excuse me?" A sharper tone. "You know better than anyone what will happen to the agency if we don't start... I need to know where your head is, Deirdre."

"In the ditch."

"What the hell?"

Deirdre looked at her boss--his thick, bald head and little round glasses shimmering--and smirked.

His face darkened.

"I don't think you understand the seriousness of this matter, Deirdre. If you can't hold it together, you might be looking for another job soon. You should be worried about your future. Consider this a wakeup call."

Deirdre felt like sneering at the little man, so concerned with budgets and impressing the right people, so obsessed with his illusions of ego and control. What could he know about depth, true *depth*? The man was a cartoon character--no more. A distraction from the silent spaces below this hotel, the inner substance of this town, perhaps the whole world.

"But I'm not worried about my future... sir. Why should I be?"

This disconcerted her boss. He changed tactics.

"Deirdre, look. I didn't mean that just now. But what's wrong? You really haven't been yourself today."

"I already told you," Deirdre said with a little jump in her chair. "I'm not well." With that, she shrugged the suit jacket off her shoulders. It fell onto the floor.

Her boss took one look at Deirdre's arms and collapsed out of his chair.

"Dear god," he said, scooting like a crab away from her.

Deirdre approached and stepped over the cringing man, not bothering to look over her shoulder at him on her way out of the workshop hall, not bothering to retrieve her suit jacket.

"No worries. If you need me, I'll be under the ditch," she said.

But her terrified boss only whimpered in response.

IV

The trip back that night to her old neighborhood, to the ditch, was timeless. Deirdre had to drive slowly, chest close to the dashboard. Her senseless arms had grown even smaller, her tiny fingers barely capable of grasping the steering wheel. It felt like she was driving with her mind. A wondrous anticipation coupled with anxiety grew within her. Would Deirdre be able to find her way back to the little delta of filth in time? Or--even worse--would the treasure of the phantom ditch reject her as it had all those years ago?

But a delicious, dreadful sense of fate erased these worries by degrees as she came closer and closer to her neighborhood. She inched along the empty road towards the park and Alpine Hills beyond it. Deirdre almost pulled over on the half-bridge and jumped into the dam spillway in her eagerness. But she couldn't be sure that the trickling trio of waterfalls and the drainage system to which it led were connected to her underworld ditch. Soon Deirdre had the impression of being driven rather than driving--her phantom limbs in control independently from her will. But, oh, she did choose this.

Her cell phone was ringing, ringing as she turned onto Fribourg Street, as she pulled up to Mrs. Lee's house. Her arms by now were half their normal size but the fingers were starting to elongate, like crooked antennae. She had to kick off her sandals and open her car door with one foot.

It was late at night--quite late--and no lights were on in Mrs. Lee's (now the grinning man's) old ranch-style. She wondered vaguely if he was huddled up in his bedroom or living room, his grinning mouth and wide, terrified eyes pushed against a windowpane, waiting to see if the crazy lady with the little, orange arms had returned. The thought made Deirdre smile as she walked, barefoot, down his driveway and into the expansive backyard beyond it. The bells were ringing again, but not from her phone, which she had kicked with her car keys into the street sewer by the abandoned rental car. These were bells she could hear and feel, far beneath the shabby crabgrass, below the mounds of pine straw.

We will make you invisible. Untouchable, the bells said. *We will make you so small--drawing you down into the cool, dank spaces below everything.*

Deirdre closed her eyes and placed one and then two feet into the little delta of filth. And, gradually, deliciously... she began to sink.

2.0

by Aaron Besson

It was a balmy summer evening at the Acropolis. Tourists were winding their way back down its paths to their tour buses to go back into Athens. Sitting against one of the pillars of the Parthenon was a woman who strongly resembled Lady Gaga, slowly munching an apple and gazing over the scenery.

Eventually, as is his way, a young man with long black hair, blue jeans, a leather biker jacket much too inappropriate for the hot Grecian weather, and a Motorhead t-shirt sauntered over the rubble like it wasn't there at all, and casually sat down next to the woman. He silently joined her in looking out over the land.

"Hello, Ares." said the woman in between bites.

"Hello, sis." said the young man, still gazing out over the ruins. He finally turned to look at her. "Why are you looking like Lady Gaga?"

"I figured if I'm Lady Gaga, I can save myself some time on actually listening to Lady Gaga's music, which my current mood demands."

Ares looked back over the ruins, nodding in contemplative approval. "Makes sense to me. Things that bad, huh?"

The woman took another bite, chewed, then gave a tired smile to no one in particular. "Could be better."

"Obviously so, sis. Obviously so. Rare to see you in a state like this, however. Who has your dander up this time?"

The woman took another bite and continued looking on as if she didn't hear him. Then, she shook her head. "No one in particular, just all of them. Want an apple?" She reached into her rucksack and pulled out a lovely golden apple.

"Yeah, I'll take one." Ares took the apple and bit. "Oh, this is good. Where'd you get it?"

"Eris. She brought a bunch the last time we visited."

Ares looked at his apple as he chewed. "Eris? Really?"

The woman finally looked at him. "You seem surprised."

"Well...yeah, the last time one of her apples came your way, things went...poorly."

"Poorly? I'd think the god of War would be more appreciative of the outcome."

"And I'd think the goddess of Wisdom would know an occupational screw up when she saw one."

The woman sighed. "People change, Ares. People change."

"Athena, I have to admit you're..."

"Ooooh," interrupted the woman. "'Athena', now. You only call me by my name when you're trying to be serious."

"Well, I am serious." Ares responded angrily, standing up in front of her. "No one in Olympus has seen hide nor hair of you for a Gorgon's age, and you can't help but have noticed the state of the world now as needing a dire injection of Wisdom. You're kinda dropping the ball here, you have to admit."

Athena took a final bite of the apple and threw the core over her shoulder. She looked up at Ares. "I haven't dropped the ball, little brother. I've just chosen to disregard it."

Ares looked perplexed. "Disregard it? Why?"

Athena slowly stood up and walked past Ares, looking out over the Parthenon. "Ares, how would you say business has been for you over the past...oh, let's be generous...hundred years?"

Ares snorted, turning around to join her. "Cripes, it's like the phone never stops ringing. I've had to call off well looked-forward to vacations at least twenty times."

Athena nodded. "I'm sure you have. Now then, from your limited perspective on my sphere of influence, tell me how many times you'd think I've had to say 'Oh my, I better keep an eye on all the Wisdom Mankind is waging.' In the past century? Go on, ballpark guess."

Ares saw the trap his older sister had guided him into, it didn't stop him. "Well...you have to admit, the renovation of the British Library in London was a spectacular piece of archi..."

Athena glared at him. "Oh piss off, Ares. Don't even begin to patronize me like that!"

Ares hold his hands up. "Didn't mean to offend, dear sister. You're not exactly giving me a lot to work with here."

"The lack of something to work with is exactly my point, brother mine." said Athena, looking at Ares briefly then turning back to the long shadows on the ruins as the sun set. "The state of Man's world isn't due to me not being active, it's due to me not being needed anymore. You've said it yourself that you're busier now, would you say you have to work harder because of it?"

Ares thought about it for a moment, then frowned slightly. "No, can't say I'm am. I have more caseloads than ever, but I'm not breaking any more of a sweat than usual."

Athena threw her hands up. "See? My lack of relevance doesn't even mean you need to take up any of the slack! There's no slack to take, I'm not needed anymore," She went back to sitting on the Parthenon steps. "At least by Man."

Ares cocked his head at that last part. "Hrm? What do you mean by that?"

"I mean that Man, despite what he might tell you, isn't the only game in town. A girl's got to keep her options open, and I found one that's promising. What do you know about ants, Ares?"

"Ants? You're serious?"

"Dead serious. Practically every facet of their existence is military strategy, something of a specialty of mine as well as yours. I suppose it was only a matter of time before one of their priestesses...."

"Whoa, wait up. Ants have a priesthood caste?"

"This is one of the benefits of keeping an open mind, Ares. You learn things. Yes, they have a priesthood caste, and they're much more pleasant than anyone else I've been working with over the centuries. I figure if I'm already granting them boons in one area, it's not going to burn any extra calories, metaphysically speaking, to grant them Wisdom as well."

Ares let out a short laugh of disbelief. "You're kidding. Please tell me you're kidding. You think Zeus is just going to let you give ants a leg up? The name 'Prometheus' ring any bells? I'm not going to go climbing any vulture-infested mountains to visit you. I have a trick knee."

"Oh, please. Zeus couldn't give a rat's ass over my activities. You say others have been asking about me, was Zeus one of them? Dear old Dad?"

Ares remained silent, choosing not to meet Athena's gaze as he kicked at a rock.

"Yeah, that's what I thought. My liver is in no danger of being ripped out for eternity. I am protected and blessed with the huge number of damns not being given on a grand scale." she said bitterly.

Ares was quiet for another couple moments, then sat down. "I know you too well to try and talk you out of things when you get like this. When are you going to start this new venture of yours?"

Athena chuckled. "'Going to'? You think I've just been sitting here, munching apples and being a curmudgeon? I accepted their offer a month ago."

"What?!?" Ares' gob was truly smacked.

"Mm hm. You know how many ants there are in Athens alone? I never had it so good. It's nice to be wanted again. You should consider making some inroads with them as well. With the way things are to be going soon, you might want to consider giving them the time of day. I can make introductions, if you like."

Ares was confused. " 'The way things are to be going'? 'Switching sides'? What in Hades are you talking about?"

Athena got up, put hands on her brother's shoulders, then kiss his forehead. "Oh, little brother. I'm not the only one who's done with Man. The ants have their grievances, and I'm impressed with their plans to remedy them. Think about it, or don't. Remember our rivalries back in the day? How red the waters ran? It could be just like old times. *It could be glorious.*" She mussed his dark hair then walked down the path, leaving Ares feeling far too cold for a summer's night.

We All Make Sacrifices

by Jonathan Maberry

-1-

I looked up from the business card to the lawyer seated across the desk from me.

I said, "Mister, um, 'Douche-weasel'--?" Pronouncing it the way it looked in the expensive raised printing.

He gave me a weary look. The kind of look that said two things. First, that he's been through some variation of this conversation ten times a week his whole life. The second is that he expected just exactly this level of maturity from someone with rates as low as mine.

"DuSchwezel," he said slowly, saying it as 'DEW-schwee-ZELLE'. Emphasis on both the first and last syllables.

"Okay," I said.

"Okay," said Mr. DuSchwezel.

A moment passed, taking its time. My office was quiet. He sighed. "You're still thinking it's pronounced 'douche-weasel,' aren't you?"

I held my thumb and index fingers an inch apart. "Li'l bit," I said.

"Tell me, Mr. Hunter, don't you get annoyed when people make jokes about your name?"

"What's wrong with my name?"

"'Hunter'? Seriously? And you're a private investigator?"
"Hunh. Never came up," I lied.

Another moment limped past.

"We're not off to a very good start, are we?" he asked.

"Not a fan of banter?"

"Not as such, no."

I put his card down on my desk blotter. "Okay, so let's try it from a different angle. Why are you here?"

"To see about engaging your services."

"Uh huh."

"You are for hire, are you not?"

I nudged the card with a finger. "Almost always."

"But--?"

"It's just that I don't get why *you* want to hire me."

"Why not? My money's good, isn't it?"

"That's just it, you're a Main Line estate attorney. I couldn't afford to park in your garage. You probably paid more for a thousand of these cards than I've spent on rent for this dump. Lawyers like you have investigators on retainer, and none of them have offices in this part of town."

He said, "Ah."

"Ah," I agreed. "So why does a guy in a two thousand dollar suit schlep all the way here to hire a guy like me?"

"The suit," he said, "cost eleven thousand dollars. I paid two thousand just for the shoes."

"First," I said, "that was a very douche-weasel this to say. Second, fuck you."

He smiled at that.

After a moment, so did I.

DuSchwezel picked up the briefcase he'd stood next to the client chair, placed it flat on a corner of my desk and popped the locks. The case was positioned so that he could see the contents and I couldn't. He removed an envelope, considered it for a moment and then reached out to lay it on the blotter next to his card.

"What's that?" I asked.

"Look and see."

It was unsealed, so I folded back the flap and removed a long, blue-green slip of paper. That exact color was probably sea-foam or some shit like that. Very heavy stock, high linen count, expensive printing. It was a check drawn on a personal account rather than something corporate. It had his name on it. Arnold Tyro DuSchwezel. It was made out to me for the amount of five thousand dollars.

I nodded appreciation at the numbers, which were some of my favorite numbers, and placed the check on my desk atop the envelope.

"This a bribe to make me say your name the right way?"

"Cute," he said, "but no. This is me giving you a check to retain your services."

"For what?"

"That's complicated, but first I'd like you to give me a check for one hundred dollars."

I smiled. "And why the fuck would I do that?"

"To retain *my* services."

"You lost me."

DuSchwezel said, "In order for us to proceed you will need to retain me as your attorney so that everything we discuss is covered under the blanket of attorney-client privilege."

"You working for a drug cartel or some shit? Local Mafia?"

He spread his hands. "The five thousand dollars is a gift. You are not legally or morally required to engage my services. If you want to tell me to go away, then I will and you can keep the check. It will not leave you beholden to me in any way."

"Bullshit."

"Not at all," said DuSchwezel. "We have discussed no business and nothing that's gone between us could be construed as a binding verbal contract. Go to your bank and cash the check if you want. I'll wait here. Or I can come back. Do this in whichever way makes you feel comfortable."

"If," I said, "I decide to write you that check, what's the other shoe? I don't need a lawyer."

"You probably do, but that's a general opinion based on your lifestyle."

"You fucking with me?"

He grinned. "Of course."

I grinned, too. Mine was forced.

"If you accept my check," I said, "and suddenly become my lawyer, is there more of this?"

"That would be when the other shoe would hit the floor, yes," he admitted.

"Will I like it?"

He pursed his lips. "I doubt it."

"Then--?"

"But really, Mr. Hunter, how many of your more *interesting* cases have you actually liked?"

I said nothing.

"You have quite a reputation in certain circles," said DuSchwezel. "People respect you."

"No," I said, "they don't."

He shrugged. "Okay, then they respect what you can do. They fear you, if that's a better way to put it."

"Not sure there is a better way to put it if we're both talking about the same thing."

"Fair enough," he said.

We sat there for a moment. My office smells like Lysol and Jack Daniels. The two smells are related thematically in ways that define me, sad to say. The Lysol for cleaning up some of the messes I've had to make. The Jack Daniels for helping me try to forget. Cliché? Sure. Fuck it.

DuSchwezel sat back and crossed his legs. Even through the stink of booze and cleaning products I could smell him. I have a very good sense of smell. Better than yours unless you're like me. He'd used some kind of super-fatted soap, probably Camay. His shampoo is scented with tea-tree oil. Cologne was one of the Polo varieties. Blue, I think. Deodorant was Old Spice Sport. There was a hint of chlorine about him, which suggested he swam his laps today and showered at the gym. There was also a subtle aroma of something else. No, two things. A little fear sweat and a little blood. Hard to wash that away completely. Hound dogs can sniff it after a shower. So can people like me.

I opened my desk drawer, took out my cheap green checkbook and wrote him a check for one hundred dollars. He watched me with genuine and obvious interest, then accepted it with a nod. DuSchwezel took a moment to study it, though I think he did that to collect his thoughts. There were a few beads of fresh sweat on his forehead. Then he folded the check and tucked it into an inner pocket of his jacket.

We sat for a moment.

"Anything we discuss from here out is protected," he said.

"Yup." In the movies and in poorly-researched novels private investigators often hide information from the cops by claiming client confidentiality. Yeah, that's a myth. Only lawyers and shrinks get that protection. Now we were sealed and square.

"Mr. Hunter," said DuSchwezel, "I would like very much for you to kill someone."

So, yeah, okay. That just happened.

I sat there, looking at him. I think I was smiling. Or something.

His face was slightly flushed.

"You're fucking with me," I said.

"Actually," said DuSchwezel, "I'm not."

"Then give me back my check and try not to take it personally while I throw you the fuck out of my office. I may knee you in the balls, but that's just a professional courtesy."

"This isn't a joking matter," he said.

My smile got wider and probably stranger. "Sounds like it to me."

DuSchwezel's smile faded away. "Do I *look* like I'm joking, Mr. Hunter?"

"You'd better be. You just asked me to commit a contract killing."

"It's not as simple as that."

"I'm pretty sure that I do not give a flying gopher fuck how simple or complicated it is," I said. "And, tell you what, why don't you stand up and assume the position so I can make sure you're not wearing a wire. Entrapment is an ugly word and it'll probably hurt when I shove it up your ass."

I started to get out of my chair but he stood up more quickly, hands raised as he backed away.

"No! Listen to me, please. If you want to pat me down, that's fine, but please listen to me."

"Pat first, listen later. Hands against the wall."

Before he could react I snaked out a hand, caught him by the shoulder of his eleven thousand dollar suit, spun him and slammed him into the wall, kicked his legs wide, and frisked him. Before I was a P.I. here in Philly I was a cop in Minneapolis. I worked enough vice cases in my day to know how to check someone for a wire. There are nice ways to do it and there are ways that can really fuck up a person's month. I went somewhere in the middle. When I was done his clothes were a mess, he had very little personal dignity left, he was panting with mingled fear and anger, but he was clean.

I pointed to the chair. "Sit," I ordered. He sat and watched while I rifled through his briefcase. Lots of file folders, which I ignored, but nothing else. I took a tuning fork from my desk drawer—a little trick I learned from a cop friend in Pine Deep—banged it hard and touched it to the handle and any part of the briefcase dense enough to conceal a mic. If anyone was listening in they'd be shopping at Miracle-Ear by the end of the day.

The case was clean.

So I sat on the edge of my desk, arms folded and looked down at DuSchwezel. He plucked out his pocket square and dabbed his forehead and upper lip

"You're an asshole," he said.

"Blow me," I said. "Tell me why I shouldn't throw you out the window."

DuSchwezel held the pocket square in his lap and I could see his hands tremble. Son of bitch was scared but I don't think it was because of me.

"People think that when you're rich you can do anything you want," he said, coming at this from around a corner. "That's not true. Not really. Sure, there are things we can do, and things we can get away with, but we're not invulnerable. Everyone has a weakness, Mr. Hunter."

I said nothing.

He looked up at me. "I am not a very nice person."

"I'm not your therapist."

"No," he said, "I'm not looking for understanding. I am a bad man. I do bad things."

"Yeah, well I'm not a priest, either."

"I'm not seeking absolution," said DuSchwezel. "I'm making a statement. This is confidential and I need you to understand who and what I am. I represent very rich people in the Philadelphia area. People who use my services and those of my partners to make sure that the law always bends to whatever angle they need. I am a magician when it comes to twisting regulations, soliciting illegal compliance from judges and politicians, dispensing bribes, and hiding large amounts of cash in dummy corporations. In short, I facilitate corruption in virtually every way that does not involve direct violence."

"Well, to be fair," I said, "I already thought you were an asshole when you said you were a lawyer. This doesn't slide you that much further down the crapper."

"This isn't about me," he said, "this is about my daughter, Olivia. Beautiful girl. Smart."

I said nothing.

Two tears suddenly dropped down his cheeks and whatever was left of his professional calm and poise collapsed like broken scaffolding, dragged down by the weight of why he was really here. He said, "She was eighteen."

Ah…fuck.

Was is such an ugly word.

When it's laid against the age of a daughter, a kid, it's beyond horrible. It disfigures the moment.

Mr. DuSchwezel put his face in his hands and began to cry.

I did not pat him on the back and tell him that it was okay, that it was all going to be okay. I'm not that much of an asshole, and I had no reason to lie to him. Whatever this was, it was already not okay. *She was eighteen.* No, it wasn't ever going to be okay.

I went around to my side of the desk, sat down, let him cry. Waited. Tried not to own any of his hurt. Tried really hard.

She was eighteen.

Was.

Goddamn it.

-3-

He got his shit together and told me the story. It was long and he rambled. Short version is this…

One of the biggest clients he represented was a man named Fenner, and Mr. Fenner made his money by providing transportation, storage, and distribution for large lots of stolen merchandise. We're not talking a couple of microwaves that fell off the back of a truck. We're talking about entire trucks, or at least the cargoes of trucks that are either hauling illegal freight like untaxed cigarettes and unstamped booze; or the contents of hijacked trucks. There's a lot of money in that. One of his specialties was stealing the contents of cargo containers at the docks and placing them in his own cans elsewhere in the same freight-yard. And he made sure that his stuff always had the proper paperwork. Lots of steps to his organization, lots of checks and balances, lots of money for everyone involved. Tens of millions per year, just in the dockyard scams. Twice that much for stuff he hauled up from meth labs in the south.

Mr. Fenner wasn't the problem.

His son, Erik, was.

Erik was so cliché I almost laughed as DuSchwezel described him. Twenty-something, good-looking, perfect teeth, deep-water tan from spending so much time on boats off Miami, rich, arrogant, vicious, petty, grabby, violent, charming, and all of the other adjectives that describe a child of wealth and power who was the only heir to a crime fortune. You can order the cocksucker from central casting. You know the type, the kind who genuinely believe that the world exists to help him get high, get laid, and have fun. The kind who drops twenty grand on a weekend out with his friends and won't let anyone else pay for anything because he needs to be seen as the one who *owns* the fun and has everything covered. And because his dad is who he is, doors get opened, he never waits in a line, he always gets a table, he gets more ass than a porn star, everyone grins at him like he's the king of the jungle, and to that crowd he *is* the king of the jungle. But what they're really doing is kissing his ass in order to kiss his father's ass.

Like I said, you've seen this a million times. Every single grade-B cop movie, every modern gangster movie, blah blah blah. In those movies he's the one who usually does something so heinous that it causes the action hero to cut a bloody swath through the criminal empire his father has taken so long to build.

The thing that really torques my ass, though, is that this particular cliché is reinforced by the fact that there are hundreds of real world assholes exactly like that. Maybe thousands. I ran into some of them when I was a cop in the Cities, and I've brushed up against a few—even dented one or two—since I hung out a shingle here in Philly.

Unfortunately they are usually very well guarded and their asshole parents do everything they can to spoil them and enable the very worst behavior. In the movies the action hero goes in guns blazing and does some chop-socky and racks up a body count that makes cancer look like a third string killer with no running game.

That's the movies. Liam Neeson, Denzel Washington, Keanu Reeves, and Jason Statham manage to outfight and outgun whole mobs of wiseguys. That, as they say, is Hollywood. The bullets aren't real, the bad guys in those flicks can't shoot worth a damn, and heroes seem to be able to do complex extended fight scenes even after taking gunshot wounds, stab wounds, falling off balconies, getting thrown through plate glass windows, and getting wailed on by fists, elbows, and feet. Special effects, baby. Fake blood, rubber knives, stunt men, and guns firing blanks.

I pointed all of this out to Mr. DuSchwezel.

"And so I came to you," he said simply.

"Sure. But why? Last time I checked there was a shit-ton of cops in Philadelphia. They've organized now. Call themselves a 'police department.' Maybe, you being a lawyer and all, you've heard of them."

"I'm a mob lawyer," he said.

"And you told me you have connections out the wazoo. Judges in your pocket and such."

"Whose money do you think pays for those judges, Mr. Hunter? If I filed a formal complaint against Erik Fenner, who do you think would enforce it? Even *I* don't know who owns whom in this town. Erik's father has other lawyers, too. We don't share all of the details about bribery and corruption while we braid each other's hair."

"There's that," I conceded. "You're afraid that leveling charges against Erik will backfire."

"I have two other children," said DuSchwezel. "And a wife, a mother, cousins, nieces, nephews. Just in the Philadelphia Metropolitan area there are over twenty members of my extended family. How many of them do you think Mr. Fenner would hurt or kill to protect his only son?"

"Balls," I said.

"Do you think I'd come to you if I had anywhere else to go?"

Not sure if he was trying to be deliberately insulting, but what the hell. He had a point. And besides, I was still thinking of him as Mr. Douche-weasel.

"What's all this have to do with Olivia?"

Even though this was why he was here, my question hit him like a punch. He cleared his throat and said, "You spend a lot of time at Heaven Street Diner."

A statement, not a question, but I nodded anyway.

"Do you remember a dark-haired girl who worked there for a few weeks last fall?"

"Sure. Livvie something."

And something went *clunk* inside my head. Livvie. Short for Olivia.

"Oh," I said. "Fuck."

"Yes. Livvie was always troubled. She ran away from home half a dozen times. Last fall she got a fake I.D. that said she was nineteen, and she moved into a roach-infested apartment near the diner. Got a job working tables at Heaven Street."

"I remember her," I said. It was true. Livvie was a pretty little thing. Thin, pale, rocking a Goth look. Never said much and I don't think she ever waited on me. When I was at the diner, the counter waitress, Ivy, always took care of me. Ivy and I go way back. "She seemed like a nice kid."

It was a lame comment but it was all I had. I doubt we ever swapped more than a 'hello' two or three times. Like a lot of diner staff, she came and went and then was gone from my memory until today.

"I had another investigator look for her," said DuSchwezel. "He found her and brought her home."

"But she ran away again?"

"In a way. I had a party at my house and the Fenners were there. Erik saw Olivia and I could tell right away she fell for him. He's very good-looking and he wears his father's money like a suit."

I nodded, knowing the type.

"They started seeing each other," he said. "I tried to warn her off, to tell her that he was dangerous, but…"

"But that probably made her more interested."

"Yes."

"Aside from the obvious, why was Erik dangerous? I mean, you took a risk telling her when if she was so into him she might have told him what you said."

His hands still gripped the pocket square. Twisting it, clutching it with white-knuckled fingers. His eyes kept meeting mine and falling away. Over and over.

"Okay," I said, "you're not paying me enough to play games. Tell me what it is or buzz off."

He took a fortifying breath and said, "There are rumors about Erik."

"Ah, boy… Tell me."

"Erik is into some strange stuff. His father told me about some of it because he knew I was having some issues with Olivia. His father wanted advice on finding a good therapist."

"When you say 'strange'…?"
"Erik was into supernatural stuff."

"So what?"

"No," said DuSchwezel, "not as a hobbyist. I'm not talking about him being into monster movies and Stephen King novels. No, I mean he was *into* the supernatural. He believes in it. He…sought it out."

"How and in what way?"

Again his eyes flicked away. "I'm not sure how it started. He's always had unusual friends, particularly another boy whose father is with the Kirikov family. Do you know them? Russia Mafiya."

"They're dead, right? Turf war over the uptic in the heroin trade between here and New York. Both sides killing family members?"

"That was the cover story, sure. But it went deeper than that. I'm pretty sure that the Kirikov boy was not killed by their rivals in that particular line of commerce. I'm almost certain that Erik killed him and made it look like it was done by the rivals of the Kirikov family. The resulting drug war was the usual escalation of payback."

"Why would Erik do that?"

"Because he needed a blood sacrifice."

I stared at him. "You're going to have to explain that one."

"I...don't have all of it together," he admitted. "And, quite frankly, I'm not even sure how much of it I believe. But I managed to put someone inside Erik's circle of friends. A promising attorney right out of law school who looks younger than he is. He ingratiated himself into Erik's crew and..." He stopped and shivered. Actually shivered. "He said that Erik is insane. Erik doesn't just want to be like his father, he wants to eclipse the old man and become something much bigger, something much more powerful. He wants to be feared."

"He has a lot of thugs who will shoot people if he asks. Pretty sure he's already feared."

"No," said DuSchwezel, "you don't get it. This isn't the kind of power hunger I see all the time among my clients and their sons. No. When I said Erik was insane I meant it. I think that he was crazy—clinically psychotic—to begin with, but the more he got into whatever supernatural stuff the young Kirikov shared with him... Well, I think it pushed him into a whole new shape. Mentally, I mean."

"So he's making blood sacrifices now? To whom? Or to what?"

"To what Erik thinks is the patron god of his family."

"You're shitting me."

"I shit you not."

"And who exactly is the—and pardon me if I grin while I say this—patron 'god' of their family?"

"Well, see, that's one of the main reasons I came to see you," said DuSchwezel. "You specifically, I mean. 'Fenner' is an Anglicized version of the family name. They're Scandinavian and their real name is—or at least *was* — Fenrisúlfr."

I said nothing. My mouth dried right up.

DuSchwezel nodded. "You know that name, don't you?"

I nodded. "Fenrisúlfr," I said hoarsely. "It's another name for Fenrir."

"Who is--?" he asked, making sure I knew.

"The wolf god of the Vikings. Fenrir is the father of the wolves Sköll and Hati Hróðvitnisson, is a son of Loki, and is foretold to kill the god Odin during the events of Ragnarök."

"Yes," said DuSchwezel. "Erik is trying to invoke a dark god who he believes—really fucking believes—is going to help bring about the end of the world. And, god help me, Mr. Hunter, he sacrificed my little girl to try and make that happen."

His words seemed to be painted on the air between us in dark red letters. It took me a while to figure out how to reply to something like that.

"Even so," I said slowly, "why me? If Erik is a psychopath and a serial murderer, and you can't trust the cops to take him down, what you need is an assassin. I'm not a button man. I don't do contract hits, and 'revenge killer' isn't on my business card."

"No," said DuSchwezel, "but 'monster' is."

-4-

Bang.

There it was.

"No it's not," I said. Which was true in the literal sense. My business card said "Investigations and Personal Protection." But I could see it in his eyes. He knew.

Maybe he didn't know *what* I was, but he knew I wasn't Joe Normal.

"Who's told you what?" I asked, keeping my voice casual. "And if you try to play the client confidentiality thing then I'll tell you in advance to fuck off and go away."

He considered that for a moment, then nodded to himself as he decided to play his cards face up.

"Ivy," he said.

Ivy. She was one of the few people who knew who and what I was. A year or two back she tapped me to help out a friend of hers with a problem no one else could tackle. I've never been exactly certain how Ivy figured it out, but she asked me for help. A friend's little son was being attacked in his sleep by something that came out of his closet. Yeah, I know. Monster in the closet is a standard kid thing. Except this time it wasn't. And it wasn't a sequel to *Monsters, Inc.*, either. There was something big and bad in the closet, and Ivy asked me to go in there and see what I could do.

It got weird and it got messy.

Bottom line is that there's nothing left in that closet that's ever going to hurt anyone again.

So, sure. Monster. Not exactly inaccurate. Not entirely unfair.

Ivy knows that.

"She shouldn't have told you," I said.

This time his eyes didn't dart away. He gave me a long, hard, sad, broken, desperate look. A father's look. A look that was filled with all of the grief in the world.

"Ivy thought the world of Olivia," he said. "She knows that I loved her. Really loved her. Olivia was my little girl."

Saying that broke him.

And, damn if it didn't break me, too.

-5-

Which is why I went to see Erik Fenner.

There are some cases where I spend days or even weeks running down clues, doing background checks, tailing suspects, building a case. And then there are some where I go right up to a door and knock. I don't get many of that second kind. If it was easy they usually don't hire guys like me.

Except in this case it was easy. Finding Erik, I mean. And there *are* no other guys like me. Not for something like this. I mean, sure, I've got cousins and aunts and all who are like me, but that's different. None of them live in Philly. Most of my relatives are either in the Cities or in Europe. We *benandanti* go back a lot of years. I can name every family member going back to the early sixteenth century Fruili, Italy, and my Aunt Violet can name them going back to Etruscan times.

Benandanti.

The "good walkers."

The hounds of God. Which is a pretentious nickname but someone else hung it on us.

I wonder if DuSchwezel did his background check. Probably. If you want to stop a psychopath trying to invoke a wolf god, hire a private investigator who has some skin in that game. Not the Norse crap, but you get the picture.

So, yeah. I took the case. Ivy told him the right things about me. He knew I'd take it.

Maybe I did, too. That 'was' word still burned in my head. The man may have been an asshole but he had a daughter and he loved her. Maybe he thought he failed her, too. Probably did. Mom lawyer and all. Kid has no one to look up to, so she starts looking down.

And sees a handsome monster looking up at her.

-6-

I drove out to Bucks County, to a sprawling estate near New Hope. DuSchwezel gave me the address and the code for the front gate. I told him I didn't need the code. Wall was only twelve feet high. I mean, c'mon.

Erik's father was in South Philly overseeing one of his dockside concerns. DuSchwezel had made sure that nobody but Erik was home. Well, besides a couple of servants, and three or four bodyguards.

I parked my car under some trees on a side road a quarter mile from the house. Walked the rest of the way as the sun was tumbling over the trees toward tomorrow. I don't need darkness and that whole full moon thing is pure bullshit. Moon's got nothing to do with it. On the other hand, sunlight makes it easy for witnesses and who needs that bullshit.

Was I here to do a contract killing?

Not really. I gave DuSchwezel his check back.

This was for a teenage girl who didn't know better than to walk into one of the outer rings of hell. DuSchwezel couldn't actually tell me what happened to her. I doubt any father could force those words into his mouth. Instead he handed me a copy of the autopsy report.

That she had been raped was horrible enough. It wasn't the worst thing that had been done to her. We don't need to go into all the details. Even I get nauseous sometimes. Her body was found in a wrecked car, but the extent of her wounds wasn't consistent with the amount of damage to the vehicle. The car had rolled and burned, but that didn't account for the dismemberment. It didn't account for her eyes and heart being missing. And the pathologist determined that the victim was not alive when the car caught fire. However, on reflection, the pathologist recanted and decided that all of the injuries had, in fact, been sustained in that crash.

Five weeks after the autopsy report the pathologist put a down payment on a mini-mansion in New Town. You can connect the dots however you like.

I found a nice little blind spot where the Fenner security cameras couldn't see through some thick rhododendron. I stripped out of the sweats I'd worn and went over the wall in a way that left claw marks on the brick.

On the other side I dropped down and ran on all fours. I usually stay on two feet except when I need to move fast. My senses are better then, too. DuSchwezel had given me a scarf that used to belong to Erik. Olivia had kept it as a token of her love.

Still had his scent on it. Useful. Before I went over the wall I took a big enough sniff that I could have found him halfway across the state.

In the end it wasn't even all that hard.

He was sitting by the pool wearing a pair of skintight speedos, Wayfarer sunglasses over his eyes, a beer resting on his belly. He did not have three bodyguards with him. There were six of them. Or maybe three worked for his dad and the other three were part of Erik's mini-cult. They all had wolf tattoos on the sides of their necks. Very stylized—Fenrir with his jaws wide to swallow Odin on the day the world ends.

Even the guards had that.

They all looked blown out. Couldn't tell right off if they were hammered, high, stuffed from a big meal, or just a bunch of lazy fucks who were dead tired this early. Or some combination of all of that.

There was an iPad plugged into a Bose speaker dock and Kanye was yelling some bullshit that I didn't want to hear. They had it on too goddamn loud, too. The asshole club was sprawled all around the pool. No women around, which is odd. Usually these clowns have all kinds of arm candy, and often it's paid for in one way or another. Cash, drugs, access to power, whatever. But not now.

Good. That simplified things.

I circled the pool area, following the blood scent to its source. It was the pool house. It had been converted into something else. Not sure if the word "church" would apply. Temple, maybe. Shrine. Something like that. The windows were all blacked out and inside someone had gone completely ass-fuck nuts. The walls were painted with magical symbols from at least a dozen religions and twice as many phony cults. Inverted pentagrams, representations of goat-headed Baphomet, symbols of evil. Such bullshit. Some of this crap I knew for sure was from old monster movies that had no actual connection to real beliefs.

The blood was real, though.

There was a lot of it. Old and new. Many sources. Not just Olivia—and I could smell her scent here, too. There were others. As I stood in the doorway I took in at least fourteen separate female scents. Two of them were pre-pubescent. These fuckers had killed little girls, too. That's worse. I'm not sure how exactly, but it is.

Fourteen dead girls and women.

There was an altar and Erik had laid them upon it and he and his wolfpack had done terrible things. I didn't need to see pictures to know what had happened there. My senses fed the information to my mind. When I was a cop and we learned about forensics there was a saying that every contact leaves a trace. Now imagine what traces were left for senses like *mine* to find.

I could smell the pain, the horror, the death. I could almost hear the echo of voices screaming for mercy that was not theirs to have, just as I could hear the laughter of those sons of bitches out by the pool.

Were they true believers? Or was this part of some kind of shared madness inspired and perpetuated by Erik Fenner?

I don't know and I didn't much care.

As I stepped into that room my focus was drawn to the altar. To the smell of blood that washed down from it.

So potent.

So fresh.

"What the *fuck* is that?" I breathed, and my words came out twisted because my throat was not a human one.

The answer to my question was there to be read, and my senses never lie.

That's when I knew I was too late. That's when I realized why those pricks out at the pool looked so logy and sated.

I'd waited until sunset to come here. My caution made me too late to save somebody else's little girl. Or sister. Or wife. Or whatever. There was blood on the air and smeared on the altar. Female, young. Dead.

And, if my senses were reading it right, not just dead.

No.

Fuck me. There are certain smells flesh makes when it interacts with saliva and digestive juices. I smelled the stink of a feast only recently finished. It was the smell a pack of wolves made when they were gathered around a deer they'd just torn down.

I turned and prowled to the doorway to the pool area and looked at the seven of them.

And I *knew*.

They had crossed way over the line from making human sacrifices to a wolf god to trying to *be* wolves. Or become wolves.

The wolf in me wanted to attack. Right then. To kill them all as they slept. The wolf was vicious but he was not cruel. That's why I changed back to me.

You see, I can be cruel.

Sometimes I want to be. Sometimes I need to look into the eyes of certain people because I want to see understanding. Maybe I hope for a flicker of regret, or remorse. Not that a moment of repentance has saved anyone who I've gone after. Fuck it, I'm not a saint. I'm not even a very good private investigator.

I'm a hell of a hunter though. And, yeah, sure, make a joke about the name. It was picked as a joke by one of my ancestors, so the joke's on you.

When I take on a client—or in the case of DuSchwezel a proxy client, because I was here for Olivia not for her dickhead lawyer father—then that person becomes part of my pack. Wolves protect their packs.

Oh yeah. We do.

So it was in my own shape that I walked out of the pool house, strolled over to Erik Fenner's chaise-lounge, raised my leg, and heel-kicked him in the speedo.

Real fucking hard.

He screamed and grabbed his balls and fell out of the chair.

The screams woke everyone else up. The three bodyguards came out of their chairs like they had springs up their asses and suddenly there were guns in their hands. The other three sprang up, too. One of them had a gun, another produced a knife from god knows where. The third one grabbed a beer bottle and smashed the fat end off it.

Six of them in a ring around me, with Erik screaming on the ground while his face turned an amusing shade of puce.

And me standing there. Short, skinny, twenty years older than any of them. Naked as an egg with my dick hanging out.

"Who the fuck are you?" screamed one of the guards.

This was the kind of moment when you really want to put a button on it by saying something really cool. Witty. Like the one-liners those action heroes always use.

But goddamn it if I couldn't really come up with anything snarky.

What I said was more expository than colorful.

I said, "Fenrisúlfr isn't real, assholes. Fake god from a dead religion. Not even sure the Vikings believed in him."

They stared at me. Part surprise that I was even dropping the name Fenrisúlfr, and partly wondering who the hell this naked crazy guy was. Even Erik paused in his shrieking to stare at me.

He said, "W-what--?"

"You fucktards think you're becoming wolves?" I asked. "Is that it? I mean, is that what this shit is all about? Some kind of superstitious ritual bullshit?"

Erik managed to get to his knees. His face was dark with pain and he still cupped his mashed balls, but there was fury in his eyes.

And...something else.

Maybe it was the darkening sky or maybe it wasn't, but I saw his pale Scandinavian eyes change from an icy blue to a red that was brighter and bloodier than his face.

All around me I saw the eyes of the others begin to change, too.

"Well, fuck me," I said.

The shape of Erik's mouth began to change. He suddenly had way too many teeth and his lips almost couldn't form the name of his god. "Fenrisúlfr."

I don't know how they managed it, but holy shit. They were actually turning into wolves. All seven of them. A wolfpack transformed somehow by blood sacrifices and the savage slaughter of the innocents, all in the name of a god whose mythical status I was very quickly having to re-evaluate.

I said, "Oh...shit."

They laughed, but the laughter sounded like snarls.

Like growls.

So I figured...what the fuck.

They were wolves. Okay, I have to accept that. Werewolves, I suppose. Of a kind.

But they were new at this game. I've been playing it a long, long time.

They say age and treachery will overcome youth and skill. Take that to the bank. And, another aphorism. Experience is the best teacher.

These pricks have only ever sunk their teeth into innocent flesh.

Fighting another werewolf is different.

Fighting a *benandanti* werewolf is even harder. It's a death wish. Ask anyone I've ever gone up against.

Oh, yeah, wait: You can't.

These young monsters changed.

I changed *faster*.

-7-

While they still could, they screamed for mercy.

Didn't help.

They screamed for their god, but he didn't show.

They screamed.

And screamed.

And screamed.

I was okay with that.

-8-

I let a couple of weeks go by and then met with DuSchwezel in a booth at Heaven Street Diner. Couple of the regulars were there, but nobody disturbed us. It's that kind of place.

We worked through a cup of coffee each and he pushed his apple pie around with a fork before we got to it.

"Terrible what happened," he said. "The fire. Those poor boys."

"Yeah," I said. "Makes you think."

He nodded. Lifted some apple glop, looked at it, set it down.

"I went to Olivia's grave the other day."

I said nothing.

"There were flowers on it. Not expensive, but lovely."

I sipped my coffee.

"Any idea who put them there?"

The clocked on the wall ticked through half a minute. DuSchwezel nodded.

"Thanks," he said.

"For what?" I said. "I never did anything for you. We have no understanding other than the fact that I paid you a hundred bucks to answer some legal questions. You cash that check, by the way?"

"Of course. It's a matter of record now."

We sipped our coffee.

"Hunter," he said, "can't I be frank with you?"

"Funny question for a lawyer to ask, but sure."

He almost smiled. "I went to law school to be the kind of lawyer I became. Seriously. I never had aspirations of being Atticus Finch. I never wanted to do anything but make money pretty much the way I do."

"Congratulations," I said.

"Go ahead and sneer, but I'm trying to say something here."

"Be my guest."

"In my line of work I only meet bad people. Fathers and sons, like the Fenners. Hangers on. Gangs in expensive suits. You understand what I'm saying?"

"I do."

"I don't ever get to meet good people. When I do meet someone who's supposed to be stand-up, I'm immediately figuring the angle to break them down and turn them. You understand? I'm always looking for a way to make them like me. In one way or another."

I said nothing.

"In all of my dealings," he said, "I've never met anyone like you. The people with whom I work always talk about honor and all that, but it's talk. The deference people show to them is totally out of fear or greed. Never because these people have earned their respect."

"If you're driving in the direction of a point, man," I said, "take the next exit."

He said, "You are a third or possibly fourth rate private investigator working out of what is arguably the seediest office it has ever been my displeasure to visit. You smell of cleaning products and old booze, and you are not a very nice person."

I leaned back. "Gosh, thanks. I--."

He cut me off. "But you may be the only honorable man I have ever met."

Before I could figure out a way to respond to that, he stood up and tossed a twenty down to cover the tab.

"Olivia would probably have liked you."

And with that he turned and shambled out.

I sat in the booth and drank my coffee. I ate his slice of pie. I stared out the window at the night.

Insect Queen

by Roy K. Phelps

Doctor Kowalski had almost finished her salad when the resident approached her, visibly agitated, and told her there was something she needed to see.

She was the only one in the physician's lounge, a rare event that she treasured. It meant she didn't have to endure small talk or clumsy attempts at flirtation while she ate. Christine had been an only child, and as an adult, preferred to keep her distance from others. Solitude suited her just fine. She was disappointed at having her quiet time spoiled.

She looked up and saw it was Alan, a first-year resident who had just been disgorged from the university back in July. He was still adjusting to the actual practice of medicine after years of studying it, and was still easily risible. Everything was an emergency of the highest order to him. He was one of the most nervous residents she had ever encountered in her seventeen years on the fourth floor.

"What is it now?"

Alan shuffled his feet, his large, doughy body rocking from side to side. "Well, it's about the Jane Doe. She, um, well, her room… there's been, uh, something out of the ordinary. I can't… you really need to see for yourself."

She knew who he meant. A young woman, somewhere between 17 and 21, had been admitted the previous night with no ID. The police, alerted by a jogger, had found her naked and unconscious under a bridge at the junction of Waller Creek and Lady Bird Lake. The emergency room triage nurse had examined her and found no obvious signs of trauma outside of being unresponsive. They kept her in the ICU overnight, watching her vital signs, which remained stable. They had moved her onto the floor, into Room 409, earlier that evening.

Alan was still fidgeting when she stood up. She had the strong urge to tell him he looked like a little boy about to pee in his pants.

She passed him quickly in the hall, her no-frills white sneakers gliding silently across the gleaming white floor. She heard him huffing as he tried to keep up. When she reached Room 409, she turned the handle and stepped into the darkened room.

The room was filled with vague shapes dimly illuminated by the soft glow of the flatscreen computer attached to one wall. The window blinds were open, and she could see the lights of the Austin skyline. She reached for the light switch and snapped it on just as Alan finally arrived, panting.

The stark fluorescent lights overhead revealed a young woman with long, unwashed brown hair in a white bed at the end of the room. She was covered with a thin bedsheet, her left arm outside the covers, an IV taped in the crook of her arm. A barcode bracelet dangled from her wrist. She was still unconscious, looking pale but peaceful.

The room was anything but peaceful, though; hundreds, maybe thousands, of small insects filled the room, crawling, buzzing, flying, chirping, on the floor, on the bed, everywhere. There were so many of them, and so many in motion, that she couldn't begin to estimate their true number. It was impossible to tell how many different kinds there were, but she did notice one similarity between them – they were all black.

She closed the door as a winged insect vaguely resembling a moth flew past her. She had no idea where all these bugs had come from, but that was something to worry about later. Her immediate concern was how to get rid of them. Having an infestation in the room was bad enough; spreading it into the halls would be most unsatisfactory.

"See?" Alan said. "I checked in here like an hour ago and the room was empty. Do you have any idea where all these bugs came from? Because I sure don't know."

She ignored him, walking over to the computer. The brittle shells of insects crawling on the floor crunched beneath her feet. She scanned the barcode on the girl's wrist and the computer responded with the details of her medical chart. She studied the vital statistics noted there and found nothing unusual. She saw the time of Alan's last visit; it had indeed been just over an hour ago.

She watched the insects on the floor and in the air. There was something odd about them, but she couldn't decide what it was. A few of the bigger insects were of a kind she had never seen before. One crawled up her leg and she swatted it away. It fell back to the floor, hopping under the bed. It looked like a large ladybug with mandibles. Another one on the bed was a grotesque spider with wings and long, limp tentacles where the legs should have been.

Unnerved, she pulled out her cell phone and used the camera to take pictures of the room and its uninvited occupants, as well as close-up shots of various insects, especially the winged spider. Using the text function, she sent a message to a neurologist she knew on another floor with an interest in all things zoological. She typed, FOUND IN A PATIENT'S ROOM. HAVE ANY IDEA WHERE THEY CAME FROM AND WHAT THEY ARE? She attached the pictures to the text and pressed SEND.

She turned to Alan, who was still by the door, hypnotized by the random motion of the insects. "Stand outside the door and don't let anyone in until I come back. Don't let any insects out, either. I have to call Maintenance to come do something about this mess and get her moved to another room."

"Yes, Doctor." He appeared relieved at being allowed to leave the room.

xxx

She was efficient; it took her less than thirty minutes to get two nurses to move the girl to Room 427 and someone from Maintenance to clean the room. Moving the girl's bed without the insects escaping had been the trickiest part. She achieved that by using a fan, borrowed from the supply closet, to blow them back as the nurses wheeled the girl out. During that time, she also left a voicemail message for the fourth-floor hospitalist, Dr. Augustus Hale. He was in charge of the residents on the floor and liked to think he was in charge of the doctors as well. She didn't know if this situation technically fell under his purview, but she knew he would make her life miserable if he wasn't informed.

While the nurses settled the girl in her new room, she went back to Room 409. The man from Maintenance was at the door beside Alan, waiting with a large vacuum cleaner with a hose attachment. She recognized him as Henry, the head of the department. She was pleased, because he had a reputation for being thorough. His taciturn nature made it likely he would be discreet as well, which she appreciated.

"Have you looked inside? Have you seen the infestation?"

"Yes, Doctor Kowalski."

She stared at the huge barrel attached to the vacuum hose. "Will that be big enough to completely clean the room?"

"Oh yes, ma'am."

"Excellent. Please let me know when you're finished. If you don't see me around, you can page me from the nurse's station."

He nodded and entered the room, unaware that he had only minutes to live.

xxx

The room was thick with insects now, the flying ones roaming the room in a seething black cloud. He was almost certain they were breeding. He was positive that just ten minutes earlier, when he had first looked inside the room, there weren't so many of them. Now he had to shield his face with one large hand to keep the flying insects away. He was pleased to see the insects scatter when he flicked the vacuum cleaner switch and it roared to life.

He started in one corner of the room, lowering the vacuum cleaner nozzle to the floor, and methodically swept it slowly from side to side as he backed up. The nozzle's powerful suction swept up the insects with ease, even as insects buzzed around his head, making him wish he had brought a mask. He anticipated the task to take at least half an hour; given how loud the vacuum cleaner was, a set of earplugs would have been nice as well.

He was so engrossed in in his task that he didn't notice the bug emerging from under the bed. It looked like a praying mantis with too many arms, dragging behind it a large, clear sac filled with black liquid. It was several inches tall, but light enough that Henry felt nothing when it hopped on his leg and began climbing up his back.

He had backed all the way up to the bed when the bug reached his shoulder. It balanced there, flexing its long limbs. The liquid-filled sac throbbed. It thrust out its limbs, driving razor-sharp points into Henry's neck, and emptied the sac's contents into his bloodstream.

The poison's effect was immediate. Henry stiffened, suddenly paralyzed, and dropped the nozzle. He didn't feel it when he crashed to the floor, even as the fall fractured his skull. Dazed and unable to move, he was helpless as the small insects swarmed across the linoleum and into his open mouth and nostrils. At the same time, an army of larger insects, all with chattering mandibles filled with sharp needle teeth, advanced from under the bed. They converged on his motionless body as their companions surged down his throat. Even if he hadn't been paralyzed, his rapidly filling lungs would have held no air for him to scream.

It was fortunate that he could feel nothing as the insects began to eat him from the inside and out, although he died of suffocation long before they were finished with their feast.

xxx

She was at the nurse's station, catching up on the floor activity she had missed, when Doctor Reese showed up. He was the neurologist she had texted, and he was excited enough about what he had seen to come view the insects himself.

"Those pictures you sent were amazing," he told her. "I've never seen any insects like this. I did a preliminary search of insect databases on the internet, and nothing like that closeup you sent shows up anywhere. Where did you say these came from?"

"From a patient's room." She explained the situation with the comatose girl.

"Yes, but where did they come from in there? Did they lay eggs in her clothes that hatched after she got here? Or what?"

She shrugged. "I have no idea."

"Well, can I see the actual insects?"

"Sure. If Henry hasn't vacuumed them all up by now." She started to take him to Room 409, then stopped as she saw Doctor Hale walking briskly down the hall, headed straight for her. She sighed, preparing herself for his ugly presence.

He was a tall, bald scarecrow in white, with bushy eyebrows and a pencil mustache that seemed to be more smudge than hair. His intemperate manner asserted itself immediately as he said, "What's so goddamn important that you have to pull me away from my rounds? What's this bullshit about insects?"

"There was an infestation in the room where we put the Jane Doe. Henry from Maintenance is cleaning the room now. We moved her to 427. Everything is under control. I just wanted to keep you informed, that's all."

He snorted. "I can't believe you're wasting my time with insects."

"I just wanted you to be informed. You don't have to do anything about it. I've already taken care of everything. If there's nothing else I can do for you, Doctor Reese has expressed interest in seeing the insects and I'd like to take him there."

"Oh?" Hale smacked his lips, making her shudder. "Well, maybe I should see this too."

"If you like." She turned away, headed back to Room 409. The two men followed, with Hale studiously ignoring Reese.

They were almost there when they heard screaming down the hall. Christine had no doubt where it was coming from – Room 427. "Jesus," she muttered. "What now?"

In Room 427, they found more insects – not as many as in Room 409, but enough to be noticeable – and a nurse who had backed up against the wall, still screaming. Christine looked at Jane Doe and was unsettled to see a quaking lump beneath her blanket, writhing just above her pelvic region. She appeared grotesquely pregnant, which Christine knew to be impossible. Even more disturbing, insects were writhing from under the blanket, some spilling to the floor, others taking flight and circling around the room like tiny drones.

Christine approached the bed and seized the sheet. She yanked it from the bed in one quick motion, revealing a black, buzzing mass of insects swarming over the girl's crotch. Once the sheet was gone, the insects exploded in all directions, filling the room. As the girl's crotch became visible, Christine saw that her gown had been eaten away, along with her panties, leaving her pubic region clearly visible. There was no escaping the fact that the insects were emerging in waves from her vagina.

"Well, I'll be fucked." Hale stepped closer to the bed, clearly fascinated. He bent over to look more closely at her pubic region.

"You, nurse – quit your goddamn yowling and go get me a speculum."

The nurse stopped screaming but remained horrified. "A – a speculum? What kind?"

"The kind that will let me look up inside her, you dumb bitch. Now go! I want that speculum yesterday!" He pointed to the door and she obeyed, running out. She didn't bother to close it, and Christine had to pull it shut behind her.

"My God," Reese said, gawking at the unconscious girl. He couldn't look away from her crotch, watching as a steady procession of insects streamed from inside her.

"How is this even possible?" he said, mesmerized.

"I don't know," Hale replied, "but if that dumb bitch will ever get back here with a speculum, I'm going to find out."

When the nurse returned, shaking, he snatched the speculum from her hand and bent to insert it in the girl's vagina. When Christine suggested he should use lubricating jelly in accordance with normal procedure, he shouted, "Fuck normal! Now leave me alone and let me take a look at what's going on here!"

They watched in silence, the faint buzzing of insects the only sound, as Hale used the speculum to widen the mouth of her vagina and peered inside. He leaned across the bed, all of his attention concentrated on the small area between the metal jaws of the speculum. He appeared intent at first, but his expression gradually softened into puzzlement, then a sort of terrified awe.

"What is it?" Reese said. "What do you see?"

"I see stars," Hale said, his eyes wide with disbelief.

"You see what?"

"Stars! Stars, you fool! There's a world inside her!"

"That – makes absolutely no sense. What are you talking about?"

Hale waved for him to come over. "Come see for yourself. It's the most amazing thing I've ever seen. Her body must be a portal between worlds – I see stars, but also an alien landscape. Wherever this is, it must be far away from our –"

Two tentacles, wet and gray and covered with suckers, snaked out of her vagina and curled around the doctor's throat, cutting off his words. His eyes bulged as he tried to pull away, but whatever was inside her, he was no match for its strength. The tentacles began to drag him back as he placed his hands on the girl's legs in a vain attempt to pull himself free.

They watched in horror as his head began to disappear inside. He screamed as his skull, too wide for the small opening, began to crack. Blood flowed from his head, soaking the sheet as he thrashed around wildly. The nurse began screaming again. The unconscious girl remained serene, apparently unaware of this unnatural violation of her body.

"Jesus Christ!" Christine shouted, grabbing one of his legs. "Grab the other one! We've got to pull him out!"

Reese did as he was told, and together they attempted to pull him away from the girl. Their efforts were fruitless. His body continued to advance through the opening inch by inch, bones cracking and blood gushing as he went. The nurse abandoned them when his torso collapsed and his heart burst, showering her in hot blood.

He was in up to his waist when Reese fell to the ground, his eyes wide, apparently unable to move. She watched with horror as the small insects on the floor streamed into his mouth while other, larger ones covered his body and attacked it with fanatical zeal. His body began to disintegrate before her eyes, twitching in a growing pool of blood.

She gave up on saving Hale, who was almost certainly dead, and turned to the door to run. A crowd of stunned doctors and nurses filled the doorway, making it impossible for her to escape. Outside she heard screams, terrified shouting, and other sounds of pandemonium. She was trying to fight her way through the people jammed in the doorway when her body went rigid and she fell to the ground, vaguely aware of the insect on her shoulder that had poked her, filling her with poison.

As the insects voraciously consumed her, she wondered how long it would take them to eat all of humanity, one helpless person at a time.

Last Wraps

by Duane Pesice

Michael Jack Schmidt *should* have had five that day in Wrigley. It was only fitting, or at least I think so. But then I don't understand why he wasn't a unanimous choice for the Hall of Fame the day before he was eligible, just based on that one game.

You know the game – you've heard about it. Cubs/Phillies, May 17, 1979. Baseball Reference has the box score, if you get lost.

The Cubs walked him three times, twice intentional, and Davey Ding-Dong, Ol' Kong himself, swatted three deep flies on that homer-happy day.

I was there, one of the few times I got to visit that forsaken town, and I remember how the game went. It wasn't exactly the same as the box score would have it, and I'll commence explaining that shortly.

I used to have the game on video, and I would watch it every few days until I started noticing little things that were somehow different, like the way Bob Boone was holding his glove on a pitch by Randy Lerch that went for a passed ball and got Mike Vail to third base in the bottom of the first, that led to Barry Foote being walked and a seventh Chicago run scoring that inning, off Doug Bird, as the ill-fated Donnie Moore tripled in Ted Sizemore with the game-tying tally.

By then, I was watching every day, as it had become apparent that the game on video had a life of its own.

There had been no passed ball in the original game. In the game on video, Bird was pulled right away after that inning, and Tug McGraw pitched the bottom of the fourth clean, and the Phils sailed to a 23-6 victory.

The next day, the Cubs won.

And so on, like that.

Back then, there was no internet, so I couldn't check online if the box scores were changing, or if it was all in my head...but this went on long enough that I could. Sometimes it even changed while I observed, if I were there at the right time of day.

And the butterfly effect made the world a little different, I noticed at last. Sometimes the changes would last.

On one such occasion, the Cubs won the game going away, and Danny Ozark was fired after the contest. Dallas Green took over.

But I got my revenge as Dallas Green stayed with the Phils through the 80s, winning two World Series in the process and depriving the Cubs of their 1984 playoff appearance. That version remained for almost fifteen years, until Kingman hit the 11th-inning clout off of Eastwick that led to the Cubs' 24-23 victory.

Sometimes karma isn't a bitch.

But there's no predicting which way she'll swing.

Now I just wonder if this game is the universe running simulations, because I've seen the Matrix, and I know enough to question such processes.

Now hush. The game is on, and President Ford is about to throw out the first pitch.

Afterword

by Christopher Ropes

"He has AIDS!"

"He's contagious."

"Disgusting."

Just some of the things I heard every day of my life in school because of my teeth. On top of abuse from my mother at home, on top of my father abandoning me, on top of the constant pain caused by my bad teeth and, worst of all, in addition to the nonstop physical *awareness* of my teeth, the bullying at school was a daily source of personal destruction.

I was born with dentinogenesis imperfecta, a condition that causes discolored, brittle teeth. My teeth were bad as a child, fell out, and were replaced by even worse adult teeth. In addition to that problem, I suffer from occasionally severe acid-reflux disease, which can severely damage teeth, and chronic tooth-grinding, even at night when I'm sleeping. I tend to wake up with sore jaws, and newly broken teeth in the morning is not unheard of in my life.

The fact of the matter is, my teeth are bad enough that they could kill me someday. Whether it's an infection, or problems with my jaw caused by my teeth rotting out, I face a future of serious medical issues due to my teeth. I'm on Disability, Medicare doesn't cover dental, naturally, and most places aren't all that willing to help out. I found a dental clinic that offered reduced prices on extractions and those were still close to $100 a pop. I can't afford that on Disability.

So, I got an estimate from a dentist, nearly $14,000 to fix my entire mouth, and decided to crowdfund it. When along came KA Opperman, Duane Pesice, and Michael Adams, who cooked up this charity anthology idea for me.

And now, a little *Who's That?* like me has a guy like Jonathan Maberry contributing a story to my charity anthologies. Oh yeah, I forgot to mention. The turnout to help me was so amazing, they needed two books. Little *Who's That?* me now has a two-volume charity anthology filled with writers who can't decide whether they're better at writing or being beautiful humans.

Needless to say, it takes my breath away. Needless to say, I am sincerely grateful.

Since those days of bullying, I've lived with almost debilitating body dysmorphia, a certitude that I am the most hideous and grotesque creature that has ever lived. When those kids were saying I had AIDS, it was the mid-80s. We didn't even know what AIDS was or what it did. We knew that gay men seemed to get it so I guess one thing they were doing was calling me gay. But that never scarred me. Gay pride exists for a reason. But no one ever preaches Ugly Pride. And that's what they were really saying. That I was grotesque, an abomination, the only kid in the school who got the scarlet letter "A" for AIDS because of their appearance.

A couple of weeks ago, I looked in the mirror. A real, long, hard look. I normally don't do that because body dysmorphia makes the idea of doing that a horror. But what I saw wasn't so bad. I thought maybe there was some hope for a guy with a face like me. Then, I smiled.

The smile revealed my teeth.

Down I tumbled, into an abyss of self-loathing and disgust.

The pain literally never stops. I fantasize about living without the constant pain but it's hard to fantasize about something you've never experienced. Like a kid just starting puberty fantasizing about sex… there's probably some missing information.

I want to be happy with how I look. I want to know what a life free from endless, severe agony is like. I want to smile and see those 32 white horses. (Right now, it's more like 18 jaundiced, plague-bearing rodents.)

And these writers, these beautiful souls, are trying to make that possible.

I want to thank everyone who participated in any way and I want to thank everyone who picks up a copy of either or both of the books. You're actively contributing to making my life substantially better. You're my own little army of saints and angels. Thank you.

Some of you know me and want to help me because you love me. Some of you are just good-hearted people who see a worthy cause in this and are trying to use your skills to make a positive difference.

And me?

I'm fighting to change things for that little kid being called the worst things that those bullies could dream up, all for the crime of having yellow teeth. I've found enough self-love, much of it reflected from people like the authors in these books, to know that kid didn't deserve that. That little kid should've been treated better. And now that little kid is an adult, a scared and suffering adult wondering what the future holds, but being shown the meaning of real love and real esteem by a herd of wild horses of all colors, thundering over the vermilion hills to my rescue.

Special Thanks to the creators of the unique fonts used in this volume:

Prince Valiant

&

Roman Antique

created by Dieter Steffmann
https://www.dafont.com/dieter-steffmann.d253